Love, Unexpectedly

Love, Unexpectedly

SUSAN FOX

BRAVA

KENSINGTON PUBLISHING CORP.
www.kensingtonbooks.com

BRAVA BOOKS are published by

Kensington Publishing Corp.
119 West 40th Street
New York, NY 10018

ISBN-13: 978-0-7582-3826-9
ISBN-10: 0-7582-3826-6

First Kensington Trade Paperback Printing: April 2010

10 9 8 7 6 5 4 3 2 1

Printed in the United States of America

ACKNOWLEDGMENTS

It's been great fun writing the "trains" segment of my sexy "planes, trains, automobiles, and a cruise ship" Wild Ride to Love series starring the Fallon sisters. (The first book in the series, *Sex Drive*, written under the name Susan Lyons, is available from Kensington Aphrodisia.)

As always, I want to thank my critique group, who accompanied me on this journey and provided guidance each step of the way: Elizabeth Allan, Michelle Hancock, and Nazima Ali. Special thanks for research assistance goes to Nisha Sharma, Alice Valdal, and Laura Resnick for providing facts that I then proceeded to twist to suit my story. Thanks also to my agent, Emily Sylvan Kim, and to Audrey LaFehr and Martin Biro at Kensington.

And of course, thanks to my readers, and especially the ones who take the time to drop me a note. It always brightens my day to hear from you.

Readers can e-mail me at susan@susanlyons.ca, write c/o P.O. Box 73523, Downtown Postal Outlet, 1014 Robson Street, Vancouver, BC, Canada V6E 4L9, or contact me through my website at www.susanfox.ca, where you'll also find excerpts, behind-the-scenes notes, a monthly contest, my newsletter, and other goodies.

Chapter 1

"**W**hat's new with me? Only everything!" Nav Bharani's neighbor Kat widened her chestnut brown eyes theatrically. She dropped her laundry basket in front of one of the half dozen washing machines in the basement laundry room of their apartment building, then hopped up on a dryer, clearly prioritizing gossip over chores.

Nav grinned and leaned back against his own washer, which was already churning his Saturday-morning laundry. "I saw you Wednesday night, Kat." She'd taken him to one of her girl-friends' to supply muscle, setting up a new bookcase and rear-ranging furniture. "*Everything* can't have changed in two days."

Though something major had happened in his own life yesterday. A breakthrough in his photography career. He was eager to tell Kat, but he'd listen to her news first.

She gave an eye roll. "Okay, *almost* everything. My baby sister's suddenly getting married."

Even in the crappy artificial light, with her reddish-brown curls a bed-head mess and pillow marks on one cheek, Kat was so damned pretty she made his heart ache.

"Merilee? I thought she and . . . what's his name? always in-tended to marry."

"Matt. Yeah, but they were talking next year, when they

graduate from university. Now it's, like, *now*." She snapped her fingers.

"When's now?" he asked.

"Two weeks, today. Can you believe it?" She shook her head vigorously. "So now I have to take a couple weeks off and go to Vancouver to help put together a wedding on virtually no notice. The timing sucks. June's a really busy month at work." She was the PR director at Le Cachet, a boutique luxury hotel in Old Montreal—a job that made full use of her creativity, organizational skills, and outgoing personality.

"Too bad they didn't arrange their wedding to suit your workload," he teased.

"Oops. Self-centered bitch?"

"Only a little."

She sighed, her usual animation draining from her face. Lines of strain around her eyes and shadows under them told him she was upset about more than the inconvenience of taking time off work. Nav knew Kat well after two years. As well as she let anyone know her, and in every way but the one he wanted most: as her lover.

He dropped the teasing tone and touched her hand. "How do you feel about the wedding?"

"Thrilled to bits for Merilee. Of course." Her answer was prompt, but she stared down at their hands rather than meeting his eyes.

"Kat?"

Her head lifted, lips twisting. "Okay, I *am* happy for her, honestly, but I'm also green with envy. She's ten years younger. It should be me." She jumped to the floor, feet slapping the concrete like an exclamation mark.

That was what he'd guessed, as he knew she longed for marriage and kids. With someone other than him, unfortunately. But this wasn't the time to dwell on his heartache. His best friend was hurting.

He tried to help her see this rationally. "Your sister's been with this guy a long time, right?" Kat didn't talk much about her family—he knew she had some issues—but he'd heard a few snippets.

"Since grade two. And they always said they wanted to get married."

"So why keep waiting?"

She wrinkled her nose. "So I can do it first? Yeah, okay, that's a sucky reason. But I'm thirty-one and I want marriage and kids as badly as she does." She gave an exaggerated sniffle and then launched herself at him. "Damn, I need a hug."

His arms came up, circling her body, cuddling her close.

This was vintage Kat. She had no patience for what she called "all that angsty, self-analytical, pop-psych crap." If she was feeling crappy, she vented, then moved on.

Or so she said. Nav was dead certain it didn't work that easily. Not that he was a shrink or anything, only a friend who cared.

Cared too much for his own sanity. Now, embracing her, he used every ounce of self-control to resist pulling her tighter. To try not to register the firm, warm curves under the soft fabric of her sweats. To fight the arousal she'd so easily awakened in him since they'd met.

Did she feel the way his heart raced or was she too absorbed in her own misery? Nav wished he was wearing more clothing than thin running shorts and his old Cambridge rugby jersey, but he'd come to the laundry room straight from an early run.

Feeling her warmth, smelling her sleep-tousled scent, he thought back to his first sight of her.

He'd been moving into the building, grubby in his oldest jeans and a T-shirt with the sleeves ripped out as he wrestled his meager belongings out of the rental truck and into the small apartment. The door beside his had opened and he'd paused, curious to see his neighbor.

A lovely young woman in a figure-hugging sundress stepped

into the hall. His photographer's eye had freeze-framed the moment. The tantalizing curves, the way the green of her dress complemented her auburn curls, the sparkle of interest in her brown eyes as they widened and she scanned him up and down.

As for the picture she saw—well, he must've made quite a sight with his bare arms hugging a tall pole lamp and a sandalwood statue of Ganesh, the elephant god. *Nani*, his mum's mother, had given him the figure when he was a kid, saying it would bless his living space.

The woman in the hallway gave him a bright smile. "*Bonjour, mon nouveau voisin,*" she greeted him as her new neighbor. "*Bienvenue. Je m'appelle* Kat Fallon."

Her name and the way she pronounced it told him that, despite her excellent Québécois accent, she was a native English speaker like Nav. He replied in that language. "Pleased to meet you, Kat. I'm Nav Bharani."

"Ooh, nice accent."

"Thanks." He'd grown up in England and had only been in Canada two years, mostly speaking French, so his English accent was pretty much intact.

His neighbor stretched out a hand, seeming not to care that the one he freed up in return was less than clean.

He felt a connection, a warm jolt of recognition that was sexual but way more than just that. A jolt that made him gaze at her face, memorizing every attractive feature and knowing, in his soul, that this woman was going to be important in his life.

He'd felt something similar when he'd unwrapped his first camera on his tenth birthday. A sense of revelation and certainty.

Already today, Ganesh had brought him luck.

Kat felt something special, too. He could tell by the flush that tinged her cheekbones, the way her hand lingered before separating from his. "Have you just moved from England, Nav?"

"No, I've been studying photography in Quebec City for a

couple years, at Université Laval. Just graduated, and I thought I'd find more . . . *opportunities* in Montreal." He put deliberate emphasis on the word "opportunities," wondering if she'd respond to the hint of flirtation.

A grin hovered at the corners of her mouth. "Montreal is full of opportunity."

"When you wake up in the morning, you never know what the day will bring?"

She gave a rich chuckle. "Some days are better than others." Then she glanced at the elephant statue. "Who's your roommate?"

"Ganesh. Among other things, he's the Lord of Beginnings." Nav felt exhilarated, sensing that this light flirtation was the beginning of something special.

"Beginnings. Well, how about that."

"Some people believe that if you stroke his trunk, he'll bring you luck."

"Really?" Her hand lifted, then the elevator dinged and they both glanced toward it.

A man stepped out and strode toward them with a dazzlingly white smile. Tall and striking, he had strong features, highlighted hair that had been styled with a handful of product, and clothes that screamed, "I care way too much about how I look, and I have the money to indulge myself."

"Hey, babe," he said in English. He bent down to press a quick, hard kiss to Kat's lips, then, arm around her waist, glanced at Nav. "New neighbor?"

Well shit, she had a boyfriend. So, she hadn't been flirting?

Her cheeks flushed lightly. "Yes, Nav Bharani. And this is Jase Jackson." She glanced at the toothpaste commercial guy with an expression that was almost awestruck. "Nav, you've probably heard of Jase—he's one of the stars of *Back Streets*." She named a gritty Canadian TV drama filmed in Ontario and Quebec. Nav had caught an episode or two, but it hadn't hooked him, and he didn't remember the actor.

"Hey, man," Jase said, tightening his hold on Kat. Marking his territory.

"Hey."

"Jase," Kat said, "would you mind getting a bottle of water from my fridge? It's going to be hot out there."

When the other man had gone into the apartment, Nav said, "So, you two are . . . ?"

"A couple." Her dreamy gaze had followed the other man. "I'm crazy about him. He's amazing."

Well, hell. Despite that initial awareness between them, she hadn't been flirting, only being friendly to a new neighbor. So much for his sense of certainty. The woman was in love with someone else.

Nav, who could be a tiger on the rugby field but was pretty easygoing otherwise, had felt a primitive urge to punch out Actor Guy's lights.

Now, in the drab laundry room, hearing Kat sigh against his chest, he almost wished he'd done it. That rash act might have changed the dynamic between him and Kat.

Instead he'd accepted that she would, at most, be a friend and had concentrated on getting settled in his new home.

He'd just returned from a visit to New Delhi and a fight with his parents, who'd moved back to India when his dad's father died last year. In their eyes, he'd been a traitor when he'd rejected the business career they'd groomed him for and moved to Quebec City to study photography. Now that he'd graduated, his parents said it was time their only child got over his foolishness. He should take up a management role in the family company, either in New Delhi or London, and agree to an arranged marriage.

He'd said no on all counts and stuck to his guns about moving to Montreal to build a photography career.

Once there, he had started to check out work opportunities and begun to meet people. But he'd moved too slowly for Kat, at least when it came to making friends. She'd figured he was shy, taken him under her wing, kick-started his social life. Enjoying her company—besides, who could resist the driving force of a determined Kat Fallon?—he'd gone along.

But even as he dated other women, his feelings for Kat grew. He'd known it was futile. Though her relationship with Jase broke up, and she ogled Nav's muscles when he fixed her plumbing or helped her paint her apartment, she went for men like Actor Guy. Larger than life—at least on the surface. Often, they proved to be men who were more flash than substance, whose love affair was with their own ego, not their current girlfriend.

No way was Nav that kind of man. In the past, growing up in England with wealthy, successful, status-oriented parents, he'd had his fill of people like that.

Though Kat fell for other men, she'd become Nav's good buddy. The couple times he'd put the moves on her when she'd been between guys, she'd turned him down flat. She said he was a really good friend and she valued their friendship too much to risk losing it. Even though he sometimes saw the spark of attraction in her eyes, she refused to even acknowledge it, much less give in to it.

Now, standing with every luscious, tempting inch of her wrapped in his arms, he wondered if there was any hope that one day she'd blink those big brown eyes and realize the man she'd been looking for all her life was right next door.

She gave a gusty sigh and then pushed herself away. She stared up at him, but no, there was no moment of blinding revelation. Just a sniffle, a self-deprecating smile. "Okay," she said. "Five minutes is enough self-pity. Thanks for indulging me, Nav."

She turned away and opened two washing machines. Into one she tossed jeans and T-shirts. Into the other went tank tops, silky camisoles, lacy bras, brief panties, and thongs.

A gentleman would never imagine his friend and neighbor in a matching bright pink bra and panties, or a black lace thong.

Nor would he fantasize about having hot laundry-room sex with her.

Glad that the loose running shorts and rugby shirt disguised his growing erection, he refocused on Kat's news. "So you're off to Vancouver." That was where she'd grown up, and where her youngest sister lived with their parents. "When are you leaving? Are you taking the train?" She hated to fly.

She flicked both washers on, then turned to him. "I plan to leave Monday. And yes, definitely the train. It's a great trip and I always meet fascinating people. It'll take my mind off my shitty love life."

"No problem getting time off?"

"My boss gave me major flack for leaving in June and not giving notice. Gee, you'd think I was indispensable." She flashed a grin, and this one did sparkle her eyes.

"I'm sure you are." He said it teasingly, but knew she was usually the center of the crowd, be it in her social life or at work.

"We sorted it out. My assistant can handle things. But it's going to be a crazy weekend. There's tons to organize at work, as well as laundry, dry cleaning, packing."

"Anything I can help with?"

"Could you look after the plants while I'm gone?"

"No problem." He'd done it before, along with playing home handyman for her and her friends. She in turn sewed on buttons, made the best Italian food he'd ever tasted—she'd once dated a five-star chef—and shared popcorn and old movies.

"Thanks. You're a doll, Nav."

A *doll*. Also known as a wimp. As one of his friends said, he was stuck in the buddy trap.

Brushing away the depressing thought, he remembered his good news. "Hey, I have exciting news, too."

"Cool. Tell all."

"You know the Galerie Beau Soleil?"

"Yeah. Ritzy. Le Cachet buys art there."

"Well, maybe they can buy some of my photographs." He fought to suppress a smug smile, then let go and beamed.

"Nav!" She hugged him exuberantly, giving him another tantalizing sample of her curves. "You got an exhibit there?"

"Yeah, in three weeks." He scraped out a living doing freelance photography and selling stock photos, but his goal was to build a career as a fine art photographer. He wanted his photos to display his vision and perspective, and eventually to hang on the walls of upscale businesses, private collectors, and galleries.

This would be his first major exhibit of fine art photography. "They called yesterday. Someone had to cancel at the last minute, and they asked if I could fill in."

"That's fabulous." She gave him another squeeze, then stepped back. "This could be your big breakthrough."

"I know."

For a long moment, while washing machines chugged and whirred, they smiled at each other. Then she asked, "Do you have enough pieces for an exhibit?"

"I'll need a few new shots. Everything has to fit the theme."

"You already have a theme?"

"We're calling it 'Perspectives on Perspective.' " His photographs featured interesting lighting and unusual angles, and often incorporated reflections. They were accurate renditions of reality but from perspectives others rarely noticed. He liked shaking people up, making them think differently about things they saw every day.

"Ooh, how arty and highbrow. It's great. I am *so* happy for you. This is going to launch your career, I just know it. You're going to sell to hotels, office buildings, designer shops, private collectors." Her eyes glittered with enthusiasm. "And I'm going to be able to say 'I knew him when.' "

Nav chuckled. "Don't get ahead of yourself."

Kat hopped lithely up on the closest washer, catlike, living up to her nickname. Sitting cross-legged, she was roughly on eye level with him. "You're a fantastic photographer and you deserve this. You've made it happen, so believe in it. Don't dream small, Nav."

If only that would work when it came to winning Kat.

"Believe in how great you are." She frowned, as if an interesting thought had occurred to her, then stared at him with an expression of discovery. "You know, you really are a great guy."

It didn't sound as if she was still talking about his photography, but about him. Nav's heart stopped beating. Was this it? The moment he'd longed for? He gazed into her brown eyes, which were bright, almost excited. "I am?" Normally he had a fairly deep voice, but now it squeaked like an adolescent's.

Her eyes narrowed, with a calculating gleam. "You know how unlucky I've been with my love life. Well, my family blames it on me. They say I have the worst taste in men, that I'm some kind of jinx when it comes to relationships."

"Er . . ." Damn, she'd changed the subject. And this was one he'd best not comment on. Yes, of course she had crappy judgment when it came to dating. The actor, the international financier, the Olympic gold-medal skier, the NASCAR champ? They swept her off her feet but were completely wrong for her. It was no surprise to him when each glittery relationship ended, but Kat always seemed shocked. She hated to hear anyone criticize her taste in men.

"Merilee said I could bring a date to the wedding, then got in this dig about whether I was seeing anyone, or between losers. I'd really hate to show up alone."

He'd learned not to trust that gleam in her eyes, but couldn't figure out where she was heading. "You only just broke up with NASCAR Guy." Usually it took her two or three months before she fell for a new man. In the in-between time she hung out more with him, as she'd been doing recently.

Her lips curved. "I love how you say 'NASCAR Guy' in that posh Brit accent. Yeah, we split two weeks ago. But I think I may have found a great guy to take to the wedding."

Damn. His heart sank. "You've already met someone new? And you're going to take him as your date?"

"If he'll go." The gleam was downright wicked now. "What do you think?"

He figured a man would be crazy not to take any opportunity to spend time with her. But . . . "If you've only started dating, taking him to a wedding could seem like pressure. And what if you caught the bouquet?" If Nav was with her and she caught the damned thing, he'd tackle the minister before he could get away, and tie the knot then and there.

Not that Kat would let him. She'd say he'd gone out of his freaking mind.

"Oh, I don't think this guy would get the wrong idea." There was a laugh in her voice.

"No?"

She sprang off the washer, stepped toward him, and gripped the front of his rugby jersey with both hands, the brush of her knuckles through the worn blue-and-white-striped cotton making his heart race and his groin tighten. "What do you say, Nav?"

"Uh, to what?"

"To being my date for the wedding."

Hot blood surged through his veins. She was asking him to travel across the country and escort her to her sister's wedding?

Had she finally opened her eyes, opened her heart, and really seen him? Seen that he, Naveen Bharani, was the perfect man for her? The one who knew her perhaps better than she knew herself. Who loved her as much for her vulnerabilities and flaws as for her competence and strength, her generosity and sense of fun, those sparkling eyes, and the way her sexy curves filled out her Saturday-morning sweats.

"Me?" He lifted his hands and covered hers. "You want me to go?"

She nodded vigorously. "You're an up-and-coming photographer. Smart, creative." Face close to his, she added, eyes twinkling, "Hot, too. Your taste in clothes sucks, but if you'd let me work on you, you'd look good. And you're nice. Kind, generous, sweet."

Yes, he was all of those things, except sweet—another wimp word, like doll. But he was confused. She thought he was hot, which was definitely good. But something was missing. She wasn't gushing about how *amazing* he was and how *crazy* she was about him, the way she always did when she fell for a man. Her beautiful eyes were sharp and focused, not dreamy. Not filled with passion or new love. So . . . what was she saying?

He tightened his hands on hers. "Kat, I—"

"Will you do it? My family might even *approve* of you."

Suspicion tightened his throat. He forced words out. "So I'd be your token good guy, to prove you don't always date assholes."

"Ouch. But yes, that's the idea. I know it's a lot to ask, but please? Will you do it?"

He lifted his hands from hers and dropped them to his sides, bitter disappointment tightening them into fists.

Oblivious, she clenched his jersey tighter, eyes pleading with him. "It's only one weekend, and I'll pay your airfare and—"

"Oh, no, you won't." He twisted away abruptly, and her hands lost their grip on his shirt. Damn, there was only so much battering a guy's ego could take. "If I go, I'll pay my own way." The words grated out. He turned away and busied himself heaving laundry from his washer to a dryer, trying to calm down and think. What should he do?

Practicalities first. If he agreed, would it affect the exhibit? No, all she was asking for was a day or two. He could escort her, make nice with her family, play the role she'd assigned him. He'd get brownie points with Kat.

"Nav, I couldn't let you pay for the ticket. Not when you'd be doing me such a huge favor. So, will you? You're at least thinking about it?"

Of course he'd already accumulated a thousand brownie

points, and where had that got him? Talking about *roles*, she'd cast him as the good bud two years ago and didn't show any signs of ever promoting him to leading man.

He was caught in freaking limbo.

The thing was, he was tired of being single. He wanted to share his life—to get married and start a family. Though he and his parents loved each other, his relationship with them had always been uneasy. As a kid, he'd wondered if he was adopted, he and his parents seemed such a mismatch.

He knew "family" should mean something different: a sense of warmth, belonging, acceptance, support. That's what he wanted to create with his wife and children.

His mum was on his case about an arranged marriage, sending him a photo and bio at least once a month, hoping to hook him. But Nav wanted a love match. He'd had an active dating life for more than ten years, but no matter how great the women were, none had ever made him feel the way he did for Kat. Damn her.

He bent to drag more clothes from the washer and, as he straightened, glanced at her. Had she been checking out his ass?

Cheeks coloring, she shifted her gaze to his face. "Please, Nav? Pretty please?" Her brows pulled together. "You can't imagine how much I *hate* the teasing." Her voice dropped. "The *poor Kat can't find a man* pity."

He understood how tough this wedding would be for her. Kat had tried so hard to find love, wanted it so badly, and always failed. Now she had to help her little sister plan her wedding and be happy for her, even though Kat's heart ached with envy. Having a good friend by her side, pretending to her family that she'd found a nice guy, would make things easier for her.

Yes, he was pissed that she wanted only friendship from him, but that was his problem. He shouldn't take his frustration and hurt out on her.

He clicked the dryer on and turned to face her. "When do you need to know?"

"No great rush, I guess. It's two weeks off. Like I said, I'll probably leave Monday. I'll take the train to Toronto, then on to Vancouver."

"It's a long trip."

"Yeah." Her face brightened. "It really is fun. I've done it every year or so since I moved here when I was eighteen. It's like being on holiday with fascinating people. A train's a special world. Normal rules don't apply."

He always traveled by air, but he'd watched old movies with Kat. *North by Northwest. Silver Streak.* Trains were sexy.

Damn. He could see it now. Kat would meet some guy, fall for him, have hot sex, end up taking him rather than Nav to the wedding.

Unless . . .

An idea—brilliant? insane?—struck him. What if he was the guy on the train?

What if he showed up out of the blue, took her by surprise? An initial shock, then days together in that special, sexy world where normal rules didn't apply. Might she see him differently?

If he analyzed his idea, he'd decide it was crazy and never do it. So, forget about being rational. He'd hustle upstairs and go online to arrange getting money transferred out of the trust fund he hadn't touched since coming to Canada.

It had been a matter of principle: proving to himself that he wasn't a spoiled rich kid and could make his own way in the world. But now, principles be damned. Train travel wasn't cheap, and this was a chance to win the woman he loved.

Unrequited love was unhealthy. He'd break the good buddy limbo, stop being so fucking pathetic, and go after her.

But first, he had to set things up with Kat so she'd be totally surprised when he showed up on the train. "Yeah, okay." He tried to sound casual. "I'll be your token good guy. I'll fly out for the wedding."

"Oooeeee!!" She flung herself into his arms, a full-body tackle that caught him off guard and almost toppled them both. "Thank you, thank you, thank you." She pressed quick little kisses all over his cheeks.

When what he longed for were soul-rocking, deep and dirty kisses, mouth to mouth, tongue to tongue. Groin to groin.

Enough. He was fed up with her treating him this way. Fed up with himself for taking it. Things between them were damned well going to change.

He grabbed her head between both hands and held her steady, her mouth inches from his.

Her lips opened and he heard a soft gasp as she caught her breath. "Nav?" Was that a quiver in her voice?

Deliberately, he pressed his lips against hers. Soft, so soft her lips were, and warm. Though it took all his willpower, he drew away before she could decide how to respond. "You're welcome," he said casually, as if the kiss had been merely a "between friends" one.

All the same, he knew it had reminded her of the attraction between them.

She would be a tiny bit unsettled.

He had, in a subtle way, served notice.

Token good guy? Screw that.

He was going to be the sexy guy on the train.

Chapter 2

The buzzer on Nav's dryer went off, but he hadn't returned to the laundry room yet.

He'd said yes to coming to M&M's wedding, then just when I'd been gushing thanks all over him, he'd taken off, saying he needed to do something upstairs.

Well, first, he'd given me that look. The one that downright sizzled. Then he'd kissed me and I'd almost expected . . . almost wanted . . . I touched my lips, still burning from that one brief brush of his.

No, that was crazy.

What Nav and I had was perfect just as it was. Though I'd always had lots of friends, I'd never felt as connected to any of them as to him. Other women said boyfriends come and go, but it's your friends you can count on. I'd never understood what they meant because I'd never had that close a friend. Now that I did, I wasn't risking our friendship, not when every romantic relationship in my life had ended in disaster.

Besides, while I was looking for a husband, Nav's dating behavior was pure player. He hadn't got serious with anyone in the two years I'd known him. Every month it was someone new: a female smorgasbord. He gave lip service to believing in marriage, but whenever I commented that his revolving-door policy wasn't the best way of finding a wife, he'd say—wink, wink—he was holding out for the perfect woman. Yeah, right.

He still hadn't returned and his laundry would be getting wrinkled, so I opened the door of his dryer and got to work. I folded sweatpants, jeans, T-shirts. Nary a designer label. Nav's clothes sense was pretty much "starving artist" even though I kept telling him about reasonably priced consignment stores that carried stylish outfits.

Into the hamper went the running shorts that showed off his lean, muscular legs and awesome butt. Faded rugby jerseys with their Cambridge red lion crest. A Cambridge man. How cool was that?

Boxer briefs. Black and navy, plain old Stanfield's. Soft cotton that hugged his private parts. Damn, it would be so much easier if my best friend was a woman.

I shouldn't be thinking about Nav's package, but the thing was, he had an excellent one. In fact, his whole bod was pretty fine, as I'd discovered bit by tempting bit. Like, when I hugged him. Or when he ran down the street for his morning jog, and I just happened to be at the window when he left. Or when he stretched up to hang my new light fixture, or hefted my new desk, or fixed the plumbing under my kitchen sink . . . No, I wasn't creating *I need a man* chores; it was just so much nicer to have his help than to figure things out on my own.

The view didn't hurt one bit, either. He had strong shoulders, firm pecs, and a breathtakingly tight butt, as well as the aforementioned package.

Which I shouldn't be thinking about. None of it. Not that, nor the drop-dead sexy English accent, nor that gorgeous skin the color of cinnamon. I should focus on the unstylish clothes, the shaggy hair that always needed a trim, the beard and mustache that hid half his face.

Even if he hadn't been my best friend, and even if he had been into marriage, Nav wouldn't be my type. I went for the polish of a successful, cosmopolitan man mixed with the edgy excitement and unpredictability of a bad boy. A man who'd grab me and kiss me senseless rather than give me a brotherly peck on the lips.

So, I was glad Nav had only done the peck thing. Of course I was. Because if he'd really kissed me, I might have kissed him back. And if we'd done that, we'd have crossed a line I had no intention of crossing.

Once, a few years ago, I'd fallen for a neighbor. When we broke up, I'd moved out of the building because I couldn't stand seeing him. I wasn't about to repeat the mistake and risk ruining the best relationship in my life.

All of which meant the size of Nav's package was utterly irrelevant to me, and no way was I going to think about it.

"Kat, what are you doing?"

I swung around, boxer briefs in my hands, to see their owner, still clad in those skimpy shorts. Fighting back a flush, I said, "Folding your laundry."

"You didn't have to do that." He tilted his head, studying me. "You're blushing."

Damn. I folded his undies and put them in his hamper. Totally casually. And lied. "I was thinking about the wedding. My family."

"Ah." He turned toward his dryer. "They really get to you." Muscles flexing in his forearms, he heaved the rest of the dry items on top of the ones I'd folded, guaranteeing wrinkles.

Distracted by his muscles, I tried to remember what he'd said. "Yeah. Isn't that what family's for?" I gave him a rueful grin. "In my family, love's unconditional, but it sure isn't nonjudgmental. There's a reason I don't visit more than every year or so."

Home was no longer the family house in Vancouver. It was my apartment in this renovated brownstone off St. Catherine near the heart of vibrant Montreal, where I lived side by side with my best friend.

"I know exactly what you mean." He leaned against a washer, all casual male strength and grace, albeit with faded running clothes and shaggy hair. Not that I, who hadn't expected to see anyone this early in the morning, looked much better, though at least my sweats were Lululemon.

"Got another e-mail from Mum," he said, "pressuring me to move to New Delhi. Since she and Dad moved back there, they're getting more and more traditional."

"Uh-uh." I shook my head vigorously. "You're not allowed to." We'd repeated this exchange three or four times over the past year, and I knew—almost—that he'd never move. But I also realized that living in Canada was a bone of contention between him and his parents. Nav was continually getting flack for being a disrespectful son.

His face tightened, and I tensed. Surely he wasn't considering moving. My apartment, Montreal, my *life* wouldn't be the same without him.

Slowly he shook his head, his glossy black curls catching the light. "No, I won't move to India. I love my family, but having half a world between us is a good thing."

I let out the breath I'd been holding. "Great. How would I survive without you?"

"You couldn't," he teased back. Then his gaze gentled. "Kat, you'll always survive. You're a strong woman."

"Yeah, that's me. Tough girl," I joked. But he was right. I'd survived growing up in my weird family, moving to a new province, working in French, and I'd survived having my heart broken more than a dozen times. But I didn't want to have to survive being without Nav.

One of my dryers went off, and I turned to deal with my load of delicates. As I was folding things neatly, my second dryer buzzed.

Nav opened the door and hauled out a pair of cotton pants and a tee. When he started to toss them on top of my careful pile, I grabbed them out of his hands. "Thanks, but I believe in folding clothes. Unlike *some people*, I'm not overly fond of wrinkles."

One side of his mouth kinked up. "*Some people* put too much weight on appearance, material goods, all that crap."

"*Some people* like to make a good impression."

We'd long ago established that we were opposites in a lot of ways, and the appearance thing was a running joke.

I took over the folding, then glanced at my watch. "I need to get to the hotel and reorganize timelines, leave instructions for everyone, rearrange some meetings." My job was challenging, but I loved it. Loved having a key role in the team of bright, dynamic people who were determined to make Le Cachet the best hotel in Montreal.

We hefted our laundry baskets and headed for the elevator.

When we reached the third floor, I put my basket down so I could fish in my pocket for my door key. "Got a hot date tonight?" I asked.

I certainly didn't. It was only a couple weeks since I'd been dumped by my last dating mistake, Jean-Pierre. The handsome, dashing NASCAR champ had said he was seriously interested in me, and his flattery and expensive gifts told the same story. But he'd moved on—either because he was a deceptive bastard or because I'd bored him—and my heart still felt battered.

"You're asking about my love life because . . . ?" Nav raised his eyebrows.

"Thought we might get together for a late-ish dinner." After a long, hectic day at Le Cachet, it would be great to unwind with him. Besides, we should celebrate his exhibit.

He studied me for a long moment. "One of our good old food-and-a-movie nights?" There was a strange edge to his voice.

Was he afraid I wanted another favor? "Yes, that's all. No more favors to ask, honest. If you have a date or whatever, don't cancel it."

He reflected, perhaps mentally reviewing his social calendar.

Not only did he date lots of women, his breakups usually seemed to be friendly and he'd as often be grabbing coffee with an ex as dating someone new. As well, he had three or four close guy friends he hung out with.

Finally he said, "Alas, no date. No whatever."

Ridiculous to feel glad. As ridiculous as the fact that, on the mornings when I was leaving for work as he dragged home with the drained glow of a man who'd had sex all night and desperately needed sleep, it'd put me in a foul mood for the rest of the day. This business of being best friends with a cute guy could be damned complicated, but Nav was so worth it.

"I'll have to settle for you," he joked.

"Hey, watch it with the insults. I was going to bring home a bottle of champagne to celebrate your exhibit."

His chocolate eyes sparked with mischief. "In that case, I can't think of a woman in the world I'd rather spend the evening with."

I chuckled. "Oh, I'm *so* flattered. Okay, champagne it is."

"I'll pick up tourtière from Les Deux Chats."

He knew the spicy pie, a Québécois specialty, was my favorite comfort food. "I probably won't make it home until around nine. Is that okay?"

"Sure. I've got a busy day, too. Knock on the door when you get home."

"You're a doll."

Was that a grimace on his face? He'd turned away before I could get a second look.

It was more than twelve hours later when, pump-clad feet dragging with weariness, stomach grumbling about the hours that had passed since my lunchtime salad, I knocked at Nav's door.

He opened it, wearing gray sweatpants and a faded T-shirt with the sleeves ripped out. "Hey, Kat."

"Tired. Hungry." I sagged against his doorframe and tried not to notice his brown, well-muscled shoulders. "Long, *long* day." I held up the bag I carried. "I come bearing champagne."

"Great. Go get changed, and I'll bring the food."

I grinned. How nice it was to not have to be *on*. To relax, be myself.

After going into my apartment, I left the door unlocked for him. His place was smaller than mine and cluttered with photography gear, so we always hung out at mine.

I stripped off my business suit, shoes, and bra, and gave a head-to-toe wriggle of relief. The business day was over; time to unwind.

The June night was warm, so rather than sweats I chose a light cotton salwar kameez—a midthigh-length tunic in blues and yellows over loose, drawstring waist blue pants. Light, floaty, feminine. I'd seen Indian women wearing them in Montreal and commented to Nav.

He'd said that, according to his mother and aunties, they only fit properly if they were custom made. The next time he'd visited his family in India, he'd taken my measurements and brought me back three outfits. The clothes were so comfy and attractive, I'd become addicted.

Knuckles tapped on my bedroom door. "Dinner's ready."

"Coming."

We never ate at the small dining table tucked into the space between galley kitchen and living room. I only used it to serve elaborately prepared dinners to impress dates. Instead Nav and I sprawled on the couch, food and feet fighting for space on the coffee table.

I flopped down on my side of the couch, cozy and relaxed amid the interesting furniture I'd picked up at auctions and garage sales—woven rugs, Quebec folk art, a half dozen flowering plants. Although this morning Nav and I had mentioned a movie, he had put on a CD instead. One he'd given me. Pleasant and new-agey, with piano, flute, and sitar, it suited my mood.

As did the scent of the spicy pork pie that sat on the coffee table. Not to mention the sight of Nav carrying plates and silverware from my kitchen. It was always a pleasure to watch him move. A rugby player in school, a jogger now, he had an athlete's strength and grace. Just as much as the Olympic skier I'd once dated.

As Nav put the plates down, the spicy scent made my tummy growl. Thank heavens he didn't avoid pork.

He'd found the bottle of champagne I'd put in the fridge. Moët et Chandon Grand Vintage 2000 Brut. It sat unopened on the coffee table along with two flute glasses.

"You sure you want to drink this tonight?" he asked. "It's pretty fancy. I have a Beaujolais in my apartment."

"You deserve fancy. God, Nav, your first major exhibit. This is big."

A quick smile flashed. "Thanks. Okay, consider my arm twisted." He peeled off the foil, loosened the wire cage, then, using a towel and rotating the bottle, eased the cork out as deftly as any sommelier could have. Golden liquid foamed into our glasses.

I lifted my glass to him. "To a huge step on your road to success."

"To steps forward. And success." He clicked his glass to mine.

There was something in his voice—determination, fire—that sent a shiver, the good kind, down my spine. A man with that passion and drive would get what he wanted.

We tasted the wine and I sighed with pleasure. This champagne was one of my favorites. Fruit, honey, yeast, a touch of spice. Fresh, rich, elegant. Perfect for a celebration. And speaking of which . . .

I raised my glass once more. "And here's to M&M as well. May they have a long, very happy, life together." I knew they would. They'd been joined at the hip since they were seven and were each other's most loyal supporter.

Nav drank that toast, too. "This is great wine, Kat."

I suspected he'd rarely, if ever, drunk such an expensive one. He refused to discuss finances—and always fought me for the check—yet it was clear he lived on a shoestring budget. "Glad you like it." Hopefully his exhibit would be a huge success, and he'd finally be able to afford some of the better things in life.

"Awfully fancy for a quiet night at home with a buddy and a plate of tourtière, though."

Maybe so, but tonight everything seemed just right. "Nav, this is perfect. Coming home to food, music. You look after me like, oh, a 1950s housewife."

He had leaned over to cut the pie and there was an odd tone to his voice when he said, "That's what friends are for." When he glanced up, however, his face wore its usual quiet smile, half hidden by his mustache and beard.

"I really wish you'd shave," I said for the zillionth time. I was dying to know what his face really looked like under all that curly black hair. With it, he was round faced and youthful, cute more than handsome. Of course, perhaps he was disguising a weak chin or acne scars.

"You're too obsessed with appearance." He came back with his usual response as he handed me a plate with a hearty serving of tourtière.

He dished some out for himself, and we both dug in.

"Have a good day at the office, dear?" he asked in a saccharine-sweet voice.

I looked up to see a twinkle in his eyes. He was playing off my housewife comment.

"Cute." I wrinkled my nose. "My day was stressful. Leaving on short notice is hard."

"And so is thinking about Merilee getting married." Nav's hand brushed my bare forearm. No doubt he meant it as a comforting gesture, but it felt almost like a caress, sending a quick thrill through me, of recognition, of . . . arousal. Damn.

His hand dropped away, reached for his glass, and I shivered, banishing the sensation.

"I know you want the same thing yourself," he said. "Yet you keep dating men who are . . ." He shrugged.

"I know, I know. I have the worst luck."

"You go for, uh, pretty dramatic men."

That was true. "I can't help who I'm attracted to." Attraction of opposites was normal. I was such an average person. Not brilliant like my parents and my one-year-older sister Theresa, not gorgeous like my one-year-younger sister Jenna. It made sense I'd be drawn to men who were amazing. And when one of those men was attracted to me, it blew me away.

A humorless grin quirked Nav's mouth. "Too true."

Said him, who was attracted to someone new each month. "And, unlike you," I said, "I date seriously." To me, it was a waste of time to date casually. I only went out with men I could imagine a future with. "I want a forever guy."

"And you think these men you hook up with are forever guys?"

Obviously none had turned out that way. "When I met them I thought so." Which only proved I was a bad judge of character, or didn't have what it took to hold their interest and keep them faithful.

"Why?"

"Because I'm an optimist." I sounded a bit snappish, but I was sensitive about this. I was used to my family joking about my crappy taste and the jinx thing, but did Nav have to pick on me, too? Usually he was good about offering a shoulder to cry on, sans judgment. Why was he acting different tonight?

"I know, Kat, and that's a great quality. But you also need some common sense. You meet Olympic Guy or NASCAR Guy, and suddenly you're crazy about them and thinking in terms of forever. What is it about them? Or is it less about them and more about you being so desperate to get married?"

"I'm not *desperate*, damn it. Just because I want to be married and you don't—"

"I do. I just don't—"

"Yeah, sure, I know." Maybe in five or ten years. His current revolving-door policy was so *not* aimed at finding a wife.

"I'm sorry I said that," he said gently. "I know you're not desperate. But maybe when you look at those guys, you see what you want to see. A prospective husband. Rather than what's really in front of your eyes."

Was he right? Damn, this was heading into pop psych self-analysis, the kind of stuff that, in my humble opinion, only made people depressed.

When my family trotted out the old stuff about my rotten taste, and me being a relationship jinx, I always tried to brush it aside. It hurt too much to think that my dating life consisted of attracting either losers or dynamite guys who quickly tired of me.

God, I hated this introspective stuff. "Let's watch a movie."

Normally, Nav would comply, but tonight he said, "Don't feel like it."

At least he changed the topic of conversation. "Have you booked the train yet?" he asked, holding the pie plate toward me and offering me the last serving of tourtière.

His muscular arm was even more tempting than the pie. I shook my head firmly. "No, thanks. And yes, I booked this morning."

He dished the pie onto his plate. "What's your plan?"

I rattled off my timetable for the tenth time today. "Work Monday morning, then the three forty train to Toronto. It gets in around eight thirty, and I'll stay at the Royal York across from the train station. Then I'm on the morning train to Vancouver, arriving there first thing Friday."

"I hope you meet one or two fascinating people." There was an odd note in his voice, but he was looking down at his plate, and that shaggy hair made it so hard to read his expression.

Speaking of that hair, and his general appearance . . . Earlier today, I'd e-mailed my sister Theresa and told her I was bringing Nav as a wedding date. Claiming bragging rights, I'd described him as good looking and successful. Which he was, in his way.

His career was taking off, and I was thrilled for him. Now it was time he dressed for success. For being a flauntable wedding date, too.

For us, discussions about appearance had been a running joke, a stalemate. How could I now get him to listen?

I swallowed the last bite and put my empty plate on the coffee table. "By the way," I said casually, "do you own a suit?" I'd never seen him in one, but didn't every guy have a suit?

His lips curved, then smoothed out. "For the wedding? I can manage something."

Given what I'd seen of his taste in clothes, I hated to think what he might *manage*. "Hmm." I chewed my lip. Could I possibly persuade Nav to let me buy him a classy suit? No, not the guy who fought me for pizza bills.

I respected male pride, but damn it, this was about my pride, too. He needed a makeover before he met my family. They were rough on dates. I'd yet to bring a man home they approved of, and Nav's scruffy appearance would be a big strike against him.

Maybe if I bought a suit and had it delivered, and there was no receipt that would let him return it . . . Still trying to act casual, I asked, "What size are you, anyhow?"

Chapter 3

What *size* was he? Nav almost choked on his last bite of tourtière. Exactly which portion of his anatomy was Kat inquiring about?

Then it dawned on him. She meant suit size. Damn, the woman was trying to dress him so he'd impress her family. What the hell was wrong with him just the way he was?

He'd been raised by a mum who was all about this kind of shit, and he'd gone to school with kids who judged by appearances. By image, status, job prospects, not by what kind of person you were inside. He fucking hated it.

He and Kat had different views on appearance, and it was one of the things that had become a joke between them. But tonight, she'd gone beyond teasing and was starting to piss him off.

Nav slapped his empty plate on her coffee table and stared at her through narrowed eyes. "I can dress myself without your help."

Her eyes widened with surprise. Then she stared right back. "Nav, I'm totally grateful you're coming, but face facts. This is a wedding. You've shot wedding photos. You know the starving-artist jeans and tee don't cut it for a guest. You need grown-up clothes."

Grown-up clothes? What made a suit more grown-up than

jeans? As a boy and young man, he'd worn enough suits to last him a lifetime. She did have a point though. As a guest at her sister's wedding, he should conform to the dress code. "Yeah, fine," he said grudgingly. "I'll check out a couple consignment shops."

"Consignment shops." She eyed him warily. "I'll write down the names of the best ones."

The best, meaning stores that carried once-worn designer clothes. The kind of shop where she bought much of her own classy wardrobe. Okay, maybe he'd follow her suggestion. He didn't want to embarrass her in front of her family.

Maybe he'd even wear a suit on the train. He stifled a grin. That'd shake her up.

Maybe he'd get a haircut and shave off his beard. He hadn't seen his face in four years. Probably wouldn't even recognize himself.

Nav wasn't entirely sure why he'd agreed to this friends-hanging-out evening, but it was giving him interesting ideas. If he wanted Kat to see him differently, a designer suit might help.

Rather than conceding her point, he decided to have some fun with her. "Salvation Army has a thrift shop."

She slumped back, shaking her head. "Appearances matter, damn it." After a moment, she sat up again. "Let's take this morning."

"Uh . . ." What about this morning?

"In the laundry room. I was wearing sweats, right?"

Made of a soft fabric, clinging to her curves. Like the way the light cotton of tonight's salwar kameez did. Enough for him to have noticed that under the flimsy top she wore only a camisole. No bra. He cleared his throat and shifted position as his groin tightened.

She made a face. "Yeah, sure, you don't even remember. Anyhow, take it from me, I was wearing sweats. I'd just got out of bed, pulled on the first thing that came to hand."

Oh, man, the image of her climbing out of bed all warm and

soft—did she sleep naked?—messed with his mind. If his train plan succeeded, he'd find out what she wore to bed. Casually he tugged his loose tee down over his baggy sweatpants to conceal his growing erection.

She was going on, oblivious to her effect on him. "Then you saw me when I got home from work. You probably don't remember *that,* either, but I was wearing a business suit, heels, makeup."

Looking great then, too, in a totally different way. When he saw her dressed for work, all sleek and professional, he had an overwhelming urge to strip off her clothes. To tousle her, tumble her, and—

"Nav?" Her tone was sharp. "Are you paying attention?"

"Sure." He bit back a grin. "Go on."

"I'm saying appearance counts. Trust me on this."

Same old, same old. "It's not the façade that matters, it's what lies beneath." Look at Margaret, the English girl he'd planned to propose to. Turned out she'd been all about image. When he'd chosen photography over the high-powered corporate career his parents had groomed him for, Margaret had taken off.

And so, when he'd moved to Quebec City to go to school, he hadn't mentioned his family's multinational business, he'd lived on a tight budget rather than dipping into his trust fund, and he'd dressed for comfort rather than style. *What you see is what you get. Take it or leave it.* Lots of women were happy to take it. Why the hell wasn't Kat?

"I'm a woman and I work in PR, and I'm telling you both things count," she said firmly. "Look at Le Cachet. We offer a lovely, luxurious image, and what lies beneath matches up. It's pure quality. And every one of us who works there conveys that image with our clothes, our grooming, our attitude."

Hmm. That did kind of make sense. But . . . "How about those guys you date? You go for façade there."

"I do not! I want substance. Depth." The protest came quickly, then she pressed her lips together, frowning a little.

He waited, giving her time to reflect. To his mind, any guy with depth would see how amazing Kat was, and not let her get away.

Slowly she said, "Okay, maybe I do get blown away by style, charm, good looks. Successful, fascinating men with exciting careers. I suppose I'm a little, uh, dazzled."

Dazzled into blindness so she didn't look beneath the surface. "Gee, you think?"

"What's wrong with wanting someone who's attractive and presents themselves well?" she said heatedly. "Someone who does interesting things, who's successful?"

Damn. Now she'd made him think. Yes, of course he found Kat attractive and there was no question she presented herself well, whether in stylish business suits, slinky evening wear, camisoles matched up with designer jeans, or the salwar kameezes he'd had made for her in New Delhi. Oh, yeah, he liked looking at her.

Of course he found her interesting, and no question she was successful. Grudgingly he admitted, "I guess there's nothing wrong with that. But shouldn't you look at personality first, not appearance? And if you care about someone, does it matter whether they're beautiful or plain? Whether they're an Olympic gold medalist or a, er . . ." He couldn't say "photographer."

"Schoolteacher? Ditch digger? Maybe it shouldn't, but I want someone who's more than just . . . average." She muttered something under her breath that sounded like, "I'm average enough myself."

He must have misheard. About to ask, he stopped when she said, "It's like when I go window-shopping. It's not the plain dresses that catch my eye, it's the gorgeous ones."

Gorgeous dresses and dazzling, successful men.

What was he thinking, with this crazy plan of his? Even if he did show up on the train in a suit, he'd still be Nav. A man three years younger than her, just starting his career, who was anything but dazzling. She'd give him the same old line about seeing him as a friend, yada yada.

Speaking of his career, he should stay at home and concentrate on the exhibit that might well launch it to the next level. Why put that in jeopardy to tilt at the windmill of winning Kat's love?

Let's face it, it was time to get on with his life. He should put his feelings for Kat behind him and give other women a fair chance. He'd thought he'd been doing that, but maybe his efforts had been doomed because he'd still been hoping Kat would one day return his love.

He was too sunk in his own gloom to realize she had been quiet for a while, too.

Then she said, "It's not necessarily the gorgeous men I go for. It's the ones who make the most of what they've got. The way I do. I'm not beautiful—"

He couldn't hold back a sound of protest.

She chuckled. "Aw, that's sweet, but I know I'm not. Jenna's the beauty in our family. I have a decent build, okay features, nice hair. If I stay in shape, get my hair styled, wear a little makeup, and dress well, I look more attractive than I really am."

"You always look great to me." He tried not to sound hopelessly besotted and resisted glancing toward her, afraid his face would give him away.

"Spoken with the loyalty of a good friend."

Nav gritted his teeth, *buddy trap* echoing in his head.

"A male friend." She jabbed him lightly in the shoulder. "A woman would've made a detailed assessment of my strengths and weaknesses, like my sisters and I did when we lived at home. Women are more analytical and objective about appearances than men."

"More obsessed." He crossed his arms.

"But this stuff is important for guys, too." She curled up on the couch, facing him. "Nav, you ought to be able to relate to this. Your work is all about visual representation and the message it conveys. What did you say the name of the exhibit is?"

He glanced at her. What was she getting at? " 'Perspectives on Perspective.' "

"Right. Perceptions, messages. Image, and what's beneath it."

His brain was trying to come to terms with what she was saying, but she rushed on. "Think about the opening night of your exhibit. That elegant gallery, your work on the walls, framed, lit, displayed to perfection." Kat waved her hands, as if conjuring up the scene. "People with glasses of champagne." She lifted hers in a toast. "Admiring your photos."

Oh yeah, he had to smile at that vision.

"They want to meet the artist," Kat said. "And there you are, *ta da*! Naveen Bharani, the brilliant photographer. Dressed in . . . sweats? An old rugby jersey?"

"Of course not."

"What then? Jeans and a shirt?"

He hadn't thought about it. But now that he did . . . "Not a business suit. Too stuffy."

Her face lit up like he'd handed her a box of Godiva chocolates. "Exactly! Now you're thinking about image. You shouldn't look stuffy, nor like a starving artist. You need to look like a successful photographer. Jeans could be okay, but they need to be designer jeans. Paired with a classy shirt, or a light sweater. A V-neck sweater, maybe black. Something that shows off your great build, your wonderful coloring."

She thought he had a great build and wonderful coloring?

"You need to do what I do," she said. "Make the most of what you've got."

He'd written off her obsession with appearance as the same kind of snobby thing he'd grown up with and hated. However, now that she was explaining, her viewpoint made some sense. Yes, he of all people ought to understand about perspectives and perceptions.

When he looked at his problem from that angle . . . from Kat's perspective, he was an old friend. He needed to alter that perception and make her see him as someone different.

As . . . a stranger? Part of the mystique of trains was meeting a fascinating stranger.

Excitement rushed through him. This was brilliant. He could show up on the train as a stranger, the kind of man who dazzled her. Ritzy clothes, a haircut, a shave. The flashy diamond ring his parents had given him for his twenty-first birthday, which he kept stored in a safe-deposit box. He'd create a radically different image, not just Nav-in-a-suit.

She'd know it was him, yet it wouldn't be him. Could he create a sexy "stranger on a train" game and persuade her to buy in?

He glanced at Kat, who was sipping champagne. Could he sweep her off her feet? Did he have the guts to do something so bold?

He might be an easygoing guy, but he was no coward. In England, he'd spent his childhood being ruled by parental expectations. Then he'd reached the breaking point. He couldn't be what his mum and dad wanted, so he'd left to follow his passion for photography even though it had cost him their approval.

Well, his passion for Kat was even stronger, and he was fed up with letting her expectations govern their relationship. Things between them damned well *had* to change.

Hell, yeah. He could reinvent himself. As the old saying went, *All's fair in love and war.*

Adrenaline fizzing through him, he leaped to his feet. "Time to head home. I have things to do, and you need a good night's sleep."

"But we still have wedding details to work out," she protested. "Your suit. Airline tickets. We need—"

"We'll work things out later." He cut her off and held out his hand. "Come on."

She put her hand in his and let him haul her to her feet. "There's something different about you tonight."

"Is there?" The good buddy would have gathered the dishes and stacked the dishwasher, but Nav walked straight to the door.

Kat followed. "I can't put my finger on it."

"I have a lot on my mind." He fought to keep a straight face.

"I know. Congrats again on the exhibit. It's fabulous. And thanks again, too." She threw her arms around him. "You're the best, Nav."

"That I am." The best man for her. On a subconscious level she had to know it.

He couldn't resist brushing her cheek with the lightest of kisses. Oh, yeah, there was a disadvantage to his facial hair. He could barely touch her skin. That would change very soon.

She stepped back quickly, gave a nervous laugh. "Tickles."

"Does it?" The next time he kissed Kat, he'd make damned sure she had a very different reaction.

Chapter 4

The VIA Rail train from Montreal to Toronto was an old friend. I took it at least once a month on Le Cachet business.

Settling into a cushy window seat, I sipped the skinny latte I'd bought in Central Station and stretched luxuriously. Yes, there would be family stresses over the next couple of weeks, but the bottom line was, my baby sister was getting married and I was on two weeks' holiday.

I'd changed clothes at Le Cachet, leaving my work persona behind in my office. Now I wore my favorite Miss Sixty jeans topped by a bright pink camisole with a gauzy sleeveless blouse over it.

I gazed out the picture window at the intriguing hustle and bustle of the underground station, wondering who would sit beside me.

Funny how sisters could be so different. Theresa preferred academic texts to human beings, Merilee mostly hung out with Matt, and Jenna and I were true extroverts.

This afternoon I hoped I'd get a seatmate who felt like chatting for at least part of the four and a half hours it would take to get to Toronto.

Perhaps a handsome, charming man? No. It wasn't three weeks since Jean-Pierre had dumped me. My heart didn't rebound that quickly.

Thinking about relationships reminded me of my conversation with Nav on Saturday night. He was right that I tended to fall head over heels. It was like seeing a lovely designer dress that I just had to have. With men, I'd see an Olympic champion or a NASCAR winner, handsome and sexy and fascinating, and if he was actually attracted to me, how could I not fall for him?

Of course with the lovely dress, once I tried it on, I knew if it fit well, and the designer label assured me of quality. With a man, perhaps I did fail to look below the surface, to check for true quality and a good fit in terms of personality and values. Perhaps that was why so many men ended up disappointing me.

In other cases, I feared it was me who disappointed them. I wasn't pretty enough, exciting enough, sexy enough, to hold their attention. They'd move on to another woman as Jean-Pierre had.

A depressing thought. But, being a woman of action, I wasn't going to dwell on it. Instead, I needed an action plan to ensure I didn't repeat the same mistake.

What I needed to do was avoid the head-over-heels part. Attraction was fine, but I had to hold off on love until I'd known the guy for . . . oh, maybe a month. Yeah, that made sense. In four weeks of dating, I'd focus on getting to know the man behind the façade, and with luck I'd identify any major flaws. Also, if he was tiring of me, likely there'd be signs of it by then.

Satisfied by my proactive approach, I focused my attention out the window, enjoying the bustle of activity in the busy station.

My gaze was caught by a birdlike woman with white hair and skin as brown and creased as a pecan, wrapped in a gorgeous burgundy and gold sari. Facing her, his back to me, was a man who, at least from the rear view, warranted a second look. His jeans—I recognized the 7 For All Mankind logo—and fitted white shirt looked great on a body with broad shoulders, slim hips, and long legs. He had glossy black hair, longish and pulled neatly back, and I guessed he might be Indian like the woman.

Beside the pair were two wheeled bags, one neatly upright,

the other toppled over. The woman carried a big embroidered tote and the man had a couple of black bags over his shoulder, which he juggled as he bent to deal with the fallen luggage. Nice butt, I noted.

As he righted the bag, he turned slightly and I saw his profile. Wow. I sucked in a breath. That was one hot-looking guy, with strongly cut features and cinnamon-colored skin that was set off by the stylish white shirt. Handsome, masculine, purely wow!

There was something familiar about him. Had I met him? No, this man I would definitely remember.

White teeth flashed in a smile as he listened to his companion.

Ah, that was it. He reminded me a bit of Nav, with his athletic build, his coloring, the attentive way he listened.

He gestured the woman, likely his grandmother, toward the ticket window, then followed behind, towing the wheeled bags. I squinted, hoping he'd look back this way.

"Bonjour." A male voice made me jump. A distinguished man with silvery hair and a beautifully cut gray suit stood in the aisle. In Québécois French, he said, "I believe I'm sitting beside you."

"Bonjour." I held out a hand. *"Je m'appelle* Kat Fallon."

"Philippe Martineaux. *Enchanté.*"

He took the aisle seat, then we did the "who are you and why are you on this train?" chat. Philippe was a lawyer going to Toronto for a series of meetings dealing with a corporate merger. I was ready to settle in for a chat, but he gave me a polite smile and said he needed to work. As the train pulled out of the station, he snapped open his briefcase and extracted a file folder.

So much for passing the trip in conversation. I might as well get my head into wedding mode. I plugged in my laptop and turned it on.

Merilee was busy making up her university semester after missing time due to illness, Mom was preparing to present a

case in the Supreme Court of Canada next week, and Dad, a research scientist, was hopeless when it came to girlie stuff. So
the three-pack—as our family called Theresa, me, and Jenna,
each born a year apart—had volunteered to organize the wedding.

I doubted Jenna'd be much help. She didn't even believe in
marriage, not to mention she was hopelessly disorganized. We'd
be lucky if she even made it back from Santa Cruz, where she'd
been counting peregrine falcons and surfing, in time for the
wedding. So, it was up to Theresa and me.

We had a lot to do in the next ten days. As the train crossed
the Lachine Canal, I pulled up the last family e-mails, sipping
coffee as I reread them.

On Saturday I'd e-mailed Theresa. After giving her my travel
itinerary, I said:

How often does a Fallon girl get married? So far, only once, and you
didn't even invite us. (Bad girl!) And that obviously jinxed your
marriage, so we can't let that happen to Merilee. Not that anything
could jinx her and Matt, right? I mean, they've only been each other's
"one and onlys" for how long? 15 yrs!

Poor Theresa. My professor sister was, quite literally, a genius. She'd done a Doogie Howser dash through school, acing
her studies and failing social skills, and had fallen in love an
exact total of one time in her life. She'd married the guy—a
professor—and he'd turned out to be an asshole, appropriating
her research and passing it off as his own.

The experience had soured Theresa on men.

I went back to my e-mail to my sister.

Do have to wonder why the kid has all the luck . . . You thought you'd
found your guy and he turned out to be a loser. And me, yeah, I can
hear exactly what you're saying. I keep repeating the same mistake,
and you at least learned from yours.

But Theresa, I don't WANT to be cynical like you. I want to believe there's a great guy out there for me. That I deserve love, and that I'll find it.

It was true. And because I refused to be cynical, I kept giving my heart, and having it tossed back, bruised and battered. One day—fingers crossed for sooner rather than later—I'd meet Mr. Right-Forever.

And in the meantime, thanks to Nav, at least I could fake it with my family. I was fed up with the ribbing. And the pity. I read my e-mail to Theresa.

So, anyhow, guess what? I'm bringing a date to the wedding!!!! Yes, it's a guy, and he's good-looking and successful. And very, very nice. His name is Nav. Honestly, Theresa, this man is NOT another of my bad choices. You and the 'rents and the sisters will all approve of him. HONEST!! <G> He'll probably fly out a day or 2 before the wedding.

Nav was so amazing to do this for me. Could a girl have a better friend? I was so going to owe him.

To tell the truth, I couldn't believe he'd agreed, and didn't really understand why. Sometimes the man seemed transparent as glass, and other times I suspected still waters that ran deeper than he let me see.

He was kind of like his photographs. On one level, they were merely excellent pictures of buildings, scenery, people—a bit unconventional when it came to angle and lighting. If you looked deeper, however, there were all sorts of things to be seen, and you never knew if you'd found them all. When you asked Nav, he'd smile enigmatically and say, "The observer makes the picture."

Like with his photo of a giant modern office tower. You couldn't see in the tinted windows; you were left to guess about who worked there. Instead, the windows reflected images: a flock of suited businesspeople, a couple of designer-clad women with shopping bags, a homeless guy sprawled on the sidewalk, begging.

Nav's work was brilliant, and it made you think. I was thrilled about his exhibit at Galerie Beau Soleil.

The man beside me gave a snort and I glanced over to see him dashing bold black question marks in the margin of a document. I turned back to my e-mail to Theresa.

> BTW, re the wedding. We'll need invitations, right? M&M need to come up with a guest list ASAP. I know Merilee always wanted hand-calligraphied invitations with RSVP cards enclosed, but there won't be time. Phone calls would be a hassle, having to provide all the info and get people to write it down. So I was thinking, why don't we do e-vites? I'm really good with graphics, I could design something in the next couple days, if you get the list from M&M. Oh, and we could use the list to plan the bridal shower and make sure one of Matt's friends is arranging a bachelor party. Let me know what you think.
>
> Hugs, Kat.

Theresa, flying to Vancouver from Sydney, Australia, where she taught sociology at the university, had picked up my e-mail in Honolulu and responded.

> Hi Kat. Glad you got the tickets. I should be able to borrow someone's car and meet you at the station.
>
> Yes, you're right about invitations. I think e-vites are a good idea. I talked to Merilee and she agrees. She and Matt are going to put together a guest list. So, when you have time, go ahead and do something up. I'm sure it'll be great.
>
> Just remember, this is M&M, not some ritzy hotel you're promoting!

I gave a snort of my own. Having a superachiever for an older sister was a pain in the ass. She never gave me credit. Of *course* I'd design especially for my kid sister and her guy.

> Oh, BTW, I won't be in Vancouver until tomorrow night. I'm in
> Honolulu overnight. There's e-mail (obviously!) and you can reach
> me by cell.

Overnighting in Honolulu had been a change of plans. She'd intended to connect straight on to Vancouver. Normally, my control freak sister would be royally pissed if something messed up her plans, yet she sounded surprisingly copacetic.

> Heard anything from Jenna? I told her to call you. She's trying to work
> out her travel plans.
>
> Talk soon. Theresa

Ah, Jenna. No, I still hadn't heard from her. The word "flaky" had been invented for the third sister in our three-pack. She was almost thirty, yet she'd never had a real job or a real relationship. Her motto was *Variety is the spice of life.* And she liked her life very, very spicy.

The next e-mail was from Merilee—the unexpected child who'd come along eight years after Jenna, making us a three pack plus one. Her message said she and Matt were working on a guest list and loved the idea of e-vites. I had e-mailed her and Theresa back.

> Been doing some thinking, and there's a couple of ways we could
> go. Merilee, those mags you scattered around the house were all
> hearts/flowers/lace, so maybe you want to go with the whole soft,
> romantic, traditional kind of thing. But then I was thinking how you
> and Matt have been M&M forever, and how you always include a bag
> of M&Ms whenever you give each other a birthday or Christmas
> present, and I thought it might be fun to use the candy as a theme.
>
> Let me know what you think. I can do either. Whatever you guys want.
>
> Hugs and smooches, bride to be!

Merilee had responded with,

Squeee!!!!!! Oh yeah, M&Ms! What a cool idea. It's so "us." You're the best, Kat.

I smiled. Theresa might have put herself in charge of the wedding—she'd said she was drawing up a spreadsheet—but I was the one who'd made Merilee *Squeee* with six exclamation marks.

Last night I'd started to draft an e-vite. Now I pulled it up to work on.

Glancing out the window, I saw we were passing through the western suburbs of Montreal. Sure enough, moments later we pulled into Dorval station and some passengers gathered their belongings.

A burble of sexy female laughter distracted me from the computer screen, then the unseen woman said, in French, "Oh, I definitely want to hear more about that."

A male voice, deep and so low I couldn't make out the words, replied.

Then the woman came into view, sauntering toward me down the aisle as she headed for the exit. Long blond hair, vivacious features, a lush body, and a killer suit I guessed to be Armani. In her hand was a gorgeous and very feminine red leather bag—either a Birkin or an excellent knockoff—that made me drool. She did a hair toss and glanced behind her flirtatiously, then her companion came into sight.

It was the man from the train station. The hot Indian grandson, as I'd thought at the time. And now here he was with a different travel companion.

He came closer; I looked at his face, and—oh, my God! "Nav?"

Or was it? If so, he'd been transformed.

His gaze flicked to mine. He raised his brows in puzzlement

rather than smiling in recognition, but there was definite appreciation in the wickedly male gleam in his eye, the hint of a smile tugging at full lips.

No, it wasn't my neighbor. The eyes were very similar, but this man—the one whose fashion sense and budget were the polar opposite of Nav's—was older. He had a higher forehead, sharper cheekbones, a stronger jawline. An utterly sensual mouth.

My lips curved. How could I not respond to the flattery of that eye-gleam, from such a striking, sexy guy? Even if he was with another woman, one who topped me on the beauty scale.

He moved on, pulling a Louis Vuitton wheeled carry-on. I caught the flash of gold on his wrist. An expensive watch.

I glanced out the window to watch the departing passengers. Expecting to see the striking couple, I was surprised when only the woman—now pulling the Vuitton bag herself—headed for the shuttle. Walking confidently, with a sexy sway to her hips, she paused to toss a laughing remark over her shoulder.

I wondered at their relationship. Were they a couple, or had they just met on the short train trip, hit it off, exchanged phone numbers?

Would he be walking back down the aisle?

Pretending to study my computer screen, I glanced up under my eyelashes as a family bustled noisily past. The train started to move and then, there he was. Pausing to stare at me until I couldn't pretend any longer.

I lifted my head and met his gaze.

The interested gleam was still in his eyes and it shot a tingle of acknowledgment—let's face it, of lust—rippling through me.

Oh, wow, was he fine. But also, hauntingly familiar. Was this my neighbor, playing a joke on me?

If Nav's hair was pulled back, his mustache and beard shaved off, and if he could be persuaded to wear designer labels, might he look like this? Surely it was too much coincidence that a near look-alike would show up on my train. But had I even told

Nav my schedule? Last night I'd knocked on his door, but there'd been no answer.

"Nav?" I asked again, speaking in English, hearing the uncertainty in my voice. "Come on, it's you. Isn't it?"

His eyes—Nav's eyes—danced. When he spoke, his voice was deep like Nav's, but he didn't speak English, nor Québécois French. In Parisian French, he said, "You break my heart." His gesture, placing his right hand over his heart theatrically, was not one I'd ever imagine Nav making. Nor was the ring, heavy gold with a flashing diamond, something my antimaterialism neighbor would ever, in a million years, wear, or be able to afford. "I'd like to think that if you'd met me, lovely lady, you would remember."

Then he said, "Pardon me. I'm assuming you speak French. Yes?"

"*Oui.*" Baffled, I switched to French. "I'm amazed by the resemblance. Are you related to Naveen Bharani?"

"No, I'm not related to Naveen Bharani, but everyone has a double. Who is this man? Your boyfriend?" Again he put his hand to his heart. "Tell me you don't have a boyfriend."

I chuckled and was about to respond when the lawyer in the aisle seat said, "Excuse me for *interrupting*, but would you two like to sit together?" He put a slight but pointed emphasis on the word "interrupting."

"I'm so sorry," I said. "I know you're trying to work."

"I apologize, too," the flirtatious man said. "Perhaps we might exchange seats? If the lady agrees?" He tipped his head to me, nicely shaped eyebrows raised, eyes sparkling with appreciation and challenge. He was polite, yet his confident manner suggested he was sure the lawyer and I would agree.

"I . . ." This person who could almost be Nav's twin had just said good-bye to a beautiful woman, and now he was hustling me. I shouldn't go along.

All the same, it was a long trip and my current seatmate

wasn't into chatting. The Indian guy intrigued me, and not only because of his resemblance to Nav. He was distinctly hot, and his attention was flattering.

"Well?" The lawyer's voice was edged with impatience.

"Fine," I said. "Thanks. And again, I'm sorry we disturbed you."

"Not a problem." He gathered his things, stood, then the two men headed down the aisle together.

Quickly I closed the file on my computer, touched up my lipstick, and got rid of my empty coffee container.

And then the hot guy was back. As he stowed his bags overhead, I thought that he moved the way Nav did, with strength and fluid economy.

I loved his style. Modern, classy, expensive, but not over the top. Immaculately groomed, yet not the slightest bit metrosexual with his strong features and athletic build. No, he was purely masculine, and my body tingled with sexual awareness.

He slipped into the seat beside me and a hint of sandalwood, one of my favorite scents, drifted toward me. In my apartment, I always had sandalwood candles. That spicy, earthy scent coming off a sexy man stirred my senses in a way the candles never had.

His movements reminded me of Nav's; his scent was different. His eyes were like Nav's, but his face was leaner, stronger. Or at least I thought it was. As best I'd been able to tell, given Nav's overgrown hair, my friend had rounder features.

"No," the man said, "I'm not related to your friend. Do I look that much like him?"

He'd caught me staring. "Sorry." I made an apologetic face. "There really are some similarities."

"As I said, everyone has a double." He adjusted his seat and I got a closer look at his watch—a gold Piaget that had to be worth a small fortune.

I chuckled at the thought of shaggy-haired Nav in his old jeans and battered Timex side by side with this man. "You're not exactly doubles." For a moment, the thought made me feel disloyal to my friend. But that was silly. Sweet, cute Nav with his "you're too obsessed with appearances" philosophy had chosen his style just as much as this man had.

"We're not?" My companion crossed one leg over the other, his knee brushing my leg. Not accidentally. If there was one thing this man wasn't, it was shy. He gazed at me, a teasing challenge in his eyes. "How am I different?"

Through my jeans, my flesh tingled pleasantly. But I drew my leg away. I wasn't going to make this too easy for him. Besides, my heart was still bruised from Jean-Pierre—though I had to admit it was healing under the flattering balm of this hot guy's attention.

How should I respond to his question? This man needed no boost to his male ego, and I wasn't about to tell him he was better looking, better dressed, richer, and more confident than Nav. Keeping my face straight, I said, "You're older." Nav was twenty-eight, three years younger than me. This man, with his angular features, expensive style, and sophisticated aura, had to be older than me.

"Older?" One side of his mouth curved up.

"And his French is Québécois while yours is Parisian." Though I did recall Nav telling me that as a child in London he'd learned continental French. When he'd moved to Quebec, he'd worked hard to change accents so he'd fit in with his fellow students. Doubt crossed my mind again. Those eyes were so much like Nav's.

I narrowed my own eyes. "You're absolutely positive you're not him?"

He chuckled. "Would you like me to be Naveen? I can pretend, if that's what you want."

"I'm not sure you could. He's a very nice person." I said it teasingly. This man knew I was attracted to him, but I wanted him to know I had reservations.

"Ouch." His brow wrinkled. "What did I do to deserve that?"

"You abandon your grandmother, then you see your girl-friend off at Dorval, and five minutes later you're flirting with someone else?"

"Ma grand-mère?" He frowned in puzzlement. Then his face lightened and he snapped long, well-shaped fingers. Fingers just like Nav's except for the excellent manicure. "You saw me at the station. How did I not notice you?" His Parisian French was so elegant, so much better suited to this kind of compliment than Québécois or English.

"Don't go overboard on the flattery," I said dryly, though I was a sucker for it. "And I wasn't in the station, I was on the train." I gestured toward the big window beside me. Outside, I saw fields of farmland bordered by lush forest. Soon we'd cross from Quebec into Ontario.

"Ah, yes. Well, the woman you saw, Mrs. Chowdary, isn't my grandmother. I was crossing the station when her bag fell over, so I stopped to help."

A Good Samaritan. Nav would have done the same thing. "That was kind."

He shrugged. "The bag was far too heavy for her. She's going to visit family in Quebec City and packed gifts for her daughter and son-in-law and six grandchildren."

She'd told him her life story, and he'd listened. Points to him for being nice to the old lady, but that didn't let him off the hook. "And what about the girlfriend? The Armani blond with the Birkin bag."

"Observant, aren't you?" He smiled and touched my bare forearm quickly. Casually. Except, I sensed that nothing this man did was casual. If his intent had been to make my skin burn, my breath quicken, to make me even more physically aware of him, he'd succeeded. "And you jump to conclusions," he added.

"Do I?"

"She's no more my girlfriend than Mrs. Chowdary is my grandmother. My seat was beside hers, we got talking. You know how it goes."

"*Certainement.* I suppose the women you sit beside always give you their phone numbers?" I guessed the blonde had, from the comment I'd overheard. And because he was that kind of man.

The kind of man I went for. The dangerous kind.

"It's been known to happen." Humor danced in his eyes.

I wished those eyes weren't so like Nav's. They made me want to trust him. I firmed my jaw. "And is that what you want from me? My phone number?" One more to add in his PDA? If so, he wouldn't get it. I didn't need a man who, like Jean-Pierre—and Nav—went through women the way I went through a box of Godiva chocolates.

He gave me a knowing smile. "What do I want from you? Many things. Starting with pleasant company on a long train trip. Fair enough?"

I'd have happily spent the trip chatting with the silver-haired lawyer, so why not with this sexy, flirtatious man? "Fair enough." I held out my hand. "I'm Kat Fallon."

He took it, but rather than shaking, held on to it. "Just to be clear, you don't want me to be Naveen?"

A warm glow spread up my arm. "Cute. No. There's only one Nav, and he's my best friend."

"Best friend." He echoed the words slowly, thoughtfully.

He must think it unusual for a woman to have a male best friend, but it was the truth. A truth I'd never actually told Nav. It seemed kind of pathetic that an outgoing woman of my age had never had a friend I felt as close to as I did him.

"Well, then." My seatmate lifted my hand to his lips and pressed a slow, soft, sexy kiss to the back of it. "You can call me Pritam."

My breath caught. God, he had sensual lips, and that kiss had me imagining the way they'd feel on other, more intimate parts of my body. As he'd no doubt intended.

I tugged my hand away. "No last name?"

He shook his head. "I use only Pritam."

"Really?" The single name, the clothes, the jewelry—he definitely wasn't the normal guy you met on the street. "What line of work are you in?"

"Entertainment. And what do you do?"

Entertainment? That fit his image. I was curious, but answered his question. "I'm director of public relations at a hotel in Old Montreal. Le Cachet. Do you know it?"

"I do. It's charming."

"Have you stayed there? Or do you live in Montreal?"

"I've eaten there a time or two. And yes, at the moment I'm based in Montreal."

"At the moment?"

"I'm doing business in Montreal. How about you? Did you grow up there? Your French is perfect, yet I sense you're not a native Québécoise."

"No, I'm from the West Coast. Vancouver."

"Ah. Mountains and ocean. I hear it's lovely. What brought you to Quebec?"

I was about to give him the edited version that had nothing to do with escaping family pressures, when a uniformed steward stopped beside us. "*Madame, Monsieur,* would you care for a drink before dinner?"

"I'd like a glass of white wine," I told him.

"For me also," Pritam said. "And it's my treat."

"We have a chardonnay from Château des Charmes or an Inniskillin pinot grigio," the steward said.

"I'll take the pinot grigio," I said. Then, to Pritam, "Thank you."

"My pleasure. I'll have the same."

The steward poured our wine. "I'll leave dinner menus and check back shortly."

We thanked him, then when he'd gone Pritam raised his wineglass. His shirt cuffs were unbuttoned, his wrist brown and masculine.

Very, very masculine and touchable. My nipples tightened against the silky fabric of my camisole.

"To two strangers meeting on a train." There was a seductive huskiness to his voice that told me, if he had his way, we wouldn't stay strangers long.

My body responded with another thrill of arousal. I touched my glass to his. "And to a pleasant journey."

"A very pleasant one." He drew the words out slowly and, over the glasses, our gazes met. There was no mistaking the sexual spark in his.

And no mistaking the sparks that heated my blood and made my pussy throb. This was exactly the kind of man who attracted me. Charismatic, sexy, and sure of himself. Attracted to me, and totally focused on going after what he wanted. Pritam's attention both soothed my heartache and ignited my sexuality. I hadn't felt so alive, so feminine and desirable, in months.

I could allow myself this indulgence, and give him my phone number at the end of the trip if I wanted, but I had to remember my new one-month rule. Attraction was one thing, but no head-over-heels stuff.

He took a sip of wine. "Speaking of which, do you go all the way?"

I choked on my own wine. "Excuse me?"

Eyes dancing, he said, "All the way to Toronto, I hope?"

He'd set me up neatly. In fact, wasn't that a line from the movie *Silver Streak*? I chuckled. "Yes, all the way to Toronto."

"Good, then we have lots of time to get to know each other. Now, where were we?" He gave me an encouraging smile. The man really did have the sexiest lips, full and sensual and very, very kissable.

"Uh . . ." Damned if I could remember. "Tell me what you do in the entertainment industry."

"First, you were going to tell me how a girl from Vancouver ended up in Montreal."

"Oh, right." Yes, that's what we'd been talking about. "By the way, do you speak English?" The first thing I'd said to him had been in English, and he'd understood.

"*Avec compétence, mais je préfère Français.*"

"Then we'll stick with French."

"It is, after all," he said in French, "the language of love."

I chuckled. "Give me a break."

He laughed, too. "What can I say? Frenchmen are known for being outrageous, especially when a beautiful woman is involved. And for the moment I live in Montreal, so I'm a Frenchman and entitled. Now, tell me why you moved so far from home."

Most men I'd dated had been more eager to talk about their exciting lives than my more mundane one. And I'd hung on their words, fascinated. Curious as I was to learn about Pritam, it was refreshing that he was interested in me.

All the same, I didn't want to bore him to tears, so I gave him the short version. "I went to the University of Toronto for undergrad. I wanted to see a new place, meet new people."

"Toronto? For a particular academic program?"

"No. I didn't know what career I wanted." Which had pissed off my parents no end. They were career driven and so was my older sister. But I'd had no outstanding talent and hadn't felt really drawn to any subject in school, nor to a particular line of work. Trying to show myself in the best light, I said, "I'm creative but practical, too, and I'm very social."

"An excellent combination. So, how did you decide on your career?"

"Through experimentation." I sipped wine. "I took different courses, worked at part-time and summer jobs, figured out what I liked and what I was good at."

He nodded. "An intelligent approach."

It had felt more like muddling around, and my parents had complained about my lack of focus. They'd urged me in the direction of law, my mother's field. Not medical research, my dad's specialty, because I didn't have a scientific brain.

"And how did you end up in Montreal?" Pritam leaned toward me, his sleeve brushing my bare arm on the armrest.

I tried to focus on the question rather than on the way I thrilled to his touch. "I wanted to be fluently bilingual, so after two years in Toronto I went to study in Montreal, at McGill. I loved Montreal. After I graduated, I worked in several hotels, and was assistant to the director of PR at Le Cachet. Then he moved to New York. I got his job, and I love it."

"What do you love about it?" His expression was attentive.

How to put it into words? I wasn't big on analyzing feelings, I just experienced them. Like, when I walked toward the front doors of Le Cachet, my step was bouncy and I felt like singing. It would sound silly to say that though. "It makes good use of all my skills. The other staff are great to work with, and I love the hotel itself. I'm challenged, alive; each day is different."

As I spoke, Pritam had begun to smile. Now he rested his hand on my forearm, making me tingle again. "You've found your niche. It feels wonderful when that happens, *n'est-ce pas?*"

"Yes, you're right, that's exactly it." If he could relate to the feeling, he must consider the entertainment industry to be his niche. Again, I was about to ask him what he did, but he was going on, a quizzical expression on his face.

"Your niche in your career, *oui.* Now, what about your personal life? You're a beautiful, intelligent woman who has chosen to be single."

Chosen? No, I sure hadn't *chosen* being single.

I must have frowned, because he said, "Wait, I'm making an assumption. You're not single?"

"Yes, of course I am. I wouldn't be—" Flirting with him.

And then something occurred to me. The question I should have asked before I let him flirt with me. "Are you single?"

"*Mais oui.*" His brows drew together. "If I was married, I'd never behave this way with you. How could you think that?"

"Because I don't know you. You could be one of those men

who takes off his wedding band the moment he's away from his wife."

He frowned. "You can't know, of course. But I give you my word. When I marry, fidelity will be part of the deal." His dark eyes looked sincere, and in that moment exactly like Nav's. It was so disconcerting.

Then he gave a small, mischievous smile. "And no, as you say, you don't know me. I hope to remedy that in the hours of this trip, Kat."

Kat. I stiffened. It was the first time he'd spoken my name. My heart raced. It seemed to me, he'd said Kat exactly the way Nav did. With a Brit accent, not a Parisian one.

One syllable. I stared at him. Maybe I'd been mistaken. How much could I read into one syllable? "Say my name again. All of it. Kat Fallon."

Muscles tightened beside his eyes; amusement flickered in their depth.

I realized I was holding my breath.

"Katherine Fallon," he said, giving it a Parisian flair.

I puffed out breath, shook my head, glared at him. "Uh-uh. In English. Kat Fallon."

A grin started on his face. Widened. Speaking in Nav's posh English accent, he said, "Kat Fallon, it took you long enough."

Oh! I was right. "Nav! Oh, my God! What are you doing? What's going on? Where did you get those gorgeous clothes and the expensive jewelry?"

I put my hands to my cheeks, laughing, shaking my head in amazement. "What crazy game are you playing? I can't believe you took me in. And here I said you were older, by years. It's your face; it looks so much leaner without all the hair. Why did—"

"Kat," he broke in.

His tone was so serious, I lowered my hands and stared at him. At that totally intriguing face that was his, yet not his. My friend Nav's, yet also the sexy stranger Pritam's. "Yes?"

"You meet fascinating people on a train," he said in English. "A train's a special world. Normal rules don't apply."

The words were my own. And now, the truth really sank in. He'd deceived me. Stiffly, I said, "So you decided to play a trick on me?"

His lips twisted in a small, wry smile.

Even though I was growing increasingly pissed off, I had to marvel at the sensual, expressive mouth he'd been hiding behind the mustache and beard.

"A game," he said. "I knew you'd call me on it eventually."

Remembering how I'd responded to his flirting, the way I'd become aroused, I flushed. "Not a very kind game. You made a fool of me." Nav would never let me live this down. If he'd finally listened to my advice about cleaning up his appearance, he ought to have been honest with me. Instead, he'd tricked me, and even borrowed fancy jewelry to do it.

Annoyance was rapidly turning to anger.

He shook his head. "No, that wasn't my intent, Kat. I only—"

"You *jerk*, Nav! What the hell were you thinking?"

He gazed steadily into my eyes. "That you might enjoy Pritam's company on the train trip to Toronto. And I knew Pritam would enjoy yours."

Confused, I shook my head. "I don't understand." Maybe he hadn't meant it as a nasty joke. After all, Nav had never, in two years, done anything mean to me.

"Nav and Kat are good friends, and that friendship is important to them. Right?"

"Of course." Why was he speaking in that one-step-removed fashion?

"But there's an attraction between them, right?"

Did he have to talk about it? I tried to avoid thinking about that attraction. "Okay, sometimes," I admitted. "But the friendship is more important." For me, our friendship was unique and wonderful.

"Kat doesn't want to risk losing that friendship, and Nav doesn't want to risk losing her."

I nodded, glad that he, too, valued what we had together. But I still didn't understand what he was up to with this game of his.

"But Pritam's a stranger," he said. "A stranger she met on a train. If he and Kat flirt, if they—" he waved a hand in one of Pritam's suggestive continental gestures—"what does that have to do with what she and Nav have together?"

"But you're both of them. Pritam and Nav. I don't understand."

"Pritam is a . . . fantasy. People can enjoy a fantasy without it affecting reality."

This reminded me of Nav's photography, which was all about different perspectives and realities.

What was he saying? If he played this Pritam role, we could flirt as if we were strangers and—oh, God, maybe even have sex—without jeopardizing our relationship back home? My breathing quickened. "You mean, afterward it'd be as if Pritam never existed? We—Kat and Nav—go back to being good friends as if . . . as if Nav had never left Montreal?"

He swallowed. "Do you like that idea?"

It was crazy.

But tempting. Because he was Nav, I could trust him. But with the "stranger," Pritam, I could let go, give in to the powerful attraction I felt.

I could satisfy my curiosity. The sexual curiosity I'd felt since the day I'd first seen Nav in the hallway, eyes sparkling, muscular brown arms clasping an elephant. When I'd begun to flirt with him before Jase Jackson had come along and I'd remembered I was in love with him.

Nav and I could even, if we wanted, be lovers in an anonymous hotel room in Toronto and not jeopardize our friendship. If I could buy into this game and pretend he was a sexy stranger named Pritam.

His face was all lean, unfamiliar angles, his eyes dark with a determination and challenge I'd never seen before. A very male and very appealing one.

"Who do you want to sit beside on this journey to Toronto?" he asked. "Nav or Pritam?"

Chapter 5

How would she answer? If she said "Nav," he'd be flattered, but his fingers were crossed for Pritam.

Pritam. The name he'd chosen because it meant darling, beloved. How he enjoyed hearing Kat call him by that name rather than referring to him as a doll.

She had definitely been attracted, and had interacted with him differently, but she'd only had an hour with Pritam. That wasn't enough to break a two-year pattern. When she thought of him as Nav, she was still all about the friendship.

Nav needed this game. Needed her to opt into a fantasy world he'd create.

He wanted Kat to relate to him as if he were a man she'd just met. A man who made her eyes spark, her nipples tighten. Like NASCAR Guy, Actor Guy. She'd said she was dazzled by style, good looks, charm, success, exciting careers. So that's what he would give her.

For Kat, he had done the thing he'd sworn to never do: he'd used his wealth to create a façade.

He had also lied when he'd said things would be the same, back in Montreal. Yes, he'd always be her friend—probably always love her—but he couldn't live in good buddy limbo any longer. Either he won her love or he'd get on with his life and put some distance between them. He felt crappy about deceiving her, but he didn't know how else to win her.

Finally, she opened her mouth to respond. Her voice was soft, breathy. "You want us to pretend Pritam really exists?"

The man had damned well better exist. Nav had spent a small fortune on clothes, train tickets, and a fancy watch, and he'd done appallingly metrosexual stuff like getting a manicure. He'd also devoted a couple of hours to researching an intriguing career.

He'd been speaking to her in Nav's English, but now he switched back to Parisian French, which was so deeply ingrained it had come back easily. "But I do exist. And I was having a great time getting to know a beautiful stranger. I thought she was having fun, too."

"She was," she said in English. Then, after a moment, in French, "I was having a good time with Pritam."

"Then let's get back to that."

"But how can I? You're Nav."

"Have you no imagination, woman? Were you never in a school play?"

"I was. I played Betty Rizzo in *Grease*. I've told you that."

Of course she had, and he knew she'd enjoyed getting into the role. "No, you're mistaken. So far, all you've told me is about how you moved from Vancouver, and your job. But I'd very much like to hear more about your life."

She stared at him intently, then her lips kicked up at the corners. "I think I'd rather hear about *Pritam's* life. Like, what do you do in the entertainment industry, for example? Oh, wait." She touched a finger to her cheek, widened her eyes disingenuously. "Let me guess. You're a photographer."

Nav gave a mischievous grin. "No. Try again."

"Excuse me," a male voice interrupted, and Nav turned to see the steward. "Have you decided what you'd like for your entrée?"

"Oops," Kat said, and hurriedly opened her menu.

Nav did the same. He saw that today's appetizer was prosciutto with melon and asiago cheese, and dessert was strawberry ginger cheesecake. They had options for their entrées: beef tenderloin with morel mushrooms, Atlantic salmon with lemon butter, or four-cheese spinach tortellini in alfredo sauce. "What are you going to have?" he asked Kat.

Knowing she loved rich, cheesy pasta, he was surprised when she said, "The salmon. How about you, *Pritam?*" Her eyes gleamed as she said his name.

"The tortellini." He'd be sure to offer her a taste.

After the steward had refilled their wineglasses and moved on, Kat said, "Tortellini. Are you vegetarian, *Pritam?*"

A number of Indo-Canadians were, but she knew Nav wasn't. For him, a Sindhi, there were no particular food taboos, though his family avoided beef on religious holidays like Diwali. He decided to make Pritam vegetarian, to emphasize that he wasn't Nav. "Mostly, but I'm not rigid about it." If she offered him a taste of her salmon, he wouldn't refuse.

"Well, we've established one fact about Pritam. An encouraging start. Now, let's get back to your job. In *entertainment.*" She raised her eyebrows in an exaggerated query.

"Have you heard of Bollywood?" Knowing she was attracted to larger-than-life men, he'd figured, what was bigger and more glamorous than Bollywood? He'd be Bollywood Guy.

A surprised, pleased laugh. "Indian movies. Glitzy musicals that go on for hours."

"Yes. Have you seen any? Do you like them?"

"A couple, with my friend *Nav.*" Her eyes glinted mischievously. "He's Indo-Canadian and has a relative in India who's involved with Bollywood. He's not that keen on the movies. Says many are more glitz than substance. I gather you think differently, *Pritam?*"

It was true, Nav wasn't big on musicals in general, whether

they were Bollywood or Hollywood ones. But today he was Pritam. "Some have substance, but those tend to be difficult for Westerners to relate to, because Indian values and culture are so different. But, anyhow, there's a place for substance and a place, too, for escapist entertainment."

"I totally agree. So, you're involved with Bollywood?" She leaned close eagerly, her bare arm brushing his sleeve on the armrest. Making a show of her play-acting.

She was so pretty, with auburn curls framing her heart-shaped face, her full pink lips parted. That seductively see-through top, worn over a tight pink camisole that hugged soft curves and perky nipples, which, right now, unfortunately weren't budded with arousal. Slim legs clad in body-hugging denim, her thigh tantalizingly close to his. Smelling the way she always did, of jasmine.

Damn, but he wanted to touch her.

It was too soon, though. She still saw him as Nav. Pritam had to spin a story, draw her into the fantasy. Get her to buy in, to flirt genuinely as she'd been doing earlier.

"I'm a producer." His cousin Laksha was married to a Bollywood producer, Vijay. On Nav's last trip to India, he'd visited them in Mumbai, where he'd had a tour of the studio and heard lots of talk about the movies. And about the growing ties between Bollywood and Canadian filmmaking. Yesterday he'd supplemented his memories with a couple of hours' research, and now could talk the talk, to a point.

Kat widened her eyes theatrically. "Wow, a producer! How cool is that?"

"I enjoy it."

The steward served their appetizers. Kat tasted hers, murmured, "Nice," then said, "Do go on, *Pritam.* You're a Bollywood producer, yet you're living in Montreal? Why are you in Canada?" It was a definite challenge. She hadn't bought into his game yet, but she was intrigued.

"Bollywood is expanding its scope." He paused, cutting matching slices of prosciutto and melon, capturing a sliver of asiago cheese, then savoring the mouthful. "The concept of the movies has changed a little over the years, but most are still based on the idea that the best entertainment is a mix of music, dance, romance, and violence, wrapped up in a glamorous shell. An escapist fantasy, usually with a dollop of poetic justice at the end."

She nodded reflectively. "That fits the couple I've seen. Bollywood movies have been quite successful, haven't they?"

He chuckled. "As in, 'Bollywood produces more films and sells more tickets than Hollywood'?"

"You're kidding."

He shook his head. "Not at all. And that's with an audience that's mostly South Asian. The movies appeal to different castes, occupations, income levels."

Her expression was attentive as she listened, nibbling her appetizer. "I know they're gaining more of a distribution and audience in Canada, and I assume the States as well."

"Yes, which is great." And now that he'd set some background, he needed to make it personal. Pull her focus back to Pritam. "As a producer, I want my movies to be traditional enough to be popular to their core audience but also appeal to North Americans."

He was really warming to his role. "As well as considering subject matter, I'm looking into joint production efforts. Filming Bollywood movies in Canadian locations, with some stars from India but using mostly local actors. And local crews. Then bringing some of those actors and crews back to Mumbai to make films there."

"That's fascinating." Kat seemed totally engaged, hanging on his words as if he really were a glamorous producer.

"Canada and India have an agreement designed to encourage joint projects, with tax incentives on both sides." He'd learned this from Vijay, who was actually considering coming to Canada to explore opportunities.

"But isn't most of the Canadian film industry in Toronto and Vancouver, not Montreal?"

"Yes, but think about this. Bollywood's about song and dance, drama, color, pageantry, right? It's vivid, exciting, fun."

A smile flashed. "Oh, yeah."

"And isn't that what Montreal's like? Wouldn't it be a great location?"

"You're right." She stared at him, excitement written on her face. "That's brilliant!"

It was. He'd have to suggest it to Vijay.

So, he'd got her interested, and he'd impressed her with his brilliance. It was time to get back to the seduction. Was she invested enough in the game that she'd flirt with Pritam?

Time to find out. The steward was clearing away the appetizer plates and delivering dinners.

Nav tasted his tortellini, which was creamy and delicious. Hmm, there was a benefit to his newly shaven face. He didn't have to worry about cream sauce catching in mustache and beard hairs. His naked face still felt a little raw and exposed, though, and it was a shock every time he passed a mirror. He'd lost the chubby cheeks he'd had as a younger man. No surprise Kat had thought Pritam was older than Nav.

He took another bite of pasta. "This is excellent. How's the salmon?"

"Very good." She cast a sideways glance at his tortellini.

"Do you like tortellini?"

"Love it. But there's so much rich food on trains, I try to eat light."

"A taste won't hurt. Want one?"

"Yes, please." Her answer came promptly.

Rather than shoving his plate toward her as her buddy would have done, he swirled a stuffed shell around in the rich sauce, then extended his fork to her. An offer of intimacy.

Would she accept it? Eat off the fork where, a moment ago, his mouth had been?

Her gaze met his, then tentatively she raised her hand and touched his, gripping it lightly as she bent toward the fork.

How many times had Kat touched him? Poking him in the ribs when he told a bad joke, claiming a hug when she was upset, playfully slapping his fingers when he reached for the last slice of pizza.

But never had she touched Nav the way she did now. This touch sizzled with meaning. He could tell from the way her fingers trembled. This wasn't a practical steadying of his hand; it was an acceptance of physical intimacy. She was opting into the strangers-on-a-train fantasy.

His dick surged to attention as if she'd touched it rather than his hand, and he was grateful for the napkin on his lap.

He didn't look away as she slipped the pasta off the fork, between those rosy pink lips. Color rose to her cheeks. He'd made Kat Fallon blush.

Well, his alter ego, Pritam, had. Which was the next best thing.

She chewed, swallowed, and her cheeks grew pinker as he watched intently.

"Good?" he asked, deepening his voice. Telling her he meant more than just the pasta.

She nodded. "Yes." Her voice was barely more than a whisper.

"More?"

Now her cheeks were flaming. "I'd like that."

He swirled another bite of tortellini and offered it to her. As she again touched his hand, the artist in him approved the contrast between her white-tipped nails and his dark skin. The man in him savored the press of her soft fingertips and imagined them drifting across his belly and curling around his now-erect shaft.

He struggled not to squirm in his seat.

She slid the pasta into her mouth, and he thought of those full lips parting wider, taking his dick between them.

He bit back a groan.

After she chewed and swallowed, she said, voice husky, "Would you like to taste my salmon? Or do you eat fish?"

"Occasionally, and I'd love a taste. And please, Kat, call me by my name. Pritam."

"Pritam." It was barely more than a breath, but she had obeyed. Now, would she offer the food as he had, off her own fork?

She did.

This was his excuse to clasp her wrist lightly as he closed his mouth around her fork and slipped the salmon into his mouth.

He didn't let go of her hand. Instead, after he'd finished the fish—which he didn't even taste—he leaned down farther and turned her hand over so it was palm up. Softly he kissed the center of her palm, then flicked his tongue across her skin, making her shiver. He glanced up. "Thank you. It's delicious."

Her eyes had widened, and he saw how quickly her breasts rose and fell, noted the hard tips of her nipples pressing through her camisole.

"Are you . . ." She freed her hand from his. "Are you trying to seduce me, Pritam?"

Her blunt question caught him by surprise. "Trying? I'd hoped I was doing it."

"I'm still confused." Her chestnut eyes showed an unusual vulnerability.

Normally, even when she was upset about something, Kat played things for drama. She was "shattered" or "pissed off," with exclamation marks. Rarely did she let down her guard, expose her doubts and uncertainties. Often he'd wished she would, but this wasn't one of those times.

"You're being too analytical, *chérie*," he teased, still in Pritam's voice.

She gave a soft laugh. "That's sure not like me."

"What's your biggest fear?"

"Fear?" A startled look. The word clearly surprised her.

"What's the worst thing that could happen?"

"Now you're asking me to be analytical. Make up your mind."

"Just for a moment. Let's identify the fear, see if it's realistic."

"I . . . don't want to make a fool of myself," she said softly, cheeks flushed.

"You aren't. You won't." Awkwardly, because their trays were in the way, he caught her hands and squeezed them. "Yes, I want to seduce you, and I think you want to be seduced. You're attracted; you can't hide it." Deliberately he let his gaze linger on her flushed cheeks, then move down to her breasts. When he raised it again, she was even pinker. "So, how is it foolish to give in and enjoy?"

Her lips quivered into an almost-smile. "I guess it isn't." Gently she freed her hands. "But *Pritam*, I have this friend named Nav. He's very important to me. I don't want to ruin my relationship with him."

All's fair in love and war, he reminded himself. "You won't. What happens on the train stays on the train." Unless she wanted to carry it back to Montreal, as he hoped would happen. "Pritam and Kat can have some fun, take it wherever they want it to go. That doesn't need to affect Nav and Kat." But he sure as hell hoped it would, for the better.

He dropped back into English and spoke as Nav. "Kat, I promise." If his plan didn't work, he'd seek some distance and eventually they'd both marry, but there was one thing he knew. "As long as you want me as your friend, I'll be there for you."

"Oh, Nav, me, too." Her eyes glowed with affection, and for a long moment, they just smiled at each other.

His heart warmed, but he knew this was a key point in his campaign. If she spent too long seeing him as Nav, she wouldn't be able to get back into the Pritam game.

As Pritam, he said, "What do you say, my lovely seatmate? Are you open to seduction?"

She bit her lip. "Dinner's getting cold."

So, she hadn't decided. As she forked up salmon, he turned back to his tortellini. They ate in silence for a few minutes, though he was too tense to even taste the food. He'd said everything he could to persuade her. Now he must wait for her to make up her mind.

Finally she glanced up. "All right, Mr. Producer, let's hear more about Bollywood. What you were saying was fascinating." Her tone was neutral. Not a buy-in, but not a rejection, either.

The wisest approach now, he figured, was subtlety. He wouldn't overtly seduce her, but try to engage her interest, help her relax again.

As they finished their entrées, he drew on his scant knowledge. "Let's start with the music. *Filmi* music, as it's called. In Hollywood, the soundtrack is an important part of the package, but in Bollywood, it's often critical to a movie's success. You know how movie trailers are released to promote interest in advance? Well, Bollywood soundtracks are released in advance, and sales of the soundtrack may outgross those of the movie."

"I had no idea." Again she was listening intently.

"Here's another difference from Hollywood. In the Bollywood movies you've seen, did you notice any lip sync?"

"Yes. What's the deal with that?" She had finished her dinner and leaned closer to him.

Her soft cheek was temptingly near. If he stretched over a few inches, he could kiss it. His blood heated at the thought. It was hell to focus on the conversation. "Until the turn of this century, Bollywood didn't record sound simultaneously with filming. The sound was done later. So the actors would go into a recording studio after filming and dub the dialogue."

"And sing the songs, I guess."

"Actually, vice versa for the songs. The songs are rarely sung by the actors, but by professional singers called playback singers. They record the songs before filming, then the actors lip-sync.

Some of the *filmi* playback singers are as big stars as the actors."

"Wow." She was hanging on his every word. "You said things
changed recently?"

"Yes, with a groundbreaking film called *Lagaan*. Since then
the industry has been moving to new technology, and more A-
list movies are made with simultaneous on-location sound. Dialogue dubbing isn't done. But we still generally use playback
singers for the songs."

The steward cleared their plates and they both accepted top-
ups on their wine.

Kat lifted her glass in a toast. "Here's to Bollywood. Now,
tell me more about your job. It must be so exciting."

He drank the toast, then expanded on his fake career. They
both reclined their seats slightly, and Kat curled sideways so
her jean-clad knee brushed him. When he dared to caress her
arm lightly, her cheeks flushed and she didn't draw away.

Her face was bright with interest, her expression admiring,
and he could just imagine her with NASCAR Guy or the
Olympic skier. With the men talking about their dramatic lives
and Kat getting sucked in deeper and deeper.

She was so impressed by accomplishments and charm, she
didn't look below the surface to see if the man was actually a
decent person.

Damn, he was tired of talking about Pritam. Yes, his alter
ego needed to be larger than life in order to tempt Kat into the
fantasy game, but he didn't have to be a self-centered ass.

So, after the steward had served strawberry ginger cheesecake and coffee, Nav said, "Enough about me. Tell me more
about your job."

"It's nowhere near as interesting as yours."

That was strange. At home with Nav, she'd often relate stories about her work. But with Pritam, she was diffident. Almost
as if his glamorous career intimidated her. What was up with

that? "Come on," he urged. "Give me an insider's view of the hotel business."

"Mmm, let's see."

While she mused, savoring a mouthful of cheesecake, he tasted his dessert. The spice of the ginger, the sweetness of the strawberries, and the slight edginess of the creamy cheese made for an unexpected but perfect combination.

"In a way," she said, "running a hotel is similar to making a movie. There are so many things and people to organize. The general manager coordinates everything, with other managers—like me for PR—reporting to him. It takes an incredible amount of organization to keep things running smoothly, but most of that takes place behind the scenes."

He nodded. "As with a movie, what matters to the audience is the end product."

"Exactly. Le Cachet is about luxury, comfort, being looked after. For many guests, their stay is an escape from real life. People change, either a little or a lot, when they're in a hotel."

She'd told Nav stories about bizarre or humorous incidents at Le Cachet, but never before commented about people changing. "How do you mean?" he asked. "Like actors playing a role?" Or like he was doing on this train, trying to reinvent the way he and Kat related to each other?

"Not exactly, because there's no script or director. They make it up as they go along." She chuckled, warming to her topic. "And no cinematographer, so they're more liberated. They do things in hotels they wouldn't do at home."

He took another bite of cheesecake. "For example? Tell me a story."

"Mmm, let me see. Okay, there's this dignified older couple who stay with us a few times a year. They dine out, go to the theater. They're wonderful to the staff and we all love them. Anyhow, one night around midnight, the wife phoned the front desk in a panic, saying her husband was having a heart attack.

The concierge phoned 911 and rushed up to the room because he has first-aid training. And what do you think he found?" She widened her eyes dramatically.

"I hope nothing terrible."

"The wife was dressed up in a black leather dominatrix outfit and he was naked, handcuffed to the bed. She was hunting frantically for her glasses because she couldn't see to unlock the cuffs."

"Must have been a shock for the concierge."

"Trust me, concierges have seen everything. He took it in stride. Unlocked the handcuffs, suggested she get changed, and even managed to get the man's pajamas on before the paramedics arrived. It turned out to only be indigestion, thank heavens. After, she told the concierge that they never do that sort of thing at home because it wouldn't feel right."

Nav gave a delighted laugh. "Talk about drama. There's more in your work than in mine." Then he snapped his fingers. "A hotel would be a great setting for a Bollywood movie." For a moment, he felt almost as if he really were a producer.

Kat nodded vigorously. "What a wonderful idea. Let me know if you need a consultant." She sounded sincere, as if she really were talking to a Bollywood producer.

"You'll be the first person I call." He gave her a flirtatious look and rested his hand on her forearm. "That is, if you give me your phone number."

Automatically she bent to reach for her purse. And then froze. When she straightened, purse in hand, her expression said she'd come back to reality. Remembered he was Nav.

What would she do?

Her hand fiddled with the clasp of the purse. "In the beginning, I expected you to ask for my number," she said slowly. "Then I forgot about it." The words were ones she'd address to Pritam, but she spoke hesitantly, as if debating whether to keep on with the game.

He wasn't going to break character. In Pritam's voice, he said seductively, "I never forgot, *chérie*. But I wanted to make certain that, when I got around to asking, you'd be sure of your answer." Trying to summon the go-for-broke ballsiness he'd always had on the rugby field, he added, "And you are." Making it a statement, not a question.

She gave a soft laugh. "You're full of yourself, aren't you?"

"You want a confident man." As he said the words, he realized they were true.

Furthermore, he knew that when he'd first moved to Montreal, Kat hadn't seen him as self-confident. Though it had taken guts to start a new career in a new city, not knowing a soul, his confidence was of the quiet, not showy, variety. It was his nature to find his way and make friends slowly, and he was happy being that way.

But Kat had thought he was shy, and she had taken pity and pulled him into her world.

She'd formed her opinion early and never changed it even as he developed his career and social life.

Pritam, unlike Nav, was a cocky bastard. So he held her gaze and said, "Confidence is sexy."

"It is." She stared into his eyes, again seeming open to the possibilities between them.

He gave her his most charming, appreciative smile. "You're sexy, Kat Fallon. Everything about you is sexy."

"Such as?" The breathy question told him she welcomed flattery.

He didn't want to give her the same lines she'd heard from every other guy who'd tried to hustle her. "Such as the way your lipstick matched your camisole. Before you ate it all off."

Her soft laugh trembled, and beneath that pink top her nipples tightened again. He ached to touch her breasts, but instead captured her hand, clasping it gently in his, feeling that tingly glow he always felt when he touched Kat. A glow that was arousal and love and tenderness all wrapped together. Without looking down at her hand, he said, "Such as those white-tipped nails, perfectly manicured except for one that's broken. On your middle finger."

"I got them done yesterday." Her voice was husky, wondering, turned on. "I caught one when I was zipping my bag. You really do notice things."

"I notice things about you. Now, let's see what else I've discovered. For one thing, you don't like sharing a man with another woman."

"Lucky guess. What woman does?"

"Some do. Like, if what they want is sex, company, fun, but no commitment, no pressure. I wondered, since you're single, if that might be you. But I think not."

"Because?"

"Your reaction to Marie-Thérèse."

"Marie-Thérèse? Oh, the Armani blonde." She nodded. "You're right. I like men who are attractive to women, but I expect fidelity. And some degree of commitment. If a man cheats on me, he's toast." Expression fierce, she said, "Been there, done that—and I do *not* like it."

She drew her hand from his, leaned sideways, and put both hands on his shoulders. Face only a foot from his, she stared into his eyes. "*Pritam*, what do you want from me?"

"That's not hard to guess." If he removed one of her hands from his shoulder and placed it on his lap, under the napkin, she'd know. "And it's *with* you, not from you. I want to taste you." His voice came out husky with need. "Smell you. Touch you. Listen to you moan with pleasure, make you cry out with ecstasy."

Flushed, lips parted, she listened.

"I have a hotel room in Toronto," he said. "Share it with me."

She didn't look startled, so he knew the idea had already occurred to her, but she did nibble her lip. "I'm not a one-night-fling kind of person."

Should he tell her he was booked all the way through to

Vancouver and wanted to continue their adventure? No, he needed to stay flexible. He might have to adjust his strategy tomorrow. "What's so wrong about letting me make you happy for a night?"

She tilted her head. "What kind of man are you, *Pritam*? A player who enjoys a night here, a night there with a different woman?"

He'd created a Bollywood producer who had almost managed to seduce her, and now, if she was going to buy into the game for a night's worth of lovemaking, she wanted to know if Bollywood Guy was a decent man. It was interesting how she opted in and out of the game as the mood struck her.

He gave her a smile full of charm. "No. I'm very discriminating. I only go for women who are beautiful, sexy, intelligent, successful, interesting, fun."

"Yeah, right." The words were cynical, but her mouth twitched to hold back a smile.

"And Kat? I, like you, am serious about relationships. I'm looking for the right person, as I sense you are."

"Uh-huh," she said skeptically. "Okay, tell me this. Have you ever been in love?"

She really did take Pritam for a player.

"Yes."

"Really?" Her eyebrows rose. "What happened?"

I'm still waiting to find out. Of course he couldn't say that, but he could share something else. A piece of himself he'd never before revealed to anyone. For Nav, Margaret's rejection had cut so deep, it was painful and embarrassing to talk about. Pritam, though, who was a man women drooled over, could be more forthcoming.

"I was in love and she said she loved me back. I was going to propose." He paused, trying not to remember the pain. "But she dumped me."

Chapter 6

I stared at the fascinating, sexy man beside me. "You're kidding." What woman in her right mind would dump a guy like him?

On the other hand, Pritam didn't really exist.

Except, I was looking at him. A man who could talk knowledgeably about Bollywood movies, who looked like a movie star, who kissed my hand. He so wasn't Nav.

Was this story about being dumped by the woman he loved merely another tall tale, one designed to arouse sympathy?

"Sadly, no," he said, keeping in character. Playing his role.

And yes, it was a role. He'd proposed a game, and I was having fun. While Nav's friendship had helped me through several breakups, the flirtatious attentiveness of the sexy Pritam was balm to my ego after Jean-Pierre's humiliating rejection.

"I'm sorry about your ex," I said. "What happened?"

He toyed with his fork for a few seconds, then, as if he realized he was fidgeting, put it down. "You know what we were saying earlier, about finding your career niche? I was well along on a career path, and that path—especially the income and status—appealed to Margaret. But not to me." Bitterness edged his voice.

Bitterness that sounded genuine. Was this true? Had Nav once loved this Margaret? If so, why had he never told me? I felt a twinge of hurt, maybe even jealousy that some other woman had been so important to him. "What happened?" I asked softly. And why was he telling me now, as Pritam?

"I refused to be stuck doing something I hated." He swallowed. "I changed course."

This fit with the few things Nav had told me about his parents. They'd wanted him to work in some big company—the one his dad worked for—rather than be a photographer. He could have studied photography in London, where his family had lived at the time, but the relationship was so strained, he'd come to Canada instead. Things hadn't improved since then, and Nav didn't talk much about his folks.

"Turned out," he went on, "Margaret was more interested in the status than in me as a person." The edge to his Pritam voice would have been impossible for anyone but an excellent actor to fake.

Margaret was real. The bitch. "That's awful. I'm so sorry. But you're better off without her."

"Yeah, well." He gazed at me, a baffled expression in his eyes. "She said I betrayed her."

"Betrayed?" I mused, thinking about my own love life. "Maybe she thought you wooed her, uh, kind of under false pretences. She believed you were one man, then you turned out to be someone else." My Olympic skier had done that, saying he wanted a serious monogamous relationship when in fact he had lovers in France, Italy, and God knows where else.

Pritam—Nav—winced.

"Sorry," I said quickly, realizing the comparison was unfair. "I don't mean you did it intentionally." Nav would never deliberately mislead a woman. I knew that from my own experience, and from the way his former lovers remained friends with him.

"She didn't want to see who I really was."

Was this why Nav got so annoyed about the idea of people judging by appearance? "Her loss." I touched his hand.

"Thanks." He threaded our fingers together. "But at the time, it really hurt."

Such a simple thing, linked fingers, and yet how complex the sensations. Warmth and connection. Sexual heat, and the suggestion of other body parts interlocking.

"Breaking up always does." I squeezed his hand.

How many times had I ranted to Nav and cried on his shoulder when I went through a breakup? Why had he never shared this story? I wanted to ask, but if I did, I'd be talking to Nav rather than Pritam. I'd have to let go of his hand, banish the delicious sexual feelings.

The steward came to clear our dessert plates and pour more coffee.

After, my seatmate picked up his coffee cup and said, still in Pritam's voice, "It took me a while to get over Margaret."

And perhaps he never had. Was that why Nav only dated casually? Was he afraid of risking love again? "Has it made you cautious about dating, Pritam?"

His expression lightened and he gave me a sexy twinkle. "Do I strike you as cautious?"

I chuckled. "I meant, about dating *seriously.*"

"No. Other than making sure the woman is interested in who I am, not who she thinks I should be."

"Have you been in love since Margaret?"

The hand that held mine tensed. "Once. But she didn't feel the same way."

"I'm sorry." Another story he'd never told me, and another reason for Nav to resist serious relationships. How ridiculous that I felt jealous of those two women who had meant so much to my friend.

I squeezed his hand until it relaxed, then let go and picked up my coffee cup. "What was your previous career?" I asked. "The one Margaret was so keen on?"

"Boring corporate stuff. Nowhere near as much fun as Bollywood. But the movie biz is a risky way to make a living. Everything in the arts world is. Margaret came from a wealthy family. She liked the things money could buy, and definitely liked status. She and my parents got along famously."

He slanted me a glance from those gorgeous brown eyes. "How about you, Kat? Could you imagine hooking up with a starving artist?"

The question took me by surprise. "I've never dated anyone like that." Anyone who was, in fact, what Nav had been when he'd arrived in Montreal. Was I as shallow as Margaret?

"Why not?"

I couldn't tell him my opposites attract theory, about average me being drawn to amazing men, and I didn't want a replay of our Saturday-night conversation, so I just shrugged, hoping he'd drop the subject.

"You've never dated a man who was just a nice normal guy?"

"Not really," I admitted. Then I corrected myself. "Well, my first boyfriend, Bob." I gave a soft laugh. "He even had an average name." Bob Johnson. "He was a little chubby, a bit of a nerd. I was having trouble with algebra and he helped me after school. He was a really nice guy."

"Nice guys finish last," my companion said wryly. "So what happened to poor Bob?"

"I took him home for dinner, excited I had a boyfriend. My older sister has this genius IQ and was—is—the family superstar. But Theresa wasn't dating, so for once I'd one-upped her."

"I guess it's human nature for siblings to compete."

And in my family we did it in part by claiming different niches: brains for Theresa, beauty for Jenna, being half of M&M for Merilee, and being Ms. Sociability for me.

"After dinner, when Bob had gone home, my family dumped on him. He planned to work in his dad's hardware store after high school, and my parents said I should look for a boy who was more ambitious. Theresa said he was a dummy, and my sister Jenna said he was a dork."

He grimaced. "You ditched the poor guy?"

Ashamed, I nodded. "Yeah. It was a shitty thing to do, but family pressure is . . ." I shrugged, surprised at myself for having shared this much personal stuff. Why on earth would anyone be interested in my family history?

He nodded understandingly. "Believe me, I get it." The corner of his mouth twitched. "Family pressure have anything to do with why you moved across the country as soon as you finished high school?"

"Oh, yeah. And with why I'm still here." Quickly I said, "Look, I love my parents and sisters. But it's like, in Vancouver I was a kid, and when I left I became a woman. In control of my own life. When I go back, I get sucked into the old patterns."

"Yeah. It's hard to figure out how to be an independent adult and still respect and love your family."

We smiled at each other, and I felt a strong sense of connection.

Hurriedly I glanced away and picked up my coffee cup. This was very strange, what was happening between me and this man.

When he'd been spinning his Bollywood tales, I could buy into the Pritam game.

But then he'd told me about Margaret, a Nav story I'd never heard before. Though in the past Nav and I had chatted a bit about my family, it had been superficial. Today he'd got me thinking about things, sharing things I normally kept quiet about.

Yes, there was something about sitting on a train with nothing else to do that got people talking in a different way. More reflectively than my normal light and breezy conversation.

To be honest, though, I couldn't attribute it all to the train. There was something about this Pritam-Nav person beside me.

When "Pritam" had said he wanted to seduce me, I'd expected dazzling stories, charismatic charm, and sexy flirtation. The kind of thing new boyfriends typically did to impress me.

And yes, he'd given me all that, but he'd gone further. He made me feel as if he really wanted to get to know me, not just hustle me into bed, and that he'd try to understand rather than judge. I hated being judged because I always feared I'd be found lacking.

My companion also seemed willing to share some painful truths. More than Nav had ever done. Or had Nav held back because I hadn't been forthcoming myself?

People in relationships—family, business, or social—did get into patterns. I'd liked the easygoing, supportive one Nav and I had formed.

But I also liked the way Pritam and I related.

"What are you thinking, Kat?" he asked gently.

Flushing, I put down the cup I'd been toying with. "I like being with you."

A surprised laugh jolted out of him. "Well, thank God. I mean, if we're talking about . . ." He kinked an eyebrow suggestively and caught my hand again, resting our clasped hands on the armrest and shifting closer so our arms brushed all the way down from our shoulders.

I quivered at the contact, sensual and arousing. "For you, does seduction require liking?" At this point, I had no idea whether I was asking the question of Nav or Pritam.

His head tilted. "Interesting question. Yes, it does. Otherwise it's only lust." His eyes gleamed with humor. "Which, when I was young, was enough. But the older I get, the more I think seduction—sex—should be about liking, sharing, having fun together."

Did that answer come from Nav or Pritam? Both, I suspected. As for me, when I went to bed with a guy, I was usually falling in love. Occasionally, after I'd broken up with a man, I'd even realized that while I'd fancied myself in love, I hadn't actually liked him that much. I missed the excitement of the romance more than the man himself.

"Even if both people know it's not going anywhere," he

said, "it still should be more than just orgasm." He gave me a teasing wink. "No matter how wonderful that orgasm might be."

I swallowed, imagining the kind of climax he might give me with those long, strong fingers, that sensual mouth. And then there was that excellent package. The one I'd tried not to think about when he was Nav. The one I had full permission to think about if he was Pritam.

Oh, God, I wanted him. Wanted what he was proposing.

We had both turned in our seats, facing each other. He leaned closer and caressed my cheek, making me tremble. "Between us, it would be more. You feel that, don't you, Kat? There's been a connection ever since we got on this train and our eyes first met."

He was reminding me of the game. I could accept Pritam, and we might end up in bed. Or I could treat him like Nav, my good friend and neighbor—the one I'd forbidden myself from having sex with—and call it quits now.

His face moved closer as I watched, fascinated. Nervous. Hopeful.

He was going to kiss me. Should I let him?

I wanted that kiss. Really, really wanted it.

And yet, it would be a make-or-break moment. What if our lips touched and things didn't click? Or the kiss was clumsy? Or it was nice but no passion sparked? Or, if it was great but I got hung up obsessing about my friendship with Nav? If any of those things happened, then so much for the game, the fantasy, the scarily glorious sense of possibility.

Oh, damn, I believed in action, so why was I doing all this uncharacteristic analysis? I tilted my head and moved closer in clear invitation.

His eyes, warm and brown, filled with something that looked almost like wonder. Then, those sensual lips met mine, soft and gentle, tentative for a moment. But only a moment.

They firmed, and confidently he took possession of my mouth

in a kiss that seared me from head to toe, especially all the deliciously sexy places in between.

His tongue demanded entry and I accepted it eagerly, answered back with my own. All the attraction I'd felt since I'd seen this man—whether he was Pritam on a train or Nav holding an elephant—came together with relief, hunger, passion. This kiss was more than thrusting tongues, nips and nibbles, the liquid heat in his eyes. Something sparked, flamed, between us.

My body tightened, ached, moistened. Talk about possibilities. Our kiss more than hinted at them, it promised, and I threw myself headlong into it.

Suddenly he broke away. He scrubbed a hand across his face, sucked in a long breath, and then blew it out again.

I was trying to catch my own breath when he said, eyes twinkling, "Now that was a damned presumptuous first kiss."

I laughed softly at his wording. "You didn't see me objecting, did you?"

A quick grin flashed. "No, thank God. But we *are* on a train. We don't want to get booted off before we get to Toronto."

I flushed. I'd been so caught up in the sexy world we'd created together, I'd forgotten our surroundings. "This is embarrassing."

"You know what people say when they see that kind of public display of affection." His eyes gleamed seductively. "Get a room."

Oh yes! "Um . . ."

"We're almost to Toronto. My room at the Royal York has a king-size bed."

That's where the kiss had been leading. The two of us in bed. I couldn't think of anything more appealing. But . . . This was insane, wasn't it? Indecisively, I said, "I booked a room, too."

His fingers trailed down my arm in a gentle, arousing caress. "Cancel it. I want to make love with you, Kat."

"What if it doesn't work out?"

He gave me a wicked, knowing smile and shook his head

slowly, deliberately. "After that kiss, you can ask that question?"

If the kiss was a fair sample, the sex would be fantastic. He—Pritam—was gorgeous, sexy, confident. Even better, he found me attractive and desirable. His kiss hadn't been smooth and practiced, it had been raw and needy.

I glanced sideways. His napkin had fallen to the floor and an impressive erection pressed against the front of his jeans. My pussy pulsed and moistened at the thought of feeling him deep inside me, and I squeezed my thighs together.

Pritam was promising me great sex. The game was time limited. Without consequences.

"We're adults," he said, "and we know what we want."

Everything he did—the compelling gleam in his eyes, the soft brush of his fingers, of his voice—stimulated my senses, sent ripples of sexual need pulsing through my body. My nipples, my pussy, ached for his touch. He was right. We both wanted sex, so why pretend otherwise?

Two weeks from now, back in Montreal, my old world and my friendly neighbor would be waiting for me. For now, what was wrong with enjoying a sexy stranger?

"Phone and cancel your room," he urged.

The steward collected our cups, but I barely noticed. I was so focused on my seatmate.

When it came to men, trusting my instincts often proved to be a mistake. And yet, I hadn't felt so wonderful in a very long while. It was only one time. A special time, with its own special rules.

"I won't cancel my room, but I will come to yours." No matter how tempted I might be, I wouldn't spend the whole night with him. I only did that when I believed a relationship was becoming serious, which this one never could.

"Good." A relieved expression crossed his face.

I'd expected a smug, masculine smile, a grin of victory. Relief was a bigger ego boost.

"When we get there," I said, "I'd rather not go in with you. I have a professional relationship with the hotel, and some of the staff know me. I don't want them thinking . . ." I shrugged.

"After I check in, I'll call your room and let you know my room number."

"All right."

Around us, passengers were stirring restlessly. I turned to glance out the window, seeing the CN Tower in the distance and the first blush of a peach-colored sunset painting the sky. "We're almost there." I had completely missed more than four hours of sunlit landscape. Lakes, rivers, farmland—as scenic as it all was, the view inside had been much nicer.

The train crossed the Don River, and I turned back to him, nervous again.

Across the aisle, a petite woman struggled to retrieve her bag from the overhead storage. My companion sprang to his feet and did it for her, body lithe and powerful. She smiled and thanked him.

"Kat? Any bags I should bring down?"

"Yes, please," I told him. "A black wheelie with a pink scarf tied to the handle."

"Got it." He lifted it down easily, then collected his own bags as the train pulled into Union Station.

When I rose and stepped into the aisle, he pulled me to him in a quick, close hug. The press of his firm body through his clothes was tantalizing. The times I'd hugged Nav, I'd always been aware of his muscular body, but had forced myself to think of him only as a friend.

Now, I wanted to see him naked. See every inch of that superhot body.

Pritam's body, I reminded myself.

Leaning down, his breath warmly erotic against my ear, he murmured, "Can't wait to do this properly," and then he stepped away, freeing me.

"Me, too."

We maneuvered our luggage off the train, into the underground station.

"Let's go aboveground," he said. "Get some fresh air. See the sunset."

"Yes, that's nicer than the tunnel." In winter, I was glad for the tunnel connecting Union Station and the Royal York, but on this lovely June evening his idea was much better.

We emerged into warm air, a busy street, deepening color in the sky. Across Front Street stood the grand old hotel. I gazed at it appreciatively—and with anticipation.

My companion squeezed my hand.

Could I really pretend he was Pritam? Play the game and separate this adventure from real life? Nervously I said, "D'you know, when the CPR built this hotel eighty years ago, it was the tallest building in the British Commonwealth?"

"Really? Times have sure changed. It's classic, though."

"As a *Bollywood producer*, you'll be interested to know that lots of movies have been made here. Wait until you see the inside. Or have you stayed here before?" It was well beyond Nav's normal budget, and I wondered how he'd managed to afford a room.

"No, this is my first time." He turned his gaze from the hotel to me. "And it's not the hotel architecture and décor, or moviemaking, I'm most interested in."

Tingles of sexual awareness raced through me. Oh, yes, I wanted this. "I'll go ahead and you follow in a couple minutes."

He bent down and brushed his lips across mine in a quick, hard caress that made me crave more. "See you soon."

His kiss still burning on my lips, I headed across the street.

For the first time since I'd been introduced to Pritam, I was free of his compelling presence. This was the time to reflect and make sure what I wanted.

Sex with him? Oh, yes. But not at the risk of losing my best friend.

When I'd first moved to the apartment building off St. Catherine, I'd been saving up a down payment, shopping for a condo. Then Nav had moved in. Now, I had a huge amount of money saved and I'd long ago stopped checking the real estate listings. Because *home* didn't mean a fancy condo, it meant living next door to Nav.

But, okay, he'd said our friendship wouldn't change. Though my grandmother had always said you couldn't have your cake and eat it, too, Nav had promised me differently.

The doorman—not one I recognized—tipped his hat as he ushered me in. "Good day, miss. Enjoy your evening."

I gave him a nervous smile. "I plan to, thanks."

When I'd first entered this hotel more than ten years ago, I'd stood and gaped at the grandeur: chandeliers and a painted ceiling, pillars with light sconces, ornate furniture. Tonight I didn't pause to admire the golden opulence but strode toward the registration desk.

The check-in was efficient, and in less than five minutes I was in my room. Quickly I freshened up, awaiting his call.

When my room phone rang, I hurried to answer.

He told me his room number and I said, "I'll be there in a minute."

Taking only my purse and key, I went to the elevator.

My heart raced as the elevator rose, floor by floor.

The doors slid open and I took a deep breath, then walked down the hall. When I located his room, the door was ajar. I stepped inside, closing it behind me. "Wow!"

I'd assumed he'd be in one of the standard rooms like mine, an upscale version of the traditional hotel room with a bed, dresser, TV cabinet, and so on. But no, he had an expensive suite with a sitting room area and a bedroom—the king-size bed visible, already turned down for the night.

Decorated in the hotel's Victorian style, the suite was elegant and warm in shades of gold and garnet. Two ornate lamps were lit, but the curtains hadn't been drawn across the window. Outside, the sunset had deepened, a striking backdrop to tall buildings sparkling with lights.

He turned from admiring the view and came toward me. "*Oui, c'est une chambre agréable, n'est-ce pas?*" A knock sounded behind me, and he veered to swing open the door.

Nav couldn't possibly afford a room like this, much less the train tickets and the clothes. One day I'd learn the truth, but for now, I was with Pritam.

From this moment on, this man was Pritam. I wouldn't allow myself to think otherwise, or I couldn't go through with this.

A room service waiter came in bearing an ice bucket, a bottle, and two flutes. Champagne. Pritam had ordered champagne.

The waiter displayed the bottle, and I saw the lovely painted anemones that graced Perrier-Jouet's La Belle Epoque, and noted the excellent vintage. This was very good, and very expensive, champagne.

"Do you like this wine?" Pritam touched my shoulder.

I jumped nervously and cleared my throat. "Oh, yes. It's a subtle, perfectly balanced champagne. One for a sophisticated palate." Great, I sounded like a sommelier.

Pritam gave a teasing grin. "Well, then, since we're both so sophisticated, it should be perfect." Still speaking Parisian French, he said to the waiter, "Please go ahead and open it."

"*Bien sûr, monsieur.*" The waiter did so deftly, the cork easing out with a hushed puff of air. Pritam thanked him and said we'd pour the wine ourselves. Then he signed the tab and the waiter left with a quiet, "*Merci, et bon soir.*"

When I'd left Montreal five hours earlier, I'd imagined a quiet night in my room checking e-mail, working on the wedding e-vite, going to bed early.

Now here I was in a gorgeous suite, with as sexy and fascinating a man as I'd ever met, and a bottle of excellent champagne.

Not to mention the memory of that sizzling first kiss.

Chapter 7

Nav's heart beat so fast and hard, it was a wonder Kat couldn't hear it. The love of his life stood beside him in his hotel room.

A suite that had cost, for one night, almost as much as a month's rent in Montreal. But a normal room wouldn't do. The trappings of this seduction had to be extravagant. He must keep Kat from seeing him as Nav and slamming him back into the buddy trap.

He poured champagne into two elegant flute glasses. Not having drunk much champagne in the past few years, he hadn't relied on memory but had asked room service to bring something special that would appeal to a lady with excellent taste. The flowered bottle was certainly pretty, feminine, and he'd seen Kat's smile of recognition.

Now he presented a glass to her, holding it by the stem. When she took it, he made sure their fingers touched before he let go. Then he raised his own flute. "To meeting each other and beginning a wonderful adventure."

"I'll drink to that, Pritam." Her voice was light, breathy. Nervous? Excited? Or both?

They sipped. The bubbles fizzed on his tongue as he savored the elegant complexity of the wine. Once, he'd drunk fine wines on a regular basis, and his palate appreciated this one even as he thought that no wine in the world was worth the kind of money he'd laid out.

Seducing Kat, on the other hand, was worth whatever it took.

"Come over here." With a hand on her lower back—touching her the way a confident lover would and Nav never had—he guided her to the window. "Isn't this a wonderful view?"

They stood side by side, sipping champagne and looking at the cityscape. Lights glittered in hundreds of windows, bright against the deepening purple sky of approaching night.

If he hadn't been with Kat, he'd have been reaching for his camera. But now his hand still rested on her back, just above the waistband of her jeans, and he felt the heat of her skin through the thin layers of camisole and filmy blouse. He longed to touch her naked flesh, and his dick pulsed at the thought.

"The city's shifting from her daylight persona to her evening one," he commented.

She glanced at him. "What a lovely way of putting it."

"Inside all those windows, people are making that same shift. Getting dressed up to go out, or changing into comfy clothes to curl up with a book or TV show." He smiled down at her. "And then there's us."

He put his glass on a table by the window, took hers and did the same, then rested his hands lightly on her shoulders. "We aren't going out."

Gazing up into his eyes as if mesmerized, she shook her head. "No."

"Nor watching TV or reading."

Another head shake. Her pulse fluttered in the hollow of her throat. A spot he very much wanted to kiss.

"Here's what we're going to do while the sun finishes setting." He tilted his head and bent down, letting his intent show on his face.

She came up on her toes, rising to meet him. "Yes." Her soft breath whispered against his mouth. Wine, mint. She'd brushed her teeth for him, as he had for her.

Her lips were pink, gleaming, full. Parted the tiniest bit. And then his lips touched them. Softly, but with no tentativeness. He claimed her mouth with a gentle, sure kiss.

When she responded, he angled his head and explored her lips thoroughly, kissing and nibbling, darting his tongue around the outside rim but not plunging inside. He'd wanted to kiss her for so long, and now they were alone together, so he could savor every moment. He sucked on the fullness of her bottom lip and she gave a soft moan.

His blood thickened, surged through his veins. Finally, he had no need to fight back an erection, to conceal the effect she had on him. He wrapped his arms around Kat and, as his dick grew, pressed the front of his body against hers.

She didn't hesitate before returning the pressure.

Her cheeks were flushed; her eyes drifted shut; her hands stroked down his back. He wished he wasn't wearing a shirt; longed to feel her flesh against his.

Now that her eyes were closed, he could stare at her face all he wanted and not bother to hide his joy and love. Holding her securely around the waist with one arm, he touched her face with wonder. Arched brows. Slim nose. Cheeks that were rosy with passion. For him.

A firm jaw on that heart-shaped face, to suit the determined, independent woman she was. He stroked it, featherlight, then tightened his grip, holding her where he wanted her as his tongue dipped between her lips.

Her tongue met it, delicately at first, then with fervor.

As they kissed, his hand continued its exploration, drifting down the slender column of her throat as she stretched her neck in encouragement. Circling the silky soft hollow at the base where her pulse now throbbed wildly. As he traveled uncharted territory, places Nav had only gazed at and hungered for, he delighted in each sensation.

Reaching between them, he unbuttoned her filmy blouse, hands fumbling as he felt the curves of her breasts, the hard nubs of her nipples under her camisole.

She stepped away so she could peel off the blouse, and he cupped her breasts through the thin pink fabric. Firm, with a deliciously soft, feminine weight, they filled his hands perfectly.

She arched her back and dragged her hands through her hair, pulling it away from her face, tousling it. The movement was sensual, abandoned. It lifted her breasts and thrust them even more firmly into his hands.

Nav went down on his knees and, through her camisole, ran the edge of his thumb over a pert nipple. Back and forth. Heated skin under the thin fabric, a scent of jasmine and woman. He put his mouth to the silk and sucked the areola into his mouth.

She gasped.

He applied more suction, nibbled the tight bud gently.

She moaned softly. "That feels so good."

Lifting his head from the wet patch on her camisole, he gazed up at her. Breasts rising and falling rapidly under her top, a long, beautiful stretch of naked chest and neck, raised arms, flushed cheeks, glittery eyes, hair in sexy disarray. "I want to make you feel good, Kat."

He turned his attention to her other breast as she pressed her hands to the top of his head, holding him there.

Then, hooking his fingers in the hem of the camisole, he began to peel it upward. When it cleared the waistband of her jeans, he paused to swirl his tongue in her delicate navel. Then he tugged the fabric higher, baring her taut stomach and rib cage, the bottom curves of her breasts.

Impatient now, he rose from his kneeling position and started to pull the camisole free of her breasts.

Her arms crossed over her chest, stopping him.

Damn, what had gone wrong? "Kat?"

Freeing one hand, she gestured toward the window. "We need to pull the drapes."

He glanced out. An indigo night had fallen. Facing them were hundreds of windows, some lit, some dark. He felt a primitive urge to beat his chest like Tarzan and declare to the world that the beauty beside him was his woman. He shook his head. "No, we don't."

"Someone could see in. Our lights are on."

"Only if they had binoculars or a telescope. And who cares if they do? No one would recognize us; we'd just be an anonymous woman and man. An erotic image. Let them look."

Her lips parted; her eyes gleamed. "You want people to see us?"

"Yeah. Let them envy us."

The arm across her chest eased away and dropped to her side. "All right." Her whisper was so low he could barely hear it.

Wasting no time, he went back to peeling the camisole over her head. And there she stood, half naked in golden lamplight. "You take my breath away."

"I feel self-conscious." But she didn't cross her arms over her chest again. She reached for the front of his shirt. "I want to see you, too." Her fingers trembled as she undid buttons.

Impatient, Nav wanted to help, yet he also wanted her to do this herself. He wanted Kat to hunger for him the way he did for her.

Finally, she reached the last buttons, her fingers brushing against the front of his jeans, inadvertently stroking his erection. Or maybe not so inadvertently, because they lingered.

He wanted to thrust into her hands, but restrained himself. Kat deserved to be worshipped. No matter how much he wanted her, how long he'd wanted her, he wouldn't act like a horny boy.

She spread the sides of his shirt and now her fingers were dancing up his body, quick and light, touching here, there, everywhere.

He yanked his shirt off as he watched her face, read the appreciation, the lust, on it.

"Nice," she murmured as she ran her fingers through curls of chest hair. "Strong," as she gripped his shoulders. "Oh, yes, very nice." Then she closed the distance between them and came into his arms, her naked breasts against his naked chest, the way he'd imagined so many times.

Sensation jolted through him. Even in his wildest erotic fantasies, she hadn't felt this good. His imagination hadn't captured the heat of her skin, the silky slide of it against his as she shifted position. The combined scent of jasmine and mint. The "mmm" sounds she made as their bodies moved together.

He ran his hands through her hair, lifted her face to his, and then plunged his tongue inside her mouth, letting her feel his pent-up passion.

Hungrily, she returned the kiss.

He reached between them, found the fastenings of her pants, and undid them. When he tried to shove the snug jeans down her legs, she took over. He went to work on his own pants.

Breathless, laughing, they stepped apart to kick out of their jeans. She looked so hot in only a brief pair of pink panties. Then they were pressed together again, kissing frantically.

His hands caressed every inch of her back, dipped under her panties, cupped her curvy ass, yanked her tight against his rigid erection.

She moaned and squirmed, trying to get even closer. Her hands paralleled the course his had taken, coming to rest under the expensive Armani underwear he'd bought just for her. His buttocks tensed under her touch, and he wanted to thrust against her. Into her.

He squeezed his eyes shut, fighting for control. Kat was such a turn-on. But what he really wanted was to turn *her* on. To make love to her in a way that showed her how beautiful she was. How special to him. How lovable.

Trying to forget his own driving need, he eased his mouth from hers and trailed kisses across her cheek and over to her

ear, where he circled and teased with his tongue. Then slowly
he tracked soft, damp lip prints down her neck, coupled with
flicks of his tongue against skin that quivered at his touch.

He swirled his tongue in the pulse-point hollow at the base
of her throat, then continued down, unable to resist the lure of
her lovely breasts. First, the soft creamy upper curves, then rosy
areolas puckered with arousal. Then raspberry pink nipples,
begging to be sucked.

"So beautiful," he murmured. On his knees again, his hands
at her waist to steady her, he took one nipple in his mouth, applying soft, rhythmic pressure. Suck and release, suck and release. He scraped his teeth gently across the engorged bud, then
soothed it with his tongue.

"Oh, God," Kat whispered. "Oh, yes." She gripped his shoulders and her torso arched back. Under his hands, her skin rippled with each jerky breath she took.

He moved to her other breast, lavishing it with the same attention.

"I can't believe how good that feels," she said breathlessly.
Focused on sensation, she was speaking English now.

He slid a hand across the front of her tiny panties. Felt the
springy curls of her bush pressing against the thin silk. Then
the plump firmness of her mound. Then his fingers stroked the
soaking wet fabric between her legs, and she let out a whimper
of pleasure.

Nav wanted to whimper, too, partly from the joy of being
with her like this and partly from the painful pressure in his
groin.

Abandoning her breast, he kissed his way downward, dipping his tongue into her navel, moving across her quivering
belly and then the front of her panties. The heady musk of her
arousal drew him on until he was kissing her sex through a
layer of moist silk.

She shuddered and widened her stance, allowing him better

access, thrusting her groin into his face, body telegraphing her need. Her fingers bit into his shoulders as she struggled to stay upright.

He licked back and forth, then in circles, tongue pressing the fabric against her swollen flesh. Firmly, to give her maximum stimulation. Then lightly, to tease her. Then harder again.

"Oh, yes," she panted. "More. So good." Heat rose off her, and she wriggled against his tongue.

He circled the hard nub of her clit with his lips and breathed hot, moist air on it. Because of the barrier of her panties, he couldn't take it in his mouth, but he flicked his tongue across it, strumming it.

"Oh, God!" She gasped, tensed, froze.

He imagined how she felt. The pressure building inside. Waiting for him to give her the final stimulus to tip her over the edge.

He firmed his tongue, flicked it harder. Then once more.

She came apart. In surging pulses against his mouth. In a high, wordless cry of elation.

He almost did, too. It took every ounce of self-control not to join her.

Then he realized her legs were trembling so hard she might fall. He rose quickly and pulled her into his embrace.

Kat clung, head sagging against his shoulder, chest heaving, struggling to breathe.

He stood rigidly, fighting the need to strip off their underwear and thrust into her. To the hilt.

She raised her head, eyes dazed, and lifted a shaky hand to drag it through her hair. Her cheeks were flushed, dewy. "Wow. That was something."

"Only the beginning." It was an effort to remember to speak in French. "I think it's time we tried out that bed."

"Bed," she echoed, speaking French now, too. Then her eyes widened, sharpened, her gaze jerked to the window. "Oh, my God!" Her body clamped itself more tightly against his as if she could hide in his arms. "I can't believe we did that in full view of— What were we thinking?"

"I was thinking it was sexy. How about you?"

"I wasn't thinking about anything except how good it felt. But now . . ."

Nav couldn't wait any longer. He lifted her and strode toward the bedroom.

He'd barely registered the searing imprint of her curvy body against his near-naked one before he was tossing her onto the turned-down bed and reaching for one of the condoms he'd left on the bedside table. In one swift motion, he ripped the package open. Then he yanked down his underwear and sheathed himself.

Kat had arranged herself on the bed, still wearing those pink panties. With a hand behind her head and one knee up, her pose said, "Look at me," but right now he wasn't into looking.

He needed to be inside her.

She must have seen the fierce determination on his face, because she gasped, then spread her legs in invitation.

He fitted his body between them and captured her lips in a searing kiss. With one hand he yanked aside the crotch of her panties, and then he plunged inside her without an iota of finesse.

There. Deep inside Kat. That's where he'd wanted to be since that first day in the hall.

He held still a moment, savoring the bliss of it. But the way her heated channel gripped him, her moan of pleasure, the knowledge that this was the woman he loved, all combined in an irresistible urge to move.

Now. Hard. Fast. Deep.

In and out, relentlessly, as the pressure built at the base of his spine, as his balls tightened and drew up.

Their mouths parted, both of them panting, making wordless sounds.

He reached between their bodies, found her slippery, swollen clit. Stroked it urgently. Heard her cry out. Felt her body spasm as he plunged into her core and exploded in a climax that almost took off the top of his head.

When the jerky spasms finally ended, he collapsed on top of her. Barely conscious—was any oxygen getting to his brain?—he managed to take some of his weight on his knees and arms so he didn't crush her.

Under him, her body heaved as she, too, struggled to get air. Finally, she lifted a hand and stroked his back. "That was amazing."

"*Oui, vraiment.*" A smile curved his lips. "Not exactly elegant, but effective."

She chuckled. "Definitely effective."

He studied her face. Eyes closed, a grin of smug satisfaction.

He rolled off her and went to deal with the condom. Then he retrieved the champagne bottle and glasses from the sitting room. "Sit up."

She opened her eyes. "Oh, yum, champagne." She raised up, shoving pillows behind her back, and took the glass he offered. A sip. A happy sigh. "Mmm, sex makes me thirsty."

"Me, too." He sat on the edge of the bed beside her. He sipped from his own glass, then tilted it so a trickle of bubbly golden wine spilled onto her stomach.

"Hey, what are you doing? That's too expensive to waste."

"Believe me, it won't be wasted." Now he'd satisfied his immediate sexual hunger, he wanted to get back to worshipping her.

He put the glass on the cabinet by the bed, then bent over her. Though her arms, legs, and face were lightly tanned from the June sun, her stomach was pale in the warm lamplight. Private skin, exposed to his eyes only.

He licked, tasting champagne and a slight saltiness, tracing the trail of drops to where wine had pooled in her navel. When he lapped it out, she giggled, shifted, murmured, "Ticklish."

Lifting the glass again, he held it over her pelvis. "Don't want to get those panties wet. Maybe you should take them off."

"Like they're not already wet." She slid the scrap of pink down her shapely legs.

Nav didn't see where she tossed it, he was absorbed in the perfection of the view revealed by her spread legs: a nest of neatly trimmed auburn curls and the slick, pouty lips of her sex.

Lovely. Utterly feminine. And he'd been inside there.

When he drizzled a stream of bubbles onto her belly, he hoped she didn't notice his hand was shaking. Her beauty, her trust, the intimacy, all stunned him. While he had fantasized countless times about making love with Kat, and had hoped his strangers-on-a-train plan would succeed, it was almost impossible to believe this was real.

Maybe he was dreaming. If so, he intended to enjoy every second before he woke up. Though his body was again heating to arousal, he was more interested in savoring her and making this special for her.

Again he bent to lap droplets of champagne, and this time he caressed her with his fingers, too. Combing through the springy curls of hair, cupping her fleshy mound, he hoped she could sense she was being cherished.

With other women, he'd had recreational sex. Enjoyable, mutual, even caring. But with Kat, this was all about his love for her.

"I'm being lazy," she murmured. "Tell me what you'd like."

"This. Exactly this."

When he touched his tongue to the swollen folds between her legs, her juices were sweeter than the wine. The taste of her sexual arousal, an arousal he'd created, was ambrosia.

Letting her response guide him, he licked the sensitive folds, at first gently, then flattening his tongue to apply firmer pressure as she writhed and pressed against him. Then he eased a finger inside her, and another. He stroked and circled, feeling the texture of her secret flesh.

Her hips lifted. "I can't stand it."

Unable to tell if that choked cry was pain or pleasure, he slid his fingers out.

"No!" she protested. "More."

He thrust in again, three fingers this time, and felt her walls grip him, pulse around him.

Now he did what he hadn't been able to through her panties. He laved her swollen clit with his tongue, then sucked it gently into his mouth.

She arched. "Yes, oh, yes!"

Her thighs gripped his head; her hips thrashed; she pressed herself against his face.

Still thrusting with his fingers, he held her tiny, sensitive clit carefully between his lips. Applying suction around it, he flicked his tongue across the tip. Back and forth, faster and faster.

With a shout, she climaxed, sweet and wet and pulsing against his mouth.

Chapter 8

Helpless in the grip of a shattering climax, I clutched the sheet below me with both hands and rode the waves that crashed through my body.

And through all of it, he held me.

What a rare, generous lover he was. That was twice that he, his cock hard and thick with arousal, had put my satisfaction first. "Hey." My voice came out husky. "Come kiss me."

His head lifted, a smile quirking his full lips. "I thought I was."

"Oh, yeah. And very nicely, too. But now I want—" I broke off at the thought of what I really wanted from him.

"What do you want, Kat?" Gleaming dark eyes challenged me.

"I want to feel you inside me again. It's so good."

His eyes squeezed shut for a moment, the angles of his face almost harsh as if he was gripped by a strong emotion. Then he was moving, shifting lithely from the cramped position he'd been in.

He'd given me gentle lovemaking, and he'd given me vigorous passion. Right now, his tender ministrations had whetted my appetite for passion. I doubted he'd object.

Grabbing the box of condoms on the bedside cabinet, I said, "Now. I want you now." I pulled out a package and tossed it to him. "Hard and fast."

Surprise lit his face, made him fumble the catch so he had to use both hands to secure the condom package. "Hard and fast?"

"Don't you want to?"

He swallowed, muscles in his throat rippling. A fire lit his eyes. "Hell, yeah." With quick motions he ripped open the packet and sheathed himself.

I'd barely spread my legs wider when he covered my body with his.

I gasped at the contact. He was so muscular, so hot, so purely male. My arms circled him and I stroked his back, caressed his taut butt.

When he kissed me, I responded hungrily. Lips, tongues, teeth met, dueled, clashed, mated in a frenzied dance.

His cock plunged inside me in one sure, forceful stroke that made me cry out with pleasure against his mouth. I'd asked for hard and fast, and that's what he was giving me.

Clinging to him, I met each thrust with one of my own, drawing him deeper, urging him to move faster, ever faster. And all the time we were kissing, mouths mashing together with desperate fervor.

That pre-orgasmic achy need built inside me, demanding release.

He tore his mouth from mine. Gasped, "Slow down, Kat. You'll make me come."

"I want you to." I gripped his butt harder, not letting him stop. "I want us to come together. Now."

"Jesus!" His eyes were wild, impassioned.

He let go in powerful strokes that hit every sensitive spot, plunged to my very core, drew everything inside me to one point of pure, focused sensation. Sensation where pain and pleasure mingled so closely, I couldn't separate them. But I couldn't stay there long. I couldn't survive it.

Then he gave one final thrust, a guttural cry of triumph, and took me over the edge. I exploded at the same moment he jerked and spasmed inside me. Both our climaxes seemed to go on forever.

My legs were weak and trembling when I managed to un-hook them from around him. They fell heavily to the bed. I sank into the mattress, and he collapsed on top of me as he'd done before. Still inside me. Both of us panting as if we'd run a marathon.

He managed to hoist himself on his elbows, and then planted a kiss on my lips. "My God."

"Yeah." My chest heaved as I tried to find breath. "Wow."

"You're amazing."

"You, too," I told him.

"I wanted to make it last longer."

"I wanted it hard and fast."

He chuckled. "I noticed. And it felt damn good."

Gradually our breathing slowed.

"I'm too heavy," he said.

"You're not." He felt perfect. With his knees and forearms taking much of his weight, he wasn't heavy. Just firm, hot, sexy. Smelling a little of sandalwood and a lot of sex. If someone bottled that scent, lots more men would be getting lucky.

"Sorry, but I need to deal with the condom." As he pulled out of me and rolled off, I resented the necessity, the intrusion of practicality into this sexy adventure.

On the other hand, as he strolled naked toward the bath-room, I got to appreciate the rear view. What a perfect male back, from the broad shoulders to the narrow waist, lean hips, breathtakingly tight butt . . .

Oh, God, I'd had sex with Nav. It was the butt that brought me back to reality. Nav's butt, naked. As fabulous as I'd imag-ined it to be.

I squeezed my eyes shut and pressed my hands over them. No, no, no. This wasn't the time to think about Nav.

The man in this ritzy hotel suite, the one who'd bought Belle

Epoque champagne, who wore a flashy diamond ring on his manicured hand, was Pritam.

The man who'd seduced me into climaxing in front of all of Toronto, then fucked me senseless in a king-size bed, was *Pritam*.

From the bathroom, I heard the toilet flush, water run.

Quickly I sat upright, drained my glass of champagne, and clicked off the bedside lamp. Enough light seeped in from the sitting room so I could see to refill my glass. And his. The glass from which he'd dripped champagne onto me. Then licked it off.

Pritam had done that. Pritam, the Bollywood producer. The man with clean-shaven cheeks and a Piaget watch.

I drank more champagne, slugging it back rather than giving it the appreciation it deserved. Life had gone topsy-turvy, and I had no clue how to deal with it. But excellent champagne could only help.

The bathroom door opened. And now I regretted having turned off the light, because I didn't have a crystal-clear view as he walked, with that confident athletic stride, across the bedroom and into the sitting room.

He came back in a moment with a bottle of water and two glasses. Cautiously my eyes darted upward. Yes, his face was shaved, angles rather than curves, and no curls of hair hung over his eyes. Pritam's face, not Nav's.

He poured water into a glass and offered it. "Want a drink?" The Parisian French was Pritam's.

"Thanks, but I'm happy with the champagne." Actually, I realized I was exhausted. Satiated, worn out from both stress and pleasure. Maybe a little tipsy. A gigantic yawn shuddered through me and, too late, I tried to cover my mouth.

He chuckled and took my flute glass from me. "Lie down."

"I should go." But not quite yet. I yawned again and slid down in the bed. Mmm, the pillow was so soft. My eyes slid shut.

Dimly I was aware of him lying beside me and gathering me close so my head rested on his shoulder, and tucking covers around us.

Of his kiss on the top of my head.

I should leave. Couldn't spend the night here. I'd get up in a moment, but right now I was too tired. Too content.

I woke in the darkness with a champagne headache and a parched mouth.

And a male arm wrapped around me. What? I was lying in bed in the dark with a man. A man who smelled of sex and sandalwood.

Oh, my God. Pritam. Nav. What had I done?

Gingerly, I extracted myself from under his arm. He stirred and made a grumbly sound. No, no, no. I didn't want him to wake up, didn't want to talk, didn't want to make love.

I held my breath as he rolled over and settled back into sleep. His hair had come loose from the band that had held it back. Black curls—Nav's—tumbled across the white pillowcase.

Shit. Maybe my headache wasn't from wine, maybe it was pure stress.

I couldn't stay here. Couldn't wake up beside him in the morning. I needed distance, a chance to work things through in my head. Once it stopped aching.

I slipped cautiously out of bed and tiptoed out to the sitting room.

He hadn't drawn the drapes—oh, my God, I'd let him go down on me in front of all of Toronto!—and the light of the night city brightened the room enough that I could find my purse. And my discarded clothing, except for my panties. They were somewhere in the bedroom, and I wasn't going back in case he woke up.

When we did talk, what would we say? He'd promised nothing would change, but . . . but we'd had sex. Incredible sex. The best I'd ever had.

No, that had been with *Pritam,* I told myself. Nav was my friend, and being lovers would ruin that.

The next time I saw Nav would be in Vancouver. If he was still willing to come. But how could Nav be my wedding date after this . . . fling with his alter ego, Pritam? We'd have to talk.

Maybe I should take some aspirin and stay and wait for him to wake up.

No, leaving was best. We'd played out his strangers-on-a-train game, and it was over. Easier for both of us to not endure an awkward morning-after conversation.

In fact, maybe we didn't need to talk about this at all. Could we pretend it had never happened? I could take my cue from him. If he didn't mention it . . .

I'd have to e-mail or phone about the wedding. If Nav acted like his old self and didn't refer to Pritam, maybe I wouldn't, either.

Damn. This was confusing. What had I been thinking?

I hurried toward the door, already fumbling my room key out of my purse.

Five minutes later, after taking aspirin and drinking two glasses of water, I pulled off my clothes, set the alarm clock, and fell into bed. For the moment, I just needed to sleep.

What was done was done, and I'd worry about it in the morning.

Chapter 9

Nav woke, feeling the most wonderful sense of well-being. He lay on his side with his eyes closed, savoring the sensation and the memories.

His plan had worked even better than he'd hoped. He and Kat were lovers.

He turned his face into the pillow, smelling a hint of jasmine. God, she was delicious. Every inch of her. Every scent, every sound she made. Better than he'd ever imagined.

The lovemaking had been incredible.

He opened his eyes to check the clock by the bed. Almost seven. Yes, there'd be time for morning lovemaking before they had to leave for the train station. And then there'd be three romantic days, three sexy nights on the train. If she still bought into the game.

Or would she have regrets? Would she call it off? How would she handle the whole Nav/Pritam thing? He was almost reluctant to roll over and wake her.

Slowly he shifted onto his back, then to his other side. Then he jerked upright. Damn! Her side of the bed was empty. He glanced toward the bathroom. An open door, no light on.

He leaped out of bed and rushed into the sitting room. Crap. No Kat. She'd run away.

He slammed his fist on the mahogany table that, last night, had held their champagne. So much for that romantic train trip to Vancouver.

What the hell was he going to do now?

Chapter 10

When I woke, my headache was gone.

As I took a long, lovely shower, I felt more philosophical about what had happened yesterday. It had been a game, and I'd had fun. I slid my hand between my legs, where my body still hummed from that fun.

Nav had told me there'd be no consequences, that we'd go back to being friends. I trusted him, so I was going to believe that was true.

I hoped he wasn't mad or hurt that I'd left in the middle of the night without a good-bye. I'd never intended to stay—that was why I'd kept my room—but had he realized that?

Should I call him? No, he was probably sleeping in.

Maybe he'd hang around Toronto for a day or two, taking photographs for his exhibit, rather than heading straight back to Montreal. Later today, or maybe tomorrow, I'd phone and make sure everything was cool. No hurt feelings, no regrets, no issues.

With any luck, we'd both pretend the whole Pritam thing had never happened. If so, then I'd find out if he was still willing to come to the wedding.

At least now I knew he'd be eminently show-offable, with his shaved face and nice clothes.

But seeing him for the first time after last night could be

weird, with his new image a reminder of Pritam. It was going to be hard not to think about how great he looked naked, and what a fabulous lover he was.

My body heated, and I turned the shower dial to cool. I couldn't think like that. He would be Nav. My best friend. The two of us were absolutely not going to have hot sex again.

Our friendship was wonderful, and to date all my love affairs had been dismal failures. I'd never take that chance with Nav. Plus, even though Pritam had said he wanted to get married, Nav was all about playing the field.

He'd probably played the stranger game with other women. Why should that thought disturb me?

Less than an hour later, an attendant showed me into my single bedroom sleeping compartment on the VIA Rail Canadian. The room was tiny, the size of a single bed plus a little space to squish my carry-on. During the day, it held a chair, toilet, and sink, and at night an attendant would stow the chair and pull out a bunk bed. The shower was down the hall.

The cramped space wasn't a problem, because I rarely spent much time in my room, except to sleep.

Normally I'd have gone to the Park Car or Activity Car to have coffee and a muffin and watch as people boarded. But before I'd left the hotel I'd downloaded e-mail to my laptop and I wanted to read it. Besides, I needed to finish off the M&M e-vite.

As my computer booted up, I glanced out the window at the busy train station. Was Nav out there, catching a train back to Montreal, or was he staying in Toronto?

Did he still feel a sexy hum in his body, and did his mind replay images from last night? Or, for him, was it just one in a long string of casual hookups?

I forced myself to concentrate on the computer screen.

One message, from my friend Corrine in Australia who had studied at the U of T with me, had the subject line

Congrats to your sister!

How had she heard about Merilee's engagement? Maybe through my sister Theresa, who taught at the University of Sydney, though I hadn't been aware Theresa and Corrine knew each other. I clicked open the message.

Theresa's on the front page of the tabloids! Wow, did she ever snag a hottie!! I've seen her fiancé on TV and man, does he rock <g>.

Theresa? Fiancé? I shook my head. Corrine was mistaken. After Theresa's divorce from backstabbing Jeffrey, she'd vowed not to marry again. The woman didn't even date. She probably hadn't had sex in years.

Unlike me, whose body felt pleasantly worn out from so many orgasms I'd lost count.

Damn, it wasn't wise to replay last night. Pritam was gone— *poof*—as if he'd never existed. And I didn't want to think of Nav in a sexual way.

I focused again on the e-mail.

Why didn't you tell me she was engaged to Damien Black? He's been voted one of the 10 sexiest bachelors in Oz, and now she's taken him off the market. Good on her!!! (I'd hate the bitch if she wasn't your sister. LOL)

I laughed out loud, too. Yeah, like my buttoned-up sister would hook up with a man like that. He definitely wouldn't be attracted to her, and she'd figure he didn't have two brains to rub together. There must be two women named Theresa Fallon.

I always thought you were the tabloid girl in your family <g>. The way you're always dating guys like the Nascar driver and the gold-medal skier. Guess your sis goes for the same kind of guy. Tell her to get a better head shot, though. That "Uni Prof" one sucks. Makes her look like a . . . oh, wait a minute! A uni prof. LOL

Have they set the date? Are they getting married in Canada or here? If it's here, let me know when you're coming and we'll get together for drinks. (Lots of drinks!)

XO, Corrine

Uni prof? There couldn't be two Theresa Fallons who taught at Australian universities.

Well, how about that? Theresa was *engaged*? Theresa *and* Merilee? No, there had to be a mistake. Theresa would never do something so out of character.

I had to call Vancouver and find out what was going on.

I realized that, while I'd been absorbed in Corrine's e-mail, the train had started to move. Cell reception was iffy inside this steel capsule, and I stood a better chance of getting through when we reached the next station. Besides, it was only six a.m. in Vancouver.

Quickly I finished the e-vite and then shut down my computer. Might as well get some breakfast.

I checked my reflection in the mirror. Despite getting only a few hours' sleep, the great sex had put attractive color in my cheeks. I added lipstick to match the printed Betsey Johnson top I wore with a short denim skirt.

I made my way through several sleeping cars to reach the Park Car, a two-level car with a 360-degree observation dome above and a lounge and seating area below. Beverages and muffins were always available.

As I poured coffee and chose a blueberry muffin, a gray-haired woman was doing the same. I smiled at her. "Good morning. Are you traveling on your own?"

"I am." Her compact body and friendly, alert expression reminded me of a fox terrier. "How about you?"

"Yes. Why don't we eat together?"

"Why not?"

Once we'd introduced ourselves—her name was Lynn—and found seats, I said, "I'm going all the way to Vancouver. How about you?"

"To Jasper, then on to Banff."

"Banff in the summer." I pictured lovely mountain scenery, stunning Lake Louise. "It should be beautiful. Is this business or pleasure?"

"Pleasure, indeed." Her eyes twinkled. "A holiday with a gentleman friend."

"Sounds lovely." What a perfect spot for a romantic escape. "So, you live in Toronto, and he's in Banff?"

"He's from Vancouver." She tasted her coffee, then added another packet of sugar. "We met on an Alaska cruise last year."

"How romantic. But isn't it difficult, carrying on a long-distance romance?"

"Sometimes. But we do pretty well." A smug grin flashed. "Very well, actually."

"Do I hear wedding bells in your future?" Was every female I knew getting married?

She shrugged. "Maybe one day. We're in no hurry. We're both widowed and had happy marriages. We don't want to rush into anything. It's best to make sure before you say the vows."

"That's wise." Wiser than my habit of falling head over heels. "I've promised myself I won't get serious about a man until I've known him for at least a month."

"A month?" Her eyes twinkled. "An entire month?"

"For me, that's an improvement." I said it dryly, to show I could laugh at myself.

We were approaching a station, and I checked my watch. My family would be up by now. "Would you excuse me? I have to make a call."

"See you later, Kat."

When the train doors opened, I stepped onto the platform and dialed the house.

Merilee answered. "Hey, Kat. Hang on, let me put you on speaker."

That told me she and the others were in the kitchen, where my parents had installed a conference phone when the first of us, Theresa, had left home.

I heard a click, then Merilee said, "Can you hear me?"

"Sure can. Is everyone there?" As I spoke, I walked to the end of the platform, as far away from the hustle and bustle as I could get.

"Hello, dear," Mom said, and Dad said, "Good to hear from you."

Then I heard Theresa's voice. "Hi, Kat. I made it home late last night. Are you—"

"You're engaged? Why didn't you tell me?"

"I'm not. Where did you hear that?"

So it was a mistake, as I'd suspected. "A friend e-mailed me from Australia. She saw it in some tabloid."

Mom said, "This is exactly the kind of thing we're concerned about."

"It's all a big mistake," Theresa said.

"I thought it must be."

"You'd have known for sure if you'd seen the guy," Merilee said. "He's seriously hot."

"Seen him?" What was my little sister talking about? "You've met him?"

"Yeah," Merilee said. "They were on the same flight. They had some little fling or whatever." She snorted. "Can you imagine Theresa being engaged to one of the ten sexiest bachelors in Australia?"

Of course I couldn't. Nor could I imagine her having a fling.

"You guys, I'm here!" Theresa's voice was loud, annoyed. "And thanks for that vote of confidence."

"What?" I asked.

She huffed. "You think there's no way I could possibly attract a seriously hot man."

True. She was so tailored and uptight, and kind of plain. Of course I wouldn't say that, and besides, there was more to it. "It's just that you go for the professorial type. Like Jeffrey."

"Except," Merilee put in, "that since Jeffrey, you don't go for any guys at all."

"I *go* for Damien. And he goes for me." Theresa sounded defiant. "It's more than a fling. It's a relationship."

A relationship? This was for real? My head-in-a-book sister had actually met a special guy? "Oh, my gosh, Theresa has a boyfriend!" I squealed. For the moment, happiness for her triumphed over envy.

"I do." She laughed, sounding young, bubbly, thrilled to bits. "I really do. And he's not only handsome, sexy, and successful, he's smart and very nice, too."

"Sounds like the perfect man," I told her, wishing I could find one of those for myself. Like Pritam, but for real. "Even better than Matt."

"No one's better than Matt," Merilee said huffily.

Oops. Pardon me. "How did you meet?" I asked Theresa.

"At a bookstore. He's a novelist."

The bookstore fit Theresa, but it was hard to imagine her being attracted to someone as frivolous as a novelist.

"And then on the plane," she added.

After all that giddy joy, I'd have expected her to be more effusive. And what did she mean by "and then on the plane"? It sounded almost as if she barely knew the man, yet the tabloids had them engaged?

Before I could ask, she said, "And how about you and this man, Nav? Is it serious?"

What could I say? "Nav? Oh, he's great."

"The relationship must be pretty serious if he's willing to come all the way across the country to go to a wedding with you," Theresa said.

"And meet the parents," Mom added.

If I still wanted him to come. In which case, I'd have to pretend he was my special guy, though actually he was my best friend, though in fact we'd had blisteringly hot sex. Of course, at that time he'd been Pritam.

Damn, my headache was coming back.

"Right," I said. "Well, let's see. He's actually pretty much what Theresa said about her novelist. Except, Nav's a photographer. But he's, you know, all those good things." Not a celebrity, though. Theresa's guy topped mine, damn it. I rubbed my aching forehead.

"We can't wait to meet him, honey," Mom said. "Right, Ed?"

"Right," Dad said. "Though it's disconcerting to suddenly have men left, right, and center, trying to take my girls away from me."

"Nav and I aren't about to get married." The words burst out before I thought. If I wanted my family to believe Nav was my special guy, I shouldn't be so hasty to deny the possibility of marriage. With Merilee and Theresa so excited about their relationships, I wanted the family to believe I had one, too. For once, it'd be nice if there was no ribbing or pity.

"Nor are Damien and I," Theresa said.

Mom said something I didn't catch.

Before I could ask her to repeat it, Merilee said, "You'll always have Jenna, Dad. She thinks monogamy sucks."

"I don't want you girls following her example," he said quickly. "It's downright dangerous, as well as foolish, to take up with one man after another."

One man *after* another? Dad was so naïve. Jenna saw nothing wrong with having more than one lover at a time. But our parents didn't have to know that. "No news from Jenna about her travel plans?" I asked.

"Not a peep," Merilee said. "Unless she got in touch with you, Theresa?"

"No," my other sister said.

We were all quiet for a few moments. Jenna acted on impulse and didn't have a responsible bone in her body. She never worried about anything, and the result was that everyone else worried about her.

I needed aspirin.

Theresa broke the silence. "Kat, Merilee and I are going to discuss wedding plans, then I'll call or drop an e-mail and let you know where things stand."

"And I have the e-vite. I'll send it next time I get Internet access."

"Weren't you in Toronto last night?" Theresa asked. "Couldn't you have sent it from there?"

"I, uh . . . didn't have it ready then." Thank heavens my family couldn't see the flush that burned my cheeks.

The train was almost loaded, so I said a quick good-bye. As I closed my cell, I realized I hadn't found out how Theresa and her boyfriend had ended up in the tabloids.

A celebrity. She was dating a celebrity.

Too bad Pritam didn't really exist. Would a Bollywood producer top a celebrity author?

Chuckling, I stood back for a moment to admire the train. I never thought of myself as old-fashioned, but there was something magical about the string of cars stretching beyond my line of sight.

Inside the more than two dozen cars were people who, except for Lynn, were total strangers. But by the time we reached Vancouver, I'd have met a number of them and heard some version of their life stories.

On trains, people tended to talk. There wasn't a lot else to do. Plus there was something about the white noise whooshing sound, the gentle rock-and-rolling motion, that hypnotized you. That loosened tongues and inhibitions.

I headed back to my room to pop a couple of aspirin, then went again to the Park Car. A fresh cup of coffee in hand, I took the stairs up to the dome to enjoy the view and find someone to chat with.

For the next hour I did my best not to think of Nav or Pritam, or my two lucky-in-love sisters, as I talked to tourists from England and Japan. When they departed for the early seating at lunch, I settled into conversation with an older man named Terry who was heading to Victoria to visit his family.

A male voice spoke from the aisle beside me. "Hello, folks."

I glanced up, then took a second look. The newcomer was tall and movie-star handsome with blond hair, tanned skin, and blue eyes, casually elegant in jeans and a blue shirt that accented his tan. As attractive in his all-American way as Pritam was in his more exotic one.

If I hadn't just spent an amazingly sexy evening with Pritam, I'd definitely have been interested in this guy.

In the easy way of train meetings, my companion and I both said hello and we all introduced ourselves. The newcomer was Sam Wilbanks.

"What brings you on this trip?" Terry asked him.

Sam leaned a slim hip against the seat in front of me. "It's research. I'm a screenwriter, working on the script for a movie that's set on a train. I never travel by train myself, so I'm looking for details to add authenticity."

How strange that his job was so similar to the one Nav had created for Pritam. Two days, two handsome men. Two possible flirtations, because I could see the interest in Sam's eyes.

It reminded me of the way Pritam had looked at me, and of all the things we'd done in that hotel room. The heat of arousal pulsed through my veins and I shoved away the memories.

"A Canadian movie?" Terry asked.

"It'll be filmed here, mostly in Toronto, but it's a Hollywood production." Sam named a major studio.

"Wow," I said. "You're doing a screenplay for them?"

"It's my third for them."

"Well," Terry said, "I'd love to talk more, but I need to freshen up before lunch."

"Of course." Sam stepped aside so the older man could

move past me and into the aisle. "We'll get together and chat some other time."

"And I'm sure I'll see you again, too, Terry," I said.

"I'll look forward to that, both of you." He lifted a hand in farewell and headed away.

Sam slid into the seat beside me. "And I'm looking forward to getting to know you, Kat." There was a flirtatious sparkle in those vivid blue eyes.

It was impossible not to feel an answering tug of interest. And silly to have a twinge of regret that he wasn't Pritam. Pritam no longer existed, and that's exactly the way I wanted it.

The public address system announced the second seating for lunch.

"Will you join me?" Sam asked.

"Why not?"

The dining car was laid out simply, with an aisle down the middle and attractively set tables on each side. The main feature was the huge windows or, rather, the view outside.

As we walked down the aisle, the back of a head caught my eye. Glossy black hair, shoulder length, pulled back in a black band.

Oh, my God. It couldn't be.

Then I heard his voice. Or, rather, a voice that was neither Pritam's nor Nav's. "Yes, import/export," he was saying, in English with an upper-crust Brit accent that had more hard edges than Nav's.

But no question it was Nav. My heart raced, my stomach did a slow flip, and heat flooded through me. Last night I'd had sex with this man. Amazingly wonderful sex.

What was he doing here? Why was he speaking with a different accent?

He sat across from two women, one in her twenties and the other, with a fading version of the same dirty-blond hair, probably her mom.

I stopped in the aisle and Nav glanced up with a smile and a gleam in his dark eyes. "Good day, miss. My name is Dhiraj. Would you care to join us?"

Dhiraj? He was playing another stranger on a different train? Utterly confused, every cell in my body tingling from the memory of last night's sex, I could barely form a coherent thought. Except that I had to know what was going on.

Yet again, he looked drop-dead sexy, today in a charcoal sports jacket, light gray shirt, and black pants. Besides, now I'd seen his terrific body and learned how well he used it.

"Kat?" Sam said, and touched my shoulder.

Nav's—Dhiraj's—eyes narrowed as he focused on the other man, perhaps realizing for the first time that we were together. Something dark flared. Hostility? Jealousy? Hurt?

I glanced up at Sam. "I'm sorry, I have to . . . You go on, Sam."

He gave me a puzzled look, then shrugged. "Okay, Kat. Have a nice lunch."

I felt mean about bailing on Sam, but I had to find out what Nav was doing.

Knowing I needed to explain to the women why I'd ditched my prospective lunch companion to sit with three apparent strangers, I gazed at Nav. "You look very much like someone I know. Are you by chance related to Naveen Bharani?"

Muscles beside his eyes tightened, hinting at a smile. "No, I'm not related."

As I moved to slide into the seat beside him, he rose and pulled the chair back. I saw the watch and ring Pritam had worn. His hand brushed my shoulder, sending another quivering reminder through me that a dozen hours ago we'd been naked together, crying out in passion.

"But I'm glad for the resemblance," he said, "if it provided the incentive for you to sit with us." Nav's normal speech was a bit less casual than that of people raised in Canada or the States, but there was even more formality to Dhiraj's.

I wanted to lean into him, feel those wonderful hands all over my body. Stretch up and capture those sensual lips. I saw desire burn in his eyes, as well, even though he was pretending he didn't know me.

So, Pritam no longer existed, as we'd agreed. Instead, Nav had created Dhiraj? Did he hope to seduce me again? For an entire three days and nights on this train? My breath quickened.

But wait, underneath the Dhiraj façade, this was still Nav, my best friend. The guy who had a revolving-door policy when it came to dating. The man I couldn't get involved with.

Utterly confused, I sank slowly into the chair, no doubt looking a little stunned.

The younger of the two women across the table smiled brightly. "We're glad you joined us. I'm Kristin, and this is my mom, Sandra." Sandra, too, offered a welcoming smile.

"Pleased to meet you. I'm Kat. And you said you're, uh, Dhiraj?" I gazed at Nav.

"That's correct."

"He was just telling us," Sandra said, "that he's the vice president of an import/export company."

"I see." This trip certainly wasn't going to be boring. For the moment, I decided to play along. "And, pray tell, what do you import and export, *Dhiraj*?"

"Textiles."

Textiles? How on earth had he come up with that? Did he have some relative in that industry, too?

"I love your accent," Kristin said. "You live in England?"

"Part of the time. I alternate between our offices in London and New Delhi."

My body was totally aware of him, and I was intrigued to find out what he was up to. But the bottom line was, whatever role he might play, he was Nav underneath and I could trust him. Because of that simple fact, I was starting to relax.

"New Delhi." I shot him a mischievous glance. "Isn't that where they make those Bollywood movies?"

He made a sound, a choked-back laugh, but managed to stay straight-faced. "No, that would be Mumbai."

"I've heard about those movies," Kristin said. "They have a lot of song and dance, don't they? Like musicals?"

"I love musicals," Sandra said with relish. *"My Fair Lady, South Pacific."*

"Yes, there are similarities between Hollywood musicals and Bollywood movies," he said. "Romance and drama." He glanced at me, eyes dancing. "Sometimes even a secret identity to add to the fun."

"If only real life were so exciting," I said, still unsure how I felt about him being here. What was better? The memory of one fantastic night, or the tantalizing possibility of more?

Kristin laughed. "You can say that again."

A waitress came to ask if we'd like something to drink.

Nav—Dhiraj—said, "Would you ladies do me the pleasure of sharing a bottle of wine? I think the beginning of a cross-country trip calls for something special."

"I wouldn't say no," Sandra said, and her daughter promptly agreed.

"I had a bit too much to drink last night." I slanted him a glance.

A concerned, vaguely guilty expression flashed across his face, though it wasn't his fault I'd kept slugging back the champagne. "Hair of the dog is the traditional remedy," he responded.

When I agreed, everyone discussed their preferences. From the all-Canadian wine list, he ordered a bottle of unwooded chardonnay from a BC winery, Grey Monk, to go on his tab.

Again I wondered where he was getting the money for this. And why. It truly was as if he'd turned into a different person.

Another very sexy one. My body vibrated with awareness of his. Every time he shifted position so his clothing brushed me, I had to stop myself from jumping.

Over wine and smoked lake trout, accompanied by scenic views of Muskoka cottage country, the two women said that

Kristin lived in Vancouver and her mom in Toronto. Sandra was going out for a visit with her daughter's family. The younger woman's husband had volunteered to look after their kids so Kristin could fly out to Toronto and the two women could travel back by train, enjoying some mother-daughter time.

The two of them related to each other so easily and affectionately, I wished my mother and I were more like that. It reminded me of the day Mom took me shopping for a prom dress—just the two of us, an entire day together, shopping, sharing lunch, gossiping like girls, and not a hint of pressure or judgment from her. It was so rare for Mom to let down her hair like that.

Kristin brought out family photos, and I fought back another wave of envy over her happy marriage and lovely children.

Nav, too, admired the photos and seemed genuinely interested in hearing stories about the kids. Then he got Kristin talking about her part-time job as a website designer, and Sandra sharing stories about her career as a high school teacher.

Normally, I was the outgoing one, but he'd thrown me so off balance I wasn't myself.

I bit back a chuckle. I wasn't myself; he wasn't himself.

This man, this Dhiraj version of Nav, was definitely attractive. Confident and poised like the men I typically dated, yet not a spotlight hog.

He wasn't flirting with me, which was disconcerting given how aware I was of him. And yet, it would have been embarrassing if he'd acted flirtatious, if he'd shut out the mom and daughter and focused on me.

All the same, he could've shown a *little* more interest. Was Dhiraj playing hard to get?

The four of us had almost finished lunch when he finally turned to me. Touching my bare forearm lightly, making me tremble at the memory of those talented fingers caressing me in far more intimate spots, he said, "How about you, Kat? Where do you live and what do you do?"

Did he expect me to pretend to be someone else, too? I toyed with the idea. But one secret identity at the table was enough. "I'm the PR director for a boutique hotel in Montreal."

"How exciting," Kristin said. She and Sandra began to ask questions, and I told them a little about my job.

Dhiraj mostly listened—of course Nav had heard all this before—but he shifted position often, drawing my attention to him. To his well-shaped hands as he lifted his glass. To the scent of sandalwood and the brush of his arm as he slipped off his jacket and draped it on the back of his chair. To the way the silvery gray of his shirt made his dark skin even more dramatic. To the strong, beautiful angles of his face. My fingers trembled with the desire to touch him.

As fruit salad and coffee were served, he said, "Hotels are a world of their own. People lose their inhibitions in the privacy of their rooms."

He was deliberately reminding me of the way Pritam had made me come in front of that big undraped window in the elegant suite at the Royal York. My pussy tingled and dampened, and I squeezed my thighs together against the memory of—the yearning for—orgasm.

"I'd hate to be a chambermaid," Kristin commented dryly.

Grateful to her for interrupting my sexy thoughts, I joined in the laughter.

"People think of a hotel as a different world, where normal rules don't apply." Dhiraj reached for the sugar and his hand brushed mine as if by accident. But it was no accident. Nav drank his coffee black and unsweetened. "I'm new to train travel," he said, "but I heard someone say the same thing about trains."

This Dhiraj person was less overt than Pritam, but the occasional brushing touches, the gleam in his eyes when his gaze locked with mine, the innuendo in the current topic of conversation, kept me totally aware of him. And growing increasingly horny.

Sandra said, "Yes, I agree with you, Dhiraj. On a train, we passengers are on hiatus from normal life. We get to sleep in, play Scrabble all day, drink wine at lunch."

"Enjoy getting to know strangers." He raised his coffee cup in a toast.

"And I find," Kristin said, "that there's freedom in knowing we'll probably never see each other again. People reveal more personal information."

"So, there's a certain *intimacy*?" He put a slight stress on the last word, and under the table his foot nudged mine.

"Yes, that's a good word," she said.

I stifled a chuckle, but he'd made his point and I was definitely craving intimacy—of more than a conversational nature. Would I be crazy to go along with this new seduction of his?

Sam Wilbanks came down the aisle and paused. "I hope you had a good lunch, Kat."

"Yes, thanks, Sam." Conscious of Nav—Dhiraj—at my side, I wondered if I should introduce everyone.

Sam decided the matter. With an easy smile, he said, "Hi, folks. I'm Sam Wilbanks."

Kristin and Sandra smiled back and gave their names.

"Dhiraj." This time there was no smile, only a nod.

"I'm sure we'll meet up again." Sam lifted a hand in a casual good-bye.

When he'd gone, Kristin said, "He's sure good looking. I bet he's an actor."

"Close," I said. "A screenwriter. He's doing research for a Hollywood movie."

"That's almost as glamorous," Kristin said.

"Time for us to head off," Sandra said. "We have a half-finished Scrabble game calling."

Kristin touched her shoulder affectionately. "Mom's an English Lit teacher and she knows all the fancy words, but I beat her on the modern tech stuff."

Their easy camaraderie again made me envious. Even though

I was known in the family as Mommy's girl, that had mostly meant having Mom on my case about finding a career and never settling for a man who was less than I deserved. I'd felt pressure rather than the acceptance Sandra showed Kristin. Of course, maybe Kristin had never disappointed her mother the way I'd so often done mine.

When they'd gone, my companion turned to me, "Will you stay and talk a while longer?"

"With . . . *Dhiraj*?"

"Of course." He was still speaking in that crisp, formal English voice. There was an edge to it when he added, "Unless you have a prior engagement with the screenwriter."

A touch of jealousy? But no matter how attractive Sam was, the man beside me was far more tempting. "No." I gave a small grin. "It's interesting, though. It must be my week for the movies. Yesterday I met a Bollywood producer."

His eyes twinkled. "I must seem quite desperately boring, with my international import/export company."

"Boring isn't a word I'd use to describe you." It was so natural, after last night, to fall into a flirtatious rhythm. And inevitable that I'd feel so aroused I could barely sit still.

"Good." He rose to take the chair across from me. "Now I can see you properly."

And I could see him properly, too. He really did have striking features, and he looked every bit the international businessman in the stylish but moderately conservative clothes.

"And I very much like what I see," he said, eyes glowing with appreciation. Under the table, his foot nudged mine again.

Damn, I was falling into this seduction. I had to get things straight before we went any further. I drew my foot away. "Nav, what game are you playing now? I thought you were going back to Montreal. You have the exhibit to prepare for."

He gazed consideringly at me for a few moments and then answered in Nav's voice. "I never said I was going back, Kat. You made an assumption."

"I thought we agreed that last night would just be . . ." I flushed. "That we'd only, you know . . . that it was a one-time thing."

"Another assumption."

Indignantly, I said, "You said nothing Pritam and Kat did would affect Nav and Kat's friendship."

"I did. And we agreed Pritam would vanish, which he did." He switched to Dhiraj's voice. "Now you have me. A new train, a new stranger. Relax and have fun. What happens on the train stays on the train."

Slowly I said, "You're proposing the same game—rules—as with Pritam? Dhiraj will disappear, too, as if he'd never existed? My friendship with you—with Nav—won't be affected?" Even if I had sex with Dhiraj?

He gazed at me for a long moment. "If that's what you wish."

Troubled, I stared back. "This is all so unlike you." With lovers, I found unpredictability exciting. However, Nav had always been predictable, reliable, and this new behavior, along with the new look that was so *not* Nav, rattled me, body, mind, and soul.

He frowned slightly, then studied me intently. "Would you rather be on the train with your old friend Nav?"

"Yes!" I imagined the old Nav across from me. Shaggy hair, unshaven face, friendly smile. Cute, even hot, but also comfortable. And resistible.

"With him, would you have a sexy adventure?"

I shook my head vigorously. "That's a boundary I wouldn't cross."

He glanced down, watching his hand rotate his coffee cup in its saucer, then up again. "It's a long trip. Why not have a sexy adventure with Dhiraj?"

I thought about the new persona he'd created. Dhiraj turned me on, and I knew he'd be a dynamite lover. But I was confused. Wary. I needed more time to think about this.

Under the table, his foot found mine again, and this time I

didn't move away. "I'm not sure," I said softly. "After all, I've barely met *Dhiraj*."

He gave a quick nod. "Fair enough. A woman who's open to possibilities. What more can a man ask for?"

I liked that he didn't try to pressure me, or trade on the fact we'd had sex last night. Of course, Dhiraj and I hadn't. That had been Pritam.

Hmm. Last night I'd had an amazing time with Bollywood Guy, as Nav would likely call him. Now I was sitting across from Import/Export Guy and might, if I wanted, end up in bed with him. I'd always had my heart set on marriage, so I'd rarely indulged in flings, but it wasn't like I was going to meet the love of my life on this train trip. Would it be so bad to let loose?

Okay, yes, I was open to the possibility. But I needed to feel my way slowly, as I'd done with Pritam. "Why don't you tell me more about your work." What tale would he spin this time?

"I'm the vice president, Operations," he said. "It's a family company, established by my father's father. Dad is the president and his younger brother is the CFO."

I wondered if he was borrowing from the business his father worked for. If so, he'd given his dad a nice promotion. His uncle, too. I raised my brows. "What about your mother and aunt?"

"They believe in traditional roles. Mum is one of those behind-the-scenes women."

"As in, 'behind every good man there's a great woman'?"

"Exactly. She's always done a lot of business entertaining, made sure Dad belonged to the right clubs and had the right tailor. You know the kind of thing."

Thank heavens I knew Nav believed in female equality or I might have worried. No, wait, he was Dhiraj. "Not with my parents. They're both career driven. Mom always wanted to be a lawyer, and nothing stood in her way except for a little time-out to have kids. Didn't your mother want a career of her own?"

"I . . . I'm not sure."

"Really?" I cocked my head. It seemed he hadn't worked out this role quite as thoroughly as the Bollywood one. "Did she grow up in India or England?"

"India. She and Dad got married there."

"An arranged marriage?"

"Absolutely."

"It seems archaic to me." I couldn't believe his parents wanted Nav to agree to one.

He shrugged. "To my parents, it's incomprehensible that people would choose mates by chance affection. Without ensuring compatibility and matching *Janampatris*—birth star charts."

"You mean horoscopes?"

"Sort of, but more complex." He glanced around and I realized the staff were clearing tables and we were almost the last people in the restaurant.

"We should clear out and let them do their jobs," I said.

"Yes." He stood, then came around and held my chair as I got up. Then he rested his hands on my shoulders and leaned down so his breath brushed the top of my head.

My body trembled, remembering all the ways he'd touched me last night. Feeling his heat, knowing the lean strength of his body under those finely tailored clothes.

"Kat, I have a suggestion. Kristin and Sandra were heading off to play Scrabble. What say you and I play a different game?"

I took a breath, then swung around so I could see his face. "What game do you suggest?"

"It's in my room." His dark eyes gleamed seductively. "Come and take a look."

"Oh, *that* game." My heart raced. He was moving too fast. Despite his clothes, grooming, and accent, I hadn't yet bought into the Dhiraj role. I narrowed my eyes. "You think I'm easy."

He grinned. "You have a delightfully dirty mind. I was talking about a board game."

Startled, I said, "A board game?"

His eyes twinkled. "Trust me, you'll like it."

Chapter 11

Nav studied Kat's face intently. Would she agree?

He'd been disappointed that she'd fled in the night, but he was damned well going to persist. That's why he'd chosen the name Dhiraj for today's role. It meant "patience."

When he'd seen that blond guy's hand on her shoulder, he'd wished he'd picked a more forceful name. He'd wanted to break character, claim Kat as his own. Which she wasn't. Not yet.

Now, he was impatient to get her alone, to continue this flirtation and overcome her hesitation. "Just come take a look."

"You want to play a board game in one of those tiny compartments?" She gazed at him like he was nuts.

She thought he'd booked a single compartment, one of those minuscule rooms no bigger than a closet. He hid a smirk. "I promise, if you don't want to stay, we'll go to the dome car."

"Okay, let's see this game."

He walked behind her, guiding her with a gentle hand on her back. Through her blouse, he felt the heat of her skin, the shift of her muscles. Subtle sensations, yet they reminded him of last night's fiery passion, and his body hardened.

Together they walked through the narrow corridors of a few sleeping cars. Several compartment doors were open, revealing people sitting in chairs gazing out at the view, playing cards, sipping drinks. The train rocked slightly, a motion that made

Nav think of making love, and he wondered if Kat had the same thought.

He opened the door to his room and ushered her in.

"Oh, my! You got a romance room." She turned to him, expression startled. "How did you . . . ? These rooms cost a fortune. When did . . . ? What made you think . . . ?"

The Romance by Rail rooms did indeed cost a small fortune. As he'd learned when he researched the train, however, they were the only sleeping compartments that weren't totally cramped, that had any appealing ambience. If this had been a hotel room, it wouldn't have rated four stars, but it was the fanciest the train provided. And only the best would do, if he was to impress and win Kat. Luckily there'd been a last-minute cancellation, so he'd been able to reserve one of these rooms when he booked on Saturday night.

Of course Kat wanted to know what Nav thought he was doing. But he wasn't being Nav. So he replied in Dhiraj's voice. "There was always the chance I might find company."

"When you bring a woman to this room, it's pretty clear what's on your mind," she said dryly, standing just inside the door, arms crossed over her chest.

The room, which was smaller than the bedroom in her apartment, was mostly taken up by a double bed.

"There you go again with that dirty mind," he teased. "Take the chair if it makes you more comfortable." In the beginning, it had taken some effort to maintain the upper-crust accent and rather formal phrasing—the speech patterns of many of his fellow students back in England—but now they came naturally. "Would you care for some sparkling wine, or a green tea drink?"

Sparkling wine came with the Romance by Rail package, and he'd asked the attendant to also put some cold drinks in the ice bucket, including Kat's favorite green tea.

"I'll stick to nonalcoholic," she said. "I don't know you well enough, *Dhiraj*, to be drinking in your bedroom."

She took the chair, tugging down the brief denim skirt as it rode up her thighs, and glanced around. "I've never been in one of these rooms. It's much nicer than the standard sleeping compartment. They even have art, and I love the flowers."

The painting was an innocuous but pleasant landscape, and a vase filled with colorful mixed blooms sat on the vanity. He'd known these special touches would appeal to Kat. "Yes, it's not bad." He opened a green tea drink and handed it to her, along with a glass.

"These rooms are typically booked by honeymooners and people on anniversary trips," she said. "Not single men."

"Who wants to be *typical*?"

"An interesting point." She studied him, and he guessed she was mulling over the whole Nav, Pritam, Dhiraj thing, and trying to decide how to act.

He took a root beer for himself, then went to the closet to find the game. It had been purchased a year and a half ago when he'd been optimistic about his and Kat's relationship. The box was still in its cellophane wrap. Now he regretted not having opened it to check it out. He was relying on the write-up on the cover, hoping the game would set a sensual, provocative mood.

When he handed it to her, she read the title. " 'Nice 'n Naughty'?" She arched a brow. "This definitely isn't the *typical* board game. How does it work? You've played it before?"

"No, I saw it in a store and thought it would be fun to share with someone special."

He took the package back, ripped off the cellophane, and opened the box. As he did, he said, "The back of the box says the prize is whatever the players agree on ahead of time. It could be . . ." he paused suggestively, "two hours of Kama Sutra sex or—"

"What?" she yelped.

He raised his brows. "You don't want two hours of Kama Sutra? Okay, then it could be, who buys the wine for dinner."

"Let's stick with the wine." She eyed him speculatively. "You don't actually know how to, uh, do the Kama Sutra thing, do you?"

Oh, yeah, he'd hooked her. He suppressed a grin. "Naturally. Indian men have a well-rounded education." He had in fact read the Kama Sutra and tried out most of the techniques.

"Hmm. I'll file that away for future reference, in case it ever becomes relevant."

He gave a soft chuckle, but the thought of sex, combined with being alone together in a room dominated by a bed, made his dick expand inside his Armani briefs.

Right now his plan was slow seduction, so he tried to ignore his arousal as he spread the game board on the bottom of the bed and sat beside it. "The squares form a maze, with the goal being to work your way from the outside into the heart. The first person to arrive wins the prize."

She leaned forward and peered at the board. Then she picked up the single die from the box. "So you roll this to move."

He studied the instructions. "You roll and land on a square. Each square has either a heart, a diamond, a club, or a spade. You draw any card from the corresponding deck."

There were four small boxes, each with a symbol on top. She opened the box with the heart and took out a deck of miniature cards, each with a rosy red heart on the back.

"Don't read the cards," he said. "The idea is, when you draw one, you follow the instructions on it."

"Oh, sure. Like 'Strip off my clothes'?" she said skeptically.

"I can only hope. Of course, maybe I'll get that one."

The color that rose to her cheeks made him smile. Turning his attention back to the instructions, he said, "You can refuse, but if you do, you have to move back the number of squares on the die." He glanced up. "Shall we try it out?"

Her expression told him she was intrigued. "As long as I don't have to do anything I don't want to."

"I promise. No Kama Sutra unless you want to." Which she would, if he had his way.

"Who goes first?"

He gestured toward her. "Ladies, always."

She rolled a two, chose the red mini-Cupid figurine, and moved it a couple squares to land on a diamond.

Nav held the diamond deck toward her. "Take any card."

"Here goes." She drew one from the middle and read, " 'Describe the most deliciously sensual meal you can imagine sharing with your partner.' Okay, food. I can handle that."

She closed her eyes and a few moments later opened them and smiled. "Oysters to start. Tiny Kumamotos, not the big fleshy ones. With a squirt of fresh lemon for accent. Mmm. A slight scent of the ocean, a silky slide down the throat, the taste of sea foam."

Oh, yeah, that was sensual. In fact, it made him think of licking her all over until he finally tasted her pussy. The delicately salty scent and taste, the silky, creamy dampness on his tongue. His dick grew even harder, and there wasn't a damn thing he could do about it.

"And then," she said, "a picnic, eaten with the fingers, of course. French or Italian bread with that wonderful yeasty, fresh-baked scent. Crusty on the outside, soft on the inside. Creamy cheese, something like cambozola or blue Brie, with a subtle bite to it. Kalamata olives, sweet red grapes. Each flavor distinct, unique, and blending perfectly with the others."

He imagined the two of them in a secluded corner of Parc Angrignon or Mount-Royal Park, spreading a blanket, feeding each other picnic food with their fingers. Each nibble a kind of foreplay. He cleared his throat. "And for dessert?" Knowing Kat, it would involve chocolate.

"Bittersweet chocolate soufflé with Grand Marnier sauce. Melting on the tongue."

The way her body had melted against his tongue. "Sounds fantastic," he said hoarsely, barely remembering to keep his accent. "Especially if it's shared."

"Many things are best when they're shared," she said softly, a little flirtatiously. Then she waved the card. "What do I do with this?"

"The instructions say to put it back in the deck."

That meant glancing down, and when she did, her gaze focused on the erection his dress pants couldn't hide. Her cheeks went pink again. "Uh, it's your turn to roll."

He threw a four. His black Cupid landed on a square with a spade, and he picked a card. "It says, 'What's the one thing you want most in the world?' " Wasn't she sitting across from him right now? But of course he couldn't say that. And in fact, he did have a deeper desire. One that, if his plan succeeded, would include her.

He'd give Dhiraj that same desire, so he could be honest with Kat. "Family," he said. "Marriage and kids. A loving home." A home in which the kids' individuality and self-expression would be encouraged, not thwarted as had happened with him.

"Oh, yeah? I'd have taken you for the playboy type, Dhiraj."

"Why is that?" How had she got that impression, after he'd spent much of lunchtime listening happily to stories about kids?

"I'm sure you meet—date—lots of eligible women, yet you're still single. And you seem like a pretty good catch."

A good catch. Even though he'd created Dhiraj to be one, he hated the concept. Margaret had said he was a good catch—up until he decided to be a photographer. "So I've been told," he said evenly. "And yes, I've met many eligible women. But eligible doesn't equate to special."

Her gaze met his. "You're right." Her voice was solemn, and he realized he'd reminded her of her own failed relationships.

Damn, that had been stupid. He wanted to create a sexy, fun mood. "Your turn to roll."

She got a three, landed on a club, took a card. " 'Who's your favorite person of the opposite sex, and why?' Hmm. I need two."

He hoped he was one of them. "All right."

"I have to say my dad. Even though we butt heads, he raised

me, and I know he loves me and he'd do anything for me. And I love him, too. I really do." She shook her head wonderingly. "These questions make you think."

"And the other?"

A grin flashed. "Oh, that's easy. My friend Nav."

Relief warmed him. When she didn't go on, he prompted, "The card said you were supposed to tell why."

She chuckled. "You don't mind hearing me sing another man's praises, *Dhiraj*?"

"My self-esteem is just fine. Sing away."

"Well, he accepts me and doesn't want anything from me except to be friends."

She sure as hell didn't know him very well.

"He's easy to be with. Like, at the end of the day when I'm tired and I want to relax and unwind. He's considerate, generous, sweet."

Sweet. There was that stupid word again. "Those sound like good qualities in a friend." He paused, took a swallow of root beer, wondered if he could shake her up. "Or a spouse."

She frowned slightly. "A spouse?"

"Mmm. Do you ever want to get married?"

"Yes. Very much."

"All right, I'll give you a bonus three spaces on the board if you answer me this question. What are you looking for in a husband?"

"Um . . ." She took a breath, moved three spaces. "Okay, here goes, in no particular order. Intelligent, fun, interesting, creative. A positive attitude. Attractive, sexy, someone who turns me on. Loving, generous. Successful, motivated, energetic. In good shape."

She paused, then went on. "Someone I can relax with when I want to, but also someone who can be spontaneous, impulsive, unpredictable. If you think about spending decades with a person, you want to know you won't get bored. Right?"

He nodded. "Absolutely." And, damn it, he wasn't boring.

She studied his face intently. "Okay, Dhiraj, how about you? You say you want to get married. What are you looking for? Three spaces for you if you answer."

"Your list actually sounds pretty good to me." He moved his Cupid three squares.

"Oh, no, you don't. Seems to me like you haven't really thought about it."

"Oh, I have. Believe me." He gazed into those sparkling chestnut brown eyes, and let Nav speak through Dhiraj. "A woman who's a true equal. Independent, but not afraid to share her problems, to lean on me when she needs support. Strong enough that sometimes I can lean on her, and she won't think less of me. Together we make a team, a partnership. We're different but we complement each other. We don't compete. We're each other's biggest fan."

Her lips curved in a warm smile. "That sounds nice."

He nodded. "It does." His gaze held hers for a long moment. Was she capable of being that woman? Of forming that partnership with him? He believed it in his soul, but would she come to realize it?

She glanced away, found her glass, and lifted it toward him. "Here's to both of us finding someone like that. I hope they're really out there."

"I believe they are." *Just look in front of you.* He clicked his glass to hers and took a long swallow.

"Your turn. Roll the die."

He rolled a five, which put him on a diamond square. When he read the card, he grinned. " 'Give your opponent a foot massage.' "

"Ooh, nice. I like that one."

He smiled. "I can live with it." How often had he sat beside her in her apartment, gazing at her feet—bare in summer, sock-clad in winter—curled beside him as she snuggled in her corner of the couch, or resting beside his on the coffee table, and longed to do this very thing? It was something a friend might do, yet because he felt far more than friendly toward her, it would have been such a turn-on he'd have revealed his arousal.

But now he was Dhiraj, and Dhiraj was allowed to be turned on.

He got up, wishing he'd thought to bring massage oil, and returned with the small bottle of body lotion the train supplied. He moved the game board aside and sat on the bed. When she raised her leg, he caught her bare foot and settled it on his thigh only inches from his package. He poured a little lotion into one hand, warmed it between his palms, and then smoothed it into her skin.

Holding her foot in both hands with his thumbs on the top and his fingers on her sole, he stroked her skin, squeezing gently and then harder, working his fingers into her muscles. Her foot was slender, so much smaller than his. Almost delicate, yet strong enough to carry her around all day in those crazy high heels she was so fond of.

She closed her eyes, sighing with pleasure. "Nice." Her toes, tipped with sexy red polish, flexed. When he rubbed the top of her foot and her arch, she let out a soft moan that made his groin tighten and his dick throb.

Working slowly, he dug his thumbs into her heel, then up the back of her ankle.

When he'd finished that foot, he picked up the other one and, after pouring more lotion—its scent mildly citrus—started at her toes.

"You do that so well," she said dreamily.

As he massaged her arch, she opened her eyes. "Dhiraj, you said you want to get married. You don't mean an arranged marriage, do you?"

Nav had no intention of agreeing to one, but maybe Dhiraj should be different. "I'd prefer a love match. But if that doesn't happen . . ." He shrugged.

"Seriously?" Her eyes widened. "You'd actually marry a stranger?"

"Nowadays, usually the couple meet first. Even in the most traditional families there's at least a bride-viewing and—"

"Bride-viewing? What's that? It sounds like a meat market, or auction block." Her eyes widened further.

He chuckled. "No, it's more like a high tea. The man and his family go to visit the woman and hers at her parents' house. The prospective bride's parents greet the visitors and seat them, then she comes in and serves tea. Everyone chats politely, and the couple have a chance to check each other out."

Finished with her second foot, he carried on up her leg, kneading her strong calf muscles. The repetitive motions of working his lotion-smooth fingers into her soft, pliant flesh were as relaxing as they were arousing.

"And if the couple hate each other on sight," she said, "the wedding's off?"

A glimpse of purple fabric between her legs, visible as she shifted position in that short skirt, was purely arousing. Was she wearing panties or a thong? Would he find out?

He tried to focus on her question. "Yes, these days usually the man and woman have a say. However, if the match has been properly done, they typically get along well enough."

He'd reached the toned flesh above Kat's knee and was almost at the hem of that provocative skirt. Deliberately, he let his fingers drift upward in a touch that was more caress than massage.

She squirmed and sounded a little breathless when she asked, "And that's it? Next thing they know, they're saying wedding vows?"

"Sometimes." Much as he'd have liked to explore under that skirt, to rediscover sensitive flesh that Pritam had enjoyed last night, he was Dhiraj now. He wouldn't rush her. This was a time to build trust and arouse desire slowly. To whet her appetite until she was so hungry for him that she stopped worrying about who he really was.

He shifted to her other leg and started again at the ankle. "In some cases, if they and their parents are more progressive, they may spend more time together. They might be allowed to date, either with a chaperone or on their own."

"It still sounds archaic."

Not that he believed in arranged marriage, but in his opinion, no culture had worked out a good system for building stable, loving marriages. "As compared to Western society, where people choose mates for themselves?"

"Yes."

"And where they vow, on marriage, to be bonded until death do them part, but haven't much more than a fifty percent chance of honoring those vows?" A statistic his mum frequently cited to him.

Kat bit her lip.

He went on. "Look at the success of dating services that are supposed to help people find compatible mates. They're a recognition that we're not very good at doing it ourselves. Aren't they just a replacement for having family do the same thing, and perhaps more effectively?"

"You're actually defending arranged marriage?"

"I'm saying no system is perfect."

He squeezed her knee. "Lie on the bed and I'll massage your arms and shoulders."

"Really? The card only said feet, but I've been enjoying this so much, I'm afraid I've been selfish and just let you keep going."

"Kat, I'm enjoying it, too." It was deliciously arousing. More than that, he loved touching her in ways he'd never been able to before, and giving her pleasure.

"Honestly?" She studied his face, then rose. "I've never had a man do this before."

"You haven't?" What had her lovers been thinking, missing out on an opportunity to explore every inch of her wonderful body and bring her pleasure?

She lay down on her stomach, head turned sideways on the pillow. Her body looked tight, as if she wasn't sure what he intended and was feeling vulnerable. "Well," she said, "sometimes a quick shoulder massage if I was achy from too much time at the computer."

"Functional massage." He sat beside her, admiring the curve of her ass under the denim skirt, the slim line of her back beneath the light top, the profile of her half-turned head. Taking her hand between his, he smoothed lotion onto it and began to rub gently. "As compared to massage for mutual enjoyment."

"I'm so glad you like this, because I'm loving it. My legs have never felt so good."

He smiled, hoping soon she'd be able to say the same thing about her entire body.

After massaging her hand in silence for a few minutes, he said, "You don't believe in arranged marriage. How do you think marriages should come about?"

"Two people meet and fall in love," she answered promptly.

"When people meet and are attracted, I'd call that lust, not love." It was what he'd felt when he first met Kat, but over weeks and months of being with her it had matured into love.

"Lust can turn into love."

He smiled at the way she'd echoed his thought. "Over time, certainly. But so can compatibility. Having a similar upbringing and values, for example." He began to work his way up her forearm.

"And having your stars in alignment?" She shot him a skeptical look.

"It makes more sense than marrying based on lust. And don't twist your neck. Keep your head on the pillow."

"Yes, sir." She relaxed again, head back on the pillow. "And yes, of course a couple should wait and see if the lust turns into love. And, yes, there should be basic compatibility. I agree with you about common values, but not about upbringing. I think it's stimulating when people have different backgrounds."

"It can be. So long as there's mutual respect." He massaged her elbow, digging in gently. "How long do you think it takes to know it's really love, not merely lust that will burn itself out? And to ensure compatibility on things that are important to both people?"

It was a question he, as Nav, had never asked Kat in their rare discussions of her unlucky dating life. Now, as he worked the firm muscles of her upper arm through her blouse, he watched her profile with interest while she pondered her answer.

In Montreal, if Nav had started a conversation like this, Kat, who avoided introspection, would have turned on the TV or suggested they go out to a club. Now, as his fingers worked the muscles beneath the surface of her skin, she seemed willing to let her thoughts travel deeper and to share what she found.

Whatever the reason for it, he loved the way that, as his hands grew increasingly intimate with her body, their conversation drifted to a deeper level and she opened herself more to him.

"I guess, until both people are sure," she said. Then she gave a quick laugh. "You know, I already heard those words today. I was talking to a woman over coffee, a widow who's long-distance dating a widower. I asked if they were getting married. She said there was no rush, they wanted to take the time to be sure."

"Sounds like wise advice. Do you agree with her?" Having reached her shoulder, he moved to her other side and picked up her hand.

"I . . . think maybe I do." She twisted her head to look at him, and a gleam lit her eyes. "A *friend* once told me I let myself be dazzled by men, so I don't really see them."

So she'd been listening. "And is this friend right?"

"I've been thinking about it and yes, perhaps. Lust and dazzlement and, hey presto!" She snapped the fingers of her free hand. "I'm in love."

"Except you aren't in love," he said quietly. "You're in lust and dazzlement."

"But they can grow into love, like we said." She sounded a bit defensive.

But they often didn't. She knew that, so he didn't say it. Instead, he'd try to ease out her defensiveness with his fingers. He rested his hands on either side of her neck. "Let's put a pillow under your chest to lift you up a bit more, and I'll do your neck and back."

After helping her stuff a pillow under her body, he wove his fingers into her hair and massaged her scalp.

For a few minutes they were quiet except for her soft sounds of satisfaction as his fingers probed her temples, the back of her head, her slender neck. He hoped his fingertips were conveying the subliminal message, *If you were with me, you could have this every night when you came home from work.*

When he moved to her shoulders, he said, "Love can come about in all sorts of ways."

"Mmm? Oh, like, you're saying it can grow out of an arranged marriage?"

"It can. My parents are an example. Or it can . . ." He took a deep breath. Should he say this? "Or it can happen when a person looks at someone they've known a long time, and realizes their feelings have changed into love." Knowing her fondness for old movies, he added, "Have you seen *When Harry Met Sally*?" Of course she had; they'd watched it together.

She nodded and he felt the movement through his fingers. "All those years they kept bumping into each other," she said. "At first they didn't really like each other; then they became friends and finally they fell in love. I guess that can happen."

"I believe it can." He sure as hell hoped it could.

Stroking her back, he said, "This would feel better if you took the blouse off."

She tensed, and several seconds passed during which he could swear he heard his own rapid heartbeat. Then she reached under her chest and undid buttons. With his help she slipped her arms free.

He tossed the blouse across the bed and gazed down at her.

Thin purple bra straps crossed her back, too tempting to resist. He unfastened the back hook and eased the straps aside, not attempting to take the bra off.

Last night, every time they'd made love he'd been facing her, and he'd never seen her naked back. Gently he ran both hands down her shoulders, upper arms, sides, waist, caressing the lovely contours of her torso. "You're beautiful, Kat."

Until now he'd been in a mild state of arousal—a pleasant hum in his blood, the enjoyable stimulation of his swollen dick pressing against his pants.

Now, seeing her like this, his erection grew and the pressure went from pleasant to a painful need. God, he wanted her.

Last night he'd been inside this woman, and he sure as hell hungered to be there again.

Trying to keep the tension from his fingertips, he carried on, turning the sensual massage into an erotic one. He added lingering caresses, delicate touches designed to arouse and tantalize. A few of those, then a few deeper strokes, kneading her muscles, relaxing her again.

But as soon as the tension had eased from her body, he'd start up again with the provocative caresses.

Under his hands, she stirred restlessly, her body heated. Her scent of jasmine and woman, combined with the citrus of the lotion, drifted up to him. Her breathing quickened, and she let out the occasional needy whimper.

No, he wasn't going to restart the conversation. He wanted all her concentration on the sensations he was eliciting in her body. His fingertips roamed under the waistband of her skirt, into the soft, warm hollow at the base of her spine.

She drew in a long, shuddering breath.

He bent down to press soft, damp, nibbling kisses to her lower back and then let his fingers delve further under her waistband, feeling the lovely top curves of her ass.

She let out the breath and sighed, "Oh, yes. More." Then she lifted up a little and reached down to unfasten her skirt.

His slow seduction was working. She wanted this erotic massage to get even sexier.

He eased her skirt down her long, shapely legs. And off.

A thong. The purple he'd glimpsed before was a lace thong, setting off her curvy cheeks.

Trying to keep his hands from trembling, he cupped those firm mounds and massaged them. The thong was so enticing, he had to touch it.

She moaned softly, hips twisting, pelvis pressing into the bed.

He stroked back and forth along that lacy strip, then followed it farther, down between her legs. Where he was met with heat, moisture. A ragged "o-oh" from Kat.

The crotch of her thong was soaked, the flesh underneath plump. He stroked the fabric, pressing it against her, running his finger down the center and feeling her open to him.

Then he pulled the thong aside and eased his finger inside her. She was so hot and lush, he couldn't stifle his own groan.

"Oh, yes, please," she whispered.

He slid farther, pumped gently in and out, and then added another finger. And another, as the walls of her channel eased open to accommodate him, then gripped him tight.

Her hips rose and tilted in invitation, and he shoved the pillow farther down so it was under her pelvis, lifting her backside even higher and giving him better access.

He had a condom in his pocket and his dick was aching with the need to drive into her, but he held back. The way Kat twisted against his fingers, her panting breath, told him she was near release. He didn't want to delay her satisfaction.

Stroking inside her, he found her G-spot, and with his thumb he gently rubbed her engorged clit.

"God, yes!" she cried.

He loved hearing her but had to murmur, "Sshh, the walls of the compartment are thin."

She gave a stifled whimper, her body twisting against his hand. "Don't stop. Oh, yes, just like that."

He did as she asked, struggling to control his body as her movements grew wilder, frantic.

Then she cried out again, burying her face in a pillow to muffle the sound, and her body spasmed in climax.

He held her through it, until her spine softened, her hips relaxed.

A few minutes later, she lifted her head. "Now, let's try that again. But this time, it's not fingers I want inside me."

Chapter 12

Male weight dipped the bed beside me.

I buried my flushed face in a pillow. I'd just been given an incredible orgasm by a man I hadn't even kissed.

Or by an English-speaking version of Pritam.

Or by my good friend, Nav.

What was I doing? Even if my brain had wanted to work, I doubted it could. Easier to focus on sensation. I stayed on my stomach rather than have to face him, but savored the caress of his hands on my back.

Those warm hands pulled on my hips, urging me up on my knees.

I went, dragging the pillow out from under me. Arching my back so my butt, still clad in the soaked, twisted thong, was tilted toward him.

Strong hands gripped me. The blunt head of his cock slipped between my legs, not entering me, just sliding back and forth against my sex. Growing slick with my juices as the friction added to my arousal.

Balancing on one arm, I reached under my body and guided him to my opening.

As he slid inside, he let out a groan of relief. He leaned down, curving around my back, and kissed the nape of my neck. "Feels so good in there, Kat." The accent was Dhiraj's.

"Mmm." The massage and the orgasm had sensitized my whole body, so even the soft kisses he dropped on my neck made me shiver with need.

He straightened again so he was kneeling on the bed, and holding my hips for leverage, he began to pump slowly in and out in smooth, even strokes.

Still weak from that first orgasm, at first I rested on my hands and knees and let him do it, enjoying the pressure of his firm cock as it filled me. Feeling my body answer him in small ways. Subtle shifts of angle.

Each stroke heightened sensation, arousal. My body tightened with need.

Wrapping one arm around my waist, he straightened so we were both kneeling with our upper bodies more or less upright, his chest pressed to my back. He held me steady around the waist and with the other hand reached around to squeeze my swollen nipple.

"Oh," I sighed as sensation rippled outward. I arched, raising my hands to drag them through my hair, thrusting my breast more firmly into his hand, wanting more.

He obliged, rolling the nipple between his finger and thumb. Still he thrust into me with those long, smooth strokes, as if he could go on forever.

My body throbbed, twisted, pulled him in deeper as I climbed the slope to orgasm, impatient to get there, yet wanting to enjoy the moment.

"Kat. Look."

"What?" Then my gaze caught our reflection in the mirror of the vanity.

We looked so hot. I was pale skinned, curvy; he was dark cinnamon, muscled. My hair was a mess of auburn curls; his was black and sleek in that tight, low ponytail. Perfect contrasts, and perfectly complementary.

That was exactly how he felt inside me. Hard and strong and male, plunging into my soft, lush femininity.

His eyes, glazed with passion, met mine in the mirror.

Again I faced that paradoxical Nav-but-not-Nav enigma. The man in the mirror looked sort of like my neighbor, yet was different in key ways. It wasn't just the shaven cheeks, the pulled-back hair; it was the fierce passion on his face.

Watching was sexy, but too disconcerting. It made me think about things I didn't want to. And this was no time for thinking. This was all about sensation, pleasure, as he stroked deep inside me.

I shifted my weight forward, pulling him down with me until I was on my hands and knees again. He gripped my hips, thrusting in and out, making me gasp as he penetrated all the way to my core, each stroke in and out so powerful, so erotically charged.

I couldn't see his face. Could let myself believe he was Dhiraj.

Braced on my hands, I couldn't even touch him. Anonymous sex. Except, it didn't feel that way. It felt intimate. Maybe because of how tenderly he'd touched me earlier.

He drove into me hard, pistoning his hips, until I was helpless to do anything but stifle my moans of pleasure in the pillow.

"Damn, Kat, you feel so good," he muttered, breath hot on the back of my neck. "You're so sexy." He nipped me, closing his teeth hard enough to cause a quick tingle of pain.

That nip only heightened my arousal, made me grind against him more fiercely as I felt my climax building. I lifted my head to gasp, "Come with me."

"Oh, yeah." He stroked into me again, hard and deep. Then he reached down to finger my clit.

We came apart, him burying his cry against my shoulder and me groaning into the pillow with glorious release.

After, we collapsed slowly onto the bed. I lay on my side and he spooned my back, still inside me.

A few minutes later, he pulled out and the bed shifted as he climbed off.

Trying to hang on to the pretense of anonymity, I didn't turn to watch him walk to the tiny bathroom.

A few minutes later he curled up behind me again. "Kat? Are you all right?" His arm came around my waist, holding me gently.

"I . . . guess so."

"Don't worry so much. Just enjoy." He spoke in Dhiraj's voice. Wise advice. Could I take it? I had to find out.

I rolled onto my back and stared at the handsome face that was becoming almost as familiar as Nav's bearded one. "We're agreed on the same rule as yesterday? This is like . . . a fantasy? Not real life. In Montreal, Kat and Nav will still be friends."

A pause. "If that's what you want."

My brows drew together. How could he think otherwise? "Of course I do! You know how important our friendship is to me."

He nodded, dark eyes solemn. "Best friends. You told Pritam I'm your best friend."

"It's true. My best friend ever."

"You never said that before." I realized he was speaking in Nav's accent.

"I guess . . ." I rubbed my hand across my face. "I didn't want to sound too pathetic."

"Pathetic? Being friends with me is *pathetic*?" He thrust himself to a sitting position and punched a couple of pillows into place behind him, looking both wounded and indignant.

"No, no," I hurried to say. "Being friends with you is wonderful. I only meant, here I am, thirty-one years old, and I've never had a friend as close as you." Uncomfortable about being naked with him since he'd stopped playing Dhiraj, I grabbed the sheet and pulled it up.

"I've always had a ton of friends," I said. "Of both sexes. But mostly we go to clubs, movies, theater, shop together, play tennis in the park. Doing *stuff*, often in a group. Not just two of us hanging out. Helping each other, like the way you fix things for me and pick up tourtière, and I cook you lasagna and sew on buttons."

"We complement each other," he said softly.

"Right." Why did those words sound familiar? "And we

support each other. I'd never realized that having a best friend could be so great." I hugged the sheet tighter across my chest. "This is freaking me out. I can't talk this way to *Nav* when I'm not dressed."

He sighed and then said in Dhiraj's voice, "Does this make you feel more comfortable?"

A change in voice, that's all it was, but it was symbolic, and I did feel marginally more at ease. How ridiculous. "A bit. Yeah. If we're going to do this, you have to be Dhiraj. Or Pritam. Or someone else. I know it's artificial, but I need to draw that line. Nav—my friendship with Nav—is too important to me."

In Dhiraj's voice, he said, "Haven't you heard of friends with benefits?"

"That's not my style." As I'd told Nav, the couple of times he'd suggested we date.

He cocked a brow. "And yet, in the last twenty-four hours, you've been to bed with both Pritam and Dhiraj."

I waved a dismissive hand. "Oh, come on. It's a game. Train flings, time limited. With people who don't even *exist*. Nav exists and I want him as my friend. Long-term. I need to be able to count on him."

"And you think sex would change that?"

"Of course it would." Aside from this train game, casual sex wasn't what I wanted, and it was the essence of his dating life. If I already felt twinges of jealousy when my *friend* came home all sexed out, how would I feel if he was also my lover?

I shook my head again. "No. I bought into this game because of the rules we set in the beginning. It's the only way it'll work for me."

"I see." He rose from the bed and walked the few steps to the ice bucket, giving me a perfect view of that perfect butt. Nav's butt.

He stood for a long moment, and I wondered what he was thinking. Feeling off balance, I slid from under the sheet and began to scramble into my clothes.

Without turning to face me, he said, in Dhiraj's voice, "Would you like another cold drink? Perhaps a glass of wine?"

"No thanks. I need to do a few things before dinner." Like regain my composure.

He turned, a bottle of water in his hand. The clean-shaven face, the pulled-back hair, were pure Dhiraj. "Then I'll see you at dinner." It was a statement, not a question.

Relieved that he'd dropped the previous conversation, I said, "Yes, that'll be nice." In the dining car, with him dressed in his Dhiraj clothing, I could get back into our sexy play.

When I rounded the end of the bed in search of my shoes, I kicked the Nice 'n Naughty game board. Our energetic lovemaking had knocked it to the floor. I picked it up and put it on the bed.

"Tonight we'll finish the game," he said, a challenge in his voice.

We'd left off with massage, which had led to sex. What would another roll of the die, another card, lead to?

It was my turn to roll next.

I opened the door. "See you at dinner."

"In the meantime," he said, a wicked gleam in his eye, "the offer's still open to switch the prize. If you feel like two hours of Kama Sutra sex."

I closed the door behind me and fled back to my room.

Two hours of Kama Sutra sex, with a man as sexy as Dhiraj. The notion teased my mind as I tried to nap, then took a shower. What woman could resist that offer?

So, I wouldn't. And there'd be no more role shifting between Nav and Dhiraj. I'd made my conditions clear, and I trusted my train guy to remain Dhiraj.

Now, I really needed to focus on other things. There'd be Internet access when we reached Sudbury, and I wanted to have messages ready to send.

I typed a note to Merilee, attaching the e-vite.

Hope you and M like this, sis. If you have venue and time details,
you can fill them in yourself, or let me know and I'll revise it. But
communication on the train's pretty iffy, so it could take a while,
and I know you're in a hurry.

Next I wrote a note to Mom. Seeing Kristin and Sandra together at lunch had got me thinking about her, and I realized
we'd never talked about the wedding since Merilee's one conference call with the whole family.

Hi Mom. Just wanted to let you know I'm on the train and looking
forward to seeing you Friday. I hope you're okay with M&M moving up
the wedding date. I know they're young, but they're so obviously made
for each other.

Matt was the only boyfriend our parents had ever approved
of, perhaps because he'd been around for so long he'd almost
become part of the family already.

I'm sure you're going nuts preparing your SCC case, so don't worry
about the wedding. The 3-pack, with our many and varied talents
<g>, will pull it off. M&M deserve the best and we'll make sure they
get it.

My superlawyer mom was preparing an appeal to the
Supreme Court of Canada. And that was as big as it got for a
Canadian lawyer. Normally she'd have wanted to manage the
wedding plans herself, but she didn't have time, which was why
Theresa, Jenna, and I had said we'd handle it.

As for Merilee, she'd had surgery for endometriosis this
spring and was madly trying to make up the university semester, so she didn't have much spare time, either.

Poor kid. All her life she'd looked forward to her wedding,
and now the planning was a scrambled rush and her energy

was focused as much on her schoolwork as on looking forward to the big day.

Oh, yeah, we were going to give her a fabulous wedding. The wedding of her dreams.

And I would swallow my envy and believe—*know*—that one day I'd be walking down the aisle myself, toward the man of my own dreams.

In fact, now that Nav—or Dhiraj—had helped me understand some of the mistakes I'd made with relationships, maybe I'd have a better chance of finding that guy.

The train whistle sounded, and I realized we were almost to the station. Quickly I finished the e-mail to Mom, then I started hunting for a wireless Internet connection. When I found one, my Inbox began to fill.

My assistant at Le Cachet had reported in, and he seemed to have things under control.

There was an e-mail from Merilee to me and Jenna, no cc to Theresa.

Jenna, are you out there somewhere?

Tune in, girl, because there's MAJOR NEWS. Our Theresa came home with a MAN!!! And, OMG, what a man! Damien Black, some superpopular Aussie thriller writer, not to mention ranked one of Oz's 10 sexiest bachelors, not to mention the Aussie tabloids had them on the front page as ENGAGED!! Which they aren't. But all the same, can you believe Theresa's actually dating a guy like that??? Seriously, he is incredibly HOT. If I wasn't so totally in love with Matt, I'd give him a 2nd look myself. Met him briefly at the airport last night, and he's coming for dinner tonight (and I bet he stays in Theresa's room tonight <G>). Don'cha wish ya were here?? LOL.

Mind you, it's kind of annoying too. Like, I'm the one GETTING MAR-RIED here. Aren't I supposed to be the center of attention for once in my life???

Speaking of which, Kat, don't forget the e-vite, pretty please? Really
looking forward to seeing it. Not to mention this guy Nav you're
bringing home. He sounds nice too.

Oh, great. I had the "nice" guy and Theresa had the "incredibly HOT" one.

I paused to reflect. Could I still take Nav as my wedding date?

Damn, I couldn't imagine it. How could I face him in front
of my family after our train games? Moreover, for my peace of
mind, I'd need a little time and distance before going back to
Montreal and seeing my friend Nav. It looked as if train sex
had cost me a wedding date.

Well, it was excellent train sex. And there was more to look
forward to.

I returned to Merilee's e-mail.

Mind you, if you picked him, Kat, there's got to be a fatal flaw.
Right???

Like that he had multiple personalities, and I'd screwed two
of them? I buried my face in my hands and had to chuckle.
Now there was a new and original, and very sexy, fatal flaw.

It wouldn't be wise to share that one with my family. No
matter how much fun it would be to spill some details about
the amazing sex I'd been having, and watch my sisters turn pea
green with envy.

Merilee continued:

So, Jenna, what's the scoop? You are gonna be here for my wedding,
right??? What would my big day be, without you to tell me marriage is
a . . . how does it go again? Anachronistic, paternalistic institution? I
know I've left out a couple adjectives but I'm sure you'll remind me <g>.

Hugs, big sisses. See ya soon.

And then, surprise, there was an e-mail from Jenna.
She addressed it to all the sisters, subject line:

For God's Sake!!

I'm here, I'm here, for god's sake, you girls are the biggest nags in the
world! Just because god invented e-mail and cell phones, doesn't
mean a person has to stay glued to them 24/7. Y'all need to get a life!

Yes, of course I'm coming to Vancouver. M, there's absolutely no
way in the world I'd miss your wedding. ("A stifling, paternalistic
anachronism that subjugates women and discriminates against
homosexuals." Since you asked <G>. But now I'll shut up, except
to say I hope you and Matt will be very happy. LOL.)

So, anyhow, I sold my surfboard (boohoo!) and I've got a couple
good waitress gigs where the tips should be fabulous. I'll have gas
money in a day or two and head home. (Coast road, so it'll take me
a little longer, but the B's not exactly up to the I-5.)

Jenna had a cute, but ancient and pretty battered MGB con-
vertible. Yellow, like her hair. Thank heavens she had the sense
not to take it on the highway. And hurray that she'd worked
out her finances. Theresa and my folks had offered to pay for
her flight, but she'd refused. Jenna might be scattered, and as
unmaterialistic as Nav, but—like him—she had her pride.
    If she left in a couple of days, on Thursday, she should be
home by the end of the weekend.
    Wow, all us sisters in the same house. That hadn't happened
since the Christmas before last. We'd either tear each other's
hair out or drink way too much wine and paint each other's
toenails. Most likely both.
    I read on.

Theresa Fallon, what's this I hear about the sexy writer? (Yeah, M
spilled the beans <g>). Am I, like, living in a parallel universe????

Wasn't it just a couple days ago I was saying you had to get back in the game or your hoo-ha'd shrivel up and die, and all along your hoo-ha's been getting some excellent action with some Aussie superstud <G>.

You too, huh, Kitty-Kat. Guess you're having some fun with your new guy. But 2 weeks is a l-o-n-g time. Here's betting you find the fatal flaw, or manage to jinx things, before M&M's wedding <g>. Seriously, I sure hope it works this time, sis. One of these days your luck's gotta change.

Ack. I scowled at the screen. If I told them Nav wasn't coming, Jenna'd say I told you so. Once again I'd be the subject of teasing. Of pity. No, I couldn't stand that, not on top of watching my sisters being all romantic with their guys, and yearning to have the same thing myself.

So, I wouldn't say Nav and I had broken up. Once I reached Vancouver, I'd pretend I got a call from him about his exhibit, saying he needed to stay in Montreal to prepare.

A life of deception could certainly get complicated.

As for me, I'm starting out the drive alone, but you never know who I'll meet along the road. You know me, I live to shock. LOL.

And to worry our parents to death. Didn't she realize her behavior affected other people?

So cool you got VanDusen for the wedding. Brilliant idea SOMEONE had, eh? Glad Mom came through for us.

Yes, VanDusen Gardens, Jenna's suggestion, was the perfect place. Every Sunday afternoon when we were kids, Gran used to take us girls out for adventures all around the city, from Science World to movies to the beach. Merilee's favorite had always been VanDusen Gardens, a lovely park with natural landscaping and a huge variety of trees and flowers. Of course the place had been booked for a June Saturday, but our well-connected mom had pulled some strings and found us a scenic corner we could use.

Hope Gran will be able to make it. Well, hell, girls, we'll make sure she does. It just would be nice if she knew what was going on . . . Hey, when I get old, remind me not to lose my mind? (Yeah, yeah, no need to say it. Like I haven't already???)

Poor Gran had Alzheimer's and was in a care facility. Sometimes she recognized family and sometimes not.

"Sugar cookies," I murmured. Gran and her house had smelled of sugar. She did all sorts of baking, but her simple sugar cookies had always been my favorite. "Poor Gran."

The train jerked slightly and I glanced out the window. We were leaving the station and soon I'd lose my Internet connection. Quickly I opened the wedding e-vite and added the info about VanDusen. Then I started an e-mail to all my sisters.

Just checked messages. Great to hear you've got things organized, Jenna. Drive safe and watch out for hitchhikers <g>.

M, I sent the e-vite, but I've revised it to add venue and it's attached. Hope you like it.

Terrific news about VanDusen. Maybe Gran will remember that we all used to go there. Hope so. M, it'd be so great if she was "with it" to see you and M get married.

Theresa, how's that wedding plan? Or has Damien the hottie distracted you? <g> Let me know if there's anything I can do. (About the wedding, not about Damien. LOL.) Slot me in as soon as I get there Friday, and I'll pitch in wherever you need me.

It kind of irked me to fall into the same old pattern of letting Theresa run everything. Admittedly I'd been kind of irresponsible when I was young, but now I could be as organized and efficient as my big sister when I put my mind to it.

But, realistically, the only way to get along with Theresa was to give her control, and it wasn't like I could do much from the train anyhow. Part of the special-world quality about trains was that you were semi-isolated from the normal world.

And part was that you got to play fantasy games, like getting it on with a man you'd labeled taboo. Just so long as he pretended to be someone else.

Oh shit, I could lose Internet any moment.

Looking forward to seeing you all soon. Hugs, Kat.

I clicked SEND.

My true feeling was ambivalence. I did love them, and when we managed to relax and stop pushing each other's buttons we actually had fun together. But an awful lot of button-pushing did tend to happen.

I closed up my computer and sat back, watching the rugged scenery of the Canadian Shield flash by. The rocky outcroppings and numerous lakes must have been a challenge to the people who'd built the railroad, but now the route offered great vistas.

The first group of diners would be eating now. It was time to dress for dinner.

Now that Nav and I had got the rules absolutely straight, the idea of seeing the sexy Dhiraj—and anticipating Kama Sutra sex—made my nerves quiver with excitement.

I opened my carry-on bag. The single sleeping compartments were too tiny to hold a suitcase, so I'd checked my large bag through to Vancouver.

My whole body felt wonderful after the massage and great sex: toned, fit, sexy, almost tingling with physical awareness and anticipation. I'd packed one piece of clothing that perfectly suited my mood: the adorable Simon Chang dress I'd bought in an upscale consignment store last week. It was flowered chiffon with a loose, layered skirt and a scoop-necked top.

I slipped it on over lacy peach lingerie and tried to see my reflection in the vanity mirror.

Respectable, yet the way the dress clung and flowed was flirty and fun. I added dangly earrings, the kind I never wore to work, and then I applied light makeup to accentuate my eyes, cheekbones, and lips. For work, I usually tamed my curls, but tonight I rubbed in gel and scrunched them into a casual, sexy mess.

My shoes were high-heeled sandals, of course. Ones that showed off my pedicure. With the heels and the short skirt, I knew my bare legs were tantalizing. They'd remind Dhiraj of the massage. Of the rest of my body, naked.

Of the way he'd touched me.

His fingers would itch with the need to touch me again, and the whole dinner would be a subtle form of foreplay. It was so much fun getting dressed with a special man in mind.

And anticipating ending up naked together, exploring exotic sexual positions.

I took a light jacket from my bag, folded it over my arm, and was ready to go.

As I made my way through the swaying sleeper cars to the dining car, I wondered if he would already be there. Would he have asked for a table for just the two of us?

In the dining car, I gave the mâitre d' my name and said I was joining someone.

"Ah yes, Ms. Fallon." He stepped in front of me, blocking my view of the tables. "There's, er, perhaps a slight misunderstanding?"

"Misunderstanding?"

His mouth twitched. "Two gentlemen have requested your company."

"Two?"

"One fair haired and one dark. The fair man asked for a

table for two. You'll see him sitting a few tables down on the right-hand side."

I craned my head to peer past him and saw Sam Wilbanks talking to a waiter. "Oh, my. We hadn't arranged to have dinner together."

"He asked me to invite you to join him. As for the other gentleman, he seemed more, er, confident you would be dining together. He's sitting farther back, on the left. I'm not sure if you'll be able to see him, but—"

"It's all right. I know who he is."

"Shall I tell the fair one . . . ?"

"It's all right. I'll talk to him."

I stepped past him and walked over to Sam, who stood to welcome me with a dazzling smile. The man really was hot. Under other circumstances, I'd have had fun dining with him.

"Thanks for the invitation, but I'm afraid I already made plans for dinner."

He gave a rueful smile. "Ah well, can't blame a guy for trying."

"I'm flattered."

"You look wonderful. And that's truth, not flattery." The admiration in his eyes seemed genuine and, coming from a man who mingled with movie stars, meant a lot to me.

"Thank you." When I moved past him, I saw the now-familiar striking brown face, wearing a rather dark look that lightened as I walked away from Sam.

I was surprised to see he hadn't chosen a table for two, but was sitting across from a couple who looked to be in their late fifties.

As I approached, he sprang to his feet with a pleased smile. "Ah, there you are, Kat." The accent was Dhiraj's, and so was his appearance. Tonight he wore a stylish suit. No tie; shirt open at the neck to reveal a tantalizing glimpse of dark skin. He was so damned sexy.

When he held my chair, his fingers brushed the nape of my neck in a secret, intimate caress that made me want to press against him and beg for more. Reminding myself to think of him as Dhiraj, I wondered how soon we could start those Kama Sutra lessons.

To the other couple, he said, "This is Kat Fallon, the woman I mentioned to you. Kat, meet Maggie and Tim Farraday. They're on an anniversary trip."

"How lovely." I smiled at them, her with clear gray eyes and light brown hair, him with a pleasant, open face and thinning gray hair.

"We started our honeymoon on this train," Maggie said with a smile. "So this was our sentimental idea for celebrating our fortieth anniversary."

"Fortieth? Wow. You don't look that old."

"Thanks." The woman grinned and looked even younger. "We were children when we married. It was the summer after high school grad."

"How wonderful when first love proves to be true love," I said.

A waiter stopped beside our table. "I see you're all here now. May I take drink orders?"

Tim spoke first. "Dhiraj, you suggested an Ontario pinot noir?"

Dhiraj touched my arm. "We decided to share a bottle. Would you care to join us?"

I agreed and he placed the order. Then we studied our menus.

"Oh, my," I said. "A person can really gain weight traveling by train."

Dhiraj glanced at me. "One must look for opportunities for exercise whenever they present themselves." His tone was neutral, but the sparkle in his eyes said he was thinking of sex.

My pussy throbbed, remembering how he'd felt inside me and anticipating some exotic Kama Sutra positions.

"Such as," he went on, turning to the Farradays, "getting off at stations for a walk."

"It's too bad they don't have a fitness center on the train," Maggie said. "You'd think, in this day and age, that they would."

"Trains date back to a different age, my love," Tim said. "A time when people enjoyed luxury without guilt."

"Luxury without guilt," she repeated. "What a lovely concept. Pity you can't have luxury without high blood pressure, hardening of the arteries, all those dreadful things."

"It's a three-day trip," he said. "And our anniversary. Let's give ourselves permission to be . . . decadent."

She gave a startled laugh and her cheeks grew pink. "Decadent?" That cute grin of hers flashed. "Well, if you can't be decadent on an anniversary train trip, then there's something wrong with the world." She took her husband's hand and squeezed it.

Dhiraj touched me again, this time resting his hand lightly on the back of mine. "We don't have the excuse of an anniversary, Kat. But it seems to me, if they're going to be decadent, then we must, too."

"Hmm." I kept my mouth straight with some effort and resisted the temptation to turn my hand over and link my fingers with his. "We shouldn't be spoilsports."

He chuckled and released my hand. "Good. Now, what appeals to you?"

You. But I focused on the menu. "All right, no salad tonight. I'll go for the nice rich seafood chowder. And then, mmm . . . chicken with porcini sage sauce."

Maggie chose the same things I had; Tim and Dhiraj—who clearly wasn't vegetarian—went with prime rib; and Dhiraj chose wild mushroom soup instead of the seafood chowder.

A few minutes later we sat back contentedly, orders placed and wineglasses full. Dhiraj took off his jacket, and I saw his tailored shirt actually had cuff links. Heavy gold ones in an Asian design. The international-businessman look suited him.

I tore my gaze from him and lifted my glass to the Farradays. "To Maggie and Tim, and many more glorious years together." We all clicked glasses and drank.

Tim clasped his wife's hand. "There were days I didn't think we'd make it."

She chuckled. "Like the two months when I ran home to Mama, swearing I'd never speak to you again. Or the time you went on that weekend fishing trip and didn't come home."

"Sounds rough," Dhiraj said. Under the table, his foot slid over to rest against mine.

"No relationship is perfect," Maggie responded. "Think about the challenges of careers, having kids, aging parents, not to mention just going through all the phases of your own life as you grow from a young adult to a—" she glanced at her husband with a twinkle—"distinctly middle-aged one. There are so many things to worry about, disagree over."

"But I'd hate to go through it alone," Tim said.

She nodded. "We're a team, supporting each other. And even when we argue, the solutions we come up with together are better than either of us would reach on our own."

"Except," he teased, "I still think we should have gone to that fishing camp the year you insisted we go to Hawaii."

She rolled her eyes.

"What's your secret?" Dhiraj asked. "How did you get through the tough times?"

"Love, of course," she said promptly. "Even when I could've killed Tim, I loved him and knew my life would be horrible without him."

I'd loved men, too, but my relationships had always foundered.

"Me, too," Tim said. "But I think there's more to it. It's, uh, damn, I'm not so great putting this kind of thing into words."

"You do fine, sweetie." His wife patted his hand. "Go on."

"Love is great, but you have to, uh, hang in there and work

things out even when you're mad. You have to be good friends, not just lovers."

Hmm. When I'd fallen for men I'd seen them as lovers, potential mates, but we'd never really been friends. I had male friends, too, but I'd never had a sexual relationship with any of them. And I wasn't going to count Dhiraj, because he didn't really exist. Or, at least, he wouldn't after this train trip.

Maggie was nodding in agreement with her husband. "Sometimes you need great sex to get over being mad, and sometimes you need rational, respectful conversation. Life's full of rough patches, and it takes both love and friendship to weather them together."

She gazed at her husband with such love in her eyes, a love that his face reflected back, that I went misty. And wished, rather desperately, to find what the other couple shared.

After a long moment, Dhiraj cleared his throat.

I glanced over and saw a tender, almost wistful expression on his face as he said, "No wonder you've made it to forty years. The two of you truly deserve your happiness."

Chapter 13

Nav saw the dreamy expression in Kat's eyes and knew that she, like he, was wishing for what the other couple had. The difference was, Nav knew he wanted that future with Kat.

The bond between them was growing stronger. Surely if he persisted, she'd come to realize it herself. She would let Dhiraj, Pritam, and Nav all merge together into one man who was best friend, sexy lover, and lifetime love all combined.

Four bowls of soup arrived, and for a few minutes everyone chatted about the food and what fun it was to eat beside a picture window with constantly changing scenery outside. Nav realized how little he'd traveled since he moved to Canada and was grateful to have this opportunity to see more of the country.

Of course the scenery inside the train was even more spectacular than the rocks, trees, and lakes outside the window.

He offered Kat a taste of his mushroom soup. Though he'd have loved to feed her from his spoon, he didn't want to offend the Farradays, so he decorously passed her his bowl. He did make sure their fingers brushed, and the expression in her eyes told him she remembered the intimate way she and Pritam had fed each other yesterday.

Maggie Farraday might have noticed their silent exchange,

because she asked brightly, "Now then, how about you two? Single? Married?"

"Single and hopeful," Kat said.

"As am I," he said.

"Isn't that handy?" the other woman said, flashing her infectious grin. "You've just met, you're both single, you both want to get married. And trains are romantic, right, Tim?"

"So they say," he said with a grin of his own.

"Well, Kat," Nav said, touching her arm. "It seems we're seated with a couple of matchmakers. What do you think of that?"

"I wouldn't have thought you were the kind of man who needed any help finding women," she teased.

"Ah, but it's not *women* I'm looking for. It's one woman. The right one." He lifted his wineglass in a silent toast. She looked so sexy in a light, clingy dress, hair tousled as if she'd just climbed out of bed. Every time he looked at her he remembered making love with her, and he wanted to do it again. In fact, he had the scenario planned, when they got back to his room.

Maggie gazed from one to the other of them. "How about children? Do you want them?"

"Yes." They said the word together.

Kat's cheeks were flushed, and she looked a little embarrassed. Personally, he thought the other woman's matchmaking efforts were fun. When he'd met the Farradays in the Park Car and they'd invited him to join them for dinner, he'd figured Kat would enjoy them—and that perhaps their "happily ever after" glow would rub off.

Maggie chuckled. "Perfect. Now, how about—"

"Sweetheart," her husband said, "the two of them can take it from here if they want to."

She made a comical face. "Oh, all right."

Nav refilled their wineglasses as Kat said to the Farradays, "My turn to ask questions. You have children?"

"Three," Maggie said. "John, our oldest, is in Zimbabwe with Doctors Without Borders. We're so proud, but we worry every day."

"Children weren't put on this earth to give their parents peace of mind, that's for sure," Tim said. "Though our second child, Bronwyn, has given us an easy time."

"She and her husband own a bakery," Maggie said. "Not the most lucrative business, but they do all right. And they have a lovely baby girl. Bronwyn's about your age, Kat."

"I'm envious," Kat said.

Nav knew it was true. He reached out to straighten the candle, which was really just an excuse to brush her hand.

She gave him a surprised glance, then a smile.

"And then there's Adam," Maggie went on. She exchanged glances with her husband and they shook their heads.

"He's young; he'll settle down." But Tim didn't sound convinced.

"He's creative, intelligent, generous," Maggie said. "If only he'd *apply* all those talents."

"Sounds like my sister Jenna," Kat said.

"Is she the youngest, too?" Maggie asked. "I keep worrying we slacked off with Adam. Maybe it's our fault he's so unfocused."

"Unfocused?" Kat gave a wry laugh. "That's what my parents said about me, and they sure didn't slack off. If it's any consolation, I did settle down and find a career I love."

"That's reassuring," Tim said.

"To answer your question," Kat said, sitting back so the waiter could clear her empty soup bowl. "There were three of us in a row. Theresa, then me, then Jenna, each a year apart. Jenna was the youngest for eight years until, to my parents' surprise, along came Merilee. I guess our parents did ease off on Jenna. Sometimes she'd act out to get attention and sometimes she'd go her own merry way."

While she was talking, Nav gestured for the waiter to bring another bottle of wine.

"Just as well she and Adam don't know each other," Maggie said. "I hate to think the trouble the two of them would get into."

"She's the family free spirit, for sure," Kat said.

"Does your family do that, too?" Maggie leaned forward, elbows on the table. "Attach labels?"

"Sure. Theresa's the brainiac. I'm Ms. Sociability."

"And your youngest sister?"

"Merilee was the baby. Until she met this sweet boy, Matt, in grade two. They became M&M. How about your children? What are their labels?"

"John's the save-the-world kid," Tim said as their waiter served their dinners and poured from the fresh bottle of wine. "Bronwyn's the domestic one. Adam's our gypsy. Who's currently in Vietnam. Or maybe Thailand. Backpacking." He and Maggie exchanged glances.

The woman shivered. "You worry about them, but what can you do? It's not like they're going to listen to their parents' advice."

Cutting into his juicy prime rib—glad he hadn't made Dhiraj vegetarian—Nav heard the concern in her voice. He thought about how he forever butted heads with his own parents. "I guess there's an inevitable tension between the generations," he said slowly.

Maggie nodded. "When they're little, children depend on us completely and we protect them. As they get older, they want to be independent and we still want to protect them, even though we know they have to separate from us."

"It's tough when that separation means rejecting everything their parents stand for," Tim said ruefully.

"What their parents stand for may not be right for them," Nav said.

Maggie glanced at him, gaze sharp. "That sounds like a personal observation, Dhiraj."

"Didn't you say you work in the family business?" Kat asked, a teasing gleam in her eye. "I assume that's what your parents wanted you to do?"

Damn, she'd caught him. He'd been reacting as Nav, not Dhiraj. Slowly he chewed a bite of the succulent rosemary-flavored beef, stalling while he decided what to say. This conversation interested him, so he decided to give Dhiraj a brother who was like Nav.

"I am the oldest son and yes, in terms of labels, I'm the good son." As, in fact, Nav had been until he'd rejected his parents' plans. "My brother is the black sheep."

He'd never told Kat much about his upbringing. If she knew he'd left behind wealth and privilege to become, in essence, a starving artist, she might have thought he was nuts. Or felt sorry for him. But now, as Dhiraj, he could tell his story sideways, through a made-up brother.

"He doesn't go along with what your parents want?" Maggie asked.

"He did for a while. It's hard not to, the way we were raised. Respect for your parents is a strong tradition. But the things our parents stand for aren't things he relates to. Commerce, wealth, power, status."

No wonder Nav used to believe he was adopted; he'd been so different from his parents.

Kat nodded, expression thoughtful. "It's hard when they want you to follow in their footsteps and you can't relate."

He touched her arm. "You said your older sister was the brainiac. Did that make for more or less pressure on you?"

"Uh . . ." She put down her fork and took a sip of wine.

So often, she avoided this kind of conversation, but now she seemed to be thinking seriously about his question. He loved seeing this new openness in her.

"Different pressure," she said slowly. "Theresa took up so much of our parents' attention. She fast-tracked school, was a brilliant academic, and that's what our parents wanted."

"Did she choose the same career as one of your parents?" Maggie asked.

"No, but they're very proud of her. She's a world-renowned sociologist."

"Is she happy?" Nav asked. How nice it would be to pursue the career you wanted with your parents' blessing.

"Very." A pause. "She lives in Australia. And I'm in Montreal." To the Farradays, she said, "I manage PR for a hotel. Jenna doesn't live in Vancouver, either."

"Your parents must miss you so much," Maggie said.

"I . . . uh, I guess they do." Kat looked as if the notion surprised her. "They nag us to visit. But they're both very busy. Dad's trying to find a cure for cancer, and Mom does personal injury law, on the plaintiff side." A proud smile lit her face. "She's arguing a case in the Supreme Court of Canada next week. Which is the week before Merilee's wedding."

"Your sister's getting married?" Maggie said. "That's why you're going to Vancouver?"

Kat nodded. "The whole family will be together for the first time in a year and a half."

"Bet your folks are happy about that," Tim said.

Nav had been quietly eating the excellent prime rib, listening to the conversation and watching the expressions cross Kat's face. Love and pride, mixed with uncertainty.

It was the latter expression he saw as she murmured, "Happy. Yes, I guess . . . we all are."

There was a vulnerability to her tonight that he rarely saw. Normally, if she was upset she vented and moved on. This was new, this mood of quiet reflection, this willingness to delve into her issues rather than avoid them.

Under the tablecloth, he rested his hand on her thigh, atop

the filmy fabric of her dress. He hoped she knew he was offering support, not a come-on.

"You guess?" Maggie asked gently.

Kat gave a quick laugh. "Sorry. Of course we're happy. It's just, we don't have a lot in common, and it's easier to get along when we're at a distance."

"I can see that when kids are young and, uh, trying to find their own niches in life," Tim said quietly. "Maybe now you've all found them, you can get along better?"

It was a good point. "So long as everyone respects each other's niches," Nav said, swirling the last bite of beef to gather every drop of rosemary juice. "There's not much chance my parents will ever respect m—" Damn, he'd almost said "mine." "My brother's."

"What does he do?" Tim asked.

Oops. He hadn't thought that far ahead. As he chewed slowly, he took inspiration from the nearly empty dinner plates. "He's a chef."

"That's a fine career," Maggie said.

"Tell that to our parents."

"They're probably concerned that it's a hard way to make a living," she said.

"Maybe. I think it's more that our parents have quite traditional Indian values. Parents know best. Children should shut up and obey."

"That doesn't work so well in Canada," Tim said ruefully, and they all chuckled.

Their waiter came to clear the dinner plates. He poured the last of the wine into their glasses and said, "Another bottle?"

"Coffee for me," Maggie said, and everyone else agreed.

They discussed dessert, deciding on a couple of pastries and a cheese and fruit plate that they'd all share.

When the waiter left, Nav rested his hand briefly atop Kat's. "I asked you a question and we got sidetracked. How was it for you, as second child?"

"Oh, gosh." She waved a dismissive hand. "How did we get onto this? No one wants to hear my family stories."

Damn, she was back to her old pattern of avoidance.

Before he could prompt her, Maggie spoke up. "Of course we do. Tonight's topic of conversation is parents and children. You have to hold up your end."

"I'm really not that interesting."

The way she spoke reminded Nav of how, on Saturday night, she'd belittled her appearance, saying she wasn't beautiful but made the best of what she had.

He wanted to put his arm around her shoulders, but instead slipped his hand back on her thigh. "Come on, Kat."

"Well, if you're sure." She finished her wine and put down the glass. "Following Theresa was hard. I did okay in school, but could never measure up."

Kat was bright. In a normal family, she might have been the smart one. "It's unfair to be compared against a genius," he protested.

Her hand dropped casually to her lap, where he caught it and interlaced their fingers.

"If you have an older sibling, you're always compared to them," she responded.

"True," Maggie said. "But the oldest may bear the burden of more expectation."

Try being the only, Nav thought.

"Our kids found their niches pretty early," Tim said.

"So did we," Kat said. "Theresa was the genius academic, but she lacked social skills."

"So you became Ms. Sociability?" Nav remembered the label she'd used earlier.

"Yeah. I got along with everyone. Kids, teachers, parents of friends. That was my niche."

He'd seen the same thing in Montreal. Except, none of her friendships ran deep. Not even with him. In some ways, he'd learned more about Kat in the past two days than he had in the past two years. He was the one playing a role, yet Kat, too, was a different person. Still warm, friendly, generous, but more introspective and willing to open up about herself.

This was the woman he'd always believed lay underneath her bright, busy façade. With each truth or reflection she shared, he felt closer to her. And he loved her more.

"I was always off doing something with friends," Kat said. Her hand freed itself from his so she could cut a sliver of Camembert cheese, which she teamed with a red grape.

Maggie spoke thoughtfully. "You got your validation, your sense of worth, from having lots of friends."

Nav paused in the act of slicing cheese for himself and saw Kat's eyes widen. "I never thought of it that way." She gave a soft, nervous laugh. "You may be right. Are you by any chance a shrink?"

The other woman laughed. "No, only a mom who's gained some perspective over time."

"Her parents should have given her validation," Nav said firmly.

Kat shot him a startled glance, then the hint of a smile.

"I'm guessing they validated Kat's sociability," Tim said quietly.

"What do you mean?" Kat asked.

"They were proud you were so popular?" he suggested.

"You're right. Mom said I was a people person, like her, and Dad's always admired that quality in her. Yes, they were happy when I had so many friends and was so active, joining clubs at school, being on the student executive."

"Let me guess," Maggie said. "High school valedictorian?"

Kat flushed. "And prom queen."

Nav wondered what lucky boy had been her king. "I'm sure you were a lovely queen."

"Thanks." Her hand left her coffee cup and dropped to her lap.

He reached over and caught it.

"Of course she was," Maggie said. "She's such a beautiful girl." She shot him a meaningful look.

"I noticed." Even with the other couple right across the table, it was impossible not to get turned on by touching Kat. By imagining the two of them alone together in his room, experimenting with Kama Sutra positions. He stroked his thumb caressingly over her hand.

"What did we agree about matchmaking?" Tim teased his wife.

"And on that note," she said, rising, "we should head off."

Tim winked at them as he stood, too. "We have a date to drink Grand Marnier in the dome car and watch the moon and stars."

"It's romantic," Maggie said. "You should try it."

Her husband took her hand and tugged her toward the exit. "Sweetheart, I don't think these two need any help from you."

When they'd gone, Nav squeezed Kat's hand. "Nice people, but it's good to be alone."

She squeezed back. "I was surprised you chose to sit with other people."

"You said meeting people is part of the fun of train travel, so I thought you'd like it."

"I did. It was an interesting conversation. It made me think." She rubbed her free hand across her brow, then grinned, eyes twinkling. "Not something I'm used to doing."

He smiled back. "Then relax and just feel. For example . . ." He freed his hand from hers and edged the hem of her dress higher so he could stroke the bare flesh of her inner thigh, reminding her of the intimacies they'd shared. "Does that feel nice?"

She swallowed. "You know it does."

It felt damned fine to him, too. So fine that his dick was hardening with a desire that had been growing since he first saw her tonight. No, earlier. Since he'd planned out their evening and imagined another slow seduction, leading up to teaching her about the Kama Sutra.

"Your skin feels like warm silk," he said. "I want to lick you, right there." He ran his thumb over her in gentle circles, then went higher. "And there." Her body trembled under his touch. "Unless you'd prefer to go to the dome and watch the moon?"

Her thighs closed, trapping his hand between them, still inches short of his goal. "Too many people there," she whispered, eyes dark with need.

Thank God. He couldn't wait to be alone with her. "Then let's go to my compartment."

"Yes, please." She released his hand and started to rise.

He surged to his feet, grabbing his jacket off the back of his chair and holding it in front of himself to hide his growing erection.

She hooked her own jacket over her arm and walked ahead of him toward the exit. The blond man—his competition—had gone, he noticed. The screenwriter was just the kind of guy Kat went for, so he was relieved she'd chosen Dhiraj.

Now if he could only work her around to choosing Nav.

This time, as they walked through the sleeping cars toward his room, he put his arm around her shoulders. Although there weren't many people around, it was still a public statement they were a couple. Would she accept it?

Yes. She even tipped her head against his shoulder. The feel of her, her scent, the fact that he—or at least Dhiraj—had publicly claimed Kat Fallon as his woman, were all intoxicating.

And so arousing that, by the time they reached his Romance by Rail compartment, his whole body ached with need.

He'd barely closed the door when he pulled her into his arms, flush up against him. Thrusting both hands into her hair, he held her head firmly and tilted it up to his.

Then he kissed her. His lips seared and branded hers, and his tongue thrust into her mouth and took possession while his arms wrapped her as if he'd never let her go.

She kissed him back with the same intensity. She made little moaning sounds and her body squirmed restlessly, hands gripping his ass so hard her fingernails bit through the fabric of his pants and underwear.

Still kissing, he walked her backward the few steps to the bed, then toppled the two of them onto it. A crash told him the game board, which he'd left lying on the bed, had hit the floor.

When he'd set out for dinner, he'd planned what they'd do when they came back to this room. A glass of sparkling wine, sandalwood candles like she burned in her apartment, a few rolls of the die that would hopefully lead to provocative questions and sensuous answers, a flirtatious seduction that would result in slow, tantalizing Kama Sutra lovemaking.

Fuck that. They'd do it all later.

All he cared about now was getting inside her. Hands on either side of her head, he stared down at her face, barely visible in the dim light that came through the window. "Kat, I'm so hot for you, I can't wait. Sitting beside you at dinner, wanting to touch you . . ."

Listening to her open up and reveal herself, implicitly trusting him to understand. Yes, she'd been talking to Dhiraj, but he'd bet she had been trusting Nav.

"Me, too." Her hands scrabbled between them, tugged on his zipper.

She released his aching dick into the bliss of her warm hands, and he groaned with relief and pleasure, then fumbled under the pillow, where he'd stashed condoms.

Their bodies separated for the unbearably long moments it took for him to sheath himself and her to yank off her underwear—damn, he hadn't even seen what kind she was wearing tonight—then she lay back, dress hiked up.

Breathless with need, he kneeled between her legs, pulling his pants and briefs down his hips. With one hand he raised her skirt and caressed her, then, unable to hold back any longer, he sank inside her with a groan of relief.

As he pumped into her, her hips lifted to meet him.

They made love in a world of shadows, the only light coming from the moonlit sky outside. He could barely make out her features. Yet this sex was anything but anonymous.

Her scent, of jasmine and aroused woman, was unique. Her little gasps and whimpers, the softness of her thighs, the strength of the hands gripping his ass, all were Kat. Only Kat.

Everything he ever wanted.

"Kat," he whispered.

"Oh, yes. So good."

Not only was she opening her body to him, but bit by bit, on this trip, she'd been sharing her thoughts, her worries, opening her soul. And he knew it was to him, Nav.

They belonged together, and soon she'd realize it, too.

He moved fast, her sounds and hands driving him on, plunging deep with each stroke.

Sex. Hard, driving, needy sex.

And yet, with the total knowledge that this was the woman he loved. And the hope that, even if she wasn't ready to admit it yet, she was coming to love him.

He dipped his head, kissed the moans of passion from her lips, and absorbed the shuddering cry she gave when she came.

Then he let his own orgasm rip through him.

After, he collapsed on top of her for a moment, then rolled the two of them so they were lying on their sides, still joined. He kissed her gently, tried to catch his breath. When he could speak, he said, "That was incredible. Though not exactly what I'd planned."

"I'm sure not complaining." A pause. "What had you planned?"

"Wine and candles, a few rolls of the die, and provocative questions to answer. I seem to remember we'd discussed a prize of Kama Sutra sex."

"And here I thought you'd forgotten," she teased.

"Believe me, I'd never forget that. I'll get the candles."

He rose, dealt with the condom, and fastened his pants. Then he lit a couple of candles.

"Mmm, sandalwood," she said. She still lay on the bed but had adjusted her own clothing. "I love that scent."

"Do you? Now, how about some sparkling wine? We did say we were being decadent tonight. And on that subject—" He handed her the box of Godiva chocolates he'd brought. "I know the attendants put chocolates on the pillow, but these are better."

"Ooh, my favorite!" Then her delighted smile turned to a slight frown. Maybe the combination of sandalwood candles and Godiva chocolates was too much of a reminder that he was really Nav, who knew her taste.

He gave a casual shrug. "I figure, a guy can never go wrong with chocolates."

"True. Dhiraj." It seemed she tacked the name on deliberately. "Nor can a man go wrong with bubbly. And it goes perfectly with chocolate." She opened the box and studied the contents.

He eased out the cork, poured two glasses, and handed her one. Then he raised his. "To strangers on a train, and getting to know each other."

"I'll drink to that."

The wine wasn't up to the standard of the champagnes they'd drunk lately, but then few wines were. Its taste was pleasant, and it gleamed golden and bubbly in the candlelight.

She chose a chocolate and offered the box to him.

"No, thanks." Watching her expression as she savored hers was pleasure enough.

He put the game board in the middle of the bed, then sprawled opposite her, propping himself up on one arm. "Your turn, I believe."

She tossed the die, moved three squares, landed on a heart, and picked a card. " 'What's the most romantic gift a lover could give you?' "

Her eyes closed, and he imagined she was remembering fancy presents from other men. Yet, when she opened her eyes again and gazed at him, her expression was wistful and almost embarrassed. "The truth? A marriage proposal. Telling me he loved me heart and soul and wanted to spend the rest of his life with me."

Nav would have given her that this very minute if she was ready. "Yes," he said softly, "that's about as romantic as it gets."

He rolled and drew a card. " 'What's the sexiest place you've ever made love?' Hmm . . ."

"So many places to choose from?" She lifted her wineglass and studied him over the rim.

Did he hear a spark of jealousy, or was that wishful thinking? "Beds are great, but there's a lot to be said for variety."

He chose a memory that would work for his Dhiraj persona. "When I was seventeen or eighteen, I had sex on a midsummer night, under the stars, on an allure."

"A what?"

"It's the walkway at the top of a castle wall. One summer a chap at school invited a few of us to his family's country home for the weekend. It was near the ruins of a small castle, and some of us went for a guided tour. I was dating a girl named Anna, who was always reading historical romances. She loved the term 'allure,' and . . . well, we snuck back at night with a blanket and made love there."

"Very romantic," she said approvingly. "Was she your first lover?"

"No. That was Francesca, one of my friend's big sisters."

"How old were you?"

"Let's just say, several years younger than Francesca. She seemed very sophisticated. God knows what she saw in me, but I sure as hell was glad. For the entire two months it lasted. How about you? Who was your first?"

"The prom king, on prom night." She took another chocolate. "Could I be any more cliché? I felt like I was the last virgin in school, but I was waiting for someone special."

"Was the prom king good enough for your family?"

Her mouth twisted, and he knew it wasn't from the taste of the candy. "No, and they were right. He wasn't special. It was the magic of the night—we were even wearing crowns—that made me think so. A month later he dumped me for someone he met at his summer job."

"Sorry."

"The story of my life." She threw the single die vigorously, and he raised a hand to block it from tumbling off the board.

"Kat, they're idiots." He reached over to stroke her cheek, tuck a curl of hair behind her ear. "The men who don't appreciate you."

"That's a sweet thing to say." A sparkle hit her eyes. "And you're damned right, too." She glanced down. "What did I roll? A one. Which puts me on a diamond." She drew a card and read it. " 'Which would you rather share with your lover: a shower or a bath?' "

Images cascaded through his mind and arousal stirred again. "Both sound good to me."

"Me, too. It's hard to choose. Depends on the day and my mood. Baths are more romantic. You can play, tease, linger. Showers are immediate. Sexy, with all that rushing water."

Slick skin, soapy hands, flushed breasts. His room had a tiny bathroom with toilet and sink. The shower was in a separate room across the hall.

It wouldn't be as comfortable as this bed, but he wanted to give Kat something special. Damn it, he was a fun lover, spontaneous and inventive, not a man she'd grow bored with. She needed to realize it. If he'd had an allure handy, he'd have taken her up on it and made love to her under the starlit sky.

"The shower across the hall has room for two," he said. "So long as the two are friendly."

Her eyes gleamed with interest in the candlelight. "You want to share a shower?"

Chapter 14

A shower with . . . Dhiraj. The idea was deliciously tempting, but . . . "People are starting to turn in," I said. "Some will be taking showers before bed." It would be too embarrassing if someone saw us going in or out together.

"We'll roll the die a while longer, then have our own shower before bed."

He suited action to words, landing on a spade, and read from the card he chose. " 'What do you most fear right now?' Jesus, some of these are tough."

While he reflected, I thought how I would answer that question. Not being loved, I figured. Loved unconditionally by a special man. The idea that it would never happen was . . . terrifying. Unthinkable. I took a hefty swallow of wine.

Dhiraj was staring at the card, but his gaze was unfocused. Was this such a hard question for him?

"You don't have to answer," I reminded him. "But you'll have to move backward."

Slowly he looked up and focused on my face. "I fear not getting the thing I most want."

"Oh, no, that's not a proper answer. You have to say what you most want."

He shook his head and moved his black Cupid backward.

"Coward. Come on, Dhiraj, what do you most want?"

Picking up his wineglass, he gave me a flirtatious smile. "To get you in the shower."

"Uh-uh. They're asking for something more significant."

"Which is why I moved back." He drained his glass and got up to get the bottle.

If he'd wanted to arouse my curiosity, he'd picked the right method. He was Dhiraj. He could make up an import/export business, a brother, anything he wanted. Why didn't he make up an answer to the question?

He picked up my glass and refilled it. "Your turn, Kat."

"Okay, fine," I grumbled. I rolled, moved, picked a diamond card. " 'Taste and smell are the senses people most neglect. Describe your lover's taste and smell—and feel free to sample them to refresh your memory.' "

The question made me smile. "The scent is sandalwood. The taste . . . mmm, I think I need a refresher."

"Help yourself."

I leaned across the game board toward him, and he met me in the middle. Figuring he expected me to kiss him, I instead licked his cheek, eliciting a soft laugh. Then I gripped his head in both hands, held him steady, settled my lips on his, and probed his mouth with my tongue. With each exploratory stroke, my arousal built and his shuddering sigh said he felt the same.

I gave a purr of enjoyment, then pulled back. "Wine, with undernotes of rosemary and coffee. Yummy."

"You're saying my taste is what I last ate or drank? That's not a very good answer."

"Maybe you're right." Which meant I had to taste more than just his mouth. Not exactly a hardship. Suggestively I ran the tip of my tongue delicately around my lips.

"Jesus, Kat."

I leaned close and licked his neck, moving downward in soft, sure strokes. The top couple of buttons of his shirt were undone, and my tongue tracked the brown skin between them. I undid the next button, and the next, lapping my way down the center of his body.

Such lovely skin, with curls of black hair for accent.

When his shirt was undone halfway, I spread the sides open, licked his nipple until it hardened, then sucked it into my mouth.

He gave a soft moan. "How do I taste?"

I released him and sat back on my side of the bed. "A little salty, a little . . . musky male, that's the best I can describe it."

"You want to sample any other places?" His voice was husky with arousal.

"I'll save that for the shower." I tried to sound teasing, but the color of my cheeks, the wild pulse fluttering at my throat, would tell him I was turned on, too. "Unless you've changed your mind?"

"No way. And I think it's time for that shower now. Do you need anything? Are you okay with the train's toiletries?"

"They'll do for tonight."

He rose from the bed and quickly gathered towels and toiletries. "Come on."

We checked that the narrow corridor was empty, then crossed it and found the shower door unlocked. The room was laid out in two sections, with a small changing area as well as the shower cubicle.

After he locked the door, I peeled the flimsy dress over my head, tossed it on the bench, and stood there in a lacy peach-colored bra and thong.

"Wow." He gave a wolf whistle.

I tossed him a saucy wink.

His shirt was still open at the front, and now he removed his cuff links and put them in a pants pocket. He shrugged out of his shirt and hung it on a hook. He had the most amazing torso, all taut muscles and cinnamon skin.

Impatient to see more of him, I reached for the button at the waist of his pants, unzipped them, shoved them down to reveal the erection that thrust against his silky black underwear.

He stepped out of his pants and hung them on a hook. Then he pulled me into his arms. Our mouths joined in a soft, slow, kiss, flavored by the chocolate I'd eaten. It went on and on while our bodies snuggled close, adjusting to each other, shifting so that all the best spots pressed together.

His hands cupped my butt cheeks, left naked by the thong, and I tangled my hands in his hair, tugging it free from the band that pulled it back.

Arousal crept shimmering through my body until it filled me, burning in an urgent flame that made me gasp against his mouth.

He broke the kiss, thrust me away, and his voice was ragged when he muttered, "If we're going to have that shower, we'd better do it now." With one hand he yanked off his briefs, and with the other he reached past the shower curtain to turn on the tap.

I peeled off my bra and thong and tossed them on the bench as he stepped behind the curtain. His hand reached out and I took it.

He tugged and I let him pull me into a world of warm, cascading water, dim light, hard, heated flesh.

After a quick embrace, he put his hands on my hips and turned us so his body shielded me from the spray. He tilted his head back, into the stream of water, then forward again, his smile an exultant flash of white teeth against brown skin as water rained down his face.

Then he shook his head, scattering droplets everywhere. Soaked curls of black hair twisted this way and that around his face.

Curls like Nav's.

No, I had to think of him as Dhiraj.

"Dhiraj, where's the soap? I want to wash you."

He reached into the changing area, where he'd dropped the toiletries on the bench. But, rather than give the bar to me, he held on to it. "Me first."

"It was my idea."

"My soap." He dropped a wet kiss on my nose. "And I have less self-control than you." His eyes were mischievous behind thick black lashes beaded with droplets of water.

"Ah ha, an admission of weakness."

"Turn around."

I obeyed, closed my eyes, and sighed with pleasure as his soapy hands caressed me, slick and warm. The scent of vanilla soap rode the moist air. Gently he massaged my shoulder muscles, stroked down my back. Lingered on my butt, teased the crease between my cheeks. Slid down between my legs, focusing my arousal, making me gasp and press against his hand.

He moved on, stroking down my legs and kneeling on the floor of the shower so he could soap my feet. Then he stood up and tilted me gently into the spray, letting it rinse my body and soak my hair.

"Shampoo?" he asked.

"I can—"

"Let me." He uncapped the small bottle, and I closed my eyes. Then his fingers were in my hair, rubbing in shampoo and massaging my scalp with sure strokes that were pure bliss.

He rinsed out the shampoo, careful that none ran down my face into my eyes. "Conditioner?" he murmured.

Surrendering yet again to being pampered by this man, I said, "Yes, please."

Deftly he smoothed it through my hair; then he turned me to face him.

I opened my eyes and saw the intensity in his chocolate gaze, skimmed down his body and noted the forceful thrust of his erection. My nipples tightened, and I reached for him with both hands.

He caught my hands in one of his. "Not yet, Kat. Let me wash your front."

I dropped my hands to my sides, waiting none too patiently as he rubbed the bar of soap between his hands. Eventually he put it down and touched my shoulders with hands dripping frothy bubbles. Gently he smoothed down my arms, under them, then to my breasts.

Mesmerized, I watched. My breasts were flushed and full under the lacy coating of soap bubbles, and his fingers brushed them in a silky, seductive slide of soapy flesh against flesh.

I moaned, thrusting my breasts into his hands, and he tweaked the hard, aching nubs. Then he let go and reached for the soap, again rubbing up a froth. He slicked his hands across my belly and down into the tangle of auburn curls.

My breath caught in anticipation, and my eyes squeezed shut as I concentrated on the sensations he was creating, the spiral of arousal coiling ever tighter inside me.

His hand slid between my legs, and I gave a needy whimper as his soapy fingers stroked me, back and forth, in light drifting caresses and then firmer ones that made me press against him in an unspoken demand.

My legs trembled as need gathered inside me, desperate for release.

He ran those seductive fingers over my clit, circling, rubbing, flicking ever so gently across it. I felt that reaching sensation inside me, the I'm-so-close feeling.

Then he squeezed, and I came apart.

The climax was so intense, I cried out, hoping the pounding water would cover the sound so it didn't carry through the wall to the sleeping compartment next door.

He held me upright as my body shook with pleasure and my legs turned to jelly.

Gradually, I recovered enough to open my eyes, find my balance. Enough to admire the way the water streamed down his muscular chest and note that his erection showed no sign of faltering. "My turn." I reached for the soap, then turned him so he had his back to me.

I didn't have his patience. Much as I loved touching his body, I was in a hurry to get to the best part, so I made only a slap-dash job of washing his back, though I did linger to admire his firm butt. Then I turned him so he faced me again and brushed soapy hands across his chest, then downward toward my goal.

I curved a hand around his firm cock, gliding up and down on a skim of bubbles.

His hands were on my shoulders, gripping hard. More to steady himself now, I thought, than to help me keep my balance. "You look beautiful wet," he said.

"So do you." His back was to the shower. The water had sleeked his hair against his head, and rivulets streamed down his brown skin. "Like a seal." Or a water god.

I wanted to move him so my back was to the water, so I rose and took his shoulders to guide him. As we swapped positions, he lost his balance, reached out, and—"Oh, shit," he said, "I grabbed the alarm."

The showers had red knobs you could pull to call an attendant in case of an emergency. Quickly he shoved it back in, and we clung together, laughing breathlessly. Waiting. His cock was a rigid, enticing pressure against my belly.

In a couple of minutes we heard a male voice call, "Is everything all right in there?"

"Yes, I pulled it in error," my companion called in that classy Brit accent. "Sorry to trouble you."

"No worries. Happens all the time," was the laconic reply.

"Now," I whispered, "where were we?" We'd shifted position so I stood under the shower, my back to the showerhead, and he faced me.

"Let's start off here." He tipped my face up for a long kiss as steamy as the air around us.

When we broke apart, I sank to my knees, sliding my hands down the sides of his body as I went, then took him in my mouth. He tasted of water, smelled of vanilla soap.

He groaned. Fisted his hands in my hair. Thrust gently as my lips encompassed as much of him as I could take in.

I was under a waterfall, with water hitting my head, my shoulders, streaming down my back, my face, all around me. His cock was fiery heat, rigid strength in my mouth. I sucked, lapped the crown, and gradually the sultry taste of aroused male replaced the bland one of water.

"So good, Kat. So good." His hips tilted, and he tugged my hair. "Stop now. I have to come."

Not releasing him, I shook my head.

The sound he made was a growl. Like a leopard ready to pounce. Primitive, almost savage.

I could sense the orgasm rising in his body, gathering strength, collecting itself, then plunging forward. He jerked in my mouth and salt-sweet come exploded on my tongue.

I swallowed it, took his essence into me, and he thrust again, almost as forcefully. Once more I swallowed and then swirled my tongue gently around the head of his cock. I rode out more spasms, each less powerful than the one before.

Finally I released him and, breathless, rested my forehead against his thigh.

His hands caressed my shoulders. "Come here. Come kiss me."

I let him tug me to my feet, noticing but not minding the soreness in my knees from the floor of the shower.

His expression was tender, affectionate. He smoothed the wet hair back from my face and kissed first my forehead, then my nose, and finally my lips. Gently but thoroughly he took my mouth in a kiss that was less passion than . . .

I couldn't name it. Didn't remember ever being kissed that way before.

It made me feel warm. Loved, almost.

Discomfited, I raised my hands to his chest—God, he was firm—and pushed myself away. "We're using too much water."

He reached past me to turn off the tap, and suddenly there was silence. We stood, dripping, staring at each other. Then I turned, shoved the shower curtain aside, and reached for the towels. "Let's get dry."

He stood back and let me dry myself first. Then I stepped out into the changing area and dressed as he toweled himself.

We hadn't brought a comb, so all I could do was run my fingers through my damp hair, feeling it curl around them. My makeup must have washed off, or at least I hoped it had rather than leaving mascara streaks under my eyes.

My lover stepped out of the shower stall. His hair was a mop of black curls. Like Nav's.

Oh, damn. Dhiraj, Nav. Again the boundaries were blurring. And I couldn't let them.

He tossed down his towel. "Kat, stay with me tonight."

My breath caught. I only spent the night with a man when I believed a relationship was serious. This one couldn't be. Not with Dhiraj, because he didn't exist. And definitely not with Nav, as lovers. We'd promised each other the train games wouldn't affect our friendship.

I shouldn't feel so tempted. I forced myself to say, "I don't think that's a good idea."

Was that a shadow of hurt in his eyes? Hard to tell because he bent to put on his briefs, then stepped into his pants. Head down, tone neutral, he said, "We could play Kama Sutra."

A shiver of lust rippled through me, but all the same, I said, "Not tonight."

He slipped into his shirt. "My room's far more comfortable."

"I know. But I . . . I'm not comfortable."

A sigh, as he buttoned his shirt. "I'll trade you rooms. You can have the big one."

I shook my head. "It's sweet of you to offer, but no, thanks." Without him there, the room would feel too empty. Too lonely.

"As you wish." His voice was even. Was he annoyed with me?

I wished he'd pull his hair back, so his appearance would match his Dhiraj accent. The stranger game was fun, but I needed him to maintain the role.

We went across the corridor to his room, where I picked up my purse and jacket. "It was . . . an incredible evening." I gazed up at his strong, gorgeous face and wondered what it would feel like to spend the night in his arms.

No, I couldn't risk it. If I did, I might find myself seriously falling for him. That would be a very bad mistake. Best to stick to the fun and games. I cleared my throat. "See you tomorrow?"

Muscles flexed in his jaw. "I imagine so. As for tonight—" he gestured toward the window—"you lie in that single bed of yours and gaze out at the moon. I'll be lying in my big one, doing the same."

His tone held a challenge, and the unspoken words, *And I dare you to not think about me.*

He held the compartment door open. "Seems to me, it would be more fun doing it together. But that's your call, Kat."

He dropped a quick kiss on the top of my head and shoved me out the door before I could respond.

Chapter 15

Nav spent a restless night, frustrated that Kat wasn't there to share the double bed. Why was she so damned resistant?

Or was his plan flawed? In the beginning he'd been carried away by excitement and hope, and he hadn't realized his scheme held an inherent contradiction. Wanting to sweep Kat off her feet and make her view him differently, he'd created Pritam, then Dhiraj, the kind of men she fell for. It had worked to the extent that she'd let those guys seduce her. But whenever she found herself thinking of him as Nav, she threw up a barrier.

Even though, when he'd been playing Pritam and Dhiraj, he'd told her things he'd never shared before. Couldn't she see that the honesty and intimacy was happening between her and *Nav*? Despite the token pretense of the stranger on a train, it was him she was growing close to. Making love with.

Sighing, he figured he'd give her some space. Maybe she'd seek him out. If not, he'd pursue her once more. Remind her of the Kama Sutra prize, which he knew tantalized her.

Outside the window, the first hint of dawn was lighting the sky, the dramatic scenery of the Canadian Shield emerging from the dusk. His photographic eye sharpened.

He'd brought his camera and lenses along on the trip, knowing he needed more shots for his "Perspectives on Perspective" exhibit, but so far he'd been focused, so to speak, on Kat.

Quickly he threw on jeans and a T-shirt, unpacked his camera gear, and headed to the observation car with its 360-degree glass dome.

It was empty but for an elderly woman in a green velour tracksuit, with a crossword puzzle book on her lap. He greeted her. "Another early riser."

She smiled. "Always have been. I'm in the habit of creeping out of bed a good two hours before my husband George." She gestured toward his Nikon. "That looks like a fancy camera."

About to say he was a professional photographer, he realized he had to be Dhiraj. A train was too closed a community to allow for multiple identities. He slid a crisper English edge into his accent as he said, "It's been a passion of mine for a long time."

Her faded green eyes twinkled. "I know all about men and that kind of passion. With George, it's golf."

The train went around a curve, and a pale swath of pinkish light fell across her cheek. She turned to gaze out the window. "Dawn. My favorite time of day."

Seeing the warm light on cheeks as softly crumpled as tissue, the spectacular scenery behind her, the puzzle book unopened in her lap, Nav lifted his camera. Tough lighting to capture, but it was worth trying.

He clicked a few shots while she admired the view, apparently unaware he was taking her picture. "Amazing scenery, isn't it?" she asked.

"It is." The light shifted, the photo op gone now. He checked the images he'd taken and selected the best. "Take a look."

She glanced at the camera, and her hand flew to her throat. "Oh, my heavens! I thought you were photographing scenery."

"I was, and the view was lovely."

"Flatterer." She smiled, then studied the picture more closely. "You have a talent, young man."

"I had a good subject. If you give me your name and your address or e-mail, I'll send you and your husband a copy." He'd also send a release form asking her permission to use the photograph commercially.

"How lovely."

Nav pulled out the notebook where he recorded photo information and took down her name and e-mail, then made a few notes about the shots.

He and the woman—Elizabeth—chatted for half an hour or so. When the train approached a station, he rose. "I'm going to get off and take some photos."

"Have fun."

A few minutes later, he was on the ground, clicking pictures of the VIA Rail train from various angles, capitalizing on the early-morning light. It was a challenge to find an original way of photographing a train, yet he knew train photos were popular. To a number of people, trains symbolized a romantic, nostalgic form of travel, and now Nav was coming to understand why.

This stop was one where the crews changed, so people were milling about. Against the background of the train, he took shots of a wiry older man laughing with a girl who had tattoos up her arms. The old and the new of the railroads.

Sure enough, when he spoke to them, the man, a sleeping car attendant, said he'd worked the railways all his life and never wanted to retire. The girl, a member of the kitchen crew, was taking a year out of college to travel and make some money.

"I keep telling her she'll get hooked," the man said. "Trains get in your blood."

Before she could answer, the train gave a warning whistle. As crew members scurried aboard, Nav stood back to take a final few shots. A face stared at him out of a window, and he realized it was Kat. As he scrambled to board, he wondered if he should go to her.

No, he'd wait and see if she would come find him.

He was still in the T-shirt and jeans he'd thrown on when he got up, his hair loose and uncombed, so he went to his room to clean up before breakfast.

When he entered the dining car, he was Dhiraj, with pulled-back hair and an expensive shirt. Kat wasn't there. He sat at a table with the elderly woman, Elizabeth, and her husband. Though he saved a seat, Kat didn't appear.

She must have decided on a snack instead of a real meal. Had he come on too strong, asking her to stay with him last night? Or had the sight of him in the station this morning looking like Nav scared her off?

After breakfast, he wandered around with his camera. When he reached the Activity Car, he realized it was a great source of shots, with people chatting, playing cards or computer games, doing jigsaw puzzles.

An activity director—a perky, ponytailed blonde a few years younger than he—had gathered half a dozen kids, ranging in age from roughly six to ten, to draw train pictures. Nav took a few shots of the children with their crayons and colored pencils.

The activity director tossed him a flirtatious look. "Hey, there's a participation rule. If you want to hang out with us, you have to draw, even if you think you're not very good."

A tiny Chinese boy, probably the youngest kid in the group, gave him a shy grin. "You can share my crayons." That smile tugged at Nav's heart.

"That's nice of you." Nav hung his camera around his neck and sank down beside him. "You sure you don't mind a big kid in the group?" he asked the young woman.

"It's nice to have company." She handed him a sheet of drawing paper. "I'm Emily."

"Dhiraj." He glanced at the boy beside him. "And who are you?"

"Kevin."

They went around the circle, the kids all giving their names.

Then Nav took Kevin up on his offer to share crayons, Emily added several colored pencils, and he began to draw. Nav was a decent artist; he chose to sketch the train as it had looked standing in the station a few hours ago. He used a slightly cartoonish style, like an illustration in a kids' picture book. The children chattered about this and that as they worked, and he joined in, and also occasionally lifted his camera to take some shots.

As an only child, he'd always envied friends who had siblings, and he enjoyed the company of children. Sometimes he felt he had more in common with them—with their curiosity and spontaneity—than with other adults.

He was looking forward to being a parent. His kids would get encouragement and support. He'd provide gentle guidance rather than try to run their lives.

Emily said, "It's almost lunchtime. You have five minutes to finish up; then let's see what everyone has done."

Nav had been drawing faces peering out the train windows, making each one a cute caricature of one of the kids. Now he added Emily, with her ponytail, in the driver's seat.

As everyone showed off their artwork, he, like Emily, found enthusiastic compliments for each. When it was his turn, everyone oohed, aahed, and laughed at the funny details he'd added. He gave the drawing to the little boy, Kevin, who'd shared his crayons.

"Are you an artist?" Emily asked.

"No, a—" He stopped himself from saying "photographer." "I'm in business."

"I bet you're successful at everything you do." Her admiring look held more than a hint of a come-on.

Not wanting to encourage her interest, he said lightly, "You'd lose that bet."

As she helped the kids pack up the art supplies, he glanced around the Activity Car and was surprised to see Kat across the room beside an older man, a jigsaw puzzle in front of them.

How long had she been there, sitting behind him and watching him draw with the kids?

Quickly he went over to her. She looked great in figure-hugging jeans and a short-sleeve blouse in a flowery, feminine fabric, but he paid more attention to her expression, which was wary. "Kat, hi, I missed you at breakfast."

He smiled at the older man and held out his hand. "Hello, I'm Dhiraj."

"A pleasure. Terry." The man gave a warm, firm shake.

"Dhiraj," Kat said, "what's with the camera?" She was frowning slightly, clearly disconcerted by the reminder of Nav.

"Every businessman needs a hobby," he said, letting a spark of mischief color his tone. "It keeps me from being utterly boring."

As Nav had hoped, her lips quirked. "Yeah, I can see how that would be a problem."

Terry chuckled.

Nav addressed both of them. "There's something I need to do right now, but I wonder if we all might meet up for lunch?"

"Sounds good to me," Terry said promptly.

"I'd already arranged to lunch with a woman named Lynn," Kat said.

"Would Lynn mind the company of two gentlemen?" Terry asked.

Kat glanced at Nav as if trying to make up her mind. "I suppose not."

"Great," Nav said. "First one there claims a table. See you then." He hurried away to catch the parents as they came to collect their kids for lunch so that he could get their information and send releases if the photos turned out.

At lunch, Kat made the introductions, then the other woman, Lynn, said, "Well, isn't this fun? Four people who've only just met, looking forward to a pleasant lunch together."

"Trains are good for that," Terry said.

"This is my first time," Nav said. "It's fascinating. And getting to know people is the best part." He smiled at Lynn, then Terry who sat beside him. Then he let his eyes linger on Kat, across the table.

Whatever doubts had been worrying her, her smile suggested she'd banished them. "Speaking of which, Dhiraj, you're a man of hidden talents. Not only do you run an import/export business, you're an amateur photographer and artist." Her eyes gleamed. "Any other talents you've been keeping a secret?"

"Maybe one or two. But I'm a humble man. I don't like to talk about myself. You'll have to discover them for yourself." He hoped Kama Sutra sex leaped to her mind.

From the flush on her cheeks, he had guessed right.

Terry buried a soft chuckle against the edge of a water glass, and Lynn flashed Nav a grin.

The four of them had a pleasant lunch, the conversation coming easily. Nav had brought his camera and asked permission to take pictures, hoping it wouldn't throw Kat out of her relaxed mood. He usually left his camera at home when he was socializing, as he'd learned the hard way that friends could be offended if he seemed more interested in setting up shots than in enjoying their company.

Now he shot a few pictures of Kat, animated as she asked questions, intent as she listened. Of Lynn, face glowing as she talked about her long-distance romance. And of Terry, when he spoke with baffled resignation about his wife, who had Alzheimer's and was in a care facility in Toronto.

"I hate to leave her," the man said, "but the sad truth is, she rarely recognizes me. The grandkids in Victoria are getting older and I want to be in their lives, so I hop a train every few months and make a short visit."

"My gran has Alzheimer's," Kat said. "It's so sad what it does to people."

Lynn put her hand on Terry's arm. "You do your best. That's all anyone can do. My husband died of lung cancer, and it was a long, painful period." She patted him a couple times, then said, "Tell us about your happier days. How did you and your wife meet?"

Terry's face brightened, and again Nav lifted his camera, imagining several portraits of the man framed together. Reflections on a marriage: the optimistic beginning, the patiently loyal end, the wistful joy of memories.

It made him think about him and Kat. He hoped nothing bad ever happened to her, but he wanted her for life—whatever their lives might bring. If he ever got to say those wedding vows to her, he'd mean them with all his heart.

He realized he was staring at her, probably with a sappy expression on his face, because her eyebrows rose and she mouthed, "What is it?"

Quickly he shook his head, tuned back in to Terry's story, and raised his camera again.

They had finished dessert and were lingering over tea and coffee when the public address system announced an upcoming station where passengers could get off the train and shop.

Lynn said, "There's a lovely First Nations gift store at this station."

"Yes," Kat said, "it's great. Dhiraj, you might get some more pictures."

The four of them joined other passengers who were heading for the exit. Once in the store, each went their own way.

Nav tried for a few shots pairing the displayed pieces of art with people's reflections against the glass of the showcases. As he worked, he perused the items for sale, looking for a gift for Kat. A ring would be pushy, but he knew she liked to wear dangly earrings when she went out. The carved silver and gold hummingbirds, graceful and lively, seemed right for her.

After tucking the small package in his pocket, he moved outside to take a few shots of the train and station, then caught up with Kat as she came out of the store carrying a bag. "What did you get?"

"A T-shirt." She tugged on the strap of his camera as they strolled back to the train. "Did you get all the pictures you wanted?"

"At the shop, yes. But I have another idea." He moved closer so their arms brushed, and she didn't move away.

"Oh?"

"You."

She tilted her head up to him. "Me? You want to photograph me?"

He'd snapped shots of her occasionally in Montreal, but this time had something much different in mind. "You're photogenic."

She wrinkled her nose. "Not especially."

"Trust me." He touched her back, turning her toward the car that housed his sleeping compartment. "Let me show you."

Her "hmm" sounded curious, and she went without protest.

He opened his door and ushered her inside. "Let's play a game."

"The board game?" The corner of her mouth tipped up, perhaps thinking about that Kama Sutra prize they'd yet to reach.

The idea was tempting, but so was what he had in mind. "Let's pretend we're playing the board game, and one of us draws a card that says, 'Act out a role play where one of you is a photographer and the other's a model.' "

She gave a quick laugh. "Okay, how about I be the photographer?"

He handed her the camera. "Works for me."

After a moment's examination, she said, "Like I'd have the slightest clue how to use this? All I can do is point and shoot."

He took it back. "Then I guess I'll have to play the photographer."

"A role you're uniquely suited for, Dhiraj," she teased. She glanced around the room. "Okay, where do you want me? Let me guess, on the bed?"

"Nope. Standing. Now, you're a model, and we're shooting a spread for a magazine. It's a digital camera, so I can shoot any number of pictures and we'll delete the ones that don't work out. Don't be self-conscious, just let loose and move around."

A nervous giggle. "There isn't much room to move."

"Shift position, turn, flip your hair, flirt with the camera, make faces. Have fun." He began to click the shutter.

She scowled. Stuck her tongue out. Then laughed. Slowly she moved this way and that, at first stiffly, then beginning to relax.

He began to prompt her, as he did when he took candids or did fashion shoots. "Hands in your hair, head back. Stretch your neck. Tousle your hair. That's it, very pretty. Very sexy. Give me a smile now. Wet your lips. Oh, that's hot."

As he spoke he got down on the floor and shot upward, then sprawled on the bed and shot across at her, and then stood on the chair and shot down.

She followed his instructions, seeming to lose herself in the game and having fun with the role play. What woman had never wanted to be the object of a magazine photo shoot with a photographer who told her she was beautiful?

And she was.

"Undo a couple buttons, Kat," he said. "Now, flash me a little shoulder. Tease me. That's it; that's great." He saw the flash of a blue bra strap. "More buttons, more flesh, let's see the curve of your breasts. Oh, yeah, your skin's so pretty against the lace of your bra."

He'd done lots of nude photography, yet the sight of Kat fluffing her hair and flicking her blouse open and closed was sexier than anything he'd ever shot. Because it was her. It was personal.

Arousal throbbed in his groin, and he tried to ignore it, to concentrate on taking shots that would do her justice.

She slid the blouse partway down both arms and pulled it

back and forth in the same motion a person would use to towel-dry their back. Though she hadn't said a word, the flush on her cheeks and chest, the sultry way she moved, said she was getting into this, too.

That it was arousing for her, being worshipped by him and his camera.

"Take it off, Kat," he murmured. "Let's see you just in the bra and jeans. Yeah, that's beautiful, just beautiful. Hands on your hips, lean out from the waist, toss your hair and give me a smile. Okay, now straighten up again, turn halfway away from me, and give me a seductive look over your shoulder."

She obeyed, moistening her full lips without being prompted.

"Now, unfasten the bra and hold it in place with both hands. And then, okay now, let it drop. Cup your breasts with your hands; offer them to me."

Her areolas were rosy pink, her nipples hard.

As hard as his dick.

"Play with your breasts; touch them the way you like to be touched. God, that's lovely."

He wanted to touch her himself, but he was really getting off on photographing her. Getting off on the fact that she was letting him do it, that she was flirting with the camera and with him. That his game so obviously turned her on.

It sure as hell turned him on, too. Foreplay, without touching each other.

"Now the jeans, Kat. Undo the zipper, and slide them down your hips just an inch or two. Great. Okay, put your hands in your hair; stretch up."

She obeyed, shifting restlessly, stretching her neck, closing her eyes, tousling her hair this way and that. Making sexy little "mmm" noises like she did during lovemaking.

"Give me some hip action now. Oh, yeah, that's the way. Okay, time to get rid of the jeans. Slide them down slowly. Very, very slowly. And now, step out."

She stood there clad only in tiny lacy blue panties.

He took in the full picture. The mussed hair, the glitter in her eyes, the brightness of her cheeks. The elegant stretch of neck, her soft, full breasts, slim waist, curvy hips. The scrap of fabric, then her long, shapely legs. Was there a prettier, sexier sight in the world?

Without him prompting, she shifted position, rotated her hips, stretched her neck, tossed her head, did all the things he'd asked her to before, the moves even more erotic now because she was almost naked.

"You're the sexiest thing I've ever seen," he murmured, keeping his tone low and hypnotic to urge her on rather than distract her.

Her eyes closed and her fingers toyed with her nipples.

His breath caught, and he had to fight to hold back a groan. Did she have any idea how she was torturing him? Unable to resist any longer, he put the camera on the vanity and yanked off his clothing. Fumbling with a condom, he sheathed himself, then pulled her roughly into his arms. "Damn, Kat, I need you. Now."

Holding her around the waist with one arm, he lifted his other hand and stroked it through her wild curls. Then he anchored his fingers in her hair and held her head firmly as he lowered his mouth to kiss her.

"Oh, yes," she sighed, her lips parting for him.

He let her feel his passion, pouring it into the kiss, and she answered back. Then she broke away, but only to peel off her panties. Coming back into his arms, she raised one leg to hook it around his, pulling herself close to him, stretching her body upward like she wanted to climb him.

Desperate to bring her closer, to get inside her, he caught her under the thighs, the butt, and lifted her.

Her legs and arms curled around him, gripping tight, and he backed the two of them up so she was against the door, its firmness helping support her weight.

Somehow she managed to reach down and guide him between her slick, heated folds.

He surged inside her on a groan of satisfaction. Felt her internal muscles clasp him. Her sweet, panting breath against his ear as she whispered, "Do me. Now."

His need was so urgent, all he could do was thrust into her mindlessly, as fast and deep as he could go.

Clinging tight to him, pretty much all she could do was go along for the ride. Fortunately, her moans of pleasure told him she was enjoying that ride.

Her head tilted down, cheek against his. He closed his lips on her earlobe and nipped.

She gave a soft cry, then an indrawn "oh," and then she was coming with a long, shuddery drawn-out "oh-oh-oh" sound.

The internal spasms of her orgasm finished him off, and his own climax rushed through him.

Chapter 16

I slumped in the chair in my tiny compartment, staring out the window but barely registering the forest scenery.

I still couldn't believe what I'd done. What he'd persuaded me to do. His voice had mesmerized me. To be honest, the idea of being photographed as I stripped had been a turn-on.

The man was crazy.

Exciting. I'd never been with a lover who was so exciting.

I did trust him when he said he'd delete all the photos if I asked him to. Though, first, I wanted to take a look at them.

I hadn't had the courage, back in his room. In fact, I'd fled after we'd had sex.

He and his games had that effect on me. After, I needed to pull back and get some distance. Rationalize what was going on between us. Between me and Dhiraj.

Between me and Nav.

How could we ever go back to the way we'd been, after the things we'd done today? Did I even want us to?

This man, the one who looked fabulous, who was such fun, stimulating company and such a great lover, was special. Not Nav, yet he was Nav.

If Nav was this person, then he was a man I could really care about. As way more than just friends.

But thinking that way would be stupid. I wanted marriage,

and he'd never shown the slightest inclination to get serious about any of the two or three dozen women he'd dated since I'd known him. I shouldn't fool myself that I was that "perfect woman" who would change his mind.

After all, look at my string of ill-fated relationships.

When we were both back in Montreal, he might not even mention our train games. He'd be on to the next woman, the next game. And I'd . . . work hard at seeing him as Nav, and getting our friendship back on track.

"Be careful what you wish for," I muttered. I'd nagged him to clean up his appearance. Now he'd not only done that, he'd shown me he could be both more attentive and more exciting than any man I'd ever dated.

Damn it, I wanted him back the way he used to be.

Soon it would be time for dinner. Did I have the guts to face him? I'd done some wild things when lovers had asked me to, but nothing as outrageous as stripping—fondling my breasts—in front of a camera.

My cell phone rang, making me jump. I pulled it out of my purse. My parents' number.

Blushing, I answered.

Theresa said, "Hey, we got you," and Merilee chimed in with, "Hi, sis." I could tell they were on the conference phone in the kitchen.

"Hi, both of you. Are the folks there?" How could I talk to my parents with the thought of that erotic photo shoot so fresh in my mind?"

"No, just us."

I breathed a sigh of relief. "Can you speak up? Cell reception isn't so great on the train. So, how are things going with the wedding countdown?"

"Matt got delegated the task of sending e-vites," Merilee said, "and we're already getting RSVPs. People love the M&M invitation, Kat."

"We've decided to have the reception here at the house,"

Theresa said, "and I'm making a list of caterers, musicians, and photographers to check out."

"Great. You're being very efficient."

"Well, of course." She sounded surprised.

I gritted my teeth. So much for complimenting Theresa. "What else?"

"Matt's sister suggested a florist, who I'll talk to tomorrow," Theresa said.

"What about the wedding dress?" I asked.

"It's hard to find them off the rack," Theresa said, "but—"

"There's this place, Sandra Sung, in Yaletown," Merilee said enthusiastically. "A friend's older sister got her dress there. I took a look at gowns on the website and there are some great ones, and they're in stock now. I just know I'll find a fabulous dress, and I'm a perfect size six, so it shouldn't need alterations. We have an appointment to go in this afternoon. I can't wait!"

"Wish I could be there." It would be fun to see my little sister trying on dresses. But bittersweet to browse the racks wondering if—no, when, damn it!—my own time would come.

"The bridesmaids' dresses could be tougher," Merilee said, "especially since Jenna's not going to be home until whenever."

"Jenna's a bridesmaid?"

"Kat hasn't heard," Theresa said dryly. "It's going to be a three-pack of bridesmaids."

"What? All of us?"

"Of course," Merilee said. "And my friends Candace and Jennifer, as well. Matt's little sister is the flower girl."

"That's a lot of people walking down the aisle," I said.

"And that's not counting Mom and Dad," Merilee said. "They both have to give me away. Dad's easy; we'll get a boutonniere for his tux, but I want Mom to have a new dress so we all match. Did I tell you, the theme colors are ivory and rose? Anyhow, trying to get Mom away from the office and into the dress shop is going to be tough."

"She *is* preparing an appeal for the Supreme Court," I reminded her. "And it's being heard next week." We'd grown up knowing how important Mom's and Dad's jobs were.

"And this one's a class action suit," Theresa said, "and she has almost a hundred plaintiffs counting on her."

"Well, what about me?" Merilee complained. "Don't I ever get to count on her?"

"It's just bad timing," I said. "You know she'd love to help out if she could."

"No, I don't know that," Merilee said, sounding bitter. "How would I? Everyone's always too busy with their own shit to care about what I need."

"Uh . . ." Her outburst took me aback. Normally she was sweet tempered. And she almost never swore. "Are you having pre-wedding jitters?"

"No, I'm not having fucking pre-wedding jitters!" Her voice was loud enough that, even with the poor cell reception, I had to hold the phone away from my ear.

"Hey, don't get mad at me. It's not like I did anything." I rose, wishing there was room in this tiny compartment to pace. Why did talking to my family so often give me a headache?

"No, you never have, have you?" she said snippily.

"What's wrong with you?" I tried to remind myself she'd been sick, she was stressed out catching up with schoolwork, she was nervous about getting married. But I still felt hurt.

"She might actually have a point," Theresa said in the calm, slightly superior tone that always got my back up.

"What are you talking about?" I went over to the vanity and opened my toiletry kit, hunting for aspirin.

"Think about it, Kat. When we were growing up, who was there for Merilee?"

"There for her? All of us."

"Sometimes," Merilee said softly, sounding rational again. And sad. "But sometimes nobody. Except Matt." She paused, then said, "Theresa, I can't believe you actually *get* that."

What were the two of them talking about?

"We were self-absorbed," Theresa said. "Me, getting so much pressure from our parents to excel at school."

"But you loved all that academic stuff," Merilee said.

"True," she said. "And I'll confess, I loved being the best at something."

"No shit," I mumbled, wedging the phone between my ear and shoulder so I could uncap a bottle of water and pour a glass.

Theresa ignored my comment. "And you, Kat, always so busy with your social life. So many friends, so many activities, you hardly had time for your family."

"That's because everyone was so focused on you," I pointed out, trying not to raise my voice. "If I got any attention at all, it was only to be compared to you. Most of the time unfavorably." With a twist, I opened the pill bottle and shook out two capsules.

"I . . . Really?" Theresa said. "Is that how you saw it? But, you're Mommy's girl, right? We always said I was Dad's. The academic. And you were Mom's, with a, um, more practical kind of intelligence, and always so outgoing and sociable and interested in people."

"And I was no one's kid," Merilee said in a small voice. "Until I met Matt and had someone who really saw me and cared about me."

Wow. I'd never thought of our family this way before.

It occurred to me that none of us had mentioned Jenna. Had she felt the way Merilee had? Was her constant flitting from man to man really just an attempt to find someone who truly saw her and cared about her?

"We all cared about you, Merilee," Theresa said. "Honestly, we did. But we were too caught up in our own lives. You were so much younger. And you had Matt. You were always with Matt. It was like you didn't need us."

"Why need what you can't have?" Was it just the lousy phone reception, or was my little sister's voice quavering?

Well, damn. Had I been so busy being Ms. Sociability that I'd neglected my own sister?

"Merilee?" I said, feeling like shit. "If that's how it came across, I'm sorry. I really am. I just thought we were all really independent, and I guess . . ." I remembered what Maggie had said at dinner. "I guess you and I learned that if we wanted to feel good about ourselves, we had to look outside the family. I did it by having lots of friends. You did it by finding Matt."

I swallowed and said softly, "And you were luckier than me, because I'm still looking for that one special man." Then I held my breath, hoping that for once my sisters would forgo the jokes about my relationship jinx.

After a moment, Theresa said, "Not to play 'poor me, poor me, who got the worst deal?' but even though I got parental validation, it went hand in hand with pressure to be perfect. That's why I left home as soon as I finished high school. Yes, I wanted to achieve, but without all the stress of having the folks constantly on my back."

Another revelation. "I never thought about it being stressful for you," I confessed. "I just thought you *were* perfect." I sank into the chair, my headache easing.

She chuckled. "That'll be the day."

"I knew Mom and Dad wanted me to measure up," I said, "but I never could. At least not when it came to smarts and career decisions. They wanted so much for me, and I wasn't capable of being that person."

"Well how about that," Merilee said wonderingly. "You two are as screwed up as me."

We shared a rather shaky laugh. In some ways, I'd never felt closer to my sisters.

"Why haven't we had this conversation before?" Merilee asked.

"I don't know," I said, "but I wish Jenna could have been part of it. She's always so, you know, *out there*. I wonder if that's her way of compensating for not getting what she needed at home?"

"I think you're right, Kat," Theresa said. "That's perceptive of you."

My gosh. This might well have been the first time I'd ever heard words like that from her.

"You know what's the really strange thing about this?" she went on. "Mom and Dad are good people. They love us. We all know that. So how did everything get so . . . warped?"

I thought of what Maggie and Tim had said. "Parents want to protect their kids, and they want the best for them. I think Mom and Dad tried, but— Here's a radical thought. Maybe our brilliant folks aren't particularly skilled at parenting."

"That's . . . kind of sad," Merilee said. "For all of us. Them, too."

"But it makes sense. It's a logical explanation," Theresa said.

"Thank you, madam professor," I teased, but for once my teasing was affectionate rather than pointed.

Merilee laughed, sounding more like her usual bubbly self. "Hey, guess what, Kat? The prof's not so stodgy after all. Know what she told me?"

"What?"

"She and her new hottie, Damien, had sex on Waikiki Beach!"

"Merilee!" Theresa protested, but only halfheartedly.

"You did what?" I asked. No, that picture didn't compute. I must have misheard, due to the lousy cell reception. "Did M just say you had sex on Waikiki Beach? Like, the actual beach?"

"That's right." Theresa sounded smug. "Bet that shakes up your image of me."

"You know it." My competitive side surged forth, and I wished I could tell them about some of my adventures with . . . Nav? Pritam? Dhiraj?

I focused again on what my sisters had said. Sex on a public beach? Theresa? "Well . . . wow, Theresa. I feel like I don't know you at all." But she was a lot more interesting than I'd ever given her credit for. Going home was seeming more appealing by the moment.

The public address system announced the second seating for dinner. "Hey, I have to go eat. Is there anything I can do for the wedding before I get to Vancouver?"

"Just hold Friday afternoon clear," Theresa said. "All the bridesmaids except Jenna are going dress shopping. We'll buy one for her, too, and hope it fits. Then let's the three of us see if we can find a dress for Mom."

"Okay, you got it."

I hung up, feeling much better about my family and the upcoming visit.

Now, what was I going to do about dinner? Did I want to go play games with Dhiraj, or was it time to start distancing myself?

Before the phone call, I might have chosen distance. But hell, if my stodgy older sister could have sex on Waikiki Beach with a celebrity, the least I could do was further explore my own sexy side. We still hadn't tried out those Kama Sutra positions. Once we were back in Montreal, all I'd have was my friend, Nav, so I should take advantage of Dhiraj while I had him.

I selected a lacy black bra and thong, and paired my denim mini with a black camisole-style top. I was just picking up my jacket when a knock sounded at my door.

"May I request the pleasure of your company for dinner?" The accent was Dhiraj's, and so was the look. As he leaned against the doorframe in a sleek outfit of black pants and a thin V-neck black sweater, he looked sexy and dangerous, like a panther.

I wanted to be bold and sexy, not embarrassed by our photo shoot, so I tilted my head up, smiling. "I'd be delighted, Dhiraj."

He bent quickly and captured my lips in a kiss so skilled and potent it left me gasping for air. "I thought tonight we'd eat alone," he said confidently.

It wasn't a question, but all the same, when I caught my breath, I said, "All right."

I was used to letting the men I dated make decisions, so it was second nature to slip into this pattern with Dhiraj. It was another way in which he differed from Nav. Nav had always let me play the social organizer role that I typically took with my friends. Dhiraj, on the other hand, was a take-charge man with his own agenda.

Not that I was objecting. So far, the activities he'd initiated had been great, from sharing dinner with Maggie and Tim to playing the provocative board game to the erotic photo shoot.

He slid a hand into his pocket and brought out a small bag. "A souvenir."

I loved presents. Noting the logo on the bag, I said, "From the gift shop this afternoon. You bought me something!" Inside was a little box, which I opened. "Oh, my gosh." He'd chosen dangly earrings in silver and gold. "Hummingbirds. They're wonderful."

I threw my arms around him. "Thank you so much." Then I pulled away. "I'm going to put them on."

"You don't have to wear them tonight."

"I want to." I hurried to the vanity, removed my dangly bead earrings, and put in the hummingbirds. When I moved my head, they flitted around my neck as if they were flying, making me laugh with delight.

Then I sobered. Over the years, I'd received many gifts from men, including from Nav. But this one was from Dhiraj. The earrings would be a reminder of this trip, and the things I'd shared with the man who was—but wasn't—Nav.

How ridiculous. I shook my head firmly. It wasn't like I'd be able to forget anything that happened on this trip. I'd just remember this as a fun time with a man named Dhiraj, who'd gone his way after our journey ended. As we had both intended from the start.

Right now, though, he was still here, looking decidedly sexy.

I hugged him again, then went up on my toes for a long kiss that made my whole body hum with awareness and need. Against my belly, I felt him harden, and I was very aware that all I wore under my brief skirt was a thong.

He pulled away. "If we're going to eat, we'd better go now." He held out his arm.

I debated for a moment. Maybe we could try out one or two Kama Sutra positions? That growing erection was awfully enticing.

But then we'd miss dinner. Besides, anticipation was a nice form of foreplay. So I slipped my hand through his arm. "Lead on."

As we strolled down the corridor, I said, "No camera tonight?"

"I want to concentrate on you."

I was positive he'd downloaded this afternoon's images to his computer, and wondered how they'd come out. Were they sexy, or did I look foolish? I couldn't bring myself to ask.

We walked through the sleeping cars to the dining car, where he told the maître d', "We'll be dining alone tonight."

"Very well, sir. Madam. Enjoy your evening."

When we were seated across from each other by a window, Dhiraj shot me a wicked look. "Oh, I fully intend to enjoy it. I've got the prettiest, most interesting woman on the train for company." He glanced past me, toward the entrance to the dining car. "After Elizabeth, that is."

"Elizabeth?" Jealousy flared. Was he already looking for my replacement?

"Unfortunately, she's already taken." He sprang to his feet with a dazzling smile and stepped toward the aisle.

I turned with a frown, which changed to a grin as I saw him kiss the cheek of a white-haired lady. He introduced me to the woman and her husband, then said, "We'd invite you to join us, but I have my heart set on a romantic evening."

The elderly gent winked. "You're not the only one, young man." With a hand gently planted on his wife's hip, he steered her down the aisle.

"Such a sweet couple," I whispered.

"Too bad you didn't come for breakfast this morning. We saved you a seat." His eyes twinkled. "Elizabeth's another of my models."

"What?" I raised my brows.

"We were alone in the dome car when the sun rose this morning. I got some great shots of her in the dawn light."

"For the—" About to say "exhibit," I stopped myself. This was Dhiraj, the amateur photographer.

"Hmm?"

"Nothing. Let's look at the menu."

We both chose salad followed by chicken in Thai red curry sauce, then he asked me what wine I'd like. I chose a spicy BC gewürztraminer.

A few minutes later we were raising our glasses in a toast. "To our first dinner alone together," he said.

As I touched my glass to his, I realized with some surprise that Nav and I had never done this. Gone out for a quiet dinner in a nice restaurant, just the two of us. We'd often eaten tourtière, pizza, or lasagna on my couch watching a movie, or gone to a bar or restaurant with a group of friends.

Unexpectedly, I felt nervous. It was like a first serious date with a stranger. A wealthy, handsome, exciting stranger. How could I impress him?

I did what I always did and focused on him. "So, you've lived in both London and New Delhi, Dhiraj?"

He nodded. "They're very different. Both very old, but with such different personalities. London is more dignified. Cleaner. Much, much more expensive. And less vibrant."

"Really? Tell me more." I put my elbows on the table, clasped my hands, and rested my chin on them.

He studied me, then reached over, gently tugged my hands apart, and took my left hand in his. "I'd rather talk about you. Tell me what you did this afternoon, after I saw you."

I shrugged. "Got a phone call from two of my sisters."

"How are the wedding plans coming along?"

"You want to talk about wedding stuff? Seriously?"

"Sure."

I started out hesitantly, but under his prompting found myself relating much of the conversation, along with the insights Theresa, Merilee, and I had reached about our family.

It was an unusual and pleasant experience for me to talk so openly about myself and not fear being judged as boring.

The messages I'd been learning since I started this trip were sinking in. As a child and teen, I'd formed a pattern of looking outside the family for validation, and I'd done it by being the social organizer or the girl who tried to hold the attention of a larger-than-life date. Not by truly sharing myself. If Mom and Dad hadn't thought I measured up to Theresa, I'd feared no one would like me if I let them see who I really was.

I'd even avoided letting myself know who I really was.

As I talked to the attentive man across from me, I felt like I was only starting to get to know myself.

We'd eaten our salads while I was talking, and now our waiter took the empty plates and presented our curry, which smelled spicy and tantalizing.

After we'd taken a few bites, Dhiraj said, "That's interesting what you said about your parents. I suppose it's true, that parents can be bright, well educated, loving, and yet not be skilled or insightful about parenting." He toyed with his fork. "Do you think each child has their own idea of what makes a good parent?"

I reflected, savoring a mouthful of spicy curry. "Theresa wanted less pressure. Merilee wanted attention and support. I wanted acceptance. How about you?"

"I wanted parents who'd accept me—support me—for who I was, rather than who they wanted me to be."

I nodded. "I agree."

A corner of his mouth lifted. "We, of course, will make brilliant parents."

"I'm sure it's easier said than done." I tilted my head. "You got along well with the children this morning."

"I like kids. They're easy to relate to."

"Do you want children of your own?"

"Of course." He said it so naturally that it sounded sincere, like a Nav response rather than a Dhiraj one.

For a moment, I had a vision of Nav with a couple of cute little cinnamon-skinned children, curly black heads bent together as they worked on a drawing. The picture gave me a soft, melty kind of feeling, like a Hallmark movie.

But wait, Nav was the smorgasbord dating guy. Sometimes it was really hard to remember that much of what he said came from his Dhiraj character.

I'd been sharing myself intimately, and he'd been playing the role of Dhiraj.

A thought hit me. What would happen if I asked him to be Nav? If I said I wanted to have dinner with Nav rather than Dhiraj? To have this kind of deep conversation with Nav?

And maybe, afterward, Kama Sutra sex . . .

No! That was crazy. We had to hang on to Dhiraj, keep the boundaries in place, or we'd never be able to go back to being friends.

Nav might be quite happy to be friends with occasional benefits while he continued to date his various other women, but that definitely wouldn't work for me. If I was having trouble having a casual fling with Dhiraj, no way could I handle one with Nav.

Glancing at him, I realized he'd asked me a question that I'd missed. "Sorry, what did you say?"

"Just asked if you wanted kids."

"Yes, definitely." I'd always wanted kids, and in the past few years my biological clock had gone from ticking to sending out alarms. "Though at the rate I'm going, I'll be an aunt before I'm a mother."

"Figure your little sister and her husband will be having children soon?"

"If they have their way. They want to get started now."

He chuckled. "Sounds like you'll be an auntie within the year."

I had never mentioned Merilee's problems to Nav, in part because we so rarely spoke about our families. And in part, because thinking about them made me feel guilty. Now I found myself saying, "I hope so. Merilee was diagnosed with endometriosis this spring. It affects fertility. That's part of the reason they decided to get married now."

He gave a low whistle. "That sounds rough."

"It is." I bit my lip. If I told him the truth, would he think I was self-centered and awful?

There was something about his warm brown eyes that made me want to confess. "It should have been diagnosed earlier. We should have realized. She always had bad periods, but Mom, Theresa, Jenna, and I were all ho-hum about it and said that's just what women go through." Thank God for Matt. "It was her fiancé who finally got her to tell her doctor and get tests done."

"Don't be so hard on yourself." He gazed at me steadily across the table. "People can overlook things that are right in front of them day after day."

"We sure did."

"So, from now on, try opening your eyes a little wider." There was a spark of something—challenge?—in his eyes.

"I will." This afternoon's conversation with my sisters had already pointed me in that direction. "Anyhow, Merilee had surgery this spring and is feeling better. She's a bit run down, plus she's trying to make up a bunch of missed university assignments and exams because she doesn't want to get a semester behind Matt."

"And they're getting married in a week and a half? Busy times for her. And all of you."

"It's crazy timing for the wedding, but Matt got a last-minute deal on a Mexican Riviera cruise, and they want to do it for their honeymoon."

"A cruise ship." He winked. "Wonder if that's as sexy as a train?"

I grinned at him. "I hope so, for their sake."

We'd finished our dinners and he said, "Dessert?"

"I'm too full."

"Why don't we get coffee and a liqueur in the lounge?"

I agreed. As I stood up, I thought how differently this dinner had turned out than I'd anticipated. When he'd said he wanted a romantic evening for two, I'd expected flirtation. Instead, I'd mostly talked about myself, and he'd listened attentively.

In its own way, that was pretty romantic, too.

Now, though, as he came up behind me, his hand slid down my back, concealed between our bodies, and lightly caressed my butt. Denim slid against my naked cheeks. "Want to burn off some calories?" he murmured, leaning down so his breath brushed my ear.

My body heated. "So much for the lounge?" I wouldn't complain if we went back to his room and played Kama Sutra.

"You misjudge me. I meant, dancing in the lounge."

"Dancing?" Now there was an appealing thought. "Yes, let's." It would be a good lead-up to sex.

As we walked toward the exit, I saw Sam Wilbanks, the screenwriter, in animated conversation with three other people. He lifted a hand and gave me an appreciative smile before his gaze slid past me to my companion.

I smiled back.

"He envies me," Dhiraj murmured in my ear, "and so he should. I'm glad you met me first."

"Me, too." The other man was the kind of guy I went for—successful and attractive—and he seemed nice. Yet I doubted we'd have ended up setting off the shower alarm or discussing my sisters. I doubted I'd have this same mix of comfort and excitement with him.

When we got to the lounge, it was busy. The sound system was playing an old disco tune, and a group of Australians who looked to be in their late twenties crowded the small space available for dancing.

"Disco?" Dhiraj raised an eyebrow. "This isn't what I expected."

"They tailor the music to their audience." And clearly tonight the Aussies ruled.

We claimed a small table and ordered coffee, plus a Grand Marnier for me and a cognac for him.

He took my hand and held it lightly, easily, as if it belonged in his. "Kat, you asked me if I'd ever been in love. How about you?"

Had I asked Dhiraj or Pritam? I couldn't remember. "More times than I can count," I said lightly. "Come on, let's dance." Talking about my love life was a downer.

"Hey, wait a minute. I answered when you asked. How many times have you really been in love?"

I huffed out a sigh. On average, there'd probably been one or two men each year for more than a decade. "Honestly, I try not to count."

The table was small, and across it his dark eyes peered into mine with a serious expression. "If there were that many, my guess is you weren't in love."

"Maybe not always," I admitted. "But a number felt like love. Like the man was the special one." As I said those words, gazing into his eyes, my heart gave a lurch. If Dhiraj had really existed, I could well have been feeling that way about him, and fighting to stick to my new one-month rule so I didn't fall head over heels.

He played with my fingers. "Sounds more like you lusted after them. Sexually, and maybe in other ways, too."

"Other ways?"

"Like, if they had celebrity status or something, and you wanted to be part of it."

"To be part of the glamour." I thought briefly of Theresa and her new guy. Yes, it was exciting to be with a man like that. "I admit, that's appealing. But that's part of the package, right? You fall for a whole package. Looks, career, personality."

"Yes, but only once you know what it contains. Or do you fall for the fancy wrapping?"

He was saying the same things Nav had on Saturday night. I stirred restlessly. Hadn't we come here to dance? "Maybe, and so I have a new rule. I won't let myself fall in love until I've known a guy for a month."

"A whole month?"

"You're making fun of me."

His eyes crinkled.

"Let's dance," I said again, starting to rise.

He stayed seated. "Hang on. This brings me back to my original question. Have you ever truly been in love?"

Hmm. It was worth looking at my relationships in a new light, because it could help me figure out where I kept going wrong. Slowly I sank back into my seat. "I don't know," I said softly.

"How would you define love?"

If it wasn't that head-over-heels exhilaration, then what was it? Had I been searching all my life for something I couldn't even define? If that was true, how would I know if I found it? "How would you define it?"

His face softened, eyes glowing. "It's when you see the whole person, their strengths and their frailties, and love them for all of it. They're someone you can count on, but who's always capable of surprising you."

I nodded slowly as he went on. "It's when you look at a face and know it's the one you want to see every night and every morning for the rest of your life. You want to have kids together, muddle through being parents, muddle through everything else life throws your way, doing it together with tears and laughter and, most of all, love."

His words brought tears to my eyes.

"Kat?"

"Yes." I sniffled. "Yes, that's it."

He'd seemed to speak with such sincerity, yet the words must be part of his role play as Dhiraj. Nav, after all, was the smorgasbord dater. Or had he perhaps felt this way about Margaret and the other woman he'd loved, and being disappointed in love had made him swear off it?

"Have you felt that way about any of the men in your life?" he asked.

Refocusing on my own life, I reflected. Then I shook my head. "I don't think so. It sounds so . . . big. Maybe all my relationships have been small." Yes, small, despite the fact that more than one had rated photos in *People*, *Entertainment Weekly*, or the *National Enquirer*. Glamorous, yes, but shallow.

I took a sip of Grand Marnier, trying not to feel depressed. "They started out great, but then either I found out something about the guy that I didn't like, or he got bored with me and moved on."

He squeezed my hand. "Anyone who finds you boring is crazy."

"Oh, come on, I'm nothing special."

"Damn it, you are. Why don't you see that?" He stared at me for a long moment. "You really, honestly think you're uninteresting, don't you? That's why, when you talk about yourself, you prefer to stick to the light, fun stuff rather than get into anything too deep or personal."

His words paralleled what I'd been wondering about over dinner. Slowly, feeling my way, I said, "Don't people like talking to someone who's fun, not all self-absorbed and angsty?"

"Depends on the people. I've enjoyed the conversations we've had. About parents and kids, your sisters, arranged marriage, love. They weren't exactly superficial."

"No. But . . . I guess when I talk about some of these things, I'm afraid I sound stupid. Like, I should have figured things out earlier, made a better job of my life."

He gave a soft chuckle. "Yeah, shouldn't we all have? Welcome to the world of being human, Kat Fallon."

"I'm not sure what you're saying."

"That I hate the way you run yourself down."

"I don't!"

"You say you're not really pretty, you just make the best of what you've got."

Wait a minute. That was something I'd told Nav. Now he was definitely crossing a boundary and I was about to call him on it, but he was going on. "You're not as smart as your sister Theresa, and your job's not as important as hers or your parents'. You're not as exciting as those guys you date."

"That's not running myself down, it's just being accurate. And besides—"

"No," he cut me off. "Why compare yourself to others? You're you. Beautiful, talented, interesting, generous, fun to be with. You're unique, special, and valuable. Especially when you stop hiding behind insecurity and let your real self out."

He thought I was special. And this wasn't the kind of flirtatious flattery I'd heard from other men; I could tell he meant it. My heart warmed with a sense of acceptance I'd rarely felt.

But what was he saying? That I could simply be myself, and people would like me?

How could I buy that? I'd thought Ms. Sociability was a role that played to my strengths. Had it really been a way of hiding my insecurity?

"Hey." He stroked my hands and I realized I'd clasped them together, tight with tension. "Relax, Kat. I'll stop pushing."

I took a deep breath, let it out, and realized the sound system was playing "Dancing Queen," an ABBA song.

It made me smile. ABBA was familiar, not just from the movie, *Mamma Mia!* "My mom—my career-driven lawyer mom— loved ABBA. When I was little, sometimes she'd play their music in the kitchen and we girls danced with her." Oh, yes, there were times Mom had let down her hair and fooled around with us. Why did I so rarely think of them?

"Then we should dance." He stood up and held out his hand.

I jumped to my feet, then said, "Oh, no," realizing the song had ended. But then the next one began, and I grinned. It was ABBA again, this time "Take a Chance on Me."

The Aussies packed the floor, dancing energetically, but somehow we made a space for ourselves. With all those bodies jammed together, there wasn't much we could do but bounce around with the others, everyone bumping up against everyone else. The others were laughing, the mood infectious, and we all sang along to the chorus.

I could put the troubling conversation behind me and simply enjoy the moment. My partner in his sleek black looked so much more sophisticated than the other guys in their T-shirts and jeans, typical Nav clothing. And, though he danced as energetically, his athletic grace showed in his movements.

I'd been to clubs with Nav; we'd probably been on the dance floor at the same time, so how had I never realized he was such a great dancer?

We all chanted, "Ba ba ba ba baa" to the final chorus, ending with the plea to take a chance on me. The music ended and I grinned up at Nav. No, Dhiraj, I reminded myself.

He grinned back, then another song began and everyone whooped as they recognized the opening to "Mamma Mia."

Again, everyone sang along to the chorus, hamming it up.

More than a dozen pairs of hands went up in the air as we all chanted, "Mamma Mia."

Deliberately, I widened my eyes and put on a flirty face as I sang, "My, my, how can I resist you?" to my partner.

He laughed, and I couldn't remember when I'd had such pure fun, dancing with a sexy man amid a boisterous group of strangers, letting go and chanting lyrics even though I couldn't carry a tune. Hey, if Pierce Brosnan had had the guts to do it on-screen, why shouldn't I?

When the tune ended, everyone clapped. Laughing, gasping for breath, I let myself fall against my partner, who wasn't even breathing hard.

His arms circled me. "Hey, dancing queen, I could handle a slow one." His hips bumped mine suggestively.

Chapter 17

Though the ABBA songs had been great fun, when the next tune started, Nav was pleased to hear Frank Sinatra's "New York, New York." Now he could hold Kat in his arms.

The Australians left the floor and several couples got up to dance, but the floor was no longer crowded.

He held out his hand to Kat, she took it, and he eased her into dance position for a foxtrot. Her hand grazed his shoulder almost tentatively, then settled. He rested his hand on her upper back, bare above her black camisole top, and nudged her closer so his right side pressed gently against hers from midtorso to midthigh. A warm thrill coursed through him.

Then he stepped forward, leading her in the familiar slow, slow, quick, quick rhythm. She felt wonderful, warm and light in his arms, following his lead easily into a promenade. He stuck to the basic steps for a minute or two until they got a feel for each other. Her smile was bright, her eyes sparkled, and the hummingbird earrings caught the light as she moved.

He'd seen how uncomfortable she'd been with their earlier conversation and was glad dancing had lifted her spirits. But he didn't regret pressing her the way he had. She was coming to know herself better, and he loved having an increased intimacy with her.

Even if she wanted to pretend it was Dhiraj she was talking to.

He led her into another promenade, their hips separating on the "slow, slow" steps, then joining again, pelvises pressing against each other. He was almost glad she was wearing a denim skirt rather than last night's skimpy dress, because, even with the heavier cotton between them, he was getting aroused.

On the next promenade, he spun her under his arm, then repeated the maneuver. Completing the second turn, she gave a delighted laugh. "You really know how to dance. Not many guys your age do."

Dancing had been part of the high-society life his parents had lived in London. "Didn't I tell you Indian men get a thorough education?"

"I do seem to recall mention of the Kama Sutra," she murmured, eyes sparkling up at him. "But you've yet to follow through on that one."

"That's what you think. Didn't you recognize the Twining Position? How about the Yawning Position? Oh, and I recall Congress of a Cow, too."

"Congress of a Cow? What are you talking about?" She pulled her head back an inch—which thrust her hip forward against his pelvis—and stared up at him.

Battling against an erection, he said, "Most of the sexual positions you've ever tried are in the Kama Sutra. It's just that people generally think of the more exotic ones."

"Exotic. Hmm." Her eyelashes drifted down then up again, flirtatiously. "Perhaps you could describe one or two?"

"Well, let's see. There's the Top."

"As in, the woman's on top? What's so exotic about that?"

"Yes, she's on top and he's inside her. But that's not where the name comes from." He spun her out, then guided her back in and caught her lightly at the waist, letting their pelvises rub again. "Holding him inside her, she kind of spins around on his body. Like a top."

"Oh, my gosh, she'd have to be an acrobat." The flush on her cheeks told him she was imagining it.

The song was ending, so he dipped her, supporting her back, gazing into her eyes for a long, sultry moment, then raising her and brushing his lips across hers.

The next tune was an old romantic one, "Lady in Red." A perfect excuse to drop the more formal foxtrot position and snug Kat's body closer to his. He pulled their clasped hands in so they rested against his chest, and let his other hand drift down her back to settle at the curve of her waist. "Bet you'd like Lotus."

"That's another Kama Sutra position? Nice name."

"You know the Lotus Position in yoga, where you cross your legs?" When she nodded, he said, "Imagine lying on your back and lifting your legs up in Lotus Position. Your partner enters you. You can't move much and he has control."

Her eyes glinted up at him. "All very well for the man."

"Actually, the Lotus is really good for hitting your G-spot."

Her tongue tip emerged, circled her lips. "I'd like to try that one."

"Then we will."

The song was romantic; the sway of her body in his arms was heaven. He dropped their clasped hands to their sides, and without his urging she moved closer and rested her head against his shoulder. He tilted his head so his cheek touched her curls, glad his beard was gone so he could really feel her.

Neither of them spoke as they moved in easy harmony. He was aroused, but the feeling was a warm song in his veins, not an urgent hunger. For as long as he lived, he would remember this dance and the feel of this woman in his arms, where she belonged.

The number drifted to an end on the singer's whispered words, "I love you."

Lips against Kat's hair, Nav silently repeated those three words and longed for the day when he'd be able to say them aloud to her.

Reluctantly, they separated and he said, "I think that's a good note to end on."

She nodded, eyes dreamy. "Perfect."

"I want to be alone with you."

"Yes."

There were other people in the lounge, but he didn't look at them, only at Kat as, arms around each other, they headed toward his room.

Once inside, he pulled her close for a long, tender kiss. The way she responded told him she, too, was in the mood for romance rather than quick passion.

"Make yourself comfortable," he said.

"I'm just going to . . ." She gestured toward the tiny bathroom.

"Help yourself."

While she was in there, he lit the sandalwood candles and turned out all the other lights. Now, what would most please Kat?

He grinned as an idea struck him, then took out the hearts deck from the Nice 'n Naughty board game. When she rejoined him, he held out the deck. "Let's say you've rolled and landed on a heart. Draw a card."

"Oh, we're skipping the rolling part, are we?" She drew a card from the deck.

Before she could turn it over and read it, he took it from her. Pretending to read, he said, "It says, 'Your partner must give you anything you want. Tell him what that is.' "

She reached for it. "Is that really what it says?"

He held it away from her. "Does it matter?"

A puzzled expression crossed her face, then she said slowly, "If I said I just wanted to cuddle for a couple hours, would that be okay?"

It would take all his self-control, but the idea of holding her for two hours sounded great. Like a gift of trust and intimacy.

"Of course." He caressed her cheek, her ear, down her neck, and let his hand come to rest on her shoulder.

"Or, if I said I wanted you to—" she flushed—"make me climax with your hands and mouth?"

"Oh, yeah. Whatever you want, Kat."

She studied his face. "You were pretending to read from the card, and you could have said it the other way around. Said I had to do anything you wanted."

"Damn, why didn't I think of that?" he joked.

Her lips tipped up at the corners. "Because you're not like that. You're a generous lover, not a selfish one."

"Seems to me, lovemaking should be about generosity and sharing. Giving someone pleasure is a wonderful thing."

"True. But I guess I've always felt like I needed to impress the guy. To measure up to the other women he'd been with. Don't get me wrong, I like orgasms, but if I just lie back and . . . take them, I feel like I'm not doing enough."

Even in bed, she was trying to prove herself. "Kat, lovemaking is about two people and how they relate to each other, and it's going to be different each time. Can't you just relax and enjoy it?"

Her gaze was soft and vulnerable. "In my relationships, sometimes it's me who breaks it off. But sometimes I get dumped, and I always wonder what's wrong with me. Like, I must be boring company; I must be a bad lover."

"No." He stared deep into her eyes. "That's not true. Kat, stop trying to impress people. Be yourself; open up. Show the world the person you really are. Otherwise, even if someone likes you, it's not really you they're interested in; it's only the façade you've put on."

She gazed down at her feet and when she spoke, her voice was little more than a whisper. "What if I do as you say? And no one likes the real me?"

Her vulnerability made him feel tender and protective. Gently he tipped her chin up until she met his gaze. "That won't happen. Look at the people you've talked to on this trip. Maggie and Jim, Lynn and Terry, Kristin and Sandra. You've opened up with them, and that's led to meaningful conversations. Much more than superficial chat. They like you, Kat. The real you, not that Ms. Sociability person. And so do I. Sure, there'll be some people you don't click with. Big deal, who needs them? It's their loss."

Her eyes lit with something that looked like hope, maybe revelation.

"Now." He waved the card. "Tell me what you want."

After a few moments' silence, she said, "I'd like to dance. The way we were to that last song, but even closer and sexier, since no one's watching." A spark kindled in her eyes. "And while we're dancing, let's take off each other's clothes."

"I like the way you think." His groin tightened. "But is that it, just take off each other's clothes? Isn't there anything more you want?"

The spark in her eyes flamed. "Once we're naked and horny, I want to try that Lotus Position."

"Oh, yeah."

He eased her into his arms, holding her the way he had when they'd been dancing to "Lady in Red," and began to move them around. The tiny amount of floor space didn't allow for much more than a back-and-forth shuffle, but that was enough to let their bodies slide enticingly against each other.

She freed the hand he'd clasped in his and raised her arms, circling his neck. "You look like a panther tonight in those sexy black clothes. The fabric's so thin, I can feel your . . . mm-hmm . . . muscles as you move."

"Oh, is that what you're feeling?" He pumped his hips so his erection rubbed her stomach. Then he slid his hands between their bodies, to the button at the waist of her denim skirt. "I wouldn't mind feeling more of you." He undid the button, slid down the zipper.

The skirt fell to the floor and she stepped free of it, kicked it out of the way, and then settled her body back against his. The soft flesh of her almost naked tummy was so much more tantalizing than denim.

He slid his hands down her back, over the silky black camisole and down to, oh, yes, the bare flesh of her ass. She was wearing a thong. He was glad he hadn't known that earlier, or he'd have spent the evening with a permanent hard-on.

Cupping her firm cheeks in both hands, he felt the play of muscles as she shifted weight from foot to foot.

"I love your sweater." She tugged at the hem of it—the sweater he'd bought because, on Saturday night, she'd said a black V-neck sweater would show off his build and coloring. "But you're overdressed."

He eased away and, as he pulled off the garment, he felt her hands at his waist. By the time he tossed his sweater onto the chair, his pants were sliding down his legs. He bent to step out of them and threw them on top of the sweater. Then, naked but for a thin layer of Armani, he took Kat in his arms again.

They danced a while like that, his hands stroking her back, caressing her ass, tracing the line of the thong. Then he peeled off her camisole. Her black bra was almost as skimpy as her thong. The fullness of her breasts pressed against his chest, the lace of the bra a gentle abrasion.

He tilted her head up to his and kissed her in movements as slow and subtle as their dance.

He undid the back fastening of her bra and slid the straps down her arms. Pulled the garment free. Felt her breasts crush against him.

Her hands had found their way inside his briefs and were stroking his ass. "Let's go to bed now," she whispered.

He lifted her, placed her on the bed, and marveled at the sight of her sprawled out in the candlelight, clad only in a black thong and the earrings he'd given her. "You're so sexy."

Then he skimmed off his briefs.

"You're pretty sexy yourself," she said in a sultry tone as he lay down beside her. When he began to caress her breasts, she said, "No, I want you inside me. Enough stalling on this Kama Sutra stuff or you're going to make me think you can't deliver."

"Trust me, I can deliver." In fact his body ached with the need to deliver.

When he pulled off her thong, she was swollen, so hot and moist as she ground against his hand.

After donning a condom, he slipped a pillow under her ass to ease the strain on her lower back and spread her legs. Kneeling between them, he admired the rosy lushness of her sex in the flickering candlelight.

"Let's start with your legs up, knees bent. The Lotus is hard to hold for long if you're not really flexible, so we'll ease up to it."

"I can be flexible." There was humor in her voice, but the flush on her cheeks confirmed her arousal. She raised her legs, bending her knees.

He took hold of her knees and pressed them gently toward her chest. "Lift them as far as you're comfortable, and put your feet on my chest."

He leaned forward slightly, balancing against the soles of her feet. Then he reached between their bodies, opened her folds, and entered her in one easy plunge.

"Oh, yes," she said on an outdrawn breath. "So nice."

The position created a gentle tension between their bodies. If he put too much pressure on her legs, he could hurt her, so he controlled his thrusts as her body adapted to the position.

Control was good. If he'd been able to plunge deep and hard and fast, he'd have reached orgasm far too soon. Tonight he wanted to give Kat much more than quickie sex.

He used tantric techniques he'd learned, like focusing on deep breathing and trying to direct sexual energy away from his erection so it dispersed throughout his body. It wasn't exactly a hardship, because his own climax would be all the more powerful in the end.

She gripped his thighs, unable to reach any other part of his body, very much in his control as she gazed up at him wonderingly. "I can feel you so deep. Is this a Kama Sutra position?"

"It's Pressed Position." As he moved in and out of her, her feet on his chest, he gripped one of her ankles, helping them both maintain the position, the balance. With his other hand he caressed her leg, enjoying the long line from ankle to knee, the soft back of her thigh, the delicious curve of her buttock.

Such smooth skin, glowing golden in the candlelight. "If your legs or back start to hurt, slide your feet down from my chest."

"No, I'm—" She gave a soft gasp. "I'm good. Very good."

He thrust a little harder, but kept the rhythm slow and easy.

She moaned with pleasure and her internal muscles tightened against his shaft, increasing the delicious friction. Her torso shuddered as her breathing quickened. She tossed her head back on the pillow, the lovely column of her neck exposed to his view, the hummingbird earrings resting against her skin.

"You're beautiful, Kat. Beautiful and sexy." His own breathing was fast, too, and he deliberately slowed it, struggling to maintain control.

He thrust steadily, hard and deep, stroking to her core, finding the exact right angle to give her the stimulation she needed.

Her body clenched, then burst into waves of orgasm.

He slowed, keeping her riding the waves of climax.

When her body stopped shuddering, one of her legs, then the other, pulled away from his chest. "I can't . . ." She panted for air.

"It's okay." He eased down to cover her, taking his weight on his forearms, and dropped a kiss on her lips. "Rest. Let me do all the work."

But it was hardly work to maintain a gentle in-and-out movement, to keep both their bodies humming. It also helped him back off the intensity of his arousal.

After a few minutes, he felt the sexual tension rise in her

body again. Her legs came up to hug his sides, and her hips thrust to speed the action.

"Want to Split the Bamboo?" he asked.

She laughed. "Isn't that what you're already doing?"

He chuckled. "Not quite." He raised up on his hands. "Lift one leg up so your calf's resting on my shoulder."

Awkwardly, laughing a little, she hoisted her leg and used both hands to position it.

But her giggles stopped as he began to slide in and out. His strokes were angled now, and his dick slid across her clit.

She gave a purr of satisfaction and caressed his leg. "I don't know how bamboo feels about getting split, but this is working for me."

It was for him, too. The angle gave him intense stimulation, plus a great view of her lovely flushed face and torso.

He shifted farther forward, weight braced on one hand, and caressed her breast, with its taut rosy areola. Gently, he tweaked her nipple.

And all the time, he stroked into her, varying the timing and angle. Responding to the expressions on her face, the whimpers and moans she made, the way she tilted her hips.

Every time he felt his body build to orgasm, he eased back. Concentrating on deep breathing, he tried to cool down. Then, when it was safe, he speeded up again.

"Your leg okay?" he whispered.

"What leg?" she said breathlessly. "I can't even . . . oh, wow, do that again. Yes, there, like that."

He obliged, stroking deeply on the same angle.

Her head tossed on the pillow, her back arched, then she cried out in another climax.

Her body's convulsive spasms almost triggered his own orgasm, but he used every ounce of willpower to hold back. He'd intended to get her to switch legs, to put the other one up on his other shoulder, but he couldn't hold out much longer.

She'd asked for Lotus Position, so that's what they'd do. Once they both cooled down.

When she'd ridden out the aftershocks, he murmured, "Put your leg down."

Slowly she lowered it and let it flop to the bed. He eased down until he blanketed her body, his forearms taking most of his weight. His legs lay atop her slightly spread ones and their hips matched. Her eyes were closed and she still panted for air, breasts rising and falling under him, warm breath puffing against his face.

The band that held back his hair had come off, and black curls brushed his cheeks as he bent closer to drop a kiss on her soft lips.

He pumped his hips the tiniest bit, thrusting inside her in the most subtle of motions. "Clasping Position," he murmured against her mouth.

The hand that caressed his shoulder rose higher and twined into his curly hair.

He was too damn close to coming, and all the deep breathing in the world wasn't going to hold it off much longer. It was time for the final position. "Ready to try Lotus?"

"Mmm. I think my leg muscles have turned to jelly."

"You'll be relaxed. Flexible."

Her eyes opened. "What do I do?"

He slid out of her, regretting the necessity. "Curl your knees up to your chest like you did before. But this time, cross your legs like you were in the yoga Lotus Position."

She obeyed, treating him to a tantalizing view as her lower body rocked upward. "I can't cross my legs all the way."

"Don't push it. Be comfortable. If your legs get tired or sore, break out of the yoga position and wrap them around my waist." He kneeled, then slid inside her.

"Ooh, that's so good," she said. "I'm so sensitive."

She wasn't the only one. He bent forward over her crossed

legs, his hands on the bed by her shoulders, trying to make sure his weight was on his knees and hands, not on her legs. "I like this position." He dipped his head. "I can kiss you."

"And I can touch you." Her arms circled his neck under the long curls of hair.

As their lips met, he began to pump into her. He knew they wouldn't be able to hold the position for long, and he had run out of self-control anyhow. This time, he wanted to come, and he was going to bring her with him.

Each time he withdrew, he pulled out almost all the way. When he plunged in, he did it hard. This position was supposed to hit her G-spot, and her cries of pleasure confirmed it.

She broke the kiss, and her fingernails bit into his upper arms as she clung to him. Her eyes squeezed shut, her face went taut. Her mouth gasped for air, making wordless sounds that urged him on.

"Come on, Kat," he panted. "Come for me one more time." He thrust hard and deep, his back tensing, pressure building in the base of his spine.

He pulled out and plunged in again, balls tight, his orgasm unstoppable now.

"Oh!" she cried out. "Oh, yes, Nav!" Her body clenched and spasmed around him, milking him as he exploded inside her with an intensity he'd never felt before.

His name. She'd called his name. Joy flooded through him, as powerful as the climax that had rocked him.

He wanted to wrap her up in his arms, hold her close, and never let her go.

But Kat froze, then struggled to get free. "Oh, my God, I can't believe I did that. Dhiraj. *Dhiraj!* I didn't mean to call you Nav."

He raised himself off her so she could straighten her legs. "Kat, it's all right, I—"

"It's not!" She unkinked her body, then swung around to sit

on the side of the bed, her back to him. "That's not our deal." Her voice was high, tight with tension. "We're playing strangers on a train."

"But you know I'm Nav." He realized that, along with losing the hair band, he'd lost his Dhiraj accent during their lovemaking. "You can use my name."

"I can't." She slid off the bed and bent down to pick up her discarded clothing, still facing away from him. "I need to keep things separate. I can't think of Nav as . . . my lover." She yanked up her skirt and fastened it.

"But you know Dhiraj and Pritam are just roles." He climbed off the other side of the bed and came around so he could look her in the eyes.

He saw a sheen—tears? fear?—then she yanked her camisole over her head. Even after she smoothed it down, she averted her eyes. "Please put something on. And tie your hair back. And talk like Dhiraj again."

It was time she faced the truth. The men she'd been making love with were all him. "Do you realize how silly that sounds?"

"I don't care." She buried her face in her hands, and when she went on, her voice was muffled. "*You* started this, showing up on the train on Monday as Pritam. It's supposed to be a sexy game, and I only agreed because we set rules and you said things wouldn't change. You said our friendship—my friendship with Nav—wouldn't change."

She darted a quick glance at him. "And I can only do that if I . . . okay, *pretend*, you're Dhiraj, and you stay in character. I need the props. The accent and hair band and that fancy jewelry you borrowed."

"The watch and ring are mine," he said quietly, not reaching for either his clothing or the damned hair band.

She shook her head. "They're *Dhiraj's*. Put on the costume so I can think of you that way."

He scrubbed his hands over his forehead and cheeks. Hard.

He hated to see the distress in her face, but it was time for a reality check. "Kat, I—"

She put on her jacket and pulled it tight across her chest. "Nav is my friend in Montreal, who lives like a starving artist and is going to have a photography exhibit. Dhiraj is the rich man with the family company, whose photography is just a hobby, who—"

"The company is my family's." It was time she knew. By setting up the stranger game, he'd hoped to bring her closer. In some ways he had, but now the Dhiraj role only created distance. She had to know the real Nav, if he had any chance of winning her.

"What?" She gaped at him.

"Bharani International. Textile import/export. Based in New Delhi and London. My dad runs it, along with my uncle. I gave Dhiraj the job my parents raised me to take."

"You're . . . rich?"

He shrugged. "The family's well off. I have a trust fund, but didn't touch it when I came to Canada. I wanted to make it on my own and be liked for who I was, not my family's money."

She pulled the jacket tighter, arms crossed over her chest. "You never told me."

"I'm sorry."

"You honestly thought I was the kind of person who'd like you for your money?"

"You do tend to get dazzled by wealthy guys."

"Nav! Damn it, that's— Ooh! Okay, now I'm getting pissed off. Has anything you told me, as Nav or as Dhiraj, or bloody Pritam, been the truth?"

"Almost everything. Except the jobs."

"Yeah, sure. Like I'd believe anything you said now?"

He rested his hands on her shoulders, but she stepped back, shaking them off.

"Kat, I didn't mean to deceive you. Back in Montreal, neither of us talked much about our families or history. We both had reasons not to. But look at it from my perspective. You were more willing to share yourself with Dhiraj, your made-up lover, than you ever were with me, Nav. Your best friend."

Troubled chestnut eyes gazed up at him. "Oh, shit."

A surprised chuckle jolted out of him. "Yeah. Exactly."

"I have to think."

"We'll talk some more, try to sort this out."

"I can't. Not now, anyhow. You just confuse me."

He wasn't going to apologize. His goal had been to shake her up, to make her look at him differently, and he'd done it. "If you could have anything right now, what would it be?"

Her answer came immediately. "To go back to the way things were."

Fuck. That was the very last thing he wanted.

She opened the door. "I'm going. Please don't look for me tomorrow. If I want to see you, I'll find you. Otherwise . . . just go home. Let's take some time. I'll see you back in Montreal and we'll figure out where things stand then."

"What about the wedding? You wanted a date."

She stepped through the door and didn't turn to look at him. "Not you. I'd rather go alone than go with you."

Then she was gone, closing the door firmly behind her.

Pain stabbed through Nav. He sank down on the side of the bed and dropped his face in his hands.

Chapter 18

After I left Nav's compartment, I spent the rest of the night tossing and turning on my narrow bunk. Outside, the sky was clear, showcasing the moon and stars. It was beautiful. Romantic. And made me feel desperately lonely.

On my way to my baby sister's wedding, I'd not only lost my wedding date, I might have lost my best friend.

I'd thought I had known Nav, but now I felt as if I didn't know him at all.

Or, perhaps, I knew him better.

Even if he'd been speaking as Dhiraj or Pritam, he'd told me things I'd never known. About his family, his past loves.

And I'd opened up more to him than ever before. Partly, it was the train effect, loosening inhibitions. But also, it was the weird combination of him being both a friend I could trust and a stranger who didn't really exist. To a stranger I'd never see again, I could say anything.

But the person I'd been talking to was Nav, and of course I'd known that. I must, subconsciously, have been looking for an excuse to share more of myself with him. And he hadn't disappointed me. He'd encouraged, accepted, made me feel more positive about myself.

By the time morning rolled around, I knew I had to see him. No way would I lose our friendship just because I'd foolishly confused the game with reality, had found myself starting to long for a real relationship with a man who was a combination of Nav and Dhiraj.

My mistake, not his. Now, could we get things back on track?

I couldn't pretend we'd never had sex, and vanity made me hope he couldn't, either. But we had to put that behind us. After all, once we were home, he'd be dating other women, and I'd . . . well, of course I'd again be looking for Mr. Right-Forever.

I even had a better understanding of where I'd been going wrong.

That thought might have cheered me up if I wasn't so distraught over the possibility of losing Nav.

Needing to talk to him in private, I decided to avoid the dining room and wait until breakfast was over. It wasn't as if I had any appetite.

I took a long shower—and of course remembered every exquisite detail of the one we'd shared. When I applied jasmine lotion, I thought of his hands massaging every inch of me.

The memories were arousing, but damn it, I didn't want to think of Nav that way.

Not in the mood to dress up today, I put on jeans and a T-shirt. Then I straightened my shoulders, lifted my chin, and strode through the sleeping cars to his fancy compartment.

One of the things I'd wondered about while tossing and watching the moon was why Nav had done all this. The fancy wardrobe, the suite at the Royal York, the Romance by Rail package. I'd bet my photographer friend couldn't have afforded those things without dipping into his trust fund. He'd said it was a matter of principle not to touch that fund, yet now he had. Just so we could indulge our mutual attraction without jeopardizing our friendship?

Hoping he was in his compartment and I wouldn't have to search the train for him, I knocked firmly on the door. "Nav? It's Kat."

From inside I heard a clatter, "Damn," and then the door opened. "Kat?"

I stared at him. Barefoot, in jeans and the black V-neck sweater, his hair a mass of glossy curls and his face clean-shaven, he looked fabulous. A very classy version of my old friend.

A very sexy one, too, unfortunately.

"Kat, I'm so glad you came."

I stepped past him into the room, nervous and wishing I knew what to say. His laptop lay on the floor, and I guessed that was the crash I'd heard. "Ouch." I picked it up. "Hope it's okay." It had folded partway closed and I opened it gingerly.

"Oh!" I was staring at the photograph of a gorgeous woman in a sari.

He stepped to my side, reached for the computer. "Let me just—"

I held on tight. "Who's that?" Jealousy nipped at me. He'd just spent the past few days playing sexy games with me, and now he was gawking at another woman?

"Another of what Mum calls the prospectives," he said. "As in, a prospective bride. I picked up e-mail this morning and was going through it when you knocked."

"Oh." I sank into the chair, holding the computer on my lap. I snuck another glance at the woman's photo. Not only was she striking, but I could see intelligence in her face and a spark of humor. How could a guy resist a woman who looked like that?

Of course, I reminded myself, Nav didn't want to get married. I handed him the computer. "Why does your mom keep sending them?"

He snapped it shut. "Hope springs eternal? She wants me to marry and give her grandkids. I keep telling her I'll find my own wife." He put the computer on the bed and sat down across from me.

"Can't you just be honest and tell her you're not in the market for a wife?"

"But I am."

I shook my head and tried to find the teasing tone I'd used with Nav in the past. "Yeah, sure. Says the man with the revolving-door dating policy. That's not the behavior of a man who wants to get married."

His brows drew together. "Huh? Of course I've been dating. How else was I going to find a woman on my own, without parental help?"

"I mean, you don't date *seriously*. None of your girlfriends last more than a few weeks, unless it's to become 'just friends' after you stop dating each other."

"Yeah, because it's clear that, while we might like each other, it's not going to turn into love," he said indignantly. "I stop dating them *because* I want something serious."

He stared at me, a frown creasing his forehead. "Kat, haven't you been listening? Whenever you've said you wanted to get married, I said I did, too."

But . . . he hadn't meant it. Had he? Slowly, I said, "You said you were holding out for the perfect woman. I figured that was one of those wink-wink things, meaning you didn't believe there was such a thing."

"You were wrong." His expression was dead serious. "I do believe there's a perfect woman for me. I want to marry her, have children with her, and love her until the day I die."

So Nav really did want to get married. To some phantom perfect woman. A woman like Margaret, and that other nameless woman he'd once loved.

What woman could ever measure up to *that* expectation?

And why did I feel as if I'd been betrayed?

He'd never actually lied to me. In fact, he'd told me the truth. I just hadn't heard it.

And why was that? Maybe because, if I felt twinges of jealousy when he smorgasbord-dated, I hated to imagine how I'd feel if—when—he actually did fall in love.

Not, of course, that I wanted him to fall in love with *me*. But, as his close friend, I'd seen myself as the significant woman in his life. If he fell in love, we could still be friends, but we'd never be as close. Some other woman would always come first.

"If you get married, what happens to our friendship?" The words burst out of me in a combination of anger and fear.

His expression was shuttered. "What happens to it if you get married, Kat? You always say you want to be married."

Damn, why had I never thought this through? Maybe because doing so hurt too much. Right now my heart ached miserably. "I do, but I want you in my life, too."

One corner of his mouth tilted up ruefully. "Uh-huh. So, either we have to marry each other—" He cocked an eyebrow.

I wasn't in the mood to be teased, so just heaved an unhappy sigh.

He didn't say anything for a long moment, then gave a slow nod. "Then our friendship will change."

"I don't want that to happen." I knew I sounded like a sullen, stupid child, but it was the truth.

He reached out and took my hand, holding it gently. "It's been great being neighbors and friends, but we both want love and marriage. It's inevitable our friendship will change. And change can be a good thing, Kat. We could—"

"No!" I didn't want to hear it. "I liked things the way they were." My heart ached so much that I raised my free hand to rub my chest.

Nav caught my hand. Gripping both my hands in his, he stared into my eyes, his own chocolate ones intent and soulful. "A couple days ago, I made you a promise. I meant it then and I'll always mean it. I'll always be there for you. But I do want things to change."

He closed his eyes briefly, then opened them. "I love you, Kat Fallon."

My heart leaped. For a moment I thought . . .

But no, he meant it in the sense of loving a friend, and that was exactly the way I wanted him to mean it. We really would be friends forever. But he was right that things would change.

A strange blend of happiness and sorrow choked my throat. Tears threatened, but I managed to say, "The same goes for me. I love you, too, Nav, as my best friend. I never want to lose you."

He studied my face and then a small, sad smile touched his lips. "I know."

Why did I feel as if my heart was cracking in two? Just because our friendship would change? Because another woman would become the most significant one in his life?

Would become his wife?

My eyes swam with tears.

"I have to go," I muttered, ducking my head as I stood and made for the door.

I expected him to stop me. To say we needed to talk some more, or to pull me into a hug. Something.

All I heard was the sound of a heavy sigh.

I opened the door; glanced back. Saw him sitting on the bed, head bowed.

Hurriedly I left, almost running down the corridor between the sleeping compartments, half blind from tears that I could barely manage to hold back.

Once I reached the haven of my own tiny room, the tears washed down my cheeks. I flung myself into the chair, wishing the bunk was down so I could sprawl across it.

After sobbing for a while, I forced myself to my feet and splashed cold water on my face, trying to still the flood of tears. Why was I reacting this way? Relationships changed over time, and Nav had said he'd always be in my life.

But I wouldn't see him as often. I wouldn't be the first person he told when he got another exhibit, or made a major sale. He'd find that perfect woman, marry her, move away and build a home with her. Have children with her.

More tears escaped my eyes, and I rubbed my hand across my chest, trying to massage away the pain in my heart.

When I got home from work tired and hungry, he wouldn't be there to share pizza and a movie. When something wonderful or awful happened in my life, I could phone or e-mail him, but he wouldn't be there to give me a hug.

A hug . . . The thought of physical contact made me remember the ways we'd touched each other as lovers.

The tears kept falling.

Maybe it was just as well if he didn't live next door. How could I look at him without remembering? Without knowing how truly sexy he was, and what an amazing, generous, inventive lover?

How could I be with him without wanting more than friendship?

I gave a ragged sob, and that brought me to my senses.

This was crazy. We'd still be friends—after all, he'd said he loved me—and of course life had to change. It was time to stop being so damned melodramatic. A little sorrow was okay, but wallowing in self-pity wasn't like me.

I was on a train with hundreds of people. I needed to stop moping and go socialize. That always distracted me from my worries.

With a plan of action in place, I finally managed to halt the tears.

I rinsed my face over and over with cold water to reduce the tear-soaked puffiness. Eye makeup and concealer did a pretty good job of hiding any remaining damage, and bright lipstick would focus attention on my lips.

As I walked toward the dining car, I hoped Nav wouldn't be there. My fragile self-control wasn't up to seeing him right now.

At the entrance to the restaurant, I scanned the room, heart racing. No Nav. Not as Dhiraj, with his hair pulled back. Not as Nav, with his more casual look.

Sam Wilbanks, the screenwriter, was at a table sitting across from two Australians I recognized from the dance floor last night. He glanced up and smiled at me, a smile that widened with surprise as I walked over to their table.

The smile warmed my wounded heart a tiny bit. "Do you have room for one more?" I asked.

"For you?" He stood up and offered me the chair beside him. "Of course."

As I sat, he took a closer look at my face and frowned slightly, making me think I hadn't done such a great job with the makeup. But all he said was, "Kat, do you know Sally and Tom?"

"Only from dancing to ABBA." I forced a smile in response to their friendly ones and tried not to remember how much fun it had been to dance with . . . I tried to think of him as Dhiraj.

No, even if he'd spun a tall tale about his job, had worn clothes that weren't his usual style, he'd been Nav. I couldn't fool myself any longer.

The waiter came by to ask if I'd like a drink, and I ordered a glass of red wine.

"I was just asking Sally and Tom how they came to make this trip," Sam said.

"There's a group of you traveling together, isn't there?" I tried to focus on the tanned, attractive pair rather than on my own problems.

"Yeah, eight of us mates," Tom said.

"We all work for the same software company," Sally said, "and we like hanging out together. Last year a gang of us went to Greece."

My wine came, then our waiter served gazpacho. I sipped wine and made a token effort to eat. Prompted by Sam, the Australians talked about their friends, work, travel plans.

Usually I was the one with all the questions, the one who kept conversation flowing. Today, it was all I could do to force myself to listen, knowing that was preferable to dwelling on my own misery.

"So," Sam said to them, "you figure you'll keep doing this every year? Going someplace new together?"

"Can't beat it," Tom said, and Sally nodded vigorously.

They weren't much younger than me, but they sounded like kids. Like they were having so much fun and never planned to grow up. Didn't they think about settling down? About marriage and kids?

Nav was their age, and I'd thought he was like that, too. But I'd been wrong. He was more mature. He was gaining success in a competitive field of work and looking for a woman to share the rest of his life.

I was cutting a crab cake into tiny sections and shuffling them around my plate when Sam turned to me. "How about you, Kat? Where are you from, and what brings you on this trip?"

"I live in Montreal, and I'm traveling to Vancouver because one of my sisters is getting married."

"A younger or older sister?" Sally asked.

"Younger."

"And you're not married yourself?"

A surge of emotion choked me, and all I could do was shake my head.

Sally wrinkled her freckled nose. "My younger sister's engaged, and I'm always getting flack from my family about still being single. But I figure, I'm having way too much fun to settle down. Right, Tom?" She nudged her companion in the ribs, and he grinned at her.

Sally turned an expectant face toward me.

No, I couldn't talk about this now. Maybe I should just leave. I cleared my throat and managed to say, "I hear you, Sally," then glanced around, wondering what excuse I could make for bailing in the middle of the meal.

When I looked over my shoulder, there was Nav, his hair loose and curly, dressed the way he'd been when I left him. Across from him I saw a woman's head with sleek black hair, and beside him was the perky activity director who'd been flirting with him during the drawing session with the kids. He didn't notice me looking, because he was gazing intently at the blonde.

It sure hadn't taken him long to get over our . . . whatever it was, and find a couple of pretty women to talk to.

If I left I'd have to walk past him.

"Are you all right, Kat?" Sam leaned close to murmur in my ear so Sally and Tom wouldn't hear. "You've barely touched your lunch."

I glanced at his handsome face, saw concern in his eyes.

Time to put on my party hat. I knew how to do this. I forced a smile. "I had a touch of a stomach bug, so I'm being careful about food." I hoped that would explain my red, swollen eyes as well.

Raising my voice so the other two could hear, I said, "So, Sam what about you? You said you're doing a screenplay for a movie. Tell us about it."

I did my best to be vivacious. Sam was entertaining, the Aussies were outgoing, and I forced myself to laugh at everyone's stories. When the dessert plates had been cleared away, a couple more of the Australian group came to join the conversation, hanging out in the aisle.

As a waiter struggled to get by, Sam said, "We're in the way here. Why don't we take the party to the lounge?"

We all rose and, in a laughing, jostling group, headed for the exit.

As we approached Nav's table, I saw that people had swapped seats so the two women—the activity director and an attractive young Chinese woman—sat together, deep in conversation. Across from them were Nav and the little boy he'd been drawing with yesterday. Their heads were bent over a coloring book.

He'd make a great father.

He glanced up, and our gazes held for an instant. I thought he looked sad, just the way I felt. "Kat? Can we talk?"

"I . . ."

Tom jogged my arm. "You coming, Kat? There's a beer with my name on it waiting."

I stared at Nav. No, I couldn't deal with him, with us, right now. Tears were still too close. "I can't." Then I hurried out of the dining car.

Nav would make a great father.

The others laughed and joked, but their words didn't register. I knew he made a wonderful friend. An incredible lover. A fascinating and perceptive companion.

He'd make some lucky woman a great husband.

"Buy you a glass of wine? Kat?"

I realized we'd reached the lounge and Sam was holding a chair for me. "What? Wine? Uh, sure. Thanks." I dropped into the chair.

Nav was everything a woman could possibly want. Why hadn't I seen that before?

Because he'd only shown me the reliable, supportive, occasionally flirtatious friend. I hadn't seen the way he was with kids, had never let our conversations get into deep areas. Hadn't realized how fun and unpredictable he could be. How sexy. How handsome and poised.

He'd kept all that hidden. He hadn't even let me see his *face*, damn him.

But then, I'd hidden behind being Ms. Sociability and avoided coming to terms with my true self.

Until, on this trip, Nav made me do it.

What I'd found inside wasn't so great—there was envy, insecurity, some dark emotions—but he'd shown me I wasn't so awful, either. He hadn't rejected me. With him, I could be strong or vulnerable, playful or serious, and he would still love me.

As a friend.

I found a glass of wine in my hand and took a sip. Nav loved me as a friend. That was what I wanted.

So why did I feel so crappy? The answer hit me so hard I almost dropped my wineglass.

Because I loved him.

On this wild train ride, completely unexpectedly, I had fallen totally, utterly in love with Nav Bharani. As a lover, a partner, a potential life-mate.

This was what love truly was. It went far beyond the bedazzlement, the lust, I'd felt for other men. It was deeper, brighter, steadier. Far more exciting, in a real and lasting way.

I set the glass down with trembling hands and stared at the ruby-colored wine. Well, damn. For once, I'd fallen for a truly good, utterly wonderful man.

But, as always, the relationship was doomed.

In fact, it didn't even exist. Nav had gone to bed with me for fun, to satisfy curiosity.

Yes, now I knew he wanted to get married, but not to me. To some perfect woman who would win his heart. Someone like that damned Margaret, or the other woman he'd loved who hadn't loved him back.

Which left me . . . where? In love with a wonderful man who, at most, wanted to be friends with benefits. No way could I do that.

My grandmother had been right all along. I couldn't have my cake and eat it, too. I never should have gone along with Nav's Pritam and Dhiraj games.

But I had. And now, could I ever again look at him as just a friend?

No, but I'd have to try. Anything was better than losing him completely.

"Kat, are you okay?" Sam's low voice broke into my thoughts.

I realized I was surrounded by people who were laughing and telling jokes, the kind of party I usually enjoyed. "I'm fine. I just have something on my mind."

"Want to talk about it? Sometimes it helps to get a fresh perspective."

Perspective. I remembered that Nav had titled his exhibit "Perspectives on Perspective."

"Uh, no, Sam, but thanks."

This trip had certainly shown me some different perspectives. I had a new understanding of myself, my family, and Nav.

I couldn't deceive him. Even if it would be easier for both of us, I couldn't be dishonest with the man I loved.

In the past couple of days I'd learned that I'd spent a good part of my life hiding behind a self-protective façade. Now it was time to have the guts to face the truth.

But I didn't feel brave, I was scared shitless. I drew in a shaky breath.

Could we really remain friends if I told him the truth? Could we if I didn't?

"Kat, just go talk to him."

"Huh?" I stared at Sam. "Who?"

"Your boyfriend."

If only he was. "He's not my boyfriend."

"Sure looked like it to me. Look, I'm a writer. I observe people. I saw the connection between the two of you. Now you're feeling like crap, and I bet he is, too."

Was he? Yes, I knew it was true.

"He tried to talk to you," Sam said, "and you walked away. It's your turn."

"I don't know what to say."

"You'll figure it out as you go along. Just speak from your heart."

Could I?

He gave me an understanding smile. "The screen directions say, 'Kat rises and walks toward the exit.' "

I rose, legs shaking and stomach queasy. "Thank you. I think."

Chapter 19

Nav sat in lonely splendor in his fancy romance compartment, staring out the window at amazing mountain scenery.

Kat was off trying to cheer herself up with that ever-present screenwriter and the boisterous Aussies. Nav's preference was to retreat and lick his wounds in private.

And he felt plenty wounded.

He'd told her he loved her, and she'd responded with that damned friendship crap again. Then, when he'd gone to look for her, she'd been in the dining car chatting away with that damned screenwriter. And when he'd asked her to talk to him, she'd refused. What the hell was he supposed to do now?

Occasionally he picked up his camera to take a picture of a spectacular view, a tumbling waterfall, but he was shooting shit. His heart wasn't in it.

Besides, the camera reminded him of the incredible pictures he'd taken of Kat as she stripped so sensually.

He wouldn't look at them now. It felt like an invasion of her privacy. In her crazy mind, she hadn't been stripping for him, Nav, she'd been doing it for a stranger who didn't exist.

And it was his own damned fault for setting up the whole stupid game.

He should delete the pictures, but he couldn't bring himself to do that, either. It would be like an admission that he'd failed.

Depressed as he was, he hadn't reached that point yet.

Damn it, she'd called his name when she climaxed. Even if she didn't want to acknowledge it, she'd been making love with him.

He'd told her he loved her. Where the hell did he go from here? He was out of ideas.

"Fuck!" He wished he could go for a run. For miles and miles. Try to burn some of this tension out of his body.

When they reached Vancouver, he should probably catch a flight back to Montreal. Concentrate on his exhibit. Wait for her to return after the wedding, then see where things stood.

But that didn't feel right. He'd spent the past two years living according to her agenda. Being passive.

Until he had his *brilliant* idea and took action.

All the same, he didn't regret what he'd done. He'd taken a risk, and there was a slim chance it might still pay off.

And anything was better than being stuck in good-buddy limbo.

A soft knock sounded on his door.

He jerked to his feet and flung the door open. "Kat." Relief surged through him so forcefully he had to grip the doorframe to keep his balance. "I'm glad you came."

She stepped past him into the room, head down, subdued. "You were right about us needing to talk." She sat on the edge of the chair and darted a quick glance up at him. "But you know me, I'm better at avoidance than dealing with the tough stuff."

"You're here now." He sat on the bed across from her, realizing they were in the same positions as when they'd talked this morning.

Would she acknowledge that he'd told her he loved her? Or was she trying to pretend he'd meant it as a friend?

"I've been thinking," she said, staring down at her jean-clad knees. "And I realized something, and I need to tell you. It's . . . hard, but I have to." She swallowed. "I'm counting on what you said about always being my friend. Even if I . . . Even if something changes. Something, uh, kind of big."

What was she talking about? They'd talked about each of them getting married. What was bigger than that? "Kat, I'll always be your friend. No matter what."

She gazed up at him again, and now her expression was fierce. "Damn, I wish things didn't have to change. I liked how we were before."

He sighed. "I didn't. I needed a change." Couldn't she understand how much it had hurt to love her and be treated like a buddy?

"Oh." She sounded startled. "I didn't realize."

"I kept watching you fall for those guys." He shook his head.

"Fall for them." Her lips twisted in a grimace. "Looking back, I realize I was into the excitement, but it was never real. Never l-love." She faltered over the word. "I didn't really commit to them," she said. "When things got rough, I bailed—or accepted being dumped—rather than work on the problems. And afterward, it wasn't so much the men themselves I missed, it was the idea of love and marriage."

He was glad she'd come to see that, but still didn't have a clue about this "big" thing she wanted to tell him.

"All through those relationships," she went on, "our friendship was what gave my life stability. Warmth."

She took a breath, let it out. "Nav, when I moved into our building, I was saving to buy a condo. I'd accumulated plenty for a down payment long ago, but I never went house hunting. By then, the apartment felt like home. Because you were there."

"I didn't know that."

"I relied on you, cared about you, but I didn't really see you." She gave a small laugh. "I didn't see myself, either, not until this trip. The last few days have opened my eyes to . . ."

A spark of hope ignited. "To what, Kat?"

She gazed at him, biting her lip. Then she reached out and

took the sleeve of his sweater between her thumb and forefinger, shook it gently, and let go. "I always knew you had a great body, but look at you now. You look incredible, Nav."

"Uh, thanks. And you were right about the image thing. I overreacted to the 'judge by appearances' snobbery I grew up with. It's not so bad, wearing nice clothes and looking good. Guess maybe I have some vanity after all."

Her lips curved a little. "Don't throw out those old Cambridge jerseys, though. They're kind of sexy."

"Oh, yeah?" He grinned at her.

She smiled back, then her face tensed.

He took her hand and gripped it firmly. "You can tell me anything. Just get it over with." He took a breath then—what the hell—said it. "I'll still love you."

Her hand jerked in his. She stared down at their clasped hands and said, so softly he could barely hear, "Well, the thing is, I love you. I mean . . . really. Not just as a friend but the way a woman loves a man."

Was she saying . . . ? Or had he misheard, out of desperate longing? "Kat?"

She lifted her head slowly and gazed at him, face open and vulnerable. "That's how I know I didn't love those other men. What I felt for them was nothing compared to this."

Oh, my God. She meant it. His heart expanded so full it felt like it was going to burst out of his chest. Emotion clogged his throat so he could barely croak out, "Kat, I—"

"No, stop, I haven't finished. I want to say I'm sorry. I know we set up this strangers-on-a-train thing with the rule that we'd go back to the way we were. I tried, I really tried to keep it light and sexy, to think of you as Pritam or Dhiraj, but in the end I couldn't."

She loved him. He was so stunned, so blindsided by shock and sheer joy, all he could do was listen.

"All the time," she said in a ragged voice, "I was seeing more sides of you. And they were you, Nav, not those other guys.

And I kept falling harder and deeper. When we set up the game, I never expected that to happen, and I tried to resist it, tried to deny it, but I couldn't. And now I've messed things up, and I'm so sorry."

Her eyes were filling. "You're the most important person in the world to me, and I can't bear the thought of losing you, so can we please, please, find some way of—"

"Kat!" Finally he found his voice. "I love you, too. Love you the way you're talking about. I'm crazy about you. I want you more than any other woman I've ever met, or ever will meet."

". . . You do?"

If he hadn't been so overwhelmed with amazement and joy, the baffled expression on her face would have made him laugh. "I told you last night, but I guess you didn't understand what I meant. I've been falling in love with you ever since we met. I tried not to. Tried dating other women. But I couldn't help it. That's the reason for this whole strangers game. I had to get you past the 'just friends' thing, so you'd really see me."

"You love me?" She still looked confused, but her eyes had brightened as if it was starting to sink in.

He pulled her forward into an awkward hug. "I, Naveen Bharani, love you, Kat Fallon."

Her arms went around him and squeezed hard. "But . . . I thought you only wanted to be friends. Isn't that what you said when you were playing Pritam?"

"I figured it was the only way to get you to buy into the game. You were always so adamant about not risking our friendship." Now he realized that she'd seen him as a player, a man who didn't believe in marriage, and of course that would have put her off, too.

She pulled back a little and stared at him. "What? You wanted me to really see you, so you pretended to be a stranger? That doesn't make any sense."

"It worked, though." He cradled her face between his hands. "Kat, say it again. I've waited so long to hear it."

She gazed into his eyes, expression tender and loving. "I love you, Nav. I've finally learned how to love, because you taught me."

"And I love you. Because, once I got to know you, I had no other option."

Her lips twitched. "But you told me you were looking for the perfect woman."

"I'd found you. I was waiting for you to find me."

She ducked her head. "I'm hardly perfect."

"You're perfect for me. You're wonderful and lovable." He traced the outline of her lips with his finger.

Then he kissed her. The woman he loved and had finally won.

He kissed her gently, tenderly, with all the love and reverence and gratitude in his heart. She kissed him back the same way, lips trembling. Salty kisses. She was crying, and he realized his own eyes were damp.

"I want to make love with you," he told her. "You and me, Nav and Kat. I want to hear you call my name when you come." He rose on shaky legs, then pulled her to her feet, into a quick, warm embrace.

Fingers clumsy with awe and need, he pulled off her T-shirt, unzipped her jeans, and freed her of every item of clothing except a pair of pink panties. After pausing to admire her, he peeled them off, too, wanting nothing between them.

He tugged her into his arms again, holding her close for another kiss.

She squirmed free. "My turn." She pulled up the bottom of his sweater, leaving him to finish taking it off as she went to work on the fastenings of his jeans. "I love your new clothes, but you look—and feel—so much better without them."

When she'd stripped him, they just stood there looking at each other for a long moment. Naked together. That's how it felt. Not only their bodies, but their hearts and souls were open to each other.

He pulled back the covers on the bed, and silently they lay down, side by side, facing each other.

"I feel nervous," she said, a catch in her voice. "It's our first time."

The first time they would make love with both of them knowing, fully, that that was what they were doing. "I know."

He didn't feel at all anxious. "Don't worry. We have lots and lots of time. If we don't get it right the first time, we'll just have to try again."

As he'd hoped, that won him a small chuckle. "Then maybe it would be good if we didn't get it right the first time."

Propped up on one elbow, he stroked her arm, the curve of her hip, the soft fullness of her breasts. "You're beautiful, Kat. All I want is to make you happy."

Her hand gripped his erection. "All?" she teased.

"Okay, maybe I lied."

As he continued to caress her, her nipples tightened. Noticing and appreciating everything about her, he let his fingers speak for him.

She explored his body the same way, almost as if she'd never seen it before.

When he stroked his hand down her belly, she shifted to let him slide between her legs, where she was moist with need.

Her body twisted restlessly against his hand, telling him she was close to climaxing. "No, wait," she panted. "Nav, I want you inside me. I want us to come together."

Need raced through him, hardening him so much it hurt.

With a firm hand on her shoulder, he rolled her onto her back. Her knees came up, legs parted in an invitation he lost no time in accepting. As he sheathed himself, a thought struck him.

He leaned forward, dropped a kiss on her lips, then whispered, "One day, I want to make a baby with you."

The moment he said the words, he wished he could call them

back. Not because he didn't mean them but because he feared that, if he rushed her, he might lose her.

Her breath caught and she stared at him, then her eyes brightened, moistened. "Oh, yes. We'll make beautiful, wonderful babies."

The thought was so powerfully emotional, he surged inside her in one deep plunge that made them both cry out.

With her sheath gripping him, her arms around him, more words popped from between his lips. "Kat, will you marry me?"

Her mouth opened in surprise. "Nav, do you mean it?"

It was too much for her, too fast. But he couldn't call the words back, and he meant them with all his heart. "More than anything." If he'd planned this moment, he'd have arranged a romantic setting, a bottle of champagne. A ring.

Wait, at least he had one of those. Awkwardly he shifted his weight and managed to pull the diamond ring off his finger while she watched, looking stunned.

Then, still lodged deep in her core, bracing his weight on one elbow, he held out the ring. "We can pick out another one later, but this'll do for now."

Remembering the words she'd used when she'd talked about the most romantic gift a man could give her, he spoke the truth. "Kat, I love you, heart and soul. I want to spend the rest of my life with you. Will you do me the honor of marrying me?"

She stared at the ring, eyes wet and wide with surprise, then at his face.

He felt as if she was peering deep inside him, and into her own heart at the same time. Did she realize, as he did, how utterly right it was for the two of them to be together?

Her lips parted and he held his breath.

"Nav," she whispered, as if she could hardly believe what was happening. "Yes, oh, yes. I love you." The tears overflowed and streamed down her cheeks.

He kissed her through the tears, with love and passion mingling, then slipped the ring onto her finger.

Then he kissed her again and began to thrust into her.

He was making love with his fiancée, Kat.

He had to move faster, deeper, letting his body tell her with every stroke how much he loved her.

She wrapped her legs and arms around him, clinging tight, lifting her hips and matching his rhythm. Her internal muscles gripped him, the delicious stimulation making him struggle to hold back his climax.

Their lips clung together, kissing, panting for breath, making wordless sounds.

He angled his strokes to rub her G-spot and her body clutched; she caught her breath. Then, "Nav, oh, God, Nav, now! Come with me now."

"Yes!" He stopped holding back, gave himself over to the heady rush of arousal and emotion, and let go with wild, hard strokes that wrenched an orgasm from deep inside him and poured it into her. "Kat, I love you."

"I love you, Nav," she cried as her body came apart around him.

They clung together through shuddering spasms of pleasure that went on and on.

Long moments later, he rolled them so they were back on their sides.

She smiled at him, then studied the ring, loose on her slim finger. "Engaged. I can't believe it."

"Nor can I." He prayed she wouldn't change her mind. "How about a glass of bubbly to seal the deal?"

"Definitely."

Nav disentangled himself and rose. His sleeping car attendant was great about keeping the ice bucket stocked—possibly due to the size of Nav's tips, but more likely because of the man's pride in his job.

He held up a bottle of Canadian bubbly. "It's not French

champagne, but, like the ring, it'll do until we can get something better. I'm afraid I didn't come prepared." Even in his wildest dreams, he hadn't imagined proposing to her on the train.

After easing the cork out of the bottle, he poured the wine and brought the glasses back to bed where she'd pushed herself up on pillows. Naked, with her chest and face flushed, her nipples and mouth rosy, her hair wild and sexy, she was lovely.

As he stood beside the bed, another twinge of uncertainty, of guilt, hit him. "Kat, did I rush you when I proposed? The words just popped out."

Her hand, reaching for a glass, froze in midair. "Are you having second thoughts?"

"Me? No way! I've dreamed of it. But it was an emotional moment. It's a big step for you to go from saying you love me to getting engaged. You need to be sure."

She took the glass and held it, studying the bubbles. "I have a bad record for rushing things, don't I?" Her gaze lifted to his face, and her lips twitched. "I told you about my new one-month rule, right?"

He sighed and sat on the edge of the bed, putting down his own glass. Yes, of course this was too good to be true. "You said the next time you were attracted to a man, you wouldn't let yourself fall in love for a month. Okay, we'll wait a month so you can be sure."

She shook her head. "Actually, the rule was that I wouldn't fall in love until I'd *known* the man a month. Well, I've known you for two years. Long enough, well enough, to know you're a wonderful person, and to truly care for you."

Nav listened with relief as she went on. "Then, over the last few days, I've seen other sides to you. Like, how fun, exciting, sexy, passionate, unpredictable—in a good way—you can be. How great you are with kids, and everyone else you meet. Especially with me."

She smiled. "You can kiss me senseless, and you can make me feel . . ."

"What?"

"Cherished," she finished softly.

"You are. But, Kat, if you need more time, take it. I know you want to be married, and I do believe you when you say you love me, but you shouldn't rush into anything."

She was quiet for a long moment. "Yes, I want to be married. And you know what? This is my first proposal. After dating for more than fifteen years. After . . . I hate to think how many relationships. Those relationships . . ."

She shook her head. "They were never right."

He held his breath as she studied his face.

"My judgment sucks when it comes to men," she said. "That's what everyone's always told me. But I think it says something for my judgment that no relationship ever got to the proposal stage. Until now."

Unable to hold his breath any longer, he let it out. "What are you saying?"

"This feels right. You and me. We're already best friends and we've proved we're amazing lovers. Now we know we love each other. This train trip has been"—she broke off and gave a soft chuckle—"one hell of a wild ride. It's also been a journey of discovery, and all the discoveries are good."

"Oh, yes. Very good."

"I think that's what it'll be like for us. Marriage, kids, your career, my career, a house somewhere. More discoveries, more sharing, more love."

She met his grin with one of her own. "So, I'm staying engaged, if that's all right with you."

"It's very all right." Joy surged through him, and he pulled her into a tight embrace.

She squeaked as wine spilled from her glass, then wrapped her free arm around his neck and kissed him deeply.

When they eased apart, he raised his own glass and clicked it to hers. "Here's to us and a wonderful future together."

"To us, and a wonderful future together," she said firmly, and they both drank the toast.

He gave her a quick kiss, unable to resist those lush pink lips.

Come to think of it, all of her was irresistible. "If you have no objection, I'd like to kiss my fiancée all over, from head to toe."

Her brown eyes sparkled. "I think I could live with that."

"I warn you, I'm probably going to lick you all over, too."

"Hmm." She made a mock-serious face. "If you do, be warned there'll be consequences."

"Such as?"

"I might have to do the same to you."

Just the thought made his body, utterly satiated only a few minutes ago, stir again. "Well, all of that kissing and licking could take a long time, so I'd better get started." He took another sip of wine, then put his glass down.

Then he straddled Kat and, beginning with her forehead, began to kiss, lick, and nibble her, letting each caress tell her how much he loved her.

Just in case she wasn't getting the message—and because he reveled in being able to say the words aloud—he whispered, "I love you."

The seductive scent of jasmine drifted from skin that was tantalizingly soft and warm. That sweet but spicy aroma was, to him, a perfect embodiment of Kat's personality.

When he was circling the tender hollow at the base of her throat with his tongue, she threaded her fingers through his curly hair.

"You shaved, but you didn't cut your hair."

He lifted his head to look at her. "Do you mind? The hair stylist trimmed it but refused to cut it."

"Refused?"

He gave an embarrassed shrug. "She said I had great hair."

"She was right. It suits you. Either pulled back or loose like this. It's the shave that makes the real difference. I never knew what a strong, striking face you had." She giggled. "I thought you might be hiding a weak chin or acne. And all along, what you were really concealing was how handsome you are."

"Glad you think so." He dipped his head back down and sucked his way along her collarbone.

She toyed with his hair, running her fingers through it, twining strands around one finger as he kept worshipping her body, inch by inch.

Through her fingers, he could monitor her arousal. When they froze or gripped his skull, or yanked the hair she was twirling, it was as clear a signal as the rise and fall of her chest, her soft, panting breaths.

He tried to enjoy the slow burn of his own arousal rather than let his need become consuming. This was about Kat and his love for her.

He circled her areola over and over with his tongue, then flicked her nipple back and forth, feeling her tension mount. With gentle suction, he popped her nipple into his mouth and teased it with his lips and tongue. Then he did the same to her other breast.

Her pelvis lifted, twisted. She moaned, and then she climaxed with a low, shuddering cry.

"I've never come that way before," she murmured wonderingly.

So much for having the patience to kiss her from head to toe. He needed her now. As he sheathed himself, he said, "There's something to be said for the conventional way, too." He thrust inside her in one long, slow plunge.

"Oh, yes!" She began to rock against him, and he matched her rhythm.

He wouldn't last long, but he wouldn't have to, because already her body was tensing, her focus centering. Reaching between them, he caressed her swollen bud.

"Nav!" Her body clutched, then climaxed again, hard and long.

Those waves gripped him, drew him under, made his own orgasm as inevitable as the tides. He exploded while she was still coming.

Afterward, they flopped bonelessly on the bed, side by side on their backs, holding hands.

She turned her head to look at him. "That was incredible."

He gazed into her lovely eyes. "You're incredible. I love you."

"I love you, too, and we're incredible *together*." Then her brows drew together in a mock frown. "But what happened to kissing me from head to toe? You didn't even get halfway."

"When I recover my energy, I'll pick up where I left off."

"I'll look forward to that." Then she gave a blissful sigh. "Oh, Nav, there are so many things to look forward to."

"And if we ever run out, we'll just start that Nice 'n Naughty game again."

"Did you really buy that to play with me?"

"Yeah. But not for this train trip. I got it about six months after I met you. When I was still optimistic I could get you to go out with me."

"Wow." She shook her head wonderingly.

He squeezed her hand, the one with his bulky ring on her finger. "I have you now, and that's all that matters."

"What happens next?" she asked. "I don't want you to go back to Montreal, but I guess you have to, to get ready for your exhibit. You'll come back for the wedding, though?"

He had no intention of letting her out of his sight, but all the same, he joked, "I thought I'd been uninvited."

She punched his shoulder gently. "Oh, you're coming. For sure. And you know what? I'll even let you pay for your own flight."

He laughed. "My male pride thanks you. All the same, I think I'll just stay in Vancouver rather than go back to Montreal for a week. I'll shoot more photos, work with the ones I've been taking on the train." He paused, then said teasingly, "I got some pretty sexy ones."

She jerked up. "You wouldn't!"

He laughed. "No, of course not. But there are some great ones of you. Damn, woman, you're sexy. You'll have to see them."

"One day when I'm feeling brave." She rolled onto her side, facing him. "If you stay through to the wedding, will you really have time to get ready for the exhibit? I'll help, if there's anything I can do."

"There'll be time." He might have to work night and day, but he'd find time.

His reward was her happy smile. "Terrific!"

"Should I get a hotel room, or—"

"Oh, no. You'll stay at the house, and in my room." She winked. "My parents' bedroom's on a whole other floor."

"That's a relief."

"I should call or e-mail them. They're not big on surprises."

"What will you say?"

"Oh, gosh." She blew out air. "Last weekend I told my family you were coming as my wedding date, and said you'd be flying out. I didn't tell anyone you were on the train. I guess I'll pretend our plans changed—which they sure did!"

She raised her hand and admired the ring. "I'm getting attached to this, you know."

"We could get it remade into an engagement ring."

"Could we?" She beamed at him. "I'd like that. It's the ring you gave me when you proposed, and I love it. Oh, gosh, I can't wait to tell everyone we're engaged!"

"Two sisters engaged at the same time."

"That's right." Then she frowned. "No wait, this is supposed to be Merilee's special time. She's felt like she's been in the shadow of her big sisters for so long, she shouldn't have to share the limelight."

"You don't want to tell your family we're engaged?"

"I do! More than anything. But I think I'll wait until M&M have gone on their honeymoon. Do you mind?"

"Yes." He touched her face, thinking how generous she was and how much he loved her. "But, no. Because you're right. This is your sister's time, and her fiancé's. We'll have our own."

"I'll have to hide the ring, damn it," she grumbled.

"We'll find a jeweler and get it remade, then you'll have it to wear right after the wedding."

Her face brightened. "Great. And in the meantime, you know what I want?"

"No idea."

"Let's shower and go for dinner. I want to tell everyone on the train that we're engaged."

Oh, yeah, he wanted to tell the whole world. Except for his parents. Yes, they wanted him to get married, but a Caucasian Canadian certainly wouldn't be their choice. Oh, well, he wasn't going to let the thought of their disapproval darken this wonderful day.

"You do realize," he told Kat, "that means telling people you're engaged to Dhiraj?"

"Oh, yeah." She wrinkled her nose. "Nope. Dhiraj is a sexy guy, but it's Nav I love. I want to call you Nav. Could it be a pet name or something?"

"In Hindi it means new."

"Perfect. My new love."

"Dhiraj and Pritam have meanings, too."

She raised her eyebrows. "Ah ha. You chose those names for a reason."

"Dhiraj means patience, because after you deserted Pritam in that Toronto hotel room, I knew I'd need it."

"And Pritam?"

"Means beloved."

"You sneaky devil." She beamed at him. "You got me to call you beloved?"

"Because that's what I wanted to be."

"And you are." She stroked his face.

Then she twined her fingers into his curls and tugged. "Come on, beloved. Shower, clothes, then I get to show off my new fiancé."

Chapter 20

After two nights of very little sleep spent watching the moon from my single bunk and obsessing over what I was doing with Nav, I should have slept like a log on that third and final night on the train.

But instead, I again lay stargazing as the train rolled smoothly through southern BC, heading from Kamloops to the coast. This time, though, I was beside my fiancé, both of us spent from lovemaking but too excited to sleep.

I was so happy. This had all happened so quickly, at first I had trouble believing it was real. But the more we talked, the more we planned as, outside the window, moonlight bathed the ever-changing landscape, the more real and wonderful it became.

We talked about careers, when we should start a family, how many kids we wanted, what we should name them. Dreams and practicality blended in a perfect mix, and I'd never had so much fun in my life.

At some point we did drift off to sleep in each other's arms, and woke to find the moon had disappeared and dawn was lighting the sky.

We shared a tender good-morning kiss, then I sighed. We were almost to Vancouver. "I suppose we should get cleaned up and packed, and go for breakfast."

Nav swung out of bed—that butt only got better each time I saw it—and took something from the vanity. He came back—his front view was pretty damned fine, too—and handed me a bundle. A cloth napkin from the dining car, folded around four of the dinner rolls that had been on the table last night. Then he handed me a bottle of water.

"Bread and water?" Giving him a mock scowl, I said, "I'll have you know, *Pritam* bought me expensive champagne, and *Dhiraj* booked the Romance by Rail suite. You have big shoes to fill, and bread and water ain't gonna cut it."

Nav gave me a wicked grin. "Ah, but if we have bread and water in the room, I'll have time to do this." He slid back into bed, and hastily I put down the buns and water bottle.

He spooned me from behind, lifting the hair away from the nape of my neck and blowing gently across my skin.

I shivered with pleasure and angled my head to give him better access. His hand snuck around to fondle my breast, and against my butt his cock grew.

"That's a persuasive argument," I murmured.

An hour later, we had both showered and packed, and we'd met up again in Nav's compartment to watch out the window as the train neared Vancouver.

"You told your family that I'm on the train with you?" he asked.

"When I called home last night, Merilee answered. She said Theresa was borrowing her car to pick me up, so I told her you were with me."

I remembered my little sister's reaction. "What?" Her voice had squeaked. "Your boyfriend's on the train with you? And you didn't think to mention that before?"

I'd muttered an excuse, and she'd said, "Seems like my sisters are full of surprises these days." The edge to her voice had said she wasn't entirely thrilled.

Thinking of her reaction, I told Nav, "I'm glad we decided to

keep our engagement a secret until after the wedding." Poor
Merilee. I'd never realized how left out she'd felt when we were
growing up.

"For her sake or your own?" His voice was low.

"What do you mean?" I turned from the window to stare at
him.

"Maybe you want to gauge your family's reaction to me. If
they don't approve . . ." He stared back at me, eyes narrowed.

Anxiety skittered through me. Nav was right. They'd find
something wrong with him. They always found something wrong
with the guys I brought home.

But this was different. I was in love, engaged. I caught his
hand. "Oh, no, they're not going to talk me out of this. I love
you, Nav."

His face softened, but he didn't smile. "You thought you
loved other men, but your family found something to criticize.
And the relationships broke up."

I bit my lip. "I hate to admit this, but looking back, I really
did pick some guys who weren't a good fit. My family just
pointed out things I'd have eventually figured out myself."

"And you're so sure I'm a good fit?" In other circumstances,
the comment might have had a sexual innuendo, but his expression was dead serious.

"I am."

He squeezed my hand. "Kat, I love you. That love has been
growing for two years. You only fell for me yesterday. How can
you be so sure?"

"Because it feels right." Even as I said the words, I knew
they sounded hollow. Relationships had felt right before, then
turned out to be fatally flawed. "I told you last night, the way I
feel for you is different. You're . . . everything. I know I love
you."

"What if your parents don't approve?"

"If they don't, screw them." I thought he was wonderful,
and my opinion was the only one that counted.

His lips twitched. "Thanks, I think. But let's not forget, I intend to become part of this family."

The poor guy didn't have a clue what he was getting into. "Lucky you."

He glanced past me. "We're pulling into the station."

I gazed out to see a familiar sight: Vancouver's Pacific Central Station. As I gripped Nav's hand, excitement filled me. I going home with the man I loved, I'd started to forge a closer bond with two of my sisters, and I felt like I understood my parents a bit better. "I wonder if Theresa's here, or waiting in the car outside?"

"What's she look like?" he asked.

"An inch taller than me. Her hair's auburn but lighter than mine, and she wears it short and simple. Practical, straightforward clothes. No glamour." I was really looking forward to seeing her—not to mention curious to learn how she'd hooked up with a sexy celebrity.

Scanning people in the station, looking for a no-frills woman standing alone, my gaze skimmed over—"Oh, my God, the entire family's here!"

I gaped at them. Mom, in one of her stylish navy pantsuits, standing with her arm linked in Dad's, him in his usual L.L.Bean oxford-cloth shirt and corduroy pants. Merilee in jeans and T-shirt, clinging to Matt's arm, honey-blond curls bouncing as she said something to him.

And . . . Theresa? "That can't be Theresa."

"Where?"

I pointed.

"Hey, she looks a bit like you. Or maybe it's just the clothes."

"Yeah." I stared at my sister, slim and leggy in a denim miniskirt that was almost identical to the one I wore and a peach-colored tank top that hugged her breasts. Her short hair gleamed in the sunlight, and her lightly tanned skin glowed. Not only did she look vibrant, but she was prettier than I'd ever seen her. Sexier, too.

Or maybe I'd never looked so closely before.

Yeah, I could see a hot celebrity falling for that woman. My sister.

"It's nice they all came to meet you," Nav said. "They must have really missed you."

"Oh, it's not me." Anxiety sent a shiver rippling through me. When they'd thought it was just me arriving, they'd delegated Theresa, the person who had no work or school commitments in Vancouver. "Merilee told them I was bringing home a man, and they've all come to check you out."

Fine, so they'd meet Nav a bit earlier than planned. There was no reason to stress out.

I backed away from the window to give him a final appraisal. Jeans were perfectly appropriate for travel, and his were stylish, expensive, and they fit his awesome body as if they'd been made for him. The white shirt with rolled-up sleeves was the right cross between formality and casualness, and looked dramatic with his lovely cinnamon skin.

The Piaget watch—something he'd told me he'd bought to impress me—looked elegant on his wrist. His strong, graceful hands were bare, the engagement ring tucked safely in a zippered pocket of my purse.

His face was striking, handsome, his chocolate eyes full of affection and concern.

My God, this amazing man was actually my fiancé.

"Do I pass?" he asked, kinking a brow.

"You look wonderful."

He'd pulled his hair back in the black band, taming those glossy curls. The look suited him, but . . . I reached up, pulled off the band, and ran my fingers through his hair, freeing it to curl the way it wanted to. "I like it like that. Okay, come on and meet your future in-laws."

"Lead on." He dropped a kiss on the top of my head.

I straightened my shoulders and took a deep breath. Damn, I wished I had the engagement ring on my finger to reinforce my courage. But at least I was wearing the hummingbird earrings he'd given me.

Lugging our carry-on bags, we made our way to the exit.

I stood on the top step, waved at my family, then took another deep breath and walked down the stairs to meet them as they hurried over. Nav's solid presence behind me was reassuring.

Mom gave me a warm hug. "So good to have you home, dear." She pulled back, studied my face, and smiled. "You're looking well." Then she passed me into Dad's arms as she stepped toward Nav.

I watched from the curve of my father's arm as Mom held out her hand. "Welcome to Vancouver. I'm Rebecca Fallon."

"Naveen Bharani. I go by Nav." He took her hand and shook it firmly, meeting her gaze. Calm and confident.

I was proud of him.

Dad moved forward to meet him, and Merilee caught me up in a tight hug. "You're home! It's so great to see you."

As I embraced her, I felt a new, extra warmth in our hug. I'd always thought her so happy and even-tempered, had never recognized her insecurities. And she'd never seen mine.

"You, too, bride-to-be." I touched her pretty face. She was thinner and tired looking, but her eyes and smile were bright with happiness. "How are you feeling? And did you find a wedding dress?"

She beamed. "I'm great. And yes, an utterly gorgeous, absolutely perfect gown."

"That's wonderful, M."

"Of course she won't let me see it." Her fiancé touched my shoulder. "Hey, Kat. Good to see you." Matt was dressed for his summer job rather than in his usual jeans. With streaky dirty-blond hair, a firm athletic build, and a touch of tan, he looked fit and attractive.

"Hi, Matt." I stretched up so we could kiss each other's cheeks.

Then I turned to Theresa, marveling. "Well, look at you, sis. You look fabulous. I like your skirt. Who knew we had the same taste in clothes?"

We fell into each other's arms. "I borrowed it from Merilee," she said. "My Australia clothes are too dull, and I haven't had a chance to go shopping."

"Dull?" I pulled back to study her face. "Let me guess, this has something to do with the sexy writer?"

She glowed. "It has everything to do with Damien."

"So, where is he?"

"Today? In Boston. He's on a book tour. But he'll be back for the wedding. And we talk every night." Her eyes sparkled.

"Talk? You mean, have phone sex," Merilee said, sounding almost envious.

"We do both," Theresa said smugly.

My competitiveness surged to the fore, and I had to bite my tongue to keep from blurting out that, while Theresa might be having phone sex with one of the ten sexiest guys in Australia, I was *engaged*!

But that would have been childish and hurtful to Merilee. Maybe even to Theresa, who'd suffered from a bitter divorce and taken years to get into a new relationship.

I loved my sisters, and if I wanted them to act like grown-ups, I needed to do the same.

I darted a glance toward Nav, who was talking to my parents.

Theresa's gaze followed mine. "Speaking of sexy, you sure found a hottie this time."

Merilee leaned close. "You spent three days on the train and haven't found his flaw yet?"

"Mmm, let me think." I paused dramatically. "Nope, he's perfect." And I sure hoped they'd all think so, too.

She poked my arm. "That'd be a first."

I didn't rise to the bait, just said evenly, "It is. Come meet him."

After I'd introduced everyone, Mom and Matt walked over

to the sky train to ride a stop or two to downtown, and Dad and Merilee left to drive up to the university.

I breathed a sigh of relief.

Theresa waited while Nav and I collected the bag I had checked through to Vancouver. Then she led the way to Merilee's Toyota, where she and I insisted Nav take the front passenger seat.

While Theresa drove us home, she alternated playing tour guide and peppering Nav with questions.

"Give it a rest," I complained. "You know Mom and Dad are going to ask him the exact same things at dinner."

"I'm giving him a chance to rehearse," she retorted, and carried on with her grilling.

Nav held his own nicely, and I saw a quiet confidence I'd never appreciated before.

Maybe this time my family would actually approve of my choice. Hopefully, they'd see him the way I did and know the two of us belonged together.

When we parked outside the family home, Nav said, "What a great house."

I always enjoyed the first sight of the rambling home in which I'd grown up. "It's way too big for Mom and Dad," I said. "I wonder if they'll sell it now their last bird is flying the nest."

"They'd never find the time," Theresa said, heading toward the front door. "Besides, I think they want to keep all our bedrooms in hopes we'll visit more often."

"That's silly," I said. "When we're here, they're still so busy with their own lives."

She shrugged. "Yes, but they like having us, for whatever reason. Maybe just to boss around." She glanced at Nav. "We're not the most functional family, but I guess Kat's told you that."

He raised his hands. "Hey, you haven't met my parents."

I felt a twinge. Would his parents like me? After all, they wanted their only child to marry one of those "prospectives" his mother kept sending him. And to move to India.

Theresa was unlocking the front door. "Nav, we'll give you the guided tour so you can get your bearings."

I tried to shove my worries aside and clasped his hand as we went through the spacious downstairs. The house looked so different from when I'd lived there. Then, my sisters' and my cast-off clothes, school stuff, novels and magazines, and music had littered most of the surfaces. Now, although the furniture was attractive and everything clean and well kept, there was an air of emptiness and formality.

I got the feeling that Mom and Dad mostly spent time in their offices, and Merilee hung out in her room or at Matt's. The kitchen was the only room with a lived-in clutter.

We took the stairs to the second floor, tour-guide Theresa saying, "All us girls have bedrooms here, and there are two baths. Mom and Dad's bedroom and offices are on the third floor."

"Did they have any problem with Nav sharing my room?" I asked her.

"They gave each other *the Look*." She made a face. "They did the same thing when Damien was here. But Matt's been staying over with Merilee for years now, so we deserve equal treatment."

The three of us stood in the hall by the door to my room. "I'll give you half an hour," Theresa said in her professorial voice. "You can unpack, get organized. Then, Nav, I'm afraid I need Kat. We have to discuss wedding plans, and this afternoon we're trying on dresses. Make yourself at home. There's food in the kitchen, books in the study, I showed you the patio, and—"

He held up a hand. "I get the picture. Thanks, Theresa. I'm going to go for a run, then I'll head out with my camera."

I hugged his arm proudly. "He needs more shots for his big exhibit."

The exhibit was something he'd mentioned—with appropriate humility—when Theresa had been questioning him.

He smiled at my sister. "Just tell me when to be back. Oh,

and slot me in if there's any way I can help with the wedding preparations."

An idea struck me. "Theresa, have you lined up a photographer yet?"

"No, I have some names to call, but—" She broke off, frowning at me as she realized what I was getting at. Then she turned to Nav. "We couldn't ask you. You're attending as a guest. Besides, er, have you done wedding photography?"

She was thinking she wanted the best for Merilee's wedding, and Nav was an unknown quantity.

Before I could get my back up, Nav said calmly, "A fair bit. Check my website and see what you think. If you want, I'd be happy to do it. As my gift to Merilee and Matt."

"Thanks, Nav," she said, and I saw respect in her eyes. "I'll take a look at your website."

"Is there anything I can pick up while I'm out?" he asked. "I imagine a couple bottles of bubbly to toast the happy couple wouldn't go amiss?" He turned an inquiring look in my direction, so that only I saw the twinkle in his eyes.

"The happy couple definitely deserves a champagne toast," I told him, knowing we'd be drinking to ourselves as much as to M&M. "Nav has excellent taste in champagne," I told Theresa.

"Just all-round perfect," she said dryly. Then she grinned. "Hey, if he's as good as he looks, that means you, Merilee, and I have all found our luck this summer."

"And Jenna doesn't want a steady guy," I said, "so she won't be envious."

I wasn't looking forward to dinner. Theresa seemed to have given Nav a tentative stamp of approval, Merilee was so happy she'd probably be easygoing, and Matt was more likely to be supportive than critical. But I knew how rough Mom and Dad could be on boyfriends.

Because the weather was nice, we had set the table on the patio. It was pleasant out there, with the bright planters of geraniums, impatiens, and lobelia. The yard was, as always, well maintained by the garden service, and would make a great setting for M&M's reception.

"In your honor, sweetheart," Dad said as he transferred salmon fillets with maple syrup glaze from the grill to the platter I held out. "Hope it's still one of your favorites, though I guess you've got used to fancy food at that hotel of yours."

"I still love your salmon, Dad," I assured him, pleased my parents had planned something special to welcome me home.

When we were all seated around the patio table, Nav handed Dad one of the two bottles of Dom Pérignon he'd bought. "Perhaps you'd like to do the honors?"

Dad raised his eyebrows, then handed the bottle back. "You go ahead. If you're trying to impress us, this isn't a bad start."

As Nav opened the bottle with his usual deftness, he said, "How often does one of your daughters get engaged? I figure that's worth toasting with good champagne." He gave me a wink, and I grinned back at him.

When we all had glasses in our hands, Mom said, "Nav, you brought the wine; you make the toast."

I knew it was a test.

He raised his glass. "To Merilee and Matt. And to love, marriage, and happy endings."

Mom nodded, and we all clicked glasses and drank.

Damn, it was hard to keep quiet about my engagement. I felt like champagne myself, with fizzy bubbles of excitement rising in me, urging me to pop the cork and spill all. And yet, at the same time, my stomach clenched with anxiety as I waited for my parents to grill Nav.

I took a deep breath and sipped the excellent champagne, hoping to calm my nerves.

Theresa said, "Exciting news. We now have a wedding photographer." She paused until everyone was looking at her. "Ta da. Nav's going to do the photos. They're his gift to M&M."

Merilee squealed, then got up and ran over to throw her

arms around his neck. "You're so sweet. Thank you so much, Nav."

Matt grinned. "Yeah, thanks, man. That's really nice of you."

The sound of Mom clearing her throat drew our attention. She was frowning. "That's very kind of you, Nav, but do you have much experience photographing weddings?"

I stifled a groan.

Before Nav could answer, Theresa jumped in. "Mom, he's brilliant. Take a look at his website. He has a way of . . . how would I put it? Capturing the essence of each couple." She glanced at me. "Like Kat did with the M&M wedding e-vites. The photographs will be wonderful."

I was a little stunned, not only by Theresa's support of Nav, but also by her compliment about my invitations. We weren't big on praising each other. "Thanks," I mouthed, raising my glass to her, and she gave me a quick smile.

It occurred to me that, as Nav had helped me get a fresh perspective on myself and my family, maybe Damien had done the same for Theresa. The starchy prof had certainly softened.

"How long have you been in the photography business?" Dad asked Nav.

"A couple of years, since I graduated from Laval."

"But you're . . . how old?"

"Twenty-eight."

"Three years younger than Kat," Mom commented. "And you got a late start on your career." Her tone was neutral, but I knew she disapproved. She figured everyone should do as she, Dad, and Theresa had: decide on a career early and pursue it full steam ahead.

I opened my mouth to defend Nav, but he got there first. "Before I went to Laval, I got a Masters in Business Administration at Cambridge. My parents hoped I'd go into the family business." He paused. "An import/export company called Bharani International." I could hear the words he didn't speak: *Go ahead and Google it.*

"Your parents paid for your education?" Mom asked.

"Until I went to Laval, yes."

"They invested a lot in your schooling." This time disapproval did color her voice. "Preparing you to go into the business. And you went along with it. Then you changed your mind, rejected their plans, and started again?" In her mind, she was labeling Nav as an immature guy who couldn't figure out what he wanted to do and took advantage of his parents.

"My passion was for photography, and I knew I had a talent for it." Nav's voice remained even as he answered. "And an M.B.A. is useful for someone who runs his own business."

Mom leaned forward in what we girls thought of as her cross-examination posture. "Don't you think you owe your parents?"

I broke in. "Don't you think parents should want their child to build his career on something he's passionate about?"

Nav shot me a quick glance. He had his fair quota of pride and probably didn't appreciate my help, but I wasn't going to sit still while my mom attacked him. I'd done that too often in the past.

"I've paid my parents back for the money they spent on my education," he said quietly.

He had? He'd never mentioned that before, and I knew, given his principles, he'd have done it without touching his trust fund. No wonder he had lived on a shoestring budget.

"And," he went on, "I owe my parents love and respect. I don't owe them my life."

I nodded in agreement.

He took a breath. "None of your daughters chose law." He gazed at Mom, then over to Dad. "Nor medicine or medical research. I imagine you'd have liked it if they did?"

My parents exchanged one of those wordless communication glances they'd perfected. Dad said, "It would have been nice. But our girls have minds of their own. You may have noticed that with Kat." The dry humor in his tone lightened the mood.

Nav smiled. "I wouldn't have it any other way."

"No?" Dad glanced at Mom. "Nor would I. Life would be boring, wouldn't it?"

Mom gave a snort. "All right, Nav, you've made your point. What we want for our daughters is that each finds a career she loves. That she's happy, challenged, and financially secure."

"Which I am," I said.

"And we're proud of you, dear," she responded, giving me a warm smile.

"You are?" I was so surprised, I dropped my fork. "You've never said that before."

"We haven't?" She exchanged another glance with Dad. "We assumed you knew it."

"In my experience," Nav said quietly, "children need to hear the words. I think it meant a lot to Kat to hear you say that." He reached for my hand, and I squeezed his in a silent thank-you.

"In the past I heard more criticism than praise," I said, trying to keep my tone neutral as I gazed from one parent to the other.

They were both silent for a long moment, then Mom spoke. "After Theresa, who always knew what she wanted to do, we worried about you. You had trouble deciding what career would make you happy. And you were so determined to do things on your own, not let us help."

Help? Their idea of help had sounded like disapproval and nagging to me.

"But in the end, you worked it out and built yourself a wonderful career," Mom said.

I was basking in the warmth of this unusual praise when Dad turned again to Nav. "And you're just starting your career, not to mention photography isn't the most secure occupation. I'm sure that's a concern to your parents."

I spoke before Nav could respond. "That's between him and his parents."

"He's your boyfriend, Kat," Dad said evenly. "It's of concern to us, too."

I narrowed my eyes. "Are you seriously giving us that old-fashioned stuff about the man having a higher-paying job and being able to support the woman? Get a grip. Have you heard of women's lib? I know Mom has. I can damn—darn—well support myself."

I noted Merilee frowning, and quickly added, "I mean, you know, if we ever got serious about each other."

"But should you have to support him?" Mom asked.

Nav opened his mouth, but I cut him off. "Dad supported you when you went to law school," I said heatedly. "And now you make more than he does. You always told us it's about having an equal partnership, not who's making the most money at any particular time."

"Yes," Mom said grudgingly. "So long as neither person is taking advantage of the other."

"He—"

Nav interrupted me. "Rebecca," he said firmly, "I have no intention of taking advantage of your daughter."

"Mom, he won't even let me pay for pizza."

Theresa chuckled, and the atmosphere lightened a bit.

"I think," Nav said, "that quality of life is about more than simply income. It's about how we choose to spend our time, both in our work and outside it. It's about our values and priorities, and Kat is the top priority in my life."

I leaned my head against his shoulder. "Thanks. The same goes for me."

"You're an intelligent young man," Mom said slowly, as if she was weighing each word. "I suspect you'll do well with your photography. Intelligence, passion, and a degree in business, those are a good combination. Combined with skill, which Theresa, and I assume Kat, believe you have."

"He does," I said. "Please look at his website. And we'll

send you the catalog from his exhibit. It's the week after the wedding, at a prestigious gallery in Montreal."

"Hmm," Mom said.

It was time to quit on a high note and change the subject. "Mom, Dad, guess what?" I said brightly. "Jenna e-mailed this morning. She's on the road, heading home. She should get here Sunday night or Monday."

"That girl hasn't an ounce of sense," Dad grumbled. "She should have let us pay for her flight."

"She's crazy to be driving that old car of hers," Mom said.

Nav shot me a questioning look, and I whispered in his ear, "A 1974 MGB. It's a—"

"Hey, I grew up in England; I know what MGBs are." His soft curls brushed my cheek, and I breathed in his evocative sandalwood scent.

As our parents carried on about Jenna's lack of responsibility, I glanced at Merilee and rolled my eyes.

She stifled a giggle.

Under my breath, I said to Nav, "At least they're off your case."

"They're just worried about all of you."

I understood now that he was right, thanks in large part to Maggie and Tim on the train. Still, I joked, "Easy to say when it's not your parents."

The word "parents" fell into a lull in Mom and Dad's conversation.

Mom redirected her attention to Nav. "Tell us about your parents. They live in England?"

"They did, but recently moved to New Delhi to take care of Dad's mother after she was widowed."

"Are they traditional? What do they think of you dating a white girl?"

I felt a chill of trepidation. Nav and I hadn't got around to discussing his parents' likely reaction.

"As with my career," he said, "my decisions are my own."

"It sounds as if you don't have a very close relationship with your family," she said disapprovingly. "Any siblings?"

"I'm an only."

"No wonder they had high expectations of you," she said. "Your decisions must be difficult for them to accept."

"Mom." I spoke before Nav could answer. "If they had their way, he'd go into a career he hates, move to a country that's never been his home, and agree to an arranged marriage."

I gripped his hand tightly. "Nav's a good man. His decisions are reasonable ones, and his family should respect them."

"Perhaps so. But—"

Theresa broke in. "Mom, stop interrogating the man. Why do you two always do this? Couldn't we for once have a pleasant, relaxed meal?"

Surprised and pleased by her support, I flashed her a smile.

I was even more surprised when Nav said, "They do it because they're concerned and protective. You wouldn't want parents who didn't care who you dated, would you?"

Theresa and I shared a raised-eyebrow look, then I said, "We wouldn't mind if they cared just a little bit less."

We all chuckled.

Mom said, "Thank you, Nav. I'm glad *somebody* understands." She shot us girls a humorous look.

I realized that this dinner was a bit of a breakthrough for my family. We'd argued as we typically did, but we had also moved to a better understanding and appreciation of each other. I liked it and hoped it would continue. And that Nav would be a part of it.

"And since you do understand," my mother went on, "can we get back to the subject of your parents? I'm concerned about—"

"Mom?" This time it was Merilee who interrupted. "You've spent all of dinner cross-examining him. Don't you want to hear about the dresses we found this afternoon? Including one for you."

"Me?" Mom said. "You went shopping for me?"

I shot Merilee a grateful look. Whether she'd intervened to rescue me or because she figured it was time to be the center of attention, I was relieved by the change of subject.

All the same, I, too, was concerned about Nav's parents.

It felt like my family was struggling toward a closer relationship, and I wanted the same for Nav. I'd like to help heal the breach between him and his parents, to become accepted as a part of the family, not make the situation worse.

If his parents didn't approve of our marriage, would they cut him out of their lives?

Chapter 21

Saturday morning, Nav woke from the dreamless sleep of exhaustion to the sound of knocking.

Kat jumped out of the double bed they shared, grabbed a robe off the chair, and went to the door. She opened it a crack.

"Breakfast in ten minutes," Theresa said. "I wouldn't recommend missing it."

Kat groaned, and Nav did, too.

Dinner last night had been stressful, and he wasn't looking forward to round two, but he was determined to win Kat's parents over. They were good people, concerned for her happiness, and eventually they'd come to see he was the right man for their daughter.

He crawled out of bed and began to get ready.

Fortunately, when he and Kat went downstairs hand in hand, he discovered that breakfast at the Fallon household didn't involve a lot of conversation.

Kat's mom scratched notes on a legal pad as she absentmindedly munched toast. Her dad had his nose in some scientific journal. Merilee and Matt debated the merits of different kinds of music for the reception. And Theresa had printed out a list and started going over it with Kat.

Nav spread cream cheese on a bagel and stayed out of everyone's way.

He hoped Kat's list of things to do would allow the two of them some together time. When they'd got to her room last night, they'd both been tired and on edge, and had made swift, sweet, and very quiet love, then immediately fallen asleep.

There were things he needed to discuss with her, and that hadn't been the time. But he didn't want to wait much longer.

When her family had all departed, she poured herself another cup of coffee, then came over to him where he sat at the kitchen table. "Alone at last," she said.

"About time." He took the mug from her hand and put it on the kitchen table, then tugged her down on his lap and hugged her. Clad in shorts and a brief tank top, she felt warm and curvy and wonderful in his arms.

She snuggled close. "This is nice."

"How long have we got? What's on that list Theresa gave you?"

"Visiting three caterers and going to VanDusen Gardens to check the venue and talk to someone in admin. Would you believe it? Theresa actually said I'd probably handle these things best, given my hotel experience."

"Sounds like things are improving with you and your sisters."

She nodded. "We understand each other better, and it's nice. Hope it continues once Jenna gets home."

She looped her arms around his neck and leaned back to study his face. "What's your plan for the day? Why don't you come to the Gardens? You might find some good shots."

"Sure. And it'll help me plan the wedding photos. But I need to get some laundry done, too. Either that or clothes shopping. I didn't have time to buy many new clothes, and I'm guessing you'd rather I didn't wear my old sweats."

She stroked his freshly shaven jaw. "I'd like to wash some things, too." Then her face lit. "Hey, it's Saturday morning. What were we doing a week ago?"

He thought back, then gave a pleased laugh. "Laundry, back

in Montreal. That's when I hatched the train scheme." He gave her a quick hug, then rose, dumping her off his lap. "Let's get the wash going." When the machine was running, they'd have a chance to talk.

It turned out that the Fallons had a beautifully appointed laundry room. "Two washers and two dryers?" he said.

"That way the housekeeper can do all the laundry during her weekly visit," Kat explained.

He'd changed into sweats and a jersey so he could wash his new clothes, and now began to toss his jeans, black shirt, white shirt, silky sweater, and Armani briefs into a machine.

"Stop!" Kat grabbed his arm. "Let me introduce you to the concept of delicates. Not to mention, darks, lights, and colors. If you're going to spend a small fortune on clothes, you want them to last."

"I knew there was a hitch."

She sorted their clothes—his and hers together—explaining what she was doing.

He sighed. The new wardrobe was comfortable, and he had to admit he liked the way he looked, but his old clothes sure had been easier to look after.

Kat set both washers to run. Then, in a gesture of sappy sweetness that went straight to his heart, she patted their tops and said, "Our first shared loads."

Then she turned to him, eyes gleaming. "Ever had sex in a laundry room?"

His body went on instant alert. There was nothing he'd like better.

Except . . . "I haven't. But Kat, I want to talk to you about something."

"Talk?" Her eyebrows rose, then she backed him up against a humming machine and plastered the front of her body against his, wriggling suggestively. "You want to talk rather than make love?"

Despite his growing erection, he gripped her arms and thrust her away. "Yeah. Now go hop up on a machine like you always do, so I can think."

Her flirtatious expression vanished, replaced by a troubled one. "Is something wrong?" Slowly she pulled herself up on a washing machine as he'd asked, her legs tanned and shapely under beige shorts.

"No. Well . . . Look, how do you feel about the stuff your parents were saying last night? Like, my career and income versus yours?"

Leaning forward, legs dangling over the edge of the machine, she gave him a puzzled look. "Didn't you hear what I told them?"

"Yeah, and it sounded great. But then I thought about the kind of guys you've gone for in the past. And what you said last Saturday night about being attracted to successful men."

"You're successful."

"I'm just starting out, and like your dad said, it's an uncertain business."

"But you love it. And you're so talented. You'll make it big."

"I hope so. But what if I don't? What if I only manage to make a living, not become a big name?"

Her brows drew together. "If you still love doing it, that's what counts."

"You honestly mean that? You don't want some . . . NASCAR winner, or Bollywood producer?"

"I want you." Her mouth quirked into a grin. "Preferably with the nice clothes and smooth-shaven face."

He smiled, but he still wasn't convinced. "Thursday night, when we were dreaming about our future, we agreed we wanted to live in Montreal. But we didn't talk about whether we'd buy a house."

He leaned back against the machine across from her. "We didn't talk about how we'd afford a house."

"I told you about the down payment I've been saving."

"Kat, I—"

"Stop. Don't pull that macho pride thing on me. I won't marry a chauvinist."

"Sorry. I'm really not. Blame my mum for the way she raised me. She had pretty old-fashioned views about male and female roles."

A shadow crossed her face, and he rushed on. "I did hear what you said about an equal partnership. I want that. And here's the thing: I do have that trust fund."

"You said you wanted to make it on your own and not touch the trust fund."

"I needed to do that to prove I was independent. That I wasn't a spoiled rich kid. And I've done it. Now we're talking about our future, Kat. As a couple. Our home, our kids."

Slowly she nodded. "Independence is good, and so is investing in the future. Okay, that's something we'll take into consideration. Along with how to use the money I've saved." A warning tone had crept into her voice.

"Deal." He held out his hand, finally reassured.

"Deal." She shook it firmly.

Then he stepped toward her, lifted her hand to his lips, and gave it his best seductive kiss. "Did someone mention sex in the laundry room?"

She freed her hand. "Now I have a question." Her serious tone told him it wasn't about sex.

"Shoot."

"Will your parents be really upset? They want you to marry an Indian woman."

He shrugged. "They have to accept that it's my life and I make my own decisions."

She sighed. "I don't want them to hate me." She reached out and caught his hand again, holding it tight. "Nav, I've seen how tense you get when you talk about your family. And you know I've had issues with my parents and sisters. But things are improving for me, and that feels really good."

"I'm happy for you."

"If there's some way I can make things better rather than worse with you and your family, I'd like to do it."

Was there any hope that he and his parents would have anything more than a strained relationship?

Well, he had a pretty good idea of one thing that would go a long way. With his free hand, he touched her cheek. "You can give them pretty brown grandchildren."

A smile flickered. "I have every intention of doing that. But it would be nice if your parents would be happy about our marriage and accept me now. Not just when I produce a baby. Can you try to explain to them?" she said. "Like, not just announce it, but help them understand that we really love each other?"

"We don't do so well with that kind of conversation. They get their backs up."

Her lips twitched. "And you don't, I suppose."

He thought about it. The sharp words, and the way he and his dad would stalk off in opposite directions. The way his mom would nag at him over and over about the same damned things, and he'd refuse to listen.

"Maybe I do," he admitted. "Yeah, okay, I'll work on better communication." Was it possible that, as well as believing children should obey their parents, his were genuinely concerned about his welfare, as Kat's parents were about hers?

He studied his beautiful Kat with her troubled expression. "They should be pleased I'm getting married," he told her. "And once they meet you, you'll win them over." He made a rueful face. "As I hope to eventually do with your folks." Though he had to admit, at least her parents didn't seem to give a damn that he was Indian.

She nodded. "We'll persuade both our families. Once they see how happy we are together, they'll come around."

Oh, yes, he and Kat had some struggles ahead of them. But, as he studied her sitting on that washer, tanned legs swinging gently, he was confident they'd work things out together.

"Nav?" She tugged him closer. "Sex in the laundry room?"

"There's one hell of a good idea."

Her legs lifted to wrap around his hips, pulling him up against her, and she tugged his head down for a kiss.

How many times had he looked at her perched on a washing machine and imagined doing this? Did she know she was fulfilling one of his fantasies?

Her fingers wound through his hair, her tongue plunged into his mouth, and he couldn't think. Only enjoy and kiss her back. Feel the hot surge of blood in his veins, the hardness of his growing erection pressing against her crotch.

Breathing hard, she pushed him away and reached down to unfasten her shorts.

He stepped back to help her pull them off, and her panties went with them.

"Your turn," she said, and he hurriedly skinned his sweatpants and briefs over his hips and kicked them off.

"Damn," he said. "No condom."

"In my shorts pocket," she said smugly.

He gave an exultant laugh. She'd planned this laundry room seduction.

Quickly he found the condom and sheathed himself.

Kat had shifted position so she was sitting on the very edge of the machine, leaning back on her hands, legs spread.

He moved between her legs, erection nudging her.

Once more she hooked her legs around his waist and pulled him closer, wriggling against him. "Make love to me, Nav. I want you."

He stroked her pussy, glided a finger inside.

A sexy shiver rippled through her, and she clenched around his finger. "I'm ready, damn it. Get in here. Now."

Chuckling, he said, "It's true what guys say. Put a ring on her finger and she gets bossy."

"I don't have the ring yet," she pointed out.

"We'll find a jeweler today."

When he slid inside her, she gave a trembling sigh of satisfaction. "This feels so right. You and me."

"It does. I've been waiting for this for two years." He stroked smoothly in and out, savoring the view of her half-naked body, the soft grip of her lush channel, the little whimpers she made.

"Nav, I've been . . . waiting for you . . . all my life." Her words came out on gasps of pleasure.

"I love you, Kat."

Her gaze held his. "More than . . . them? The other two?"

Them? What was she talking about? There was only her. Then he realized what she meant. Somehow she was still insecure about his love.

Slowing his thrusts, he cupped her face tenderly between his hands. "More than Margaret. There's no comparison. And the other woman? That was you, Kat."

"Oh! I hadn't . . . realized."

"I know. I couldn't tell you. You weren't ready to hear it."

He gazed at her, letting her see all the love and passion in his heart. "You taught me what love is," he said, driving deep into her.

"You . . . too." As she came apart around him, she cried out, "I love you, Nav."

If you liked this book try INSTANT TEMPTATION, the third in Jill Shalvis's Wilder brothers series, out now from Brava . . .

"I didn't invite you in, TJ."

He just smiled.

He was built as solid as the mountains that had shaped his life, and frankly had the attitude to go with them—the one that said he could take on whoever and whatever and you could kiss his perfect ass while he did so. She'd seen him do it, back in his hell-raising, misspent youth.

Not that she was going there, to the time when he could have given her a single look and she'd have melted into a puddle at his feet.

Had melted into a puddle at his feet. Not going there.

Unfortunately for her senses, he smelled like the wild Sierras; pine and fresh air, and something even better, something so innately male that her nose twitched for more, seeking out the heat and raw male energy that surrounded him. Since it made her want to lean into him, she shoved in another bite of ice cream instead.

"I saw on Oprah once that women use ice cream as a substitute for sex," he said.

She choked again, and he resumed gliding his big, warm hand up and down her back. "*You* watch Oprah?"

"No. Annie does, and once I overheard her yelling at the TV that women should have plenty of both sex *and* ice cream."

That sounded exactly like his Aunt Annie. "Well, I don't need the substitute."

"No?" he murmured, looking amused at her again.

"No!"

He hadn't taken his hands off her. He still had one rubbing up and down her back, the other low on her belly, holding her upright, which was ridiculous, so she smacked it away. She did her best to ignore the fluttering he'd caused and the odd need she had to grab him by the shirt, haul him close, and have her merry way with him.

That was what happened to a woman whose last orgasm had come from a battery-operated device instead of a man, a fact she'd admit, oh *never*. "I was expecting your brother."

"Stone's working on Emma's 'honey do' list at the new medical clinic, so he sent me instead. Said to give you these." He pulled some maps from his back pocket, maps she needed for a field expedition for her research. When she took them out of his hands, he hooked his thumbs in the front pockets of his Levi's. He wore a T-shirt layered with an open button-down that said WILDER ADVENTURES on the pec. His jeans were faded nearly white in the stress spots, of which there were many, nicely encasing his long, powerful legs and lovingly cupping a rather impressive package that was emphasized by the way his fingers dangled on his thighs.

Not that she was looking.

Okay, she was looking, but she couldn't help it. The man oozed sexuality. Apparently some men were issued a handbook at birth on how to make a woman stupid with lust. And he'd had a lot of practice over the years.

She'd watched him do it.

Each of the three Wilder brothers had barely survived their youth, thanks in part to no mom and a mean, son-of-a-bitch father. But by some miracle, the three of them had come out of it alive, and now channeled their energy into Wilder Adventures, where they guided clients on just about any outdoor adventure that could be imagined; heli-skiing, extreme mountain biking, kayaking, climbing, *anything*.

Though TJ had matured and found success, he still gave off a don't-mess-with-me vibe. Even now, at four in the afternoon, he looked big and bad and tousled enough that he might have just gotten out of bed and wouldn't be averse to going back.

It irritated her. It confused her. And it turned her on, a fact that drove her bat-shit crazy because she was no longer interested in TJ Wilder.

Nope.

It'd be suicide to still be interested. No one could sustain a crush for fifteen years.

No one.

Except, apparently, her. Because deep down, the unsettling truth was that if he so much as directed one of his sleepy, sexy looks her way, her clothes would fall right off.

Again.

Wasn't that just her problem? The fact that once upon a time, a very long time ago, at the tail end of TJ's out-of-control youth, the two of them had spent a single night together being just about as intimate as a man and a woman could get. Her first time, but definitely not his first. Neither of them had been exactly legal, and only she'd been sober.

Which meant only she remembered.

You won't want to miss Karen Kelley's THE JAGUAR PRINCE, the first in her new series, in stores now!

This wasn't happening. Callie closed her eyes and took a deep breath. "You're not real," she repeated over and over until she could feel herself beginning to relax.

The naked hottie was only the last fragment of a delicious dream she'd been having. Right before she went to sleep, hadn't she wished he would magically materialize in her bed?

She relaxed and smiled. It had been a great dream. The way he touched her, nuzzled her neck, pressed his naked body against hers. It had been one long sensuous dream. That was probably why she'd apparently gotten rid of her hot granny gown sometime during the night. Okay, now she was back to normal. No more fantasies that a hot sexy man was in her bed. The idea was ludicrous.

Deep breath. Inhale. Exhale. She was wide awake now. She opened her eyes.

He was still there, sitting on the end of her bed, staring at her with what appeared to be . . . amusement? He laughed at her! He was in her house, her bed, and he laughed at her!

Callie sat up, and the cover fell to her waist. His gaze dropped. She grabbed the sheet and pulled it against her chest. "Get out! Who are you? How did you get into my house? Where's my gown?"

One eyebrow arched. "Are you always this emotionally unstable?"

"Emotionally . . ." she sputtered.

"Unstable," he slowly and distinctly repeated.

"I am not emotionally unstable!" Oh God, she was arguing with the serial killer. She took another deep breath, then exhaled once more. She needed to stay calm. "If you don't leave right now, I'm going to call the police."

Oh, yeah, now he really looked nervous—not! He didn't even flinch. Just sat there staring at her. And why wouldn't he? He probably weighed around one-eighty. She would be no match for him.

Maybe if she kept him talking, he wouldn't kill her right away. She'd once read somewhere that if you could befriend your abductor, then he would be less likely to kill you. Not that he'd abducted her, but he had apparently broken into her home. God, she hoped this worked.

"How . . . uh . . . did you find me?" Surely someone would've noticed a naked man following her car. For the first in her life, Callie wished her rattletrap car went faster.

She frowned. How had he followed her? Her car wasn't that slow. He probably had his own car. He'd waited for her to leave, then followed.

So, he drove around naked. And no one noticed this?

"Does it matter how I came to be here?" he asked.

"I guess not." If she knew where he came from, then maybe she could talk him into going back, though. "Where are you from?"

"New Symtaria."

"Never heard of it. Is that a suburb of Dallas?" New ones were cropping up all the time.

"It's in another galaxy."

Alrighty. "Another planet?"

He nodded, still looking amused about something.

"And you are?"

"Prince Rogar."

She nodded. Delusional. Probably escaped from the state hospital. This was worse than she ever could have imagined. Not only was he naked, but he was a nut. Automatically, her eyes strayed downward. She swallowed, then quickly jerked her gaze to a safer place. She had to stop looking . . . looking at him . . . down there. It wasn't like she'd never seen a naked man before.

This was ridiculous. She needed help, and all she could think about was staring at his . . . his nakedness. She had to call the police or something—911. Her cell phone was in her purse. From now on, she was keeping it on her bedside table. If there ever was a from-now-on in her future. Okay, keep him talking.

"And why are you here?" She smiled. At least she tried to pull it off as a smile, even though her stomach rumbled, her hands were sweating, and she was probably going to throw up any second.

"To take you home."

She looked around "I am home, so . . . bye-bye."

He grinned and she noticed his teeth were pearly white, and he had a nice smile. Ted Bundy probably had a nice smile, too.

"You're part Symtarian," he continued.

"Okayyy . . ." He thought she was from another planet, too. This was worse than she could've imagined.

"When our planet was dying, some of the people were sent to other places. An expedition went in search of a new planet to call home. Some of our people were forgotten and became integrated with the aliens. Now we're searching for them so we can bring them home."

"And you're doing it without clothes."

"It happens when I shape-shift."

"Well, of course, I should have guessed." The guy was a raving lunatic. "And what form do you take?"

A fog began to roll across her bedroom. She glanced nervously around, then looked at her crazy guy. Her mouth dropped open as he slowly began to change.

The prince dude gritted his teeth and lowered his head. His skin changed from flesh to short black hair with visible spots. He stretched out across her bed, his hand curling into a fist, becoming a paw.

Oh, God, she was crazy. Now she would never get her chance to work with the big cats—except in her warped mind. It wasn't fair.

The fog rolled in thicker until all Callie saw were patches of black fur, a glimpse of golden eyes boring into her. She couldn't move. She tried, but her legs wouldn't budge.

The fog slowly dissipated.

A black jaguar from last night lay across the end of her bed, panting slightly. It met her gaze, and seemed as though it was gauging her reaction.

She opened her mouth, then closed it when no words came out. The cat purred from deep in its throat. She swallowed past the lump in hers. What if the jag was real? Oh, yeah, now she felt better. She was going to die. Then again, she might already be dead and this was hell.

Whatever it was, the jaguar was still stretched across the foot of her bed.

The room began to tilt, then grow dark, and she knew without a doubt, she was about to faint. She'd never fainted in her life.

And here's a sneak peek at UNDONE, the historical romance anthology featuring Susan Johnson, Terri Brisbin, and Mary Wine. Turn the page for a preview of Susan's story, "As You Wish."

Fortunately for the earl's pressing schedule, the night was overcast. Not a hint of moonlight broke through to expose his athletic form as he scaled the old, fist-thick wisteria vines wrapped around the pillars of the terrace pergola. The house to which the pergola was attached was quiet, the ground floor dark save for the porter's light in the entrance hall. Either the Belvoirs were out or already in bed. More likely the latter, with only a single flambeau outside the door.

He'd best take care.

Kit had described the position of Miss Belvoir's bedchamber—hence Albion's ascent of wisteria. Once he gained the roof joists of the Chinoiserie pergola, he would have access to the windows of the main floor corridor. From there he could make his way to the second-floor bedchambers, the easternmost that of Miss Belvoir. Where, according to Kit, she'd been cloistered for the last month, being polished by her stepmother into a state of refined elegance for her bow into society a few weeks hence.

Which refinements, in his estimation, only served to make every young lady into the same boring martinet without an original thought in her head or a jot of conversation worth listening to.

He hoped there wouldn't be much conversation tonight. If he had his way there wouldn't be any. He hoped as well that she wouldn't prove stubborn, but should she, he'd stuff his handkerchief in her mouth to muffle her screams, tie her up if necessary, and carry her down the back stairs and out the servants' entrance. It was more likely, though—with all due modesty—that his much-practiced charm would win the day.

Pulling himself over the fretwork balustrade embellishing the pergola, he stood for a moment balanced on a joist contemplating which window would best offer him ingress. His mind made up, he brushed himself off, navigated the vine-draped timbers, and reached the window. Taking a knife from his coat pocket, he snapped open the blade, slipped it under the lower sash, and pried it up enough to gain a fingerhold.

Moments later, he stood motionless in the dark corridor. The stairs were to the right, if Kit's description was correct. After listening for a few moments and hearing nothing, he quietly made his way down the plush carpet and up the stairs. A single candle on a console table dimly illuminated the hallway onto which the bedrooms opened. Pausing to listen once again and distinguishing no undue sounds, he silently traversed the carpeted passageway to the last door on his right.

It shouldn't be locked. Servants required access if the bell pull by the bed was rung. For a brief moment he stood utterly still, wondering what in blazes he was doing here, about to abduct some untried maid in order to seduce her. As if there weren't women enough in London who would welcome him to their beds with open arms. Considerable brandy was to blame, he supposed, along with the rackety company of his friends who had too much idle time on their hands in which to conjure up wild wagers like this.

Bloody hell. He felt the complete absence of any desire to be where he was.

On the other hand, he decided with a short exhalation, he'd bet twenty thousand on this foolishness.

Now it was play or pay.

He reached for the latch, pressed down, and quietly opened the door.

As he stepped over the threshold he was greeted by a ripple
of scent and a cheerful female voice. "I thought you'd changed
your mind."

The hairs on the back of his neck rose.

His first thought was that he was unarmed.

His second was that it was a trap.

But when the same genial voice said, "Don't worry, no one's
at home but me. Do come in and shut the door," his pulse rate
lessened and he scanned the candlelit interior for the source of
the invitation.

"Miss Belvoir, I presume," he murmured, taking note of a
young woman with hair more gold than red standing across the
room near the foot of the bed. *She was quite beautiful. How
nice. And if no one was home, nicer still.* Shutting the door behind him, he offered her a graceful bow.

"A pleasant, good evening, Albion. Gossip preceded you."
*He was breathtakingly handsome at close range. Now to con-
vince him to take her away.* "I have a proposition for you."

He smiled. "A coincidence. I have one for you." This was going
to be easier than he thought. Then he saw her luggage. "You
first," he said guardedly.

"I understand you have twenty thousand to lose."

"Or not."

"Such arrogance, Albion. You forget the decision is mine."

"Not entirely," he replied softly.

"Because you've done this before."

"Not this. But something enough like it to know."

"I see," she murmured. "But then *I'm* not inclined to be in-
stantly infatuated with your handsome self or your prodigal re-
pute. I have more important matters on my mind."

"More than twenty thousand?" he asked with a small smile.

"I like to think so."

He recognized the seriousness of her tone. "Then we must
come to some agreement. What do you want?"

"To strike a bargain."

"Consider me agreeable to most anything," he smoothly replied.

"My luggage caused you certain apprehension, I noticed," she said, amusement in her gaze. "Let me allay your fears. I have no plans to elope with you. Did you think I did?"

"The thought crossed my mind." He wasn't entirely sure yet that some trap wasn't about to be sprung. She was the picture of innocence in white muslin—all the rage thanks to Marie Antoinette's penchant for the faux rustic life.

"I understand that women stand in line for your amorous skills, but rest assured—you're not my type. Licentiousness is your raison d'être I hear: a very superficial existence, I should think."

His brows rose. He'd wondered if she'd heard about Sally's when she mentioned women standing in line. She also had the distinction of being the first woman to find him lacking. "You mistake my raison d'être. Perhaps if you knew me better you'd change your mind," He suggested pleasantly.

"I very much doubt it," she replied with equal amiability. "You're quite beautiful, I'll give you that, and I understand you're unrivaled in the boudoir. But my interests, unlike yours, aren't focused on sex. What I do need from you, however, is an escort to my aunt's house in Edinburgh."

"And for that my twenty thousand is won?" His voice was velvet soft.

"Such tact, my lord."

"I can be blunt if you prefer."

"Please do. I've heard so much about your ready charm. I'm wondering how you're going to ask."

"I hadn't planned on asking."

"Because you never have to."

He smiled. "To date at least."

"So I may be the exception."

"If you didn't need an escort to Edinburgh," he observed mildly. "Your move."

"You see this as a game?"

"In a manner of speaking."

"And I'm the trophy or reward or how do young bucks describe a sportive venture like this?"

"How do young ladies describe the snaring of a husband?"

She laughed. "Touché. I have no need of a husband, though. Does that calm your fears?"

"I have none in that regard. Nothing could induce me to marry."

"Then we are in complete agreement. Now tell me, how precisely does a libertine persuade a young lady to succumb to his blandishments?"

"Not like this," he said dryly. "Come with me and I'll show you."

"We strike our bargain first. Like you, I have much at stake."

"Then, Miss Belvoir," he said with well-bred grace, "if you would be willing to relinquish your virginity tonight, I'd be delighted to escort you to Edinburgh."

"In the morning. Or later tonight if we can deal with this denouement expeditiously."

"At week's end," he countered. "After the Spring Meet in Newmarket."

"I'm sorry. That's not acceptable."

He didn't answer for so long she thought he might be willing to lose twenty thousand. He was rich enough.

"We can talk about it at my place."

"No."

Another protracted silence ensued; only the crackle of the fire on the hearth was audible.

"Would you be willing to accompany me to Newmarket?" he finally said. "I can assure you anonymity at my race box. Once the Spring Meet is over, I'll take you to Edinburgh." He blew out a small breath. "I've a fortune wagered on my horses. I don't suppose you'd understand."

This time she was the one who didn't respond immediately,

and when she did, her voice held a hint of melancholy. "I do understand. My mother owned the Langley stud."

"That was your mother's? By God—the Langley stud was legendary. Tattersalls was mobbed when it was sold. You *do* know how I feel about my racers, then." He grinned. "They're all going to win at Newmarket. I'll give you a share if you like—to help set you up in Edinburgh."

Her expression brightened, and her voice took on a teasing intonation. "Are you trying to buy my acquiescence?"

"Why not? You only need give me a few days of your time. Come with me. You'll enjoy the races."

"I mustn't be seen."

Ah—capitulation. "Then we'll see that you aren't. Good Lord—the Langley stud. I'm bloody impressed. Let me get your luggage."